DAVID MORRELL

THE FIFTH PROFESSION

WARNER BOOKS

An AOL Time Warner Company

WARNER BOOKS EDITION

Copyright © 1990 by David Morrell

The following publishers have given permission to use quotations from copyrighted works: *I'm So Lonesome I Could Cry*. Written by Hank Williams © 1949, renewed 1977. Acuff-Rose Music, Inc., and Hiriam Music. Used by permission. International copyright secured. All rights reserved.

Cover design by Jesse Sanchez
Cover photo by Herman Estevez

Warner Books, Inc.
1271 Avenue of the Americas
New York, NY 10020

Visit our Web site at www.twbookmark.com.

 An AOL Time Warner Company

Printed in the United States of America

Originally published in hardcover by Warner Books

First Paperback Printing: April 1991

15 14 13 12 11 10 9 8 7 6 5 4 3 2 1

ALSO BY DAVID MORRELL

FICTION

First Blood (1972)

Testament (1975)

Last Reveille (1977)

The Totem (1979)

Blood Oath (1982)

The Hundred-Year Christmas (1983)*

The Brotherhood of the Rose (1984)

The Fraternity of the Stone (1985)

The League of Night and Fog (1987)

The Covenant of the Flame (1991)

Assumed Identity (1993)

Desperate Measures (1994)

The Totem (Complete and Unaltered) (1994)*

Extreme Denial (1996)

Double Image (1998)

Black Evening (1999)

Burnt Sienna (2000)

NONFICTION

John Barth: An Introduction (1976)

Fireflies (1988)

*Limited edition. With illustrations. Donald M. Grant, Publisher,
Hampton Falls, New Hampshire.

To Sarie:
daughter,
friend

CONTENTS

"I don't understand you," said Alice. "It's dreadfully confusing."

"That's the effect of living backwards," the Queen said kindly. "It always makes one a little giddy at first."

"Living backwards!" Alice repeated in great astonishment. "I never heard of such a thing!"

"But there's one great advantage in it, that one's memory works both ways."

"I'm sure *mine* only works one way," Alice remarked. "I can't remember things before they happen."

"It's a poor sort of memory that only works backward," the Queen remarked.

—LEWIS CARROLL
Through the Looking-Glass

The Way of the bodyguard is resolute acceptance of death.

—MIYAMOTO MUSASHI
a seventeenth-century samurai

THE FIFTH
PROFESSION

PROLOGUE

ʌʌʌʌʌ

PLEDGE OF ALLEGIANCE

THE FIFTH
PROFESSION

No single historical event marks the origin of Savage's profession. The skill to which he devoted himself has its antecedents prior to fact in the haze of myth. At the start, there were hunters, then farmers, then with something to be gained by barter, prostitutes and politicians. Given some debate about precedence, those are the first four human endeavors.

But as soon as something can be gained, it must also be protected. Hence Savage's—the *fifth*—profession. Although his craft's inception has not been documented, two incidents illustrate its valiant traditions.

THE
COMITATUS

When the Anglo-Saxons invaded Britain four hundred years after Christ, they brought with them a Germanic code of absolute loyalty to a tribal chieftain. In its ultimate interpretation, this code required a chieftain's retainers or *comitatus* to defend him with their honor unto death. One of the most gripping instances of warriors displaying such total commitment to their lord occurred on the shore of the Blackwater River near the town of Maldon in Essex in 991.

Scandinavian pirates, having raided ports along the eastern coast of Britain, camped on an island that during low tide was linked to the shore by a narrow causeway. The local British chieftain, Birhtnoth, led his faithful *comitatus* to the causeway and ordered the Vikings not to cross. The enemy defied him.

Swords flashed. Blood soaked the causeway. As the battle intensified, one of Birhtnoth's apprentice soldiers turned cowardly and fled. Others supposed that the retreating figure was

Birhtnoth himself and fled as well. Only Birhtnoth and his bodyguards remained.

A javelin struck him. He yanked it out and stabbed his assailant. A Viking ax cut off his sword arm. Helpless, he was slashed to pieces. But although Birhtnoth no longer ruled, his faithful *comitatus* persisted. To protect his corpse, to avenge his death, they attacked with greater valor. Their deaths were brutal, yet joyous because the *comitatus* adhered to their code of loyalty.

The original Anglo-Saxon document that describes their heroic defeat concludes in this manner:

> Godric often let his spear fly, thrusting his slaughter-shaft toward the Vikings. Bravely he advanced among his brethren, hewed and laid low till he died in the struggle. He was not that Godric who ran from the battle.

Those two Godrics represent the principal conflict in Savage's profession. To protect was the mandate of the *comitatus*. But at what point, if the cause seemed hopeless, if the chieftain was dead, should a bodyguard protect himself? Whenever Savage debated this moral issue, he remembered Akira and an incident from a quite different culture that illustrated the extreme traditions of the fifth and most noble profession.

THE FORTY-SEVEN *RONIN*

In Japan, the equivalent of the *comitatus* were the samurai. These protective warriors came into prominence eleven hundred years after Christ when provincial chieftains, known as *daimyo*, needed fiercely loyal bodyguards to control their domains. Over the centuries, a central military ruler, called a *shogun*, exerted power over each *daimyo*. Nonetheless each *daimyo*'s samurai felt bonded to their local lord. In 1701, against this complex background of loyalties, an incident occurred that formed the basis for one of the most famous Japanese legends.

Three *daimyo* were summoned to the *shogun*'s court in Edo (now called Tokyo) with orders to pledge allegiance. However, these *daimyo* had little knowledge of court manners. Two of the three sought help from an expert in court etiquette. They bribed him with gifts and were rewarded with advice.

But the remaining *daimyo*, Lord Asano, was too innocent to bribe the etiquette instructor, Lord Kira. Kira felt insulted and ridiculed Asano in the *shogun*'s presence. Humiliated, Asano had no alternative except to defend his honor. He drew his sword and wounded Kira.

To draw a sword in the *shogun*'s presence was a grievous crime. The *shogun* commanded Asano to atone by disemboweling himself. The *daimyo* obeyed. Still, his death did not solve the controversy. Now Asano's samurai were bound by the rigorous code of *giri*, which loosely translated means "the burden of obligation," to avenge their master's death by destroying the man who'd begun the chain of insults, Lord Kira.

So compulsory was the code of *giri* that the *shogun* assumed there'd be more bloodshed. To end the feud, he sent his warriors to surround Asano's castle and demand the surrender of Asano's samurai. Inside the castle Oishi Yoshio, the captain of Asano's samurai, held council with his men. Some favored resisting the *shogun*'s warriors. Others advocated committing ritual suicide as had their lord. But Oishi sensed that the majority felt their obligation had ended with their master's death. As a test, he offered them the option of dividing Asano's wealth among them. Many unworthy warriors eagerly chose this option. Oishi paid them and urged them to leave. Of more than three hundred samurai, only forty-seven remained. With these, Oishi made a pact, each cutting a finger and joining hands, sealing the pact with their blood.

The forty-seven surrendered to the *shogun*'s warriors and claimed to disavow any obligation they felt to *giri* and their dead lord. They pretended to accept their lot as *ronin*, masterless samurai, wanderers. Each traveled his separate way.

But the *shogun*—suspicious—sent spies to follow them, to insure that the feud had ended. To deceive the spies, each *ronin* bitterly engaged in unworthy conduct. Some became drunkards, others whoremongers. One sold his wife into prostitution. Another killed his father-in-law. Still another arranged for his sister to become a mistress of the hated Lord Kira. Permitting their swords to rust and themselves to be spat upon, all appeared to wallow in dishonor. At last, after two years, the *shogun*'s spies were convinced that the feud had ended. The *shogun* removed surveillance from the *ronin*.

In 1703, the forty-seven *ronin* regrouped and attacked Kira's castle. With long-repressed rage, they slaughtered their enemy's unsuspecting guards, tracked down and beheaded the man they so loathed, then washed the head and made a pilgrimage to Asano's grave, placing the head on the tomb of their now-avenged master.

The chain of obligation had not yet ended. In obeying the burden of *giri*, the *ronin* had violated the *shogun*'s command to stop their vendetta. One code of honor conflicted with another. Only one solution was acceptable. The *shogun* dictated. The *ronin* obeyed. In triumph, they impaled their bowels with their swords, drawing each blade from left to right, then fiercely upward, in the noble ritual of suicide called *seppuku*. The tombs of the forty-seven *ronin* are revered to this day, a Japanese monument.

The *comitatus*. The forty-seven *ronin*. Savage and Akira. Codes and obligations. Honor and loyalty. To protect and if duty compelled, to avenge—even at the risk of death. The fifth and most noble profession.

ONE

∧∧∧∧∧

RETURN OF
THE DEAD

THE
LABYRINTH

1

Obeying professional habits, Savage directed the elevator toward the floor below the one he wanted. Of course, an uninvited visitor would have had to stop the elevator at the second-highest floor, no matter what. A computer-coded card, slipped into a slot on the elevator's control panel, was required to command the elevator to rise to the topmost level. Savage had been given such a card but declined to use it. On principle, he hated elevators. Their confinement was dangerous. He never knew what he might find when the doors slid open. Not that he expected trouble on this occasion, but if he made one exception in his customary methods, he'd eventually make others, and when trouble did come along, he wouldn't be primed to respond.

11

Besides, on this warm afternoon in Athens in September, he was curious about the security arrangements of the person he'd agreed to meet. Although he was used to dealing with the rich and powerful, they were mostly in politics or industry. It wasn't every day he met someone not only associated with both arenas but who'd also been a movie legend.

Savage stepped to one side when the elevator stopped and the doors thunked open. Sensing, judging, he peered out, saw no one, relaxed, and proceeded toward a door whose Greek sign indicated FIRE EXIT. In keeping with that sign, the door's handle moved freely.

Cautious, Savage entered and found himself in a stairwell. His crepe-soled shoes muffled his footsteps on the concrete landing. The twenty-seven lower levels were silent. He turned toward a door on his right, gripped its knob, but couldn't budge it. Good. The door was locked, as it should be. On the opposite side, a push bar would no doubt give access to this stairwell—in case of emergency. But on *this* side, unauthorized visitors were prevented from going higher. Savage slid two thin metal prongs into the receptacle for the key— one prong for applying leverage, the other for aligning the slots that would free the bolt. After seven seconds, he opened the door, troubled that the lock was so simple. It should have taken him twice as long to pick it.

He crept through, eased the door shut behind him, and warily studied the steps leading upward. There weren't any closed-circuit cameras. The lights were dim, giving him protective shadow while he climbed toward a landing, then turned toward the continuation of the steps. He didn't see a guard. At the top, he frowned when he tried the door—it wasn't locked. Worse, when he opened it, he still didn't see a guard.

On nearly soundless carpeting, he proceeded along a corridor. Glancing at numbers on doors, he followed their diminishing sequence toward the number he'd been given. Just before he reached an intersecting corridor, his nostrils felt pinched by tobacco smoke. With the elevators to his right, he turned left into the corridor and saw them.

Three men were bunched together in front of a door at the

far end of the corridor. The first had his hands in his pockets. The second inhaled from a cigarette. The third sipped a cup of coffee.

Amateur hour, Savage thought.

Never compromise your hands.

When the guards noticed Savage, they came to awkward attention. They were built like football players, their suits too tight for their bullish necks and chests. They'd be intimidating to a nonprofessional, but their bulk made them too conspicuous to blend with a crowd, and they looked too muscle-bound to be able to respond instantaneously to a crisis.

Savage slackened his strong features, making them nonthreatening. Six feet tall, he slouched his wiry frame so he looked a few inches shorter. As he walked along the corridor, he pretended to be impressed by the guards, who braced their backs in arrogant triumph.

They made a show of examining his ID, which was fake, the name he was using this month. They searched him but didn't use a hand-held metal detector and hence didn't find the small knife beneath his lapel.

"Yeah, you're expected," the first man said. "Why didn't you use the elevator?"

"The computer card didn't work." Savage handed it over. "I had to stop on the floor below and take the stairs."

"But the stairwell doors are locked," the second man said.

"Someone from the hotel must have left them open."

"Whoever forgot to lock them, his ass is grass," the third man said.

"I know what you mean. I can't stand carelessness."

They nodded, squinted, flexed their shoulders, and escorted him into the suite.

No, Savage thought. The rule is, you never abandon your post.

2

The suite had a sizable living room, tastefully furnished. But what Savage noticed, disapproving, was the wall directly across from him, its thick draperies parted to reveal an enormous floor-to-ceiling window and a spectacular view of the Parthenon on the Acropolis. Though Athens was usually smoggy, a breeze had cleared the air, making the pillared ruins brilliant in the afternoon sun. Savage allowed himself to admire the view but only from where he'd paused just inside the room, for he hated huge windows whose draperies were open: they gave an enemy an unnecessary advantage, inviting easy invasion with telescopes, microwave-beamed listening probes, and most crucial, sniper bullets.

The potential client he'd been summoned to meet wasn't present, so Savage assessed a door on the wall to his left. A closet perhaps, or a washroom or a bedroom. He directed his attention toward a muffled female voice behind a door on the wall to his right, and *that* door he was sure led to a bedroom. Because he didn't hear a responding voice, he assumed that the woman was using a telephone. She sounded insistent, as if she wouldn't conclude for quite a while.

With disciplined patience, Savage glanced farther right toward the wall beside the door through which he'd entered. He recognized two Monets and three Van Goghs.

His burly escorts looked bored when they realized that their employer wasn't present. No brownie points for them, no audience with their client, no compliments for supposedly doing their job. Disappointed, two of them shuffled their feet, adjusted their ties, and went back to their stations in the hall, no doubt to drink more coffee and smoke more cigarettes. The third closed the door and leaned against it, crossing his arms, trying to look diligent, though the pressure with which he squeezed his chest made it seem that he suffered from heartburn.

As air-conditioning whispered, Savage turned from the paintings toward a glass-enclosed display of Chinese vases.

The remaining bodyguard straightened.

The door on the right swung open.

A woman, a legend, stepped out of a bedroom.

3

Her official biography put her age at forty-five. Nonetheless she looked astonishingly the same as when she'd last appeared in a film a decade earlier. Tall, thin, angular.

Intense blue eyes. An exquisite oval face, its sensuous curves framed by shoulder-length, sun-bleached hair. Smooth, tanned skin. A photographer's dream.

Ten years ago, at a press conference in Los Angeles after she'd won her best actress Academy Award, she'd surprised the world by announcing her retirement. Her marriage one month later—to the monarch of a small but wealthy island-kingdom off the French Riviera—had been equally surprising. When her husband's health had declined, she'd taken over his business affairs, doubling the tourism and casinos that accounted for his island's wealth.

She ruled as she had acted, with what film reviewers had called a style of "fire and ice." Intense yet controlled. Passionate but in charge. In her love scenes, she'd always played the dominant role. The sequence in which she finally seduced the charismatic jewel thief whose attentions she'd persistently discouraged remained a classic depiction of sexual tension. She knew what she wanted, but she took it only when her desires didn't put her at risk, and her pleasure seemed based on giving more than she took, on condescending to grant the jewel thief a night he'd never forget.

So, too, her island subjects courted her attention. In response, she waved but kept a distance until at unexpected moments her generosity—to the sick, the homeless, the bereaved—was overwhelming. It seemed that compassion to her was a weakness, a fire that threatened to melt her icy control. But when politically advantageous, emotion could be permitted, indeed allowed in excessive amounts. As long as it didn't jeopardize her. As long as it made her subjects love her.

She smiled, approaching Savage. Radiant. A movie in real life. For his part, Savage admired her artful entrance, knowing that she knew exactly the impression she created.

She was dressed in black handcrafted sandals, burgundy pleated slacks, a robin's-egg-colored silk blouse (its three top buttons open to reveal the tan on the top of her breasts, its light blue no doubt chosen to emphasize the deeper blue of her eyes), a Cartier watch, and a diamond pendant with matching earrings (their glint further emphasizing her eyes as well as her sun-bleached hair).

She paused before Savage, then studied the remaining bodyguard, her gaze dismissive. "Thank you."

The burly man left, reluctant not to hear the conversation.

"I apologize for keeping you waiting," she said, stepping nearer, permitting Savage to inhale her subtle perfume. Her voice was husky, her handshake firm.

"Five minutes? No need to apologize." Savage shrugged. "In my profession, I'm used to waiting a great deal longer. Besides, I had time to admire your collection." He gestured toward the glass-enclosed display of vases. "At least, I assume it's your collection. I doubt any hotel, even the Georges Roi II, provides its clients with priceless artworks."

"I take them with me when I travel. A touch of home. Do you appreciate Chinese ceramics?"

"Appreciate? Yes, though I don't know anything about them. However, I do enjoy beauty, Your Highness. Including—if you'll forgive the compliment—yourself. It's an honor to meet you."

"As royalty, or because I'm a former film personality?"

"Former *actress*."

A flick of the eyes, a nod of the head. "You're very kind. Perhaps you'd feel more comfortable if we dispensed with formalities. Please call me by my former name. Joyce Stone."

Savage imitated her gracious nod. "Miss Stone."

"Your eyes are green."

"That's not so remarkable," Savage said.

"On the contrary. *Quite* remarkable. A chameleon's color. Your eyes blend with your clothes. Gray jacket. Blue shirt. An inattentive observer would describe your eyes as—"

"Grayish blue but not green. You're perceptive."

"And *you* understand the tricks of light. You're adaptable."

"It's useful in my work." Savage turned toward the paintings. "Superb. If I'm not mistaken, the Van Gogh *Cypresses* were recently purchased at a Sotheby auction. An unknown buyer paid an impressive amount."

"Do you recall how much?"

"Fifteen million dollars."

"And now you know the mysterious buyer."

"Miss Stone, I deal with privileged information. I'd be out of business tomorrow if I didn't keep a secret. Your remarks to me are confession. I'm like a priest."

"Confession? I hope that doesn't mean I can't offer you a drink."

"As long as I'm not working for you."

"But I assumed that's why you're here."

"To discuss your problem," Savage said. "I haven't been hired yet."

"With your credentials? I've already decided to hire you."

"Forgive me, Miss Stone, but I accepted your invitation to find out if I wanted *you* to hire *me*."

The sensuous woman studied him. "My, my." Her intense gaze persisted. "People are usually eager to work for me."

"I meant no offense."

"Of course not." She stepped toward a sofa.

"But if you wouldn't mind, Miss Stone."

She raised her eyebrows.

"I'd prefer that you used this chair over here. That sofa's too close to the window."

"Window?"

"Or else let me close the draperies."

"Ah, yes, now I understand." She sounded amused. "Since I enjoy the sunlight, I'll sit where you suggest. Tell me, are you always this protective of people you haven't decided to work for?"

"A force of habit."

"An *intriguing* habit, Mr. . . . I'm afraid I've forgotten your name."

Savage doubted that. She seemed the type who remembered everything. "It doesn't matter. The name I provided isn't mine. I normally use a pseudonym."

"Then how should I introduce you?"

"You don't. If we reach an agreement, never draw attention to me."

"In public. But what if I have to summon you in private?"

"Savage."

"I beg your pardon?"

"A nickname. The way I'm identified in my business."

"And did you acquire it when you were in the SEALs?"

Savage hid his surprise.

"Your former unit's name is an acronym, correct? Sea, air, and land. The U.S. Navy commandos."

Savage subdued an impulse to frown.

"I told you I found your credentials impressive," she said. "Your use of pseudonyms makes clear you cherish your privacy. But with persistence, I did learn several details about your background. In case I alarm you, let me emphasize that nothing I was told in any way jeopardized your anonymity. Still, rumors travel. The help you gave a certain member of the British Parliament—against IRA terrorists, I believe—is widely respected. He asked me to thank you again for saving his life. An Italian financier is similarly grateful for your skillful return of his kidnapped son. A West German industrialist feels that his corporation would have gone bankrupt if you hadn't discovered the rival who was stealing his formulas.''

Savage kept silent.

"No need to be modest," she said.

"Nor should you. Your sources are excellent."

"One of the many advantages to marrying royalty. The gratitude of the Italian financier was especially compelling. So I asked him how I might get in touch with you. He gave me the telephone number of—I suppose, in my former life, I'd have used the term—your agent.''

"You didn't learn his name, I hope."

"I never spoke to him directly, only through intermediaries.''

"Good."

"Which brings me to my problem."

"Miss Stone, another force of habit. Don't be specific in this room.''

"No one can overhear us. There aren't any hidden microphones.''

"What makes you sure?"

"My bodyguards checked it this morning."

"In that case, I repeat . . ."

"Don't be specific in this room? My bodyguards didn't impress you?''

"They impressed me, all right."

"But not the proper way?"

"I try not to criticize."

"Another commendable habit. Very well, then, Savage." Her smile matched the glint of her diamond earrings. She leaned from her chair and touched his hand. "Would you like to see some ruins?''

4

The black Rolls-Royce veered from traffic to stop in an oval parking lot. Savage and two of the bodyguards got out—the third had remained at the hotel to watch the suite. After the guards assessed the passing crowd, they nodded toward the car's interior.

Joyce Stone stepped smoothly out, flanked by her guards. "Circle the area. We'll be back in an hour," she told her driver, who eased the Rolls back into traffic.

She turned, amused, toward Savage. "You keep surprising me."

"Oh?"

"Back at the hotel, you objected to my sitting near a window, but you haven't said a word about my going out in public."

"Being famous doesn't mean you have to be a hermit. As long as you don't advertise your schedule, an accomplished driver can make it difficult for someone to follow you." Savage gestured toward the swarm of traffic. "Especially in Athens. Besides, you know how to dress to match your surroundings. To echo a compliment you gave me, you're adaptable."

"It's a trick I learned when I was an actress. One of the hardest roles . . . to look average."

She'd changed before they left the hotel. Now in place of her designer slacks and blouse, she wore faded jeans and a loose gray turtleneck sweater. Her diamonds were gone. Her watch was a Timex. Her shoes were dusty Reeboks. Her distinctive sun-bleached hair had been tucked beneath a floppy straw hat. Sunglasses hid her intense blue eyes.

Though pedestrians had paused to study the Rolls, they'd shown little interest in the woman who got out.

"You're playing the part successfully," Savage said. "At the moment, a producer wouldn't hire you, even for a walk-on."

She curtsied mockingly.

"I do have one suggestion," he said.

"Somehow I knew you would have."

"Stop using the Rolls."

"But it gives me pleasure."

"You can't always have what you want. Save the Rolls for special occasions. Buy a high-performance but neutral-looking car. Of course, it would have to be modified."

"Of course."

"Reinforced windows. Clouded glass in the rear. Bullet-proof paneling."

"Of course."

"Don't humor me, Miss Stone."

"I'm not. It's just that I enjoy a man who enjoys his work."

"Enjoy? I don't do this for fun. My work saves lives."

"And you've never failed?"

Savage hesitated. Caught by surprise, he felt a rush of torturous memories. The flash of a sword. The gush of blood. "Yes," he said. "Once."

"Your honesty amazes me."

"And *only* once. That's why I'm so meticulous, why I'll never fail again. But if my truthfulness gives you doubts about me . . ."

"On the contrary. My third movie was a failure. I could have ignored it, but I admitted it. And learned from it. I won the Oscar because I tried harder, although it took me seven more films."

"A movie isn't life."

"Or death? You should have seen the reviews of that third movie. I was buried."

"So will we all."

"Be buried? Don't be depressing, Savage."

"Did no one tell you the facts of life?"

"Sex? I learned that early. Death? That's why a man like you exists. To postpone it as long as possible."

"Yes, death," Savage said. "The enemy."

5

They followed a tour group toward the western slope of the Acropolis, the traditional approach to the ruins since the other ridges were far too steep for convenient walkways. Past fir trees, they reached an ancient stone entrance, known as the Beulé Gate.

"Have you been here before?"

"Several times," Savage said.

"So have I. Still, I wonder if you come for the same reason I do."

Savage waited for her to explain.

"Ruins teach us a lesson. Nothing—wealth, fame, power—nothing is permanent."

" 'Look on my works, ye Mighty, and despair.' "

She turned to him, impressed. "That's from Shelley's 'Ozymandias.' "

"I went to a thorough prep school."

"But you don't give the name of the school. Anonymous as usual. Do you remember the rest of the poem?"

Savage shrugged.

*". . . Round the decay
Of that colossal wreck, boundless and bare,
The lone and level sands stretch far away.*

Shelley understood precision. If he'd been Japanese, he'd have written great haikus."

"A bodyguard quoting poetry?"

"I'm not exactly a bodyguard, Miss Stone. I do more than run interference."

"What are you then?"

"An executive protector. You know, except for the sand, the ruins Shelley describes remind me of . . ."

Savage gestured toward the steps they climbed. The marble had been eroded by time, by use, by various invaders, and worst of all, by automobile exhaust.

They passed through a monument called the Propylaea, its precious decaying walkway protected by a wooden floor. Five gateways of columns grew wider and taller, leading them to a path that split right and left.

After the cloying heat of summer, September's moderate temperature brought the start of the tourist season. Sightseers jostled past them, some out of breath from the climb, others taking photographs of monuments on either side, the Precinct of Brauronia and the less impressive House of Arrhephoroi.

"Tell your guards to walk behind us," Savage said. "I'll watch ahead."

Turning right, they proceeded to the vast rectangular Parthenon. In 1687, a conflict between invaders had resulted in a Venetian bomb's igniting a Turkish gunpowder magazine in the Parthenon, which in ancient times had been a temple devoted to the Greek goddess of purity, Athena. The explosion had destroyed a considerable part of the monument, toppling pillars and much of the roof. Restoration was still in progress. Scaffolding obscured the magnificence of surviving Doric columns. Guardrails kept visitors from further eroding the interior.

Savage turned from the tourists, approaching the precipitous southern ridge of the Acropolis. He leaned against a fallen pillar. Athens sprawled below him. The earlier breeze had died. Despite a brilliant clear sky, smog had begun to gather.

"We can talk here without being overheard," Savage said. "Miss Stone, the reason I'm not sure I want to work for you—"

"But you haven't heard why I need you."

"—is that an executive protector is both a servant and a master. You control your life—where you go and what you do—but your protector insists on how you get there and under what terms you do it. A delicate balance. But you've got a reputation for being willful. I'm not sure you're prepared to take orders from someone you employ."

Sighing, she sat beside him. "If *that's* your problem, then there *isn't* a problem."

"I don't understand."

"The trouble isn't mine. It's my sister's."

"Explain."

"Do you know about her?"

"Rachel Stone. Ten years your junior. Thirty-five. Married a New England senator campaigning to be president. Widowed because of an unknown assassin's bullet. Her association with politics and a movie-legend sister made her glamorous. A Greek shipping magnate courted her. They married last year."

"I give you credit. You do your homework."

"No less than you."

"Their marriage is like the Parthenon. A ruin." Joyce Stone rummaged through her burlap purse. Finding a pack of cigarettes, she fumbled with a lighter.

"You're not a gentleman," she snapped.

"Because I won't light your cigarette? I just explained, when it comes to protection, *you're* the servant and I'm the master."

"That doesn't make sense."

"It does if you realize I have to keep my hands free in case someone threatens you. Why did you ask to see me?"

"My sister wants a divorce."

"Then she doesn't need me. What she needs is a lawyer."

"Her bastard husband won't allow it. She's his prisoner till she changes her mind."

"Prisoner?"

"She's not in chains, if that's what you're thinking. But she's a prisoner all the same. And she's not being tortured." She managed to light her cigarette. "Unless you count being raped morning, noon, and night. To remind her of what she'd miss, he says. She needs a true man, he says. What he needs is a bullet through his obscene brain. Do you carry a gun?'' she asked, exhaling smoke.

''Seldom.''

''Then what good are you?''

Savage stood from the column. ''You've made a mistake, Miss Stone. If you want an assassin—''

''No! I want my sister!''

He eased back onto the column. ''You're talking about a retrieval.''

''Whatever you want to call it.''

''If I decide to take the assignment, my fee . . .''

''I'll pay you a million dollars.''

''You're a poor negotiator. I might have settled for less.''

''But that's what I'm offering.''

''Assuming I accept, I'll want half in an escrow account at the start, the other half when I deliver. Plus expenses.''

''Stay in the best hotels for all I care. Spend as much as you want on meals. A few extra thousand hardly matters.''

''You don't understand. When I say 'expenses,' I'm thinking of as much as several *hundred* thousand.''

''What?''

''You're asking me to antagonize one of the most powerful men in Greece. What's he worth? Fifty billion? His security will be extensive, costly to breach. Tell me where your sister is. I'll do a risk analysis. A week from now, I'll tell you if I can get her.''

She stubbed out her cigarette and slowly turned. ''Why?''

''I'm not sure what you mean.''

''I get the feeling this job's more important to you than the money. Why would you consider accepting my offer?''

For a chilling instant, Savage had a mental image of steel glinting, of blood spraying. He repressed the memory, avoiding her question. ''You told your driver 'an hour.' It's just about time. Let's go,'' he said. ''And when we get back to the car, tell him to take an indirect route to your hotel.''

6

Adhering to his own advice, Savage used an indirect route to return to the Acropolis, or rather to an area immediately north of it—to the Plaka, the principal tourist shopping district in Athens. He entered narrow, crowded streets lined with myriad markets and shops. Despite the renewed bitter smog, he detected the aroma of smoking shish kebob, which soon gave way to the fragrance of freshly cut flowers. Loud vendors gesticulated toward handcrafted carpets, leather goods, pottery, copper urns, and silver bracelets. He reached a labyrinth of alleys, paused in an alcove, satisfied himself that he wasn't under surveillance, and proceeded past a tavern to a neighboring shop that sold wineskins.

Inside, the wineskins hung in bunches from hooks on rafters, their leather smell strong but pleasant. Savage bowed to pass beneath them, approaching an overweight woman behind a counter.

His knowledge of Greek was limited. He spoke in memorized phrases. "I need a special product. A wineskin of a different type. If your esteemed employer could spare a few moments to see me . . ."

"Your name?" the woman asked.

"Please tell him it's the opposite of gentle."

She nodded respectfully and turned to proceed up a stairway. Seconds later, she came back, gesturing for him to ascend.

Passing an alcove from which a beard-stubbled man with a shotgun studied him, Savage climbed the stairs. At the top, a door was open. Through it, Savage saw a room—bare except for a desk, behind which a muscular man in a black suit poured a clear liqueur into a glass.

When Savage entered, the man peered up in surprise, as

if he hadn't been notified he had a visitor. "Can it be a ghost?" Though Greek, the man spoke English.

Savage grinned. "I admit I've been a stranger."

"An ungrateful wretch, who hasn't seen fit to keep in touch and maintain our friendship."

"Business kept me away."

"This so-called business must have been truly mythic."

"It had importance. But now I make up for my absence."

Savage set the Greek equivalent of ten thousand U.S. dollars onto the desk. Spreading the bills, he covered the pattern of circular stains made by the glass refilled compulsively each day with ouzo. A licorice scent—the aniseed in the ouzo—filled the room.

The middle-aged Greek noticed Savage's glance toward the liqueur. "May I tempt you?"

"As you know, I seldom drink."

"A character flaw for which I forgive you."

The Greek swelled his chest and chuckled deeply. He showed no sign of his alcoholism. Indeed the ouzo, like formaldehyde, seemed to have preserved his body. Clean-shaven, with glinting, superbly cut black hair, he sipped from his glass, set it down, and studied the money. His swarthy skin exuded health.

Nonetheless he looked troubled as he counted the money. "Too generous. Excessive. You worry me."

"I've also arranged for a gift. Within an hour, if you agree to supply the information I need, a messenger will deliver a case of the finest ouzo."

"Truly the finest? You know my preference."

"I do indeed. But I've taken the liberty of choosing a rarer variety."

"How rare?"

Savage gave a name.

"Extremely generous."

"A tribute to your talent," Savage said.

"As you say in your country"—the man sipped from his glass—"you're an officer and a gentleman."

"*Ex*-officer," Savage corrected him. He wouldn't have volunteered this personal detail if the Greek hadn't known it already. "And *you* are a trusted informant. How long has it been since I first negotiated for your services?"

The Greek concentrated. "Six years of delight. My former wives and many children thank you for your frequent patronage."

"And they'll thank me even more when I triple the money I placed on your desk."

"I knew it. I sensed. When I woke up this morning, I announced to myself that today would be a special occasion."

"But not without risks."

The Greek set down his glass. "Every day brings a risk."

"Are you ready for the challenge?"

"As soon as I fortify myself." The Greek downed the rest of his glass.

"A name," Savage said.

"As the greatest English bard said, what's in—"

"A name? I don't think you'll like it." Savage pulled a bottle of the best-of-the-best, hard-to-find ouzo from beneath the back of his jacket.

The Greek grinned. "That name I like. And the other?"

"Stavros Papadropolis."

The Greek slammed down his glass. "Holy mother of fuck." He swiftly poured more ouzo and gulped it. "What lunacy prompts you to risk investigating him?"

Savage glanced around the almost bare room. "I assume you've been cautious as usual. Your vice hasn't made you neglect your daily cleaning chores, I hope."

The Greek looked hurt. "The day you see furniture in this room, apart from my chair and desk, you'll know I'm unworthy of trust."

Savage nodded. Not only did the Greek keep his furniture to a minimum. As well, the floor had no rug. There weren't any pictures on the walls. There wasn't even a telephone. The room's austerity made it difficult for someone to conceal a microphone. Nonetheless, each morning, the Greek used two different types of sophisticated electronic scanning devices. With one, he checked every inch of the room for radio signals and microwaves to determine if a "bug" was transmitting sounds from the room. However, that type of scanning device could detect only an active, permanently broadcasting microphone.

To discover a *passive* microphone—which stayed dormant if there weren't any sounds in the room, or which could be turned off by remote control if an eavesdropper suspected a sweep was occurring—the second scanner had to be used. It was called a nonlinear junction detector. Through an attachment that resembled the head of a portable vacuum cleaner, it beamed microwaves that located the diodes in the circuits of hidden tape recorders and transmitters. Though this second device required more time to be employed effectively, the Greek always activated it, even on those rare occasions when the first device revealed a microphone—because a skillful eavesdropper always left both active and passive monitors, in case a less skillful searcher would feel that his efforts had been successful and stop if he found only an active microphone.

With his customary humor, the Greek referred to this daily thorough search for bugs as "fumigating."

"Forgive my inquiry," Savage said. "I meant to be careful, not rude."

"If you hadn't asked, I'd have wondered if *you* were worthy of trust."

"You're understanding as always."

The Greek sipped his drink and gestured agreeably. "An obligation of friendship." He pressed his palms on his desk. "But you still haven't answered my question. Papadropolis?"

"I'm interested in his domestic arrangements."

"Not his business affairs? Thank Zeus, you had me worried. The wretch has two hundred ships. They earn a modest profit from transporting grain, machinery, and oil. But he accumulated his fortune from smuggling weapons and drugs. Anyone who inquires about his lucrative contraband becomes fish food in the Aegean."

"He may be as protective about his family life," Savage said.

"No doubt. A Greek would kill to protect the honor of his family, even if in private he didn't care for them. But business is survival. Its secrets are fiercely kept, whereas family secrets are taken for granted to be unavoidable gossip, as long as no one dares to repeat the gossip in front of the lord of the household.''

''Then find me some gossip,'' Savage said.

''Specifically?''

''About Papadropolis and his wife.''

''I've already heard some specifics.''

''Learn more,'' Savage said. ''Where she is and how she's being treated. I want to compare what you tell me with what I've been told.''

''May I ask your purpose?''

Savage shook his head. ''Ignorance is your protection.''

''And *your* protection as well. If I'm unaware of what you intend, I can't reveal it if someone questions me with a force I can't resist.''

''But that won't happen,'' Savage said. ''As long as you stay careful.''

''I'm always careful. Like you, I use intermediaries, and often messengers *between* intermediaries. I speak directly only to clients and those few assistants with whom I have a bond. You look worried, my friend.''

''Six months ago, something happened to me. It made me doubly cautious.'' Remembering, Savage felt his stomach clench.

''Commendable. However, I note the lack of detail in your revelation.''

Savage subdued his temptation to continue revealing. ''It's a personal matter. Unimportant.''

''I'm not convinced of this so-called unimportance, but I do respect your discretion.''

''Just find out what I need.'' Savage walked toward the door. ''Papadropolis and his wife. Two days. That's all the time I can give you. When I return, I want to learn everything.''

7

The Cyclades are a cluster of small Aegean islands southeast of Athens. Their name derives from the Greek word *kyklos* or "circle" and refers to the ancient Greek belief that the islands surrounded Delos, the island upon which the sun god of truth, Apollo, was supposedly born. In fact, Delos is not at the center but near the eastern rim of the islands. A few kilometers farther east of it, on the edge of the Cyclades, lies Mykonos, one of Greece's main holiday areas, where tourists worship their own sun god.

Savage piloted a two-engine, propellor-driven Cessna toward Mykonos, taking care to approach the island on an indirect course, first heading due east from Athens, then easing southward above the Aegean Sea until he flanked the eastern rim of his destination. He radioed the airport at Mykonos to notify the controller that he didn't intend to land. His flight was strictly for practice and pleasure, he explained, and if the controller would warn him which air routes to avoid, Savage would gratefully obey instructions.

The controller obliged.

At a distance and height of one-half kilometer, Savage put the Cessna on automatic pilot and began taking pictures. The Bausch and Lomb telephoto lens on his Nikon camera magnified images amazingly. The photographs would be further magnified after he developed them. The main thing, he knew from his training, was to take plenty of pictures, not only of his target but of its surroundings. Details that seemed unimportant at the moment could too often be crucial when he later constructed his plan.

Yes, plenty of pictures.

He paused frequently to readjust the Cessna's automatic pilot, then resumed his photographic surveillance. The sky was blue, the weather calm. The Cessna seemed to glide on a silken highway. His hands were rock steady. Except for the minor vibrations of the plane, conditions were perfect for taking clear photographs.

His initial objective was the town of Mykonos on the western side of the island. The town spread around two small bays, its houses projecting onto a peninsula that separated each harbor. The buildings were shaped like intersecting cubes, each brilliantly white. Here and there, red domes—sometimes blue—identified churches. Windmills lined a jetty.

But the design of the town, not its beauty, attracted Savage's attention. In antiquity, Mykonos had been a frequent target of pirates. To make their homes easier to protect, the local population had constructed the streets in the form of a labyrinth. Attacking pirates had no difficulty entering the town, but as they pillaged deeper into it, higher up its slopes, they soon discovered that the complex maze of lanes confused their sense of direction. The pirates could see their ship in the harbor below them, but to reach it, they had to test this and that route, all the while encountering ambushes set by the villagers. Eventually, after several defeats, the pirates left Mykonos alone in favor of uncomplicated prey on other islands.

Yes, a labyrinth, Savage thought. I might be able to use that.

Continuing to circle the island, all the while taking photographs, he reached a deep gulf to the north . . . perhaps a pickup site? . . . then studied a forbidding cape to the east . . . to be attempted only in an emergency . . . and finally reached his primary goal: Papadropolis's compound above Anna Bay on the southeastern side of the island.

Since he'd met with his Greek informant two days earlier, Savage had been busy and to his wary satisfaction, had learned a great deal. He'd flown to contacts in Zurich and Brussels, the two most dependable European sources of information about black-market armament sales and the security systems of the men who smuggled the weapons.

Through seemingly casual conversations—and generous

gifts to "friends" to whom Savage pretended delight when he learned that the rumors weren't true about their having been killed—he discovered what he'd already guessed. Papadropolis was controlled by his arrogance. The Greek billionaire was too consumed with power to hire protectors who had sufficient professional integrity to insist on giving orders to their employer.

Savage had also learned that Papadropolis was fascinated by gadgets and technology. Just as the shipping magnate had a passion for computers and video games, so he'd hired an expert in security systems to construct a web of intrusion-warning obstacles around his various European estates.

All Savage cared about was the *Mykonos* estate. The moment he learned who'd designed its defenses, he knew—in the same way an art historian would have recognized a Renaissance style—what barriers he faced.

His longtime and trusted Greek informant had verified what Joyce Stone had claimed. The movie legend's sister was being held captive on her billionaire husband's lavish summer estate on Mykonos.

You want to divorce me, bitch? No woman ever walked away from me. I'd be a joke. An ungrateful wife has only one use. On your back. I'll teach you.

But summer had become September. The start of the tourist season in Athens was the end of the tourist season on Mykonos—because of lowering temperatures. To force her to spend an autumn and perhaps a winter on the island was Papadropolis's idea of a further insult.

Savage lowered his camera, switched off the automatic pilot, and gripped the Cessna's controls. For six months, since the disaster he'd almost described to his Greek informant, he'd been in seclusion, convalescing. His arms, legs, head, and back still ached from the injuries he'd sustained. Nightmarish memories persisted in haunting him.

But the past could not be changed, he strained to remind himself. The present was all that mattered.

And his work.

He had to get back to his work.

To prove himself *to* himself.

He veered from Mykonos, heading north above the legendary wine-dark Aegean, patting his camera. It was good to be on an assignment again.

He felt as if he'd returned from the dead.

8

Savage rose from the waves and crept toward the shore. His black wetsuit blended with the night. He crouched behind boulders, stared at the murky cliff above him, and turned toward the sea. The speedboat's pilot, a British mercenary whom Savage often employed, had been told to hurry from the area as soon as Savage dropped into the water a half-kilometer from the island. The pilot hadn't used any lights. In the dark, with no moon and approaching storm clouds obscuring the stars, a sentry couldn't have seen the boat. Amid the din of waves crashing onto rocks, a sentry couldn't have heard it either, though Savage had taken the precaution of placing a sound-absorbent housing over the speedboat's motor.

Satisfied that he'd reached here undetected . . . unless the guards had night scopes . . . Savage pulled at the strong nylon cord cinched around his waist. He felt resistance, pulled harder, and soon withdrew a small rubber raft from the water. Behind a rock that shielded him from the spray of the waves, he unzipped the raft's waterproof compartment and took out a bulging knapsack. His wetsuit had kept the frigid water from draining his body heat and giving him hypothermia as he swam with the raft toward shore.

Now he shivered, peeling off the wetsuit. Naked, he hurriedly reached into the knapsack to put on black woolen clothes. He'd chosen wool because its hollow fibers had superior insulating ability, even when wet. His socks and cap were made of the same dark material. He slipped into sturdy ankle-high shoes with cross-ridged soles and tied them firmly. Warm again, he applied black camouflage grease to his face, then protected his hands with dark woolen gloves that were thin enough to allow his fingers to be flexible.

What remained in the knapsack were the various tools he would need, each wrapped in cloth to prevent their metal from clanking together. He secured the knapsack's straps around his shoulders and tightened its belt. The knapsack was heavy, but not as heavy as the equipment he'd been accustomed to carrying when he was in the SEALs, and his strong back accepted the burden comfortably. He placed his wetsuit, snorkel, goggles, and fins into the raft's compartment, zipped it shut, and tied the raft securely to a rock. He didn't know if he'd be forced to return to this site, but he wanted to have the raft here in case he needed it. Papadropolis's guards wouldn't notice it until the morning, and by then, if Savage hadn't returned, their discovery of the raft wouldn't matter.

He approached the cliff. A breeze gained strength, the storm clouds now completely obscuring the sky. The air smelled of imminent rain. Good, Savage thought. His plan depended on a storm. That was why he'd chosen tonight to infiltrate Papadropolis's estate. All the weather forecasters had agreed—around midnight, the first rains of autumn would arrive.

But Savage had to get to the top of the cliff before the storm made climbing difficult. He reached up, found a handhold, braced the toe of one of his boots in a niche, and began his ascent. Though two hundred feet high, the cliff had multiple fissures and outcrops. An experienced climber, Savage would not have trouble scaling it in the dark.

The wind increased. Spray from the waves stung his face and made the cliff slippery. He gripped his gloved fingers tighter onto outcrops, wedged his boots deeper into niches, and climbed with greater deliberation. Halfway up, he reached a fissure. Recalling it from the photographs he'd studied, knowing it would take him to the top, he squirmed inside it, braced his boots against each side, groped up for handholds, and strained higher. His mental clock told him he'd been climbing for almost ten minutes, but all he cared about was each second of caution. The fissure blocked the wind, but a sudden cascade of rain replaced the spray from the waves, and he fought the urge to climb faster. He groped up, touched nothing, and exhaled, realizing he'd arrived at the top of the cliff.

The rain fell harder, drenching him. Even so, it now was welcome, providing him with greater concealment in the night. He crawled from the fissure, scurried across the rim, and crouched among bushes. Mud soaked his knees. His stomach fluttered with nervousness as it always did at the start of a mission.

But it also burned with fear that despite his meticulous preparations he might fail as he had six months ago.

There was only one way to learn if he'd recovered.

He inhaled, concentrated on the obstacles he faced, and subdued his distracting emotions.

Scanning the storm-shrouded night, detecting no guards, he crept from the bushes.

9

The photographs he'd taken had revealed the first barrier he would come to—a chain link fence around the estate. From the photographs, he hadn't been able to determine the height of the fence, but the standard was seven feet. When he'd magnified the photographs, he'd discovered that the fence was topped by several strands of barbed wire attached to braces that projected inward and outward in the shape of a V.

The rain made the night so dark that Savage couldn't see the fence. Nonetheless, by studying the photographs and comparing the theoretical height of the fence with the distance between the fence and these bushes, he'd calculated that the barrier was twenty yards ahead. The photographs hadn't shown any closed-circuit cameras mounted on the fence, so he didn't worry about revealing himself to remote-controlled night-vision lenses. All the same, from habit, he crawled. The rain-soaked ground felt mushy beneath him.

At the fence, he stopped to remove his knapsack. He took out an infrared flashlight and a pair of infrared goggles. The beam from the flashlight would be invisible to unaided eyes, but through the goggles, Savage saw a greenish glow. He aimed the beam toward the fence's metal posts, scanning upward toward the projecting metal arms that secured the barbed wire.

What he looked for were vibration sensors.

He found none. As he'd expected, the fence was merely a line of demarcation, a barrier but not an intrusion detector. It kept hikers from trespassing unintentionally. Its barbed-wire top discouraged unskilled invaders. If animals—roaming dogs, for example—banged against it, there'd be no alarm needlessly attracting guards.

Savage put the flashlight and goggles into his knapsack, hoisted the pack to his shoulders, and resecured it. As the rain gusted harder, he stepped away from the fence, assumed a sprinter's stance, and lunged.

His momentum carried him halfway up the fence. He grabbed for the projecting metal arm at the top, swung his body up onto the strands of barbed wire, clutched the metal arm on the opposite side of the V, swung over the second group of barbed wire, and landed smoothly, his knees bent, on the far side of the fence. His woolen clothes and gloves were ripped in many places; the barbed wire had inflicted several irritating nicks on his arms and legs. But his injuries were too inconsequential to concern him. Barbed wire was a discouragement only to amateurs.

Staying close to the ground, wiping rain from his eyes, he studied the murky area before him. His British mentor, who'd trained him to be an executive protector, had been fond of saying that life was an obstacle course and a scavenger hunt.

Well, now the obstacle course would begin.

10

The island of Mykonos was hilly, with shallow soil and many projecting rocks. Papadropolis had built his estate on one of the few level peaks. Savage's photographs had shown that a surrounding slope led up to the mansion.

From the mansion's perspective, the bottom of the slope could not be seen. Hence Papadropolis had decided that an aesthetic barrier around his property, a stone wall instead of a chain link fence, would not be necessary. After all, if the tyrant didn't have to look at the institutional-looking fence, it wouldn't offend him, and metal was always more intimidating to an intruder than stone and mortar.

Savage tried to think as his opponent did. Because Papadropolis couldn't see this rocky slope and probably avoided its sharp incline, most of the intrusion sensors would be located in this area. The photographs of the estate had shown a second fence, lower than the first but not enough to be jumped across. The fence was halfway up the slope.

But what worried Savage was what the photographs couldn't show—buried detectors between the first fence and the second. He removed his knapsack and selected a device the size of a Walkman radio: a battery-powered voltmeter, its purpose to register electrical impulses from underground pressure sensors. He couldn't risk referring to an illuminated dial on the meter, the light from which might reveal him, so he'd chosen a device equipped with an earplug.

Lightning flashed. His earplug wailed, and he froze. The night became dark again. At once his earplug stopped wailing, causing him to relax. The voltmeter had reacted to atmospheric electricity from the lightning, not to buried sensors. Otherwise the earplug would have continued to wail even when there wasn't lightning.

But the flash of light, though startling, had been useful. He'd been given a glimpse of the fence a few yards ahead of him. It too was chain link. Not topped by barbed wire, however. And Savage understood why—anyone who'd climbed the more imposing first fence would be tempted to scramble over this seemingly less protected barrier.

He approached it cautiously. Another flash of lightning revealed small metal boxes attached to the posts supporting the fence. Vibration detectors. If someone grabbed the chain links and started to climb, an alarm would warn guards in the mansion. A computer monitor would reveal the site of the intrusion. The guards would quickly converge on the area.

In theory, the vibration sensors could not be defeated. But Savage knew that vibration sensors had to be adjusted so that a specific amount of vibration was necessary before the sensors would trigger an alarm. Otherwise, wind gusting against the fence or a bird's landing on it would needlessly alert guards. After several false warnings, the guards would lose faith in the sensors and fail to investigate an alarm. So the only way to get beyond the fence was to use a method that seemed the most risky.

To cut through the links. But it had to be done in a special way.

Savage unslung his knapsack and took out wireclippers. Kneeling, he chose a link at shoulder level and snipped it. Instead of fearing that he'd caused an alarm, instead of succumbing to second thoughts and rushing away, he calmly waited forty seconds, snipped another link, and waited another forty seconds, then snipped a third link. Each snip was the same as a bird landing on the fence or given the weather, rain lashing against it. His carefully timed assault on the fence had insufficient constancy to activate the sensors.

Twelve minutes later, Savage removed a two-foot square from the fence, eased his knapsack through the gap, then crawled through, slowly, making sure he didn't touch the surrounding links.

He put the wireclippers into his pack and resecured the

pack to his shoulders. Now, in addition to the voltmeter, he carried a miniature battery-powered microwave detector. As well, he again wore his infrared goggles. Because his photographs had revealed a further danger. A line of metal posts near the top of the slope. Nothing linked them. They appeared to be the start of a fence that would soon be completed, wires eventually attached to them.

But Savage knew better.

He stared through his goggles, anxious to know whether infrared beams filled the gaps between the posts. If his suspicion was correct, if the beams existed and he passed through them, he'd trigger an alarm.

But as he crept closer to the top of the rain-swept hill, his goggles *still* did not detect infrared beams between the posts. Which meant . . .

The moment the thought occurred to him, the earplug attached to his microwave detector began to wail.

He halted abruptly.

Yes, he thought. Microwaves. He'd have been disappointed if Papadropolis used infrared. That type of beam was too susceptible to false alarms caused by rain. But microwaves provided an absolutely invisible barrier and were much less affected by weather. This test meant nothing without a sufficient challenge.

Again, as lightning flashed, the earplug to Savage's voltmeter wailed. He paused, in case the lightning coincided with an electrical field from a buried pressure sensor. But when the wail stopped, he knew that the microwave fence was his only obstacle.

He approached his objective. The lightning had allowed him a glimpse of the nearest post. The post had a slot down its right and left side, for transmitting beams to and receiving beams from the next posts right and left. The post was too high for him to leap over the microwaves, the earth too shallow for him to dig under them.

Still, the installer—for all his cleverness—had made a mistake, for this system worked best when the posts weren't in a continuous line with each other but instead were staggered so the microwaves formed an overlapping pattern.

In such a formation, the posts were protected. If an intruder tried to use them to get past the system, he'd interfere with the microwaves. However, Savage's photographs had shown that the system was in a straight line.

It *could* be defeated.

Savage removed a metal clamp from his knapsack and attached the clamp to the post, above the slots that transmitted and received the microwaves. He screwed several sections of metal together to form a three-foot-long rod, then inserted the rod into the clamp, the rod projecting toward him. Next, he threw his knapsack over the post, gripped the rod, and raised himself onto it. For a heartpounding instant, he almost lost his balance. The rod became slippery in the rain. Wind pushed him. But the ridges on the soles of his boots gripped the rod. He managed to steady himself and dove over the top of the post, avoiding the microwaves.

He landed in a somersault. His shoulders, back, and hips absorbed his impact. So did the rain-soaked ground. He cringed from pain, however, still tender from the injuries he'd sustained six months ago. Ignoring the protest in his muscles, he came smoothly out of his roll and crouched to study the near crest of the slope.

It was haloed by faint light made misty by the rain. No sign of guards. In a careful rush, he put the clamp and rod back into his knapsack, along with the infrared goggles he no longer needed. He aimed his voltmeter and microwave detector and proceeded higher.

At the top, he lay on soggy ground and studied his target. Arc lights, dimmed by the rain, illuminated a lawn. Fifty yards away, a sprawling white mansion—a concatenation of cubes and domes that imitated the houses in the town of Mykonos—attracted his attention. Except for the arc lights on the corners of the building and a light in a far left window, the mansion was dark.

His photographs had not been detailed enough to let him know if closed-circuit television cameras were mounted above the doors, but he had to assume they were present, although in this storm the cameras would relay murky images and at three A.M. the guard who watched the monitors would not be alert.

As Savage charged toward the mansion, he saw a camera above the door he'd chosen—on the right, farthest from the lamp in the window on the opposite side of the building. The camera made him veer even farther right, rushing toward the door obliquely, clutching a canister that he'd taken from his knapsack.

When he reached the door, darting from the side, he raised the canister and sprayed the lens of the camera. The canister held pressurized water, its vapor coating the camera's lens as if a gust of rain had lanced against the house. The streaks of dripping liquid would impair but not eliminate the camera's murky image, thus troubling the guard who watched the monitor but not compelling him to sound an alarm.

Savage picked the door's lock—a good lock, a dead bolt, but freed in twelve seconds. Still he didn't dare open the door.

Instead he removed a metal detector from his knapsack and scanned the door's perimeter. Metal on the upper right, four feet above the doorknob, made his earphone wail. Another intrusion detector.

Savage understood the principle. A magnet within the door kept a metal lever in the doorframe from rising toward a switch that would signal an alarm if the door was opened.

To defeat the alarm, Savage removed a powerful horseshoe

magnet from his knapsack and pressed it upward, against the doorframe, while he gently shoved the door open. His magnet replaced the magnet within the door and prevented the lever in the frame from rising toward the contact switch. As he squeezed through a gap in the door, he slid his magnet farther across the doorframe, then eased the door shut before he removed the magnet. Now the door's own magnet prevented the lever from rising.

He was in.

But he didn't dare relax.

11

Joyce Stone had described the mansion's layout. Having memorized the floor plan, Savage proceeded tensely along a dark hallway. He studied an opening to his left and saw an illuminated clock on an oven. The kitchen was spacious, fragrant with the lingering smells of oil and garlic from the evening's meal. Passing a counter, he entered a shadowy dining room, its rectangular table long enough to seat fifteen guests on each side as well as the master and his wife at each end.

But Papadropolis was not in residence. A member of Savage's surveillance team had reported that Papadropolis and an entourage of guards had flown on the billionaire's private plane to Crete this morning. The tyrant's departure had been an unexpected gift of the Fates. Not only had Papadropolis lessened the number of guards at the mansion, but those who remained would feel a lessened sense of duty.

So Savage hoped. He'd soon find out.

At a farther doorway, he halted, hearing muffled voices. Three men. Down a stairwell on his left. Laughter echoed upward. Sure, Savage thought, they're happy to be dry and warm.

He continued through the shadows, entering a murky living room. Halfway across, he heard a chair creak and ducked behind a sofa. The sound came through an archway ahead. Holding his breath, he crept nearer and saw the glow from a rain-misted light outside two barred windows. Each window flanked the mansion's front door, and in the vestibule, another glow—red, from a cigarette—revealed a guard in an alcove on the far side of the door.

Savage raised a pistol. Its projectiles weren't bullets but tranquilizer darts, and its front and rear sights had been tipped with infrared paint that allowed him to aim in the dark, its luminous specks visible only through his goggles.

The weapon made a muffled spit. At once Savage moved as quickly as the need for silence allowed, crossing the vestibule, grabbing the guard as he slumped from a chair, and more important, grabbing the guard's Uzi before it clattered onto the marble floor. He set the guard behind his chair and folded his legs to make sure they didn't project from the alcove.

With the Uzi slung across his shoulder, Savage studied the top of a curving staircase. A light up there indicated a hallway that Joyce Stone had described. Shifting his gaze from the vestibule toward the corridor above him, then once more toward the vestibule, he slowly ascended.

At the top, he pressed against the left wall and peered cautiously through the archway, toward the right, along the illuminated corridor. He couldn't see the corridor's end, but so far he hadn't glimpsed a guard. Rachel Stone's bedroom was in that direction, however, and he took for granted that a sentry would be watching her door.

He risked leaning farther into the archway to get a better view of the corridor. Still no guard.

At last he had to show his head, his view of the hallway complete.

A guard in a chair at the end! The man read a magazine.

Having revealed himself gradually, Savage used equal care to shift back out of sight, lest sudden motion attract the guard.

Would there be a corresponding sentry at the opposite end of the corridor?

Savage stepped softly toward the right side of the archway and peered with greater caution along the left flank of the corridor.

Or started to. A noise alerted him. A gun being cocked.

There *was* a guard on the left flank of the corridor. Savage aimed reflexively. His weapon spat. The guard on the left stumbled backward, his eyes already losing focus as he pawed at the dart protruding from his throat. The guard's knees buckled.

Savage prayed that the man's cocked handgun wouldn't discharge when it hit the floor. At the same time, he pivoted into the corridor and fired at the guard on the right. This guard had seen his counterpart stagger backward. Reacting to the commotion, he'd dropped what he was reading and grabbed his pistol. He began to surge out of his chair.

Savage's gun spat yet again. Its dart struck the man's left shoulder. Though the man tried desperately to aim his pistol, his eyes rolled upward. He toppled.

The thick carpet had muffled the noise of the falling bodies. Or so Savage prayed. Pulse hammering, he hurried to the right, toward the door to what Joyce Stone had told him was her sister's room. He tested the knob; it was locked. He suspected that the bolt could not be freed from inside but only from *this* side. After picking the lock, he scanned the doorframe with his metal detector but found no sign of an intruder alarm, urgently entered, and shut the door.

12

The bedroom was luxurious, but Savage barely noticed its expensive furnishings as he scanned them in search of Rachel Stone. A bedside lamp was on. The bed had been slept in; its rumpled covers had been thrown aside. But the room was deserted.

Savage checked beneath the bed. He peered behind closed draperies, finding bars on a window, then searched behind a settee and a chair.

Where the hell *was* she?

He opened a door, found a bathroom, and turned on the light. The shower door was closed. When he looked inside, the stall was empty.

Where . . . ?

He tried another door. A closet. Dresses. Rachel Stone lunged through the dresses. Scissors glinted. Savage clutched her wrist an instant before she'd have stabbed his left eye.

"Bastard!"

Her anger-contorted features suddenly changed to a frown of surprise. Noticing Savage's black camouflage-greased face, she struggled backward.

"Who—?"

Savage clamped a hand across her mouth and shook his head. As he yanked the scissors from her grasp, his lips formed silent words. *Don't talk*. He pulled a card from his pocket. The card was sealed in transparent, waterproof plastic.

She stared at its dark hand-printed message.

YOUR SISTER SENT ME TO GET YOU OUT OF HERE.

He turned the card, revealing a further message.

THIS ROOM MIGHT HAVE HIDDEN MICROPHONES.
WE MUSTN'T TALK.

She studied the card . . . and him . . . subdued her suspicion, and finally nodded.

He showed her another card.

GET DRESSED. WE'RE LEAVING. *NOW*.

But Rachel Stone didn't move.

Savage flipped the second card.

YOUR SISTER TOLD ME TO SHOW YOU THIS.
TO PROVE SHE SENT ME.

He held up a wedding ring, its diamond enormous.

This time when Rachel Stone nodded, she did so with recognition and conviction.

She grabbed for a dress in the closet.

But Savage squeezed her arm to stop her. Shaking his head, he pointed toward jeans, a sweater, and jogging shoes.

She understood. With no hint of embarrassment, she removed her nightgown.

Savage tried to ignore her nakedness, directing his attention toward the door through which guards might any moment charge.

Hurry, he silently pleaded. His pulse hammered faster.

Glancing again in her direction, he was too preoccupied to dwell on the jeans she tugged up over smooth, sensual thighs and silken bikini panties that revealed her pubic hair.

No, Savage's attention was directed solely toward two other—the most significant—aspects of her appearance.

One: Rachel Stone, though ten years younger than her sister, looked like Joyce Stone's twin. Tall, thin, angular. Intense blue eyes. A superb oval face, its magnificent curves framed by spectacular shoulder-length hair. There *was* one difference. Joyce Stone's hair was blond whereas Rachel's was auburn. The difference didn't matter. The resemblance between older and younger sister remained uncanny.

Two: while Joyce Stone's face was smooth and tanned, Rachel's was swollen and bruised. In addition to repeatedly raping his wife, Papadropolis had beaten her, making sure his fists left marks that couldn't be concealed. Humiliate—that was the tyrant's weapon. Subdue and dominate.

Not any longer, Savage thought. For the first time, he felt committed not just professionally but morally to this assignment. Rachel Stone might be—probably had been—spoiled by luxury. But nothing gave anyone the right to brutalize her.

Okay, Papadropolis, Savage thought. I started this for me, to prove myself. But I'll end this to get at *you*.

You son of a bitch!

His skull throbbed with anger.

Turning from the door, he saw that Rachel Stone was now dressed.

He leaned toward her ear, his whisper almost soundless, conscious of her perfume. *"Take the few things you absolutely need."*

She nodded with determination and leaned close to him, her words as soft as her breath. *"I'll give you anything you want. Just get me out of here."*

Savage headed toward the door.

13

With the grace of a dancer, Rachel Stone rushed soundlessly down the stairs. In the shadowy vestibule, Savage touched her arm to guide her toward the living room, intending to reach the hallway near the kitchen and leave the mansion through the same door he'd used to enter.

But she twisted away from his grasp, her long, lithe legs taking her quickly toward the front door.

Savage rushed to stop her before she opened the door and triggered an alarm.

But she didn't reach for the door, instead for a switch above it, and Savage understood abruptly that, despite her compulsion to escape, she retained sufficient presence of mind to deactivate the alarm.

She opened the door. Rain lashed beneath a balcony. Savage followed her onto wide white steps and gently shut the door. Feeling exposed by a misty arc light, he turned to give her instructions.

She was gone, racing past pillars, down the steps, into the storm.

No! He ran to catch up to her. Christ, doesn't she realize

there might be guards out here? She can't just scramble over a fence. She'll trip an alarm!

The rain was stronger than when he'd entered the mansion, and colder. But though he shivered, he knew that some of the moisture streaming down his face was sweat. From fear.

He reached her, about to tackle her, intending to drag her toward the cover of a large statue to his left. At once he changed his mind. She wasn't fleeing at random. Rather she stayed on a concrete driveway that curved in front of the mansion. Constantly heading toward the right, she reached a short lane that intersected with the driveway. At the end of the lane, a storm-shrouded arc light revealed a long, narrow, single-story building with six large doors of a type that opened upward.

The estate's garage. *That* was her destination. They could hide behind it while he explained how he planned to get her past the sensors.

Gaining speed, Savage flanked her, his voice low but forceful. "Follow me. Toward the back."

But she didn't obey and instead lunged toward a door on the side of the garage, in view of the mansion. She twisted the knob. It didn't budge.

She sobbed. "Jesus, it's locked."

"We have to get in back—out of sight."

She kept struggling with the doorknob.

"Come on," Savage said.

He spun toward a shout from the mansion.

A guard charged out the front door, pistol raised, scanning the storm.

Oh, shit, Savage thought.

A second man charged out.

Savage hoped that the rain was too dense for the men to see the garage.

Then a third man charged out, and Savage knew the entire guard force would soon be searching the grounds.

"No choice," he said. "Your idea's lousy, Rachel, but right now I can't think of anything better. Stand back."

Rain drenched him as he frantically picked the lock. When

he opened the door, Rachel shoved past him, reaching for a light switch. He managed to shut the door just in time, before the sudden illumination would have attracted the guards.

He faced a long row of luxury cars. "Is it too much to hope you brought keys? I can hot-wire one of these cars, but it'll take me a minute, and thanks to you, we don't have that much time."

Rachel darted toward a Mercedes sedan. "The keys are already in them."

"What?"

"No thief would dare to steal from my husband."

"Then why was the door locked?"

"Isn't it obvious?"

"No."

"To stop *me* from taking a car if I somehow got out of the house."

As they spoke, Savage ran after her toward the Mercedes. But she got behind the steering wheel and slammed the driver's door before he could stop her. She twisted the ignition key she'd predicted would be in place. The car's finely tuned engine purred; acrid exhaust spewed into the garage.

At once she pressed a button on a remote control attached to the dashboard. A rumble reverberated. The door ahead of the Mercedes slid smoothly upward.

Savage barely managed to open the passenger door and scramble inside before she stomped the accelerator. His head snapped back. He slammed the door shut an instant before it would have smashed against the garage exit's frame.

"You almost left me behind!"

"I knew you'd manage."

"*But what if I hadn't?*"

Rachel spun the steering wheel to the left and skidded down the lane away from the garage. A brief glare from an arc light revealed her bruised, swollen face. She pressed harder on the accelerator and spun the steering wheel again, this time to the right, toward the driveway that led away from the mansion.

Before he could put on his seat belt, Savage was jerked in the direction of her steering.

"What if you hadn't got into the car before I sped away?" Rachel asked. "I've got the feeling you're resourceful."

"And I've got the feeling you're a bitch."

"My husband calls me a bitch quite a lot."

"I apologize."

"Hey, don't get sentimental on me. I need a savior who kicks ass."

"No, what you need right now"—Savage reached toward the controls and pressed a switch—"is to turn on your windshield wipers."

"I told you, you're resourceful."

Savage glanced all around, seeing guards try desperately to intercept the car. They carried weapons but didn't aim them.

Why?

It didn't make sense.

Then it did.

They'd be glad to blow my brains out, Savage thought. They'd get a bonus. But they don't dare shoot for fear of hitting Papadropolis's wife. In that case, the guards themselves would not be shot. Papadropolis would feed them to the sharks.

As Savage stared forward, lightning flashed, and in the stark illumination, he saw a man on the driveway ahead. The man held a rifle, and like the other guards, he refused to raise it and fire.

*Un*like the others, he held up a powerful flashlight, aiming its fierce beam toward the driver's side, hoping to blind Rachel and force her off the road.

Rachel jerked up a hand to shield her eyes and steered toward the man with the flashlight.

The guard jumped out of the way, his leap so smooth that Savage wondered if he'd had gymnastic training. Landing safely on Savage's side of the car, the guard continued to aim the glaring flashlight.

And that, too, didn't make sense. The guard couldn't hope to blind Rachel from the side.

Then the logic was obvious.

The guard directed the flashlight not toward Rachel but Savage.

To get a good look at me! So he can describe me to Papadropolis, and maybe someone can identify me!

Savage quickly covered his face with his hands. At the same time, he slumped, in case the guard decided to risk a shot at the passenger window.

The moment the car sped past the guard, Savage stared backward. Other guards ran down the road from the mansion. Every light was on in the house, silhouetting the guards in the night and the rain. The man who'd aimed the flashlight stood with his back to the house, scowling toward the Mercedes. The flashlight had prevented Savage from seeing his opponent's face, but now as the man shut the beam off, a further bolt of lightning revealed the guard's features.

The glimpse was imperfect. Because rain streaked down the back window. Because Savage's vision had not fully recovered from the glare of the powerful flashlight. Because the Mercedes was speeding away from the man.

But Savage saw enough. The guard was Oriental. His deft leap away from the car—had it been due to gymnastic training, as Savage had first suspected, or to expertise in martial arts?

Four seconds. That was all the time Savage had to study the man. The lightning died. The night concealed.

But four seconds had been enough. The man was in his midthirties: five feet ten inches tall, trim, and solid looking. He wore dark slacks, a matching windbreaker and turtleneck sweater. His brown face was rectangular, his rugged jaw and cheekbones framing his stern, handsome features.

Oriental, yes. But Savage could be more specific. The man was *Japanese.* Savage knew the man's nationality as certainly as his four seconds of shocked recognition had made him shudder at the eerie resemblance the man bore to . . .

Savage didn't want to think it.

Akira?

No! Impossible!

But as the Mercedes sped farther from the mansion, Savage analyzed his brief impression of the guard, and the major detail about the man wasn't his wiry frame or his stark rectangular features.

No, the major detail was the melancholy behind the intensity on the Japanese sentry's face.

Akira had been the saddest man Savage had ever met.

It couldn't be!

In shock, Savage pivoted toward Rachel. She supposedly was in his custody, but her hysteria controlled her. "You'll never get through the gate."

"Just watch me." She increased speed.

"But the gate's made of steel. It's reinforced."

"So is this car. Armor-plated. Grab the dashboard. When we hit the gate, the Mercedes'll be a tank."

Ahead, guards scrambled away. The chain link gate loomed quickly. With a jolting concussion, the sedan crashed through the barrier.

Savage swung to stare through the rain-drenched rear window, seeing headlights pursuing them.

He brooded.

With terrible certainty.

The man who drove the car would look impossibly like Akira.

"Did I scare you?" Rachel chuckled.

"Not at all."

"Then why do you look so pale?"

"It could be I've just seen a ghost."

14

Savage had planned several ways to get Rachel off the island. Under ideal circumstances, they'd have rushed to a motorcycle that a member of Savage's team had hidden among rocks on a slope a half-kilometer away. From there, they'd have had a choice of three widely separated coves, in each of which a small, powerful boat was waiting to speed them to a fishing trawler that circled the island.

One of the contingencies Savage had to worry about was the weather. While he'd invaded the estate, the storm had been to his advantage—the harder it rained, the better he'd been concealed. But he'd hoped that the storm would lessen during the evacuation, and instead it had strengthened. The wind would be too powerful, the sea too rough for a boat to take them to the fishing trawler, which itself would be in danger and need to seek shelter.

Of course, Savage never based a plan merely on the chance that the weather would improve, even if the forecasts were in his favor. One of his scouts had found a secluded cave in which they could hide till conditions permitted them to use a boat. Savage hadn't worried about dogs following their scent, for Papadropolis had a phobia about dogs and refused to have them on his property. But even if there *had* been dogs, the rain would have impaired their sense of smell.

Savage took into account that guards might find the boats in the coves, so he'd arranged for a helicopter to be waiting on the neighboring island of Delos. All he had to do was signal it with a radio transmitter in his pack, and the chopper would rush to pick them up at a prearranged rendezvous.

But suppose the weather stayed bad, and the chopper couldn't fly? Suppose Papadropolis's men were in the rendezvous area? Pursued, Savage had no opportunity to get Rachel to the cave. That left him with one final variation in his plan. The most desperate alternative.

"Ahead, the road soon forks. Turn left," he said.

"But that'll take us northwest. Toward—"

"Mykonos." Savage nodded.

"The village is a labyrinth! We'll be trapped before we can hide!"

"I don't plan to hide." Savage stared back toward the headlights enlarging in rapid pursuit.

Akira? No! It couldn't be!

"What do you mean, you don't plan to hide? What will we—?"

"Here's the fork. Do what I tell you. Turn left."

When they'd crashed through the gate, the concrete driveway had become a dirt road. The rain had softened the dirt. The heavy armor-plated Mercedes sank into muddy puddles. Tires spinning, rear end fishtailing, the car struggled forward. At least the pursuing car will have the same trouble we do, Savage thought. Then he noticed that farther back the headlights of other cars had joined the chase.

The mushy road had slowed the Mercedes to thirty kilometers an hour. Even then, Rachel had trouble controlling the steering wheel and keeping the car from sliding into a ditch as she obeyed instructions and took the left fork. "Satisfied?"

"For now. You drive well, by the way."

"Trying to bolster my confidence?"

"It never hurts," Savage said. "But I wasn't lying."

"My husband lies to me all the time. How do I know—?"

"That *I'm* not? Because your safety depends on me, and if you couldn't control this car, I'd insist on trading places with you."

"Compliment accepted." Frowning with concentration, she managed to increase speed.

Savage stared again toward the headlights behind him. They weren't gaining. The trouble was, they weren't receding either.

"My husband hired fools. When they had the chance back there, they weren't smart enough to shoot at the tires."

"It wouldn't have mattered."

"I don't understand."

"The tires on a car this heavy are reinforced. They can take a shotgun blast or a bullet from a forty-five and *still* support the car." A gust of wind shook the car.

Rachel almost veered off the road. Voice trembling, she asked, "What happens when we get to Mykonos?"

"*If* we get to Mykonos. Pay attention to the moment."

They reached the village of Ano Mera. At this late hour,

the village was dark, asleep. The Mercedes gained speed on its rock-slabbed road. Too soon, with the village behind them, the route became muddy again and Rachel eased her foot off the accelerator.

Savage exhaled.

Rachel misinterpreted. "Am I doing something wrong?"

"No, I was worried that the guards would have phoned ahead to warn the men your husband pays to watch for strangers passing through the village toward his estate. We might have faced a roadblock."

"You've done your homework."

"I try, but there's always something, the risk of an unknown threat. Knowledge is power. Ignorance . . ."

"Finish. What do you mean?"

"Ignorance is death. I think the headlights are gaining on us."

"I noticed in my rearview mirror. Talking helps me not to be afraid. If they catch us . . ."

"You won't be harmed."

"Until my husband returns. To beat me again before he rapes me. But you'll . . ."

"Be killed."

"Then why are you helping me? How much did my sister pay you?"

"It doesn't matter. Keep your eyes on the road," Savage said. "If we get to Mykonos—it's only eight kilometers ahead—follow my instructions exactly."

"Then you *do* have a plan."

"I had several, but this is the one I'm forced to use. I repeat"— Savage glanced toward the pursuing, possibly gaining headlights—"your life depends on total obedience. Do everything I say."

"When my husband gives me orders, I resent it. But when *you* give me orders, I'm ready to follow you to hell."

"Let's hope you don't have to prove it."

15

Their headlights gleamed off cube-shaped houses, brilliantly white even in the rain-swept darkness.

"Mykonos!" Rachel pressed her foot harder onto the accelerator.

"No!" Savage said.

Too late. The sudden increased speed caused the Mercedes to hydroplane on the mud. The car veered sideways, spun—*twice*, the steering wheel useless, Savage's stomach twisting—and crashed against a fence at the side of the road.

Rachel rammed the gearshift into reverse, tromping the accelerator again.

"Stop!" Savage said.

But the worst had been done. Instead of easing away from the fence toward the road, Rachel had made the car slip sideways onto a mound of earth that snagged the car's drive shaft, propping it up. The tires spun not on mud but air. The car was useless. Two people wouldn't be strong enough to push it off the mound.

The pursuing headlights loomed closer.

Rachel scrambled out of the car. Savage rushed to join her. His boots sank and slid in the mud. He almost lost his balance but managed not to fall as Rachel *did* lose her balance. He caught her, kept a tight grip on her arm, and urged her forward. The sensation was that of a nightmare, racing through mud and yet staying in place.

But they stubbornly gained momentum. Before them, the white cube-shaped houses enlarged as the headlights behind them magnified.

At once, the nightmare of running in place concluded. Rock slabs beneath Savage's boots made him feel as if a cable that restrained him had snapped. He and Rachel shot forward, the solid street providing traction.

The moment they entered the village, Savage realized that the Mercedes would have been useless anyhow. The street they ran along was narrow, winding. It forked, the angles so sharp and confining that the Mercedes could not have maneuvered with any speed. Hearing the engines of the pursuing cars, Savage chose the left tangent and hurried along it, suddenly confronted by two more tangents. Dismayed, he knew that no matter which direction he took, there'd soon be *other* tangents.

The maze of Mykonos, the streets arranged in a labyrinth, a means of confusing pirates in antiquity, of making it easy for villagers to trap marauders. Or for present-day hunters to trap their quarry.

Behind him, Savage heard slamming car doors, angry voices, urgent footsteps echoing along a street. He studied the tangents before him. The one to the left veered upward, the other down. His choice was inevitable. He had to keep moving toward the harbor. Guiding Rachel, he fled to the right, only to discover that the street soon angled upward.

It's taking us back to where we started!

Savage pivoted, forcing Rachel to retrace her steps. Except for the gusting rain and the angry voices of their hunters, the village was silent. Only the white of the houses, occasional lights in windows, and sporadic flashes of lightning helped Savage to see his way.

He found a lane he'd failed to notice when he'd passed this way earlier. The lane led downward, so constricting that his shoulders brushed against the walls. He emerged on a wider lane, horizontal, so flat that he couldn't tell which direction might eventually lead downward. But clattering footsteps to his left made him nudge Rachel and charge to the right.

This time, when the lane ended, there was only one exit —to the right, and *that* led upward.

No! We have to keep aiming toward the harbor!

Savage spun, staring along the lane they'd just taken. The footsteps and curses of the guards sounded closer. Flashlights blazed at the end of the lane. One guard turned to another, his beam revealing the face of the second guard.

The second man was the Japanese. Even at a distance, he still reminded Savage disturbingly of Akira. The Japanese grabbed the first guard's arm and shoved the flashlight away from his face. They rushed along the lane.

In Savage's direction.

They haven't seen us yet, but they will.

Savage's boot struck an object at the side of the lane. A ladder lay against a wall, half of which had a fresh coat of white. He braced it against the wall. Rachel scurried up. As Savage followed, he saw the flashlights checking doorways and alleys, rushing closer.

On the roof, he pulled the ladder up. It scraped against the wall. The flashlights aimed toward the noise. Savage was blinded when a beam revealed him. He ducked back, yanking the ladder with him, hearing the distinctive muffled report of a pistol equipped with a silencer, a bullet zipping past his ear. An instant later, he was out of sight from the lane.

He almost set the ladder down but quickly changed his mind.

"Rachel, grab the other end."

Awkward, they strained to hurry with the ladder across the roof, lurching to a stop when a gap before them revealed another lane.

In the distance, Savage saw murky lights in the rain-swept harbor.

"Let go of the ladder."

He swung it over the gap, setting the far end on the other roof, propping the near end securely.

Rachel started to crawl across, but the ladder's rungs were slick with rain, and her knee slipped, a leg falling through. She dangled, gasped, raised her knee to the ladder, and crawled again.

Savage steadied the ladder. He stared toward the gap below him—no flashlights, although he did hear shouts. He glanced behind him, toward where he and Rachel had used the ladder to climb the wall. No one appeared on the rim.

Rain gusted against his eyes. He squinted toward Rachel,

managing to see her on the opposite roof. Flat, he pulled himself along the ladder, its moist rungs easing his way, helping him to slide.

On the other roof, he stood and swung the ladder toward him. They struggled with it toward a farther gap between buildings, moving lower into the village, closer to the harbor.

When he crossed the next gap after Rachel did, Savage stared behind him. A flash of lightning made him flinch as a head appeared on top of a wall. The head belonged to the Japanese. Savage recalled the glint of a sword! The . . . ! Abruptly the Japanese scrambled upright.

Another man joined him, raising a pistol, aiming at Savage.

The Japanese lost his balance on the rain-slicked roof. But the Japanese had moved so gracefully at the mansion, it didn't seem likely he could ever lose his balance. Nonetheless he fell against the man with the pistol, deflecting his aim. The shot went wild. The man with the pistol toppled backward. With a wail, he plunged off the roof.

The Japanese stared down at him, then charged after Savage and Rachel, his movements once again graceful.

He'll have to stop! Savage thought. He can't get past the two gaps we crossed!

Don't kid yourself. If this is Akira, he'll find a way.

But you know he can't be Akira!

Frantic, Savage picked up the ladder. As Rachel assisted, Savage glanced again toward the Japanese, expecting him to halt when he reached a lane between roofs. Instead the Japanese increased speed and leapt, his nimble body arcing through the rain, his arms outstretched as if gliding. He landed on the opposite roof, bent his knees, rolled to absorb the impact, and in the same smooth motion, sprang to his feet, continuing to race.

Burdened with the ladder, Savage and Rachel struggled toward another lane. But this time, instead of bracing the ladder across the gap, Savage lowered it against a wall. As Rachel scurried down, Savage turned, dismayed to see the Japanese leap across another gap.

Guards shouted nearby. Savage scrambled down the ladder

and tugged it away from the wall so the Japanese couldn't use it. The lane sloped down to the right. He and Rachel sprinted along it. Behind him, Savage heard frenzied footsteps, the Japanese charging toward the side of the roof.

He'll dangle from the rim and drop, Savage thought. Maybe he'll hurt himself.

Like hell. He's a cat.

The lane ended. Savage faced another horizontal street, so level he couldn't decide which direction would take them closer to the harbor.

A light from a window reflected off water on the street. Heart pounding, Savage noticed that the water flowed toward the left.

He ran with Rachel in that direction. Shouts echoed behind him. Footsteps charged closer. Flashlights blazed ahead.

An alley on the right led steeper downward, away from the flashlights. The closer he and Rachel came to the harbor, the more the village narrowed, forming a bottleneck toward the sea, Savage knew. He'd reach fewer tangents, fewer risks of making the wrong decision and heading inadvertently upward, away from his objective.

But he had to assume that his pursuers understood where he was going. *They'll try to get in front of us.*

He prayed that the guards were as baffled by the maze as *he* was. Amid the curses behind him and the blaze of flashlights on his flanks, he heard a single set of pursuing footsteps.

The Japanese.

As if a nightmare had been dispelled, Savage broke from the village, from its confines and confusion. His way now was clear, across the beach, along the dock. No enemy awaited him. Beside him, Rachel breathed hoarsely, stumbling, on the verge of exhaustion.

"Keep trying," Savage urged. "It's almost over."

"God, I hope," she gasped.

"For what this is worth"—Savage breathed—"I'm proud of you. You did fine."

His compliment wasn't cynical. She'd obeyed him with style and strength. But his encouragement—no doubt the only

positive words she'd been told in quite a while—did the trick.
She mustered her deepest resources and ran so hard she almost
passed him.

"I meant what I said," she gasped. "I'll go with you to
hell."

16

The yacht, one of several, was moored near the end of the
dock. Savage's final option. If the boats in various coves had
been discovered, if the fishing trawler had been forced to
retreat due to hazardous weather, if the helicopter couldn't
take off from nearby Delos and pick them up at the rendezvous
site, the last possibility was a yacht that a member of his
team had left in the Mykonos harbor.

Savage sprang aboard, released the ropes that secured it to
posts, raised the hatch above the engine, and grabbed the
ignition key taped beneath the deck. He slid the key into the
switch on the vessel's controls, swelled with triumph when
the engine rumbled, pushed the accelerator, and felt a satisfying surge as the yacht sped away from the dock.

"Thank you!" Rachel hugged him.

"Get down on the deck!"

She instantly complied.

As the yacht churned away from the dock, raising waves
dwarfed by the greater waves of the storm, Savage scowled
behind him. The force of the sea made the yacht thrust up
and down, but despite his confused perspective, Savage saw
a man rush along the dock.

The Japanese. Beneath a light at the end of the dock, his
features remained as melancholy as Akira's.

He showed other emotions as well. Confusion. Desperation.

Anger.

Most of all, fear.

That didn't make sense. But there wasn't any doubt. The Oriental's strongest emotion was fear.

"Savage?" The voice was strained, obscured by the gusting storm.

"Akira?" Savage's yell broke, strangled by waves that splashed his face, filling his mouth, making him cough.

On the dock, other guards rushed beside the Japanese. They aimed pistols toward the yacht but didn't dare fire, aware of the risk of hitting their client's wife. Their faces were rain-swept portraits of desperation.

The Japanese shouted, "But I saw you . . . !"

The storm erased his next frantic words.

"Saw me?" Savage yelled. "I saw *you!*"

Savage couldn't allow himself to be distracted. He had to complete his mission and urged the yacht from the harbor.

". . . die!" the Japanese screamed.

Rachel peered up from the deck. "You know that man?"

Savage's hands cramped around the yacht's controls. His pounding heart made him sick.

He felt dizzy. In the village, he'd predicted that the Japanese would leap down from the wall like a cat.

Yes. Like a cat, Savage thought. With less than nine lives.

"Know him?" he told Rachel as the yacht fought stormy waves to escape the harbor. "God help me, yes."

"The wind! I can't hear you!"

"I saw him die six months ago!"

EXECUTIVE PROTECTION

1

Six months ago, Savage had been working in the Bahamas, an uneventful babysitting job that involved making sure the nine-year-old son of a U.S. cosmetics manufacturer didn't get kidnapped while the family was on vacation. Savage's research had made him conclude that, since the family had never been threatened, his assignment was really to be a companion to the boy while the parents abandoned him in favor of the local casinos. In theory, anyone could have served that function, but it turned out the businessman made frequent racial slurs against the local population, so Savage assumed that the supposed potential kidnappers had a skin color darker than his employer's. In that case, *why*, he'd wondered, had the businessman chosen the Bahamas at all? Why not Las Vegas? Probably because the Bahamas sounded more impressive when you told your friends you'd spent two weeks there.

Savage had disapproved but hadn't shown it. His job, after all, wasn't to like his client, but instead to provide security, and besides, despite his aversion to his employer, he enjoyed the boy's companionship extremely. While never allowing himself to be distracted from his duties, he'd taught the boy to windsurf and scuba dive. With the businessman's money, he'd chartered a fishing boat—captained by a Bahamian native, to Savage's rebellious delight—and never baiting a hook had shown the boy the graceful majesty of leaping sailfish and marlin. In short, he'd behaved like the father that the endearing boy's actual father should have been.

When the boy had flown back to Atlanta with his family, Savage had felt empty. Well, he'd thought, you've got this consolation. Not every job's as pleasant as this one. He'd remained in the Bahamas for three more days. Swimming, jogging, hardening his muscles. A vacation for himself. But then his habitual compulsion to work had taken control. He'd phoned one of his several contacts, a restaurateur in Barcelona, who'd received a call from a jeweler in Brussels, who passed the word that if Savage was available, his agent would be pleased to speak with him.

2

Savage's agent, Graham Barker-Smythe, the Englishman who'd trained him, had his home in a renovated carriage house in an elegant brick-paved lane in New York City, a half-block from Washington Square. As Graham liked to say, "At midnight, I can hear the junkies howl."

Graham was fifty-eight, overweight from too much champagne and caviar, but in his lean youth, he'd been a member of the British military's elite commando unit, the Special Air

Service, and after leaving the military, a protective escort to several prime ministers. Eventually his civil servant's income had been unacceptable compared to the guardian's fees he could earn in the private sector. America had offered the richest opportunities.

"This was after President Kennedy was shot. Then Martin Luther King. Then *Robert* Kennedy. Assassination was the major fear of anyone in power. Of course, the Secret Service had cornered the market on high-level politicians, so I chose to deal with prominent businessmen. They've got the bucks, and after the terrorists hit in the seventies, I made a bleeding fortune."

Despite his twenty years in America, Graham still retained his English accent, though his vocabulary had become an intriguing mixture of American and British expressions.

"Some of the businessmen I protected"—Graham pursed his lips—"were no more than ruffians in Brooks Brothers suits. An elegant front. No class. Not like the aristocrats I used to work for. But this is what I learned. A protector has to repress his ill opinions about his employer. If you allow disapproval to control you, you'll unconsciously make a mistake that might kill your client."

"You're saying a protector should *never* disapprove of a client?"

"It's a luxury. If we worked only for those of whom we approved, we'd seldom work. Everyone has imperfections. However, I do adhere to minimum standards. I would never help drug dealers, arms merchants, terrorists, mobsters, child molesters, wife beaters, or members of militant hate groups. I would never be able to repress my disgust enough to protect them. But unless you're confronted by unmistakable evil, you don't have a right to judge your client. Of course, you can still turn him down if the fee he offers is insufficient or the job too dangerous. Because we're tolerant doesn't mean we have to be schmucks. Pragmatism. Adapt to circumstances."

Graham always enjoyed these philosophical discussions and despite his heart doctor's orders, indulged in lighting an enormous cigar, the smoke from which hovered above his bald head. "Did you ever wonder why I accepted you as a pupil?"

"I assumed because of the training I'd received in the SEALs."

"That training was impressive, no doubt about it. When you came to me, I saw a strong young man accustomed to the stress of lethal conditions. A commendable background. Promising. Unrefined, however. I might even add, crude. Now don't look insulted. I'm about to give you a compliment. I grant that the SEALs are among the best commando units in the world, though my own SAS is of course in a class by itself." Graham's eyes twinkled. "But the military insists on strict obedience, whereas an executive protector isn't a follower but a leader. Or more exactly, a protector exists in a delicate stasis with his employer, commanding yet obeying, allowing the client to do what he wants but insisting on how he does it. The relationship is known as symbiosis."

Savage responded dryly, "I'm familiar with the word."

"Give and take," Graham said. "A protector requires the skills of a military specialist, agreed. But he also must have the talents of a diplomat. And above all, a mind. The latter—your mind—is what attracted me. You left the SEALs . . ."

"Because I disagreed with what happened in Grenada."

"Yes, the U.S. invasion of that tiny Caribbean island. It's been several years since you approached me, but if my memory hasn't failed, the date of the invasion was October twenty-five, nineteen eighty-three."

"Your memory *never* fails."

"As a Briton, I'm instinctively precise. Six thousand U.S. soldiers—coordinated units of Rangers, Marines, SEALs, and Eighty-second Airborne paratroopers—attacked Grenada, their mission to rescue one thousand American medical students held captive by Soviet and Cuban troops."

"*Supposedly* held captive."

"You sound as angry as the day you came to me. You still feel the invasion wasn't justified?"

"For sure, there'd been trouble on the island. A coup had deposed the prime minister, but *he* was pro-Cuban, and the man who replaced him was Marxist. Different shades of red. The coup caused civil unrest. A hundred and forty protesters were shot by local soldiers. And the former prime minister *was* assassinated. But the American medical students stayed in their compound—none of them was injured. Basically two Communist politicians had fought each other for power. Why Americans were studying medicine on a pro-Cuban island I don't know, but the coup hardly threatened the balance of power in Latin America.''

"What about the Cuban, East German, North Korean, Libyan, Bulgarian, and Soviet technical advisors on the island, many of whom were actually soldiers?"

"An exaggeration of U.S. Intelligence. I saw only local soldiers and Cuban construction workers. Sure, when the invasion began, the Cubans grabbed rifles and fought as if they'd had military training, but what young man in Cuba *hasn't* had military training?"

"And the ten-thousand-foot airstrip being constructed, capable of accommodating long-range bombers?"

"What I saw was less than half that long, suitable for commercial flights to bring in tourists. The invasion was show business. The U.S. looked impotent when Iran took our embassy personnel hostage in 'seventy-nine. Reagan defeated Carter because he vowed he'd act decisively if Americans were threatened again. Just after the Grenada coup, an Arab terrorist drove a truckload of explosives into the U.S. Marine barracks in war-ravaged Lebanon. Two hundred and thirty peacekeeping soldiers were killed in the blast. What happened in Lebanon was obscene, but did Reagan retaliate in that region? No, because the Mideast situation's too complicated. So what did he do to save face? He ordered American forces to attack an easy target to rescue supposed American hostages in the Caribbean.''

"But the American public perceives Grenada as a blow for freedom, an important U.S. victory against a Communist threat in the Western Hemisphere."

"Because reporters were restricted from the invasion. The only reports came from the military. In civilian life, it's called lying. In politics, it's called disinformation.''

"Yes," Graham said. "Disinformation. Exactly the word I was waiting for. As I said, what attracted me to you was your mind. Your ability to step back from your military conditioning, recognize the truth, and think independently. Why was your reaction so bitter?"

"You know that already. I was part of the first team to hit the island. We parachuted from a transport plane. Other chutes brought us rafts because we had to infiltrate the island from offshore. But the Navy misjudged the weather. The wind was stronger than predicted. At night, the waves were so fierce we couldn't see the rafts. A lot of us—a lot of my *friends*—drowned before we reached the rafts."

"Died bravely."

"Yes."

"In the service of their country."

"In the service of a movie-star president who sent us needlessly into combat so he'd look like a hero."

"So with disgust, you refused to reenlist in the Navy, despite the fifty-thousand-dollar incentive the military offered you. However, a disaffected Navy SEAL, a top-of-the-line ex-commando, *could* have asked a huge fee from mercenary recruiters."

"I didn't *want* to be a mercenary."

"No. You wanted dignity. You had the wisdom to understand your true vocation, not a soldier but a protector."

Graham leaned back behind his spacious mahogany desk, puffing his cigar with satisfaction. Though corpulent, he wore impeccably tailored clothes that minimized his bulk: a gray pinstripe suit and vest, a subdued maroon tie, and a subtle blue handkerchief tucked perfectly into the chest pocket of his suitcoat. "The tie and the handkerchief should never match," he always insisted, instructing Savage about the proper way to dress if a distinguished client had to be escorted to a semiformal occasion. "Wear clothes to match your surroundings, but never choose a suit that's more elegant than your client's."

Proper dress had been only a small part of what Graham taught Savage about the rules of executive protection. The occupation was far more complex than Savage had imagined when he first came to Graham in the fall of '83, though to Savage's credit he had not assumed that his extensive experience with one of the finest military units in the world had been all the preparation he would need. Quite the contrary. Savage's commando training had taught him the value of admitting what he didn't know, of thoroughly preparing himself for a mission. Knowledge is power. Ignorance is death. That was why he'd come to Graham in the first place—to dispel his ignorance and learn from a world-class expert about the refinements of his newly chosen profession.

Weapons: Savage required no instruction in that regard. There wasn't a weapon—firearms, explosives, ballpoint pens, or piano wire—that Savage couldn't use proficiently.

But what about surveillance techniques? Savage's training had been to assault, not follow.

And "bug" detection? Savage's experience with bugs was limited to disease-bearing pests in jungles, not miniature microphones implanted in telephones, lamps, and walls.

And evasive driving? Savage had never evaded an objective. He'd always attacked. And as far as driving was concerned, he and his unit had always been transported to whichever plane or ship would take them to their target. Driving was something he did for fun in a rented Corvette to take him from bar to bar while on leave.

"Fun?" Graham had winced. "I'll cure you of wanting that. And conspicuous vehicles are forbidden. As for bars, you'll drink only in moderation, a distinguished wine while eating, for example, and never when on assignment. Do you smoke?"

Savage did.

"Not anymore. How can you notice a threat to a principal—"

"A what?"

"A principal. In the profession you claim you wish to enter, a client is called a principal. An appropriate word, for your principal is your main—your exclusive—concern. How can you notice a threat to your principal when you're busy fumbling to light a cigarette? You think I contradict myself because I smoke a cigar? I indulge myself now that I've given up protecting in favor of teaching and arranging for my students to find employment. For an agent's fee, of course. But *you*, how can you protect a principal when your hand is compromised by a cigarette? Yes, I can see you have a great deal to learn.''

''Then teach me.''

''First you must prove you're worthy.''

''How?''

''Why did you choose—?''

''To be a bodyguard?''

''An executive protector. A bodyguard is a thug. A protector is an artist. *Why did you choose this profession?*''

Accustomed to the demeaning shouts of his Navy instructors, Savage hadn't felt angry at Graham's outburst. Instead he'd humbly sorted through his instincts, trying to verbalize his motivation. ''To be useful.''

Graham had raised his eyebrows. ''Not an inferior response. Elaborate.''

''There's so much pain in the world.''

''Then why not join the Peace Corps?''

Savage had straightened. ''Because I'm a soldier.''

''And now you want to become a protector? A member of the *comitatus*. Ah, I see you're unfamiliar with the term. No matter. You'll soon understand, for I've decided to accept you as a student. Return to me a week from now. Read the *Iliad* and the *Odyssey*. We'll discuss its ethics.''

Savage hadn't questioned this seemingly irrelevant assignment. He was used to obeying, yes. But he sensed that Graham's command was not a mere test of his discipline but rather the beginning of a new kind of knowledge. A skill that would make his previous training—as superb as it was—seem a minimum requirement for the greater demands of what Graham eventually told him was the fifth and most noble profession.

After the *Iliad* and the *Odyssey*, Graham had insisted on discussing other classics that merged military and executive-protection skills. ''You see, tradition and attitude are paramount. There are rules and codes. Ethics and yes, aesthetics. In time, I'll teach you tactics. For now, you'll learn a beautiful devotion to your principal, but as well an unrelenting obligation to control him. This relationship is unique. Perfectly balanced. A work of art."

It was Graham who made Savage read the Anglo-Saxon account of the loyal *comitatus* who fought to the death to defend their master's corpse from the ravaging Vikings at the battle of Maldon. And it was Graham who introduced Savage to the remarkable Japanese fact-become-legend of the forty-seven *ronin* who avenged their insulted dead lord by beheading their master's enemy and in victory, obeyed the *shogun*'s command to disembowel themselves.

Codes and obligations.

3

"I have an assignment for you," Graham said.

"Why so solemn? Is it dangerous?"

"Actually it's fairly routine. Except for one thing." Graham told him.

"The client's *Japanese*?" Savage said.

"Why does that make you frown?"

"I've never worked for a Japanese."

"That intimidates you?"

Savage thought about it. "With most other nationalities, I'm able to take for granted common elements of culture. It makes the job easier. But the Japanese . . . I don't know enough about them."

"They've adopted a lot of American ways. Clothes and music and . . ."

"Because of the U.S. occupation after the war. They wanted to please the victors. But their habit of mind, the way they think, that's unique, and I'm not just talking about the difference between the Orient and the West. Even the Communist Chinese, to give one example, think more like Westerners than the Japanese do."

"I thought you said you didn't know anything about the Japanese."

"I said I didn't know *enough* about them. That doesn't mean I haven't studied them. I knew one day I'd be asked to protect a Japanese. I wanted to be prepared."

"And *are* you prepared?"

"I'll have to think about it."

"You're afraid?"

Savage's pride made him tense. "Of what?"

"That you can be a *comitatus* but not a samurai?"

"*Amae.*"

Graham cocked his head. "I'm not familiar with the word."

"It's Japanese. It means the compulsion to conform to a group."

"Yes? And so? I'm puzzled."

"*Omote* and *ura*. Public thoughts and private thoughts. A traditional Japanese *never* reveals what he truly believes. He always says what he thinks the group will accept."

"I still don't—"

"The Japanese caste system, the absolute command of masters over retainers. In premodern times, the order was *shogun* to *daimyo* to samurai to farmer to merchant to untouchables, those who butchered animals or tanned hides. Apart from that hierarchy, the emperor existed with little power but great authority, the descendant of the Japanese gods. That rigid system was supposedly erased by the democratic reforms of the U.S. occupation. But it still persists."

"My compliments."

"What?"

"As usual, you've done your research."

"Keep listening," Savage said. "How am I supposed to protect a man who wants to conform to a group but won't tell me what he's thinking and who secretly believes he's better than his inferiors, which in this case is me? Add to that, the Japanese habit of avoiding favors because they impose an obligation to repay those favors in *greater degree*. And add to *that*, the Japanese habit of feeling mortally insulted whenever an underling assumes authority.''

''I *still* don't—''

''Everything you've taught me comes down to this—a protector *must* be both servant and master. A servant because I'm employed to defend. A master because I'm obligated to insist that my employer obey my instructions. A balance, you said. An artistry of give-and-take. Then tell me how I'm supposed to fulfill my obligation to a principal who won't reveal what he's thinking, who can't stand being obligated to an underling, and who won't take orders.''

''It's a dilemma. No doubt. I agree.''

''But you still recommend I accept this assignment?''

''For purposes of education.''

Savage glared at Graham and abruptly laughed. ''You *are* a bastard.''

''Consider it a challenge. A broadening of your skills. You've succeeded so far—commendably. Nonetheless you haven't achieved your full potential. Ignorance is death. To become the best you must learn the most. And the samurai tradition offers the greatest opportunities. I suggest you immerse yourself much further in the culture of your principal.''

''Does the fee he offers make the effort—''

''The challenge?''

''—worthwhile?''

''You won't be disappointed. It more than compensates.''

''For?''

''*Giri*,'' Graham said, surprising Savage by his mentor's knowledge of that essential Japanese word. ''The burden of obligation to your master and to anyone who does you a favor. Even if the assignment's uneventful, my friend, you won't be bored.''

4

A dingy drizzle fell from a soot-colored sky. It sprayed off the greasy tarmac, forming a dirty mist that beaded against the dusty windows of LaGuardia Airport.

Savage sat in a crowded American Airlines concourse and watched a DC-10 approach an arrival dock. He periodically scanned the confusion of activity around him, on guard for potential danger, sensing none. Of course, an enemy skilled in surveillance would not allow himself to attract attention, so Savage remained alert.

"What's the principal's name?" he'd asked Graham.

"Muto Kamichi."

The Japanese put their family name first, their given name last. The formal term of respect—*san* instead of "mister"—applied not to the family name but to the given name and came after the given name. Thus the principal would be addressed as Kamichi-san.

"He arrives in New York tomorrow," Graham had added, "after going through Immigration and Customs in Dallas."

"The purpose of his visit?"

Graham had shrugged.

"Come on. Is he a businessman? A politician? What?"

Graham shook his head. "*Ura.* Those private thoughts you so rightly noted the Japanese cherish. The principal prefers to keep his intentions to himself."

Savage breathed out sharply. "That's exactly why I'm reluctant to take the job. If I don't know at least the general reason for his visit, how am I supposed to assess the risks he might face? A politician has to fear assassination, but a businessman's biggest worry is being kidnapped. Each risk requires a different defense."

"Of course. But I've been assured that the threat potential is extremely low," Graham said. "The principal is bringing his own security. *One* escort. Clearly if he were worried, he'd bring others. What he wants you to do is be his driver and stand in for his escort when the escort's sleeping. A simple assignment. Five days' work. Ten thousand dollars in addition to my agent's fee."

"For a driver? He's overpaying."

"He insists on the best."

"The escort?"

"His name is Akira."

"Only one word?"

"He follows the practice I recommended to you and uses a pseudonym, so an enemy can't trace his public name to his private identity."

"That's fine. But is he effective?"

"From all reports, extremely. Equivalent to you. Language won't be a problem, by the way. Both of them speak English fluently."

Savage was only partially reassured. "Is it too much to hope that the principal's willing to confide in me enough to tell me beforehand *where* I'll be driving?"

"He's not unreasonable. And indeed you will be driving some distance." Graham looked amused. "He's authorized me to give you this sealed envelope of instructions."

5

The DC-10 reached the concourse. Its engines stopped shrieking. Friends and relatives hurried toward the arrival door, eager to meet their loved ones.

Savage assessed and dismissed them, studying observers on the sidelines.

Still no sign of a threat.

He moved toward the fringe of the waiting crowd. As usual, it took a frustrating minute for the docking to be completed. At once the empty ramp was filled with surging passengers.

Exuberant hugs of reunion. Kisses of affection.

Savage once again studied his surroundings. Everything seemed normal. He directed his attention toward the exit ramp.

Now came the test. His principal and his escort had flown first class. The extra fare meant not only bigger seats, anxious-to-please attendants, better meals, and unlimited free cocktails (which the escort should decline), but the privilege of entering and leaving the jet before the standard-fare customers.

Early boarding was a plus. Getting quickly through a possible danger in the crowd. But exiting early, *facing* a crowd and its unstudied risks, was a liability. A professional escort would insist that his principal wait until most passengers left the plane.

Avoid commotion. Maintain maximum order.

So Savage felt encouraged when he saw no Orientals among the Rolex-and-gold-bracelet, dressed-to-impress, first-class travelers, who marched past the crowd, their power briefcases clutched severely, their chins thrust high. Many wore expensive cowboy boots and Stetsons, to be expected since this DC-10 came from Dallas where an earlier 747 from Japan had landed. Evidently the Japanese passengers on the trans-Pacific 747 had either stayed in Dallas or taken connecting flights to cities other than New York.

Savage waited.

More Caucasians. More exuberant reunions.

The surge of passengers became a trickle.

An American Airlines attendant pushed an aged woman in a wheelchair through the arrival door. In theory the DC-10 was empty.

In theory.

Savage glanced behind him. The waiting crowd had dispersed. At the same time, another crowd—impatient—had boarded several departing planes.

This section of the concourse was almost empty. An airport

custodian emptied ashtrays. A young couple looked dejected because they'd been too low on a waiting list for openings due to canceled reservations.

No threat.

Savage turned again toward the exit door.

A Japanese man appeared, dressed in dark slacks, a dark turtleneck sweater, a dark windbreaker.

Midthirties. Trim but not slight. No suggestion of muscles, but a *definite* suggestion of strength. Wiry. Supple. His movements smooth. Graceful. Controlled. Economical. No needless gesture. Like a dancer—who knew martial arts, for the tips and the sides of his hands had calluses typical of someone with karate training. Equally telling, his hands were unencumbered. No briefcase. No carry-on bag. Just a handsome Japanese, five feet ten inches tall, with brown skin, short black hair, strong jaw and cheekbones that framed his rectangular face, and laserlike eyes that assessed every aspect of what he approached.

This would be Akira, and Savage was impressed. On equal terms, an enemy would be foolish to confront this man. Even on terms to the enemy's advantage. Savage was so accustomed to dealing with inferior protectors that he almost smiled at the thought of working with an expert.

Behind Akira, another Japanese emerged from the ramp. Late fifties. Slightly stooped. Carrying a briefcase. Blue suit. Protruding stomach. Streaks of gray in his black hair. Sagging brown cheeks. A weary executive.

But Savage wasn't fooled. The second Japanese could probably straighten his shoulders and tuck in his stomach at will. This man would be Muto Kamichi, Savage's principal, and evidently he too had martial arts training, for like Akira (but unlike any other principal Savage had ever worked for), the tips and sides of Kamichi's hands had calluses.

Savage had been instructed to wear a brown suit and paisley tie to identify him. As Kamichi and Akira approached, he didn't offer to shake hands. The gesture would have compromised his ability to defend. Instead he chose the Japanese custom and bowed slightly.

The two Japanese maintained impassive expressions, but their eyes flickered with surprise that this Westerner was familiar with Japanese etiquette. Savage hadn't intended to obligate them. Still, he suddenly realized that the dictates of their culture forced them to respond, though their bows were less than Savage's, Akira's just a bob of the head as he continued to survey the concourse.

Savage gestured politely for them to follow. Proceeding down the concourse, he watched travelers ahead while Kamichi stayed behind him, and Akira followed, no doubt glancing frequently around.

The moment Savage had seen his principal, he'd raised his right hand to the outside of his suitcoat pocket and pressed a button on a battery-powered transmitter. A radio signal had been sent to a receiver in a vehicle that one of Savage's associates had parked in the airport's ramp. As soon as the associate heard the beep, he'd drive from the ramp to rendezvous with Savage.

The group reached the end of the concourse and descended stairs toward the commotion of the baggage area. Weary ex-passengers hefted suitcases off a conveyor belt, impatient to get outside and into taxis.

Savage assessed the harried crowd but didn't go near its risky confusion. Instead he gestured again, this time toward a sliding door. Kamichi and Akira went with him, unconcerned about their luggage.

Good, Savage thought. His initial impression had been accurate. These two understood correct procedure.

They emerged on a busy sidewalk beneath a concrete canopy. Beyond, the drizzle persisted. The temperature, high for April, was sixty degrees. A moist breeze felt tepid.

Savage glanced to the left toward approaching traffic, reassured to see a dark blue Plymouth sedan veering toward the curb. A red-haired man got out, came quickly around to the curb, and opened the rear passenger door. Just before Kamichi got in, he handed the red-haired man several luggage receipts. Savage approved that the principal was experienced enough to perform this menial service rather than requiring

Akira to relax surveillance by reaching into his windbreaker pocket to get the receipts.

Savage slid behind the steering wheel, pressed a button that locked all the doors, then fastened his seat belt. Meanwhile the red-haired man went for the luggage. Because Kamichi and Akira had taken a prudent length of time to get off the plane, their suitcases would almost certainly be on the conveyor belt by now. A safe, efficient arrival.

One minute later, the red-haired man finished placing three suitcases in the Plymouth's trunk and shut the lid. Instantly Savage drove from the curb, checking his rearview mirror, noticing his associate walk toward a taxi. Savage had paid him earlier. The man would take for granted that Savage couldn't permit distraction by saying "thanks."

Savage himself took for granted that since the two Japanese had behaved so knowledgeably about security, they understood why he'd chosen a car that wasn't ostentatious and wouldn't be easy to follow. Not that Savage expected to be followed. As Graham had said, the risk level on this assignment was low. Nonetheless Savage never varied his basic procedure, and the Plymouth—seemingly no different from others—had modifications: bulletproof glass, armor paneling, reinforced suspension, and a supercharged V-8 engine.

As windshield wipers flapped and tires hissed along the wet pavement, Savage steered smoothly through traffic, left the airport complex, and headed west on the Grand Central Parkway. The envelope Graham had given him was in his suitcoat, but he didn't refer to its contents, having memorized his instructions. He couldn't help wondering why Kamichi had rejected Newark's airport in favor of LaGuardia. The drive would have been shorter, less complicated, because although Savage's immediate route was toward Manhattan, his ultimate destination forced him across the northern tip of the island, then west through New Jersey into Pennsylvania. Kamichi's logic, the purpose of the mazelike itinerary, eluded him.

6

At five, the drizzle stopped. Amid the congestion of rush hour traffic, Savage crossed the George Washington Bridge. He asked his principal if he'd care to enjoy some sake, which having been heated was in a thermos, the temperature not ideal but acceptable.

Kamichi declined.

Savage explained that the Plymouth was equipped with a telephone, if Kamichi-san required it.

Again Kamichi declined.

That was the extent of the conversation.

Until twenty miles west on Interstate 80, where Kamichi and Akira exchanged remarks. In Japanese.

Savage was competent in several European languages, a necessity of his work, but Japanese was too difficult for him, its complex system of suffixes and prefixes bewildering. Because Kamichi spoke English, Savage wondered why his principal had chosen to exclude him from this conversation. How could he do his job when he couldn't understand what the man he'd pledged to protect was saying?

Akira leaned forward. "At the next exit, you'll see a restaurant-hotel complex. I believe you call it a Howard Johnson's. Please stop to the left of the swimming pool."

Savage frowned for two reasons. First, Akira had remarkably specific knowledge of the road ahead. Second, Akira's English diction was perfect. The Japanese language made no distinction between *r* and *l*. Akira, though, didn't say "prease" and "Howald Johnson's." His accent was flawless.

Savage nodded, obeying instructions, steering off the highway. To the left of the swimming pool, where a sign said CLOSED, a balding man in a jogging suit appeared from behind a maintenance building, considered the two Japanese in the Plymouth's rear seat, and held up a briefcase.

The briefcase—metal, with a combination lock—was identical to the briefcase that Kamichi had carried from the plane.

"Please," Akira said, "take my master's briefcase, leave the car, and exchange one briefcase for the other."

Savage did what he was told.

Back in the car, he gave the look-alike briefcase to his employer.

"My master thanks you," Akira said.

Savage bowed his head, puzzled by the exchange of briefcases. "It's my purpose to serve. *Arigato.*"

" 'Thank you' in response to his 'thank you'? My master commends your politeness."

7

Returning to Interstate 80, Savage checked his rearview mirror to see if he was being followed. The vehicles behind him kept shifting position. Good.

It was dark when he crossed the mountain-flanked border from New Jersey into Pennsylvania. Headlights approaching in the opposite lanes allowed him to study the image of his passengers in his rearview mirror.

The gray-haired principal seemed asleep, his slack-jawed face tilted back, his eyes closed, or perhaps he was meditating.

But Akira sat ramrod straight, on guard. Like his master, his face did not reveal his thoughts. His features were stoic, impassive.

Akira's *eyes*, though, expressed the greatest sadness Savage had ever seen. To someone familiar with Japanese culture, Savage's conclusion might have seemed naive, for the Japanese by nature tended toward melancholy, Savage knew. Stern obligations imposed on them by complex traditional values made the Japanese watchful and reserved, lest they unwittingly insult someone or place themselves in another's debt. In premodern times, he'd read, a Japanese would hesitate to tell a passerby that he'd dropped his wallet—because the passerby would then feel honorbound to supply a reward much greater than the value of the contents of the wallet. Similarly Savage had read ancient accounts in which someone who'd fallen from a boat and thrashed in a river, in danger of drowning, had been ignored by people on shore—because to rescue the victim would be to inflict upon that victim an obligation to repay the rescuer again and again and *again*, forever in this ephemeral earthly existence, until the rescued victim was granted the gift of rescuing the rescuer or else had the privileged release from obligation by dying as the gods had intended at the river before the rescuer intervened.

Shame and duty controlled the Japanese personality. Devotion to honor compelled them but often also wearied them. Peace could be elusive, fatigue of the spirit inescapable. Ritual suicide—*seppuku*—was on occasion the only solution.

Savage's research made him realize that these values applied only to uncorrupted, unwesternized Japanese, those who'd refused to adapt to the cultural infection of America's military occupation after the war. But Akira gave the impression of being both uncorruptible and, despite his knowledge of American ways, an unrelenting patriot of the Land of the Gods. Even so, the emotion in his eyes was more than the usual Japanese melancholy. His sadness was seared to the depths of his soul. So dark, so deep, so black, so profound. An expanding wall of repressive ebony. Savage felt it. The Plymouth was filled with it.

8

At eleven, a country road wound through night-shrouded mountains, leading them to a town called Medford Gap. Kamichi and Akira again exhanged comments in Japanese. Akira leaned forward. "At the town's main intersection, please turn left."

Savage obeyed. Driving from the lights of Medford Gap, he steered up a narrow, winding road and hoped he wouldn't meet another vehicle coming down. There were very few places to park on the shoulder, and the spring thaw had made them muddy.

Dense trees flanked the car. The road angled higher, veering sharply back and forth. The Plymouth's headlights glinted off banks of lingering snow. Ten minutes later, the road became level, its sharp turns now gentle curves. Ahead, above hulking trees, Savage saw a glow. He passed through an open gate, steered around a clump of boulders, and entered an enormous clearing. Fallow gardens flanked him. Spotlights gleamed, revealing paths, benches, and hedges. But what attracted Savage's attention was the eerie building that loomed before him.

At first, he thought it was *several* buildings, some made of brick, others of stone, others of wood. They varied in height: five stories, three, four. Each had a different style: a town house, a pagoda, a castle, a chalet. Some had straight walls; others were rounded. Chimneys, turrets, gables, and balconies added to the weird architectural confusion.

But as Savage drove closer, he realized that all of these apparently separate designs were joined to form one enormous baffling structure. My God, he thought. How long must it be? A fifth of a mile? It was *huge*.

None of the sections had doors, except for one in the

middle, where the road led to wide wooden steps and a porch upon which a man in a uniform waited. The uniform, with epaulets and gold braids, reminded Savage of the type that bellmen wore at luxury hotels. Abruptly he saw a sign on the porch—MEDFORD GAP MOUNTAIN RETREAT—and understood that this peculiar building was in fact a hotel.

As Savage stopped at the bottom of the stairs, the man in the uniform came down toward the car.

Savage's muscles hardened.

Why the hell weren't my instructions complete? I should have been told where we'd be staying. This place . . . on a mountaintop, *totally isolated*, with just Akira and me to protect Kamichi, no explanation of why we came here, no way to control who comes and goes in a building this huge . . . it's a security nightmare.

Recalling the mysterious exchange of briefcases, Savage turned to Kamichi to tell him that *ura,* private thoughts, might be wonderful in Japan, but here they gave a protector a royal pain and what the hell was going on?

Akira intervened. "My master appreciates your concern. He grants that your sense of obligation gives you cause to object to these apparently risky arrangements. But you should understand that except for a few other guests, the hotel will be empty. And *those* guests, too, have escorts. The road will be watched. No incident is expected."

"I'm not the primary escort," Savage said. "*You* are. With respect, though, *yes*, I'm disturbed. Do *you* agree with these arrangements?"

Akira bowed his head, darting his profoundly sad eyes toward Kamichi. "I do what my master wills."

"As must I. But for the record, I don't like it."

"Your objection is noted. My master absolves you from responsibility."

"You know better. As long as I've pledged myself, I'm *never* absolved."

Akira bowed again. "Of course. I've studied your credentials. With approval. That's why I agreed when my master decided to hire you."

"Then you know this conversation's pointless. I'll do

what's necessary," Savage said. "Totally. But I will not work with you and your master again."

"Once is all that's required."

"Then let's get on with it."

Outside the car, the man in uniform waited. Savage pressed buttons that released the doors and the trunk. He stepped from the car and told the man to carry the bags inside. Nerves tingling, he glanced around at the looming darkness, then preceded Kamichi and Akira up the steps.

9

The lobby looked like a vestige from the 1890s. Antique pine lined the walls. Wagon wheels were chandeliers. A single primitive elevator stood next to an impressive old staircase that crisscrossed upward. But for all its historical charm, the place smelled moldy and stank of decay. A hotel for ghosts.

Savage kept his back to Kamichi, watching the deserted lobby, Akira doing the same, while their principal murmured to an elderly spiderweb-haired woman behind a counter.

"We won't use the elevator," Akira said.

"I advise my principals to avoid them whenever possible."

"In this instance, it's just that my master prefers the incomparable staircase."

As if Kamichi had been here before.

Third floor. And with every upward movement, Savage heard the attendant struggle with the bags. Too bad, Savage thought. The elevator would have been easier for you. But an elevator's a trap, and anyway I've got the feeling other rules apply here.

The man in the uniform stopped at a door.

"Thank you. Leave the bags out here," Savage said.

"If that is your preference, sir."

"Your tip—"

"Has been arranged, sir."

The man handed three keys *not* to Savage or Akira but Kamichi. Savage watched as the man disappeared down the stairs. Did the man have security training? He knew not to compromise the hands of the escorts.

Kamichi unlocked the door and stepped back, allowing Akira to inspect the room.

When Akira returned, he nodded to Kamichi, faced Savage, and raised his eyebrows. "Would you care to . . . ?"

"Yes."

By the standards of hotels that catered to the wealthy, by *any* standard, the room was primitive. An unpainted radiator. A dim light bulb in the ceiling. The single window had simple draperies. The floor was bare worn pine. The bed was narrow, concave, covered with a very old, homemade quilt. The bathroom had a hand-held shower attachment on a clip above dingy faucets. The moldy smell persisted. No television, though there *was* a telephone, old-fashioned, black and bulky, with a dial instead of buttons.

Savage opened the only closet. Shallow, it exuded must. He stepped toward another door, this one beside the window and the radiator. Peering out, he saw a small balcony. Spotlights at the rear of the building reflected off an oval lake directly below. Cliffs rimmed it to the right. A dock projected from the left. Beyond the water, a shadowy trail led up to pine trees, then a murky bluff. Savage's scalp shrank.

He left the room.

"Do my master's quarters meet with your approval?" Akira asked.

"If he likes to feel he's at summer camp."

"Summer camp?"

"A joke."

"Yes. So." Akira forced a smile.

"What I meant was, the room's not exactly luxurious. Most of my clients would refuse it."

"My master prefers simplicity."

"By all means, Kamichi-san's desires are paramount." Savage bowed toward his employer. "What troubles me is the balcony—and the *other* balconies. It's too easy for someone to move from one to another and enter the room.''

"The balconies on either side belong to *our* rooms, and as I explained, the hotel has few other guests,'' Akira said. ''They and their escorts are trustworthy. The principals are associates of my master. No incident is anticipated.''

"I'm also troubled by the trees on the opposite side of the lake. I can't see into them, but at night, with the hotel lit, someone would have an excellent view of Kamichi-san at a window.''

"Someone with a rifle?" Akira shook his head.

"It's the way I'm trained to think.''

"My master approves of caution, but he has no reason to fear for his life. Extreme security won't be necessary.''

"But—''

"My master will now have his bath.''

The ritual of bathing was one of the greatest Japanese pleasures, Savage knew. But bathing meant more to them than just cleansing themselves. First Kamichi would fill the tub and scrub his body. Then he would drain the tub, swab it, refill it, and soak, perhaps repeating the process several times.

"Whatever he wishes,'' Savage said, "though he won't find the water as hot as he's used to in Japan.'' He referred to the fact that the Japanese preferred a temperature most Westerners found painful.

Akira shrugged. "One must always allow for the inconvenience of travel. And *you* must learn to enjoy the solemnity of these peaceful surroundings. While my master bathes, I'll order his meal. When he's ready for bed, I'll return and permit you to rest.''

Kamichi picked up his bags, thus allowing Akira to keep his hands free. With a bow to Savage, Akira followed his master into the room and shut the door.

Savage stood watch. Alone, he became more sensitive to the stillness in the hotel. He glanced at his and Akira's suitcases. He turned his gaze toward the silent doors along the corridor, noting photographs on the walls: old, faded images of the cliff-rimmed lake before the hotel had been constructed, of bearded men and bonneted woman in buggies from another century, of long-dead families picnicking beside the lake.

Again he felt troubled. Pivoting left, he studied the top of the majestic staircase. Farther to the left, the lonely corridor went on for at least a hundred yards. Swinging to the right, he assessed the other section of the corridor. But there the hallway reached an alcove filled with antique rocking chairs, then jutted away.

Savage cautiously approached the interruption of his vantage point. At the alcove, he saw that the hallway formed a sharp angle toward the hotel's entrance, then formed *another* sharp angle that continued for a hundred yards along the continuation of the hotel's length. And *this* part of the hall felt even more lonely, not just due to a smothering accumulation of the past but because of an unnerving sense of having been trapped in a time warp, another dimension. Unreal.

Savage's shoulders felt cold.

10

Two hours later, he lay on a sagging mattress in his room, reading a pamphlet he'd found on his bedside table.

The Medford Gap Mountain Retreat, he discovered, had a fascinating history that helped explain the unreality of the place. In 1870, a Mennonite couple who owned a farm in the nearby lowlands had hiked up Medford Mountain, amazed to discover that its peak had a hollow at its tip with an oval lake fed by a spring. The place seemed touched by God.

They built a cabin where the hotel's lobby now stood and invited other Mennonite families to worship this splendor of heaven on earth. Eventually, so many worshipers accepted their request that the cabin required additions, and when outsiders heard of this retreat, the community decided to build another addition and then another to accommodate world-weary visitors who needed a respite and would perhaps find solace in the Mennonite faith.

In 1910, an unexplained fire destroyed the original cabin and its additions. By then, the couple who'd discovered the lake had gone to their reward. Their daughters and sons, committed to the ministry of their parents, had at once begun to rebuild the retreat. But farmers by training, they realized that they needed help. They advertised for a manager and hired a New York architect, who'd abandoned his profession because he couldn't bear the pressures of the city. The architect converted to the Mennonite faith and committed himself to the mountain.

But his big-city intuition told him that the retreat had to be so distinctive, so one-of-a-kind that it would compel the unconverted to leave the soot and desperation of their lives, to journey into Pennsylvania's majestic wilderness, to pay to proceed to the top of a mountain and appreciate a lake that reflected God's grandeur.

He gave each addition a separate design, and as the enterprise prospered, the building lengthened to almost two hundred and fifty yards. Visitors came from as far away as San Francisco, many requesting the same room each year. Only in 1962 had the descendants of the hotel's founders grudgingly permitted a telephone in each room. Otherwise, in keeping with strict Mennonite custom, radios and televisions were still forbidden. God's artistry in nature ought to provide sufficient entertainment. Dancing and card playing were also forbidden, as of course were alcohol and tobacco.

11

The latter restriction had inexplicably been waived on this occasion, for the following morning when Savage escorted

Kamichi to the hotel's main floor, three men waited in an enormous parlor, and two of them were smoking.

The parlor had huge wooden columns that supported massive beams. Windows filled the walls to the left, right, and center, revealing porches, the lake, and wooded bluffs. Sunlight gleamed in. Logs blazed in a spacious fireplace, dispelling the morning's chill. A grand piano stood in one corner. Rocking chairs were arranged around the room. But what Savage paid most attention to was a long conference table in the middle, where the three men stood as Kamichi approached them.

Like Kamichi, the men were in their fifties. They wore expensive suits and had the calculating eyes of upper-echelon businessmen or diplomats. One was American, the others Spanish and Italian. They were either ignorant of Japanese customs or else determined to insist on Western ways, for they shook hands with Kamichi instead of bowing. After a few pleasantries, the group sat, two on each side of the table. Their forced smiles dissolved. They began a sober discussion.

Savage remained at the entrance to the parlor, too far away for him to hear the substance of what they said, only their muffled voices. He studied the walls to his right and left and saw an Italian escort at one, a Spanish escort at the other, both standing at attention, their backs to their principals, their attention directed toward the windows and porches that flanked the parlor. At the rear of the parlor, an American escort watched the windows that provided a view of the lake.

Professional.

Savage, too, turned his back and watched the hotel's deserted lobby, on guard against intruders. He assumed that the three men Kamichi spoke with had other escorts. Some perhaps patrolled the grounds while others slept as Akira now did, having stood watch outside Kamichi's room from two A.M. till dawn when Savage took his place.

The meeting began at eight-thirty. At times, the muffled voices were agitated. Then calm tones prevailed, only to be interrupted by impatient remarks and hasty reassurances. At eleven-thirty, the conversation reached a peak of intensity and concluded.

Kamichi stood and left the parlor, followed by the other men flanked by their escorts. The group looked so dissatisfied that Savage assumed they'd soon be leaving. He hid his surprise when Kamichi told him, "I must go to my room and change clothes now. At noon, my colleagues and I will play tennis."

Akira was awake by then and took Savage's place as Kamichi and the Spaniard played doubles against the American and the Italian. The sky was clear, the temperature again sixty degrees. The energetic players soon toweled their sweaty faces.

Savage decided to stroll the grounds, in need of stretching his muscles. Besides, he was curious to learn if there were additional security arrangements.

He soon found out. When he reached a trail that led through leafless trees, past boulders, up a slope around the lake, he scanned a bluff and saw a man with a rifle and a walkie-talkie. The guard noticed Savage, seemed aware that he was on the team, and ignored him, returning his eyes to the road that led from the lowlands toward the hotel.

Savage continued along the upwardly winding path, reaching stretches of ice and snow among the woods, and stopped at the rim of a cliff that provided a stunning view of farmland in a valley surrounded by farther mountains. Wooden steps led partway down the cliff toward a ledge that a sign said was ONLY FOR EXPERT CLIMBERS.

Turning to go back to the hotel, Savage noticed another man with a rifle and a walkie-talkie hidden among pine trees on the rim of the cliff. The man assessed Savage, nodded, and continued his surveillance.

The tennis game concluded when Savage reached the hotel. Victorious, Kamichi went to his room, bathed, and ate lunch while Savage stood guard in the hall and Akira shared his master's meal. At two, the meeting continued. At five, it broke up, the principals again dissatisfied, especially the American whose face was flushed with anger.

The group went to a massive dining room on the second floor, where they sat amid a hundred deserted tables and not only smoked but broke another rule by drinking cocktails.

Their previous surliness changed to unexpected conviviality; laughter punctuated raucous remarks. After dinner and cognac, they strolled the grounds, exchanging jokes while their escorts followed. At eight, they returned to their rooms.

Savage stood watch till midnight. Akira took his place till dawn. At eight-thirty, another intense, angry meeting began, as if the fellowship of the night before had not occurred.

12

At the end of the third afternoon, the group stood from the conference table in the parlor, shook hands, and instead of going to the dining room, dispersed to their rooms. They all looked immensely pleased.

"Akira will pack my bags," Kamichi said when he and Savage reached the third floor. "We leave tonight."

"As you wish, Kamichi-san."

A sound froze Savage's heart. The subtle squeak of a doorknob.

From the room across from Kamichi's, four men surged into the hallway. Muscular. Midthirties. Japanese. Wearing dark suits. Three of the men held swords, but the shafts were made of wood, not steel, the swords called *bokken*.

Kamichi gasped.

Savage thrust him aside, yelling, "Run!"

Automatically Savage lunged to place himself between his principal and the attackers. There was absolutely no question that he, too, would run. He couldn't allow himself to fear for his own safety.

The nearest assailant swung his *bokken*.

Savage parried with a kick and struck the assailant's wrist, deflecting the wooden sword. He spun, thrust with the side of his hand, and chopped toward the neck of another assailant.

He never connected.

A *bokken* whacked across his elbow. The numbing blow slammed his arm toward his side. Bone cracked. He groaned reflexively.

Though the arm was useless, he lunged again, dodging a *bokken*, chopping with his remaining good hand. This time he managed to break the bridge of an assailant's nose.

At once he felt someone who shouldn't be next to him.

Kamichi.

"No!" Savage shouted.

Kamichi kicked toward an assailant.

"Run!" Savage shouted.

A *bokken* whacked across Savage's other arm. Again he groaned as the blow snapped bone. Four seconds had elapsed.

A door slammed open, Akira darting from his room.

Wooden swords swirled.

Akira chopped and kicked.

A *bokken* walloped against Savage's rib cage. He doubled over, unable to breathe. Struggling to raise himself, he saw Akira knock an assailant off balance.

Kamichi screamed from a wooden sword's impact.

With both arms useless, Savage had to rely on kicks but managed only one.

It struck an assailant's groin. Another assailant whacked his *bokken* across Savage's right knee. That leg collapsed, but even while falling, Savage winced in agony from a blow to his *other* knee, then his *spine*, then the back of his skull.

Savage's face struck the floor, blood spurting from his nose.

Helpless, he squirmed. He strained to look up and, through pain-blurred eyes, saw Akira pivot with awesomely coordinated kicks and blows.

Only three of the four assailants had used a *bokken*. The fourth Japanese had remained behind them, his hands apparently free. But now, his movement too fast to be glimpsed, he reached toward his side and suddenly held a *katana*, the long curved sword of the samurai. Its polished steel glinted.

In Japanese, he barked an order. The three men scurried behind him. The fourth man swung his *katana*. Its razor-sharp blade hissed, struck Kamichi's waist, kept speeding as if through air, and sliced him in half. Kamichi's upper and lower torso fell in opposite directions.

Blood gushed. Severed organs spilled over the floor.

Akira wailed in outrage, rushing to chop the man's windpipe before the assassin could swing again.

Too late. The assassin reversed his aim, both hands gripping the *katana*.

From Savage's agonized perspective on the floor, it seemed that Akira jumped backward in time to avoid the blade. But the swordsman didn't swing again. Instead he watched indifferently as Akira's head fell off his shoulders.

As blood gushed from Akira's severed neck.

As Akira's torso remained standing for three grotesque seconds before it toppled.

Akira's head hit the floor with the thunk of a pumpkin, rolled, and stopped in front of Savage. The head rested on its stump, its eyes on a level with Savage's.

The eyes were open.

They blinked.

Savage screamed, barely aware of the footsteps approaching him. At once he felt as if the back of his own head had been split apart.

His consciousness became red.

Then white.

Then nothing.

13

Savage's eyelids felt heavy, as if coins had been placed upon them. He struggled to force them open. It seemed the hardest thing he'd ever attempted. At last he managed to raise them. Light made him wince. He scrunched his eyes shut.

Even then, the glare stabbed through his lids, and he wanted to lift a hand to shield them, but he couldn't move his arms. He felt as if anvils pressed upon them.

Not only his arms. His *legs*. He couldn't move them either!

He tried to think, to *understand*, but his mind was filled with swirling mist.

Helplessness made him panic. Terror scalded his stomach. Unable to move his body, he jerked his head from side to side, only to realize that something soft and thick encased his skull.

His terror worsened.

"No," a voice said. "Keep still." A man's voice.

Savage forced himself to reopen his eyes.

A shadow rose, blocking the stabbing light. A man, who'd been sitting in a chair, turned and twisted a rod that closed slats on a window.

The mist in Savage's mind began to clear. He realized he was on his back. In a bed. He strained to raise himself. Couldn't. Had trouble breathing.

"Please," the man said. "Keep still." He stepped toward the bed. "You've had an accident."

Pulse hammering, Savage parted his lips, inhaling to speak. His throat felt filled with concrete. "Accident?" His voice was like gravel grating together.

"You don't remember?"

Savage shook his head and suddenly groaned from a searing pain.

"Please," the man insisted. "Don't move your head. It's been injured."

Savage's eyes widened.

"You mustn't upset yourself. The accident was serious. You seem to be out of danger, but I don't want to take any chances." The man wore glasses. His coat was white. A stethoscope hung from his neck. "I know you're confused. That makes you frightened. To be expected, but try to control it. Short-term memory loss sometimes occurs after massive assaults to the body, especially to the skull." He pressed the stethoscope to Savage's chest. "I'm Dr. Hamilton."

What the doctor had said was too much, too fast, too

complicated, for Savage to understand. He had to backtrack, to grasp the details of the simplest things first.

"Where?" Savage murmured.

The doctor's tone remained reassuring. "In a hospital. Accept your confusion. I know you're disoriented. That'll pass. Meanwhile it's imperative to your recovery that you try your best to stay calm."

"Not what I meant." Savage's lips felt numb. "Where?"

"I don't understand. Ah, of course. You mean *where* is the hospital located."

"Yes." Savage exhaled.

"Harrisburg, Pennsylvania. You were given emergency treatment a hundred miles north of here, but the local clinic didn't have the special equipment you needed, so one of our trauma teams rushed you here in a helicopter."

"Yes." Savage's eyelids fluttered. "Trauma." The haze returned. "Helicopter."

Blackness.

14

Pain awoke him. Every nerve in his body quivered with the greatest agony he'd ever known. Something tugged against his right hand. Savage darted his panicked eyes toward a nurse, who removed a hypodermic from a port in an IV tube attached to a vein on the back of his hand.

"A painkiller." Dr. Hamilton appeared at the side of the bed. "Demerol."

Savage flicked his eyes in acknowledgment, conscious enough to realize that a nod of his head would cause him more pain. But the pain had a compensation. It made him see with terrible clarity.

His bed had guardrails. To the right, a metal pole held an IV pump. The liquid in the tube was yellow.

"What is it?" Savage asked.

"Nourishment," the doctor said. "After all, you've been here five days, and we couldn't feed you by mouth."

"Five days?" Savage's mind reeled.

His pain-intensified consciousness made him aware of other things. Not only was his skull wrapped with bandages, but both of his legs and arms were in casts.

And the doctor—why did these details seem important?—was in his forties, blond, with freckles beneath his glasses.

"How bad?" Savage's face oozed sweat.

The doctor hesitated. "Both your arms and legs were broken in several places. That's why we put the IV into your hand. With the casts on your extremities, we couldn't reach veins in your arms."

"The bandages around my head?"

"The back of your skull was fractured. On your right side, your fourth, fifth, and sixth ribs were fractured as well."

Savage suddenly realized that layers of tightly wound tape constricted his chest. Now he understood why he had difficulty breathing, why he felt a lancing pain when he inhaled.

The Demerol began to work. His agony subsided.

But the drug dimmed his thoughts as well as his pain. No! He had too many questions!

He struggled to concentrate. "Is that the worst of my injuries?"

"Not quite, I'm afraid. Bruised kidneys. Ruptured appendix and spleen. Internal bleeding. We had to operate."

Despite the increasing numbness caused by the Demerol, Savage realized something else: a catheter had been inserted up his penis into his bladder, draining urine to an unseen container that hung at the foot of the bed.

"The rest of your injuries, thank God, are minor—multiple superficial contusions," the doctor said.

"In other words, I'm all fucked up."

"Good. A sense of humor's a sign of healing."

"I wish I could say it only hurts when I try to laugh." Savage struggled to clear his thoughts. "An accident?"

"You still don't remember?" The doctor frowned.

"It's like trying to see through a fog. Some time ago . . . Yes. I remember I was in the Bahamas."

"When?" the doctor asked quickly. "Do you recall what month?"

Savage strained to focus his mind. "Early April."

"Approximately two weeks ago. Can you tell me your name?"

Savage almost panicked again. What name was he using? "Roger Forsyth." *Had he guessed correctly?*

"The name on the driver's license we found in your wallet. And your address?"

Savage's thoughts focused. He gave the address on the driver's license, a farmhouse outside Alexandria, Virginia. Graham owned it under a pseudonym, allowing Savage and various other protectors to claim it as a residence.

Graham? Savage's heartbeat quickened. Yes. *He remembered Graham as well.*

The doctor nodded. "That *is* the address on your driver's license. We got the phone number from information. We kept calling. No luck. The Virginia state police sent an officer there, but no one's home."

"There wouldn't be. I live alone."

"Do you have any friends or relatives you want us to contact?"

The Demerol made Savage more groggy. He feared he'd make a mistake in his answers. "I'm not married."

"Parents?"

"Dead. No brothers and sisters." Savage's eyes drooped from sleepiness. "I don't want to worry my friends."

"If you're certain."

"Yes. Absolutely."

"Well, at least your answers correspond to the information we found in your wallet. It proves what I told you yesterday. You've suffered short-term memory loss. It doesn't always happen after trauma to the skull, but it's not unusual either. And it *will* be temporary."

Savage fought to stay awake. "But you still haven't answered my question. What kind of accident?"

"Do you recall the Medford Gap Mountain Retreat?"

Despite the haze drifting over him, Savage felt a shock of recognition. "Medford Gap? Yes. A hotel. A strange . . ."

"Good. It's coming back to you already." Dr. Hamilton stepped closer. "You were a guest there. You went hiking."

Savage *did* remember walking through woods.

"You fell off a cliff."

"What?"

"The hotel manager insists the stairs down the cliff were clearly marked. 'Only for expert climbers.' You went down the steps. It appears you lost your footing on a patch of ice. If it weren't for a ledge thirty feet below, you'd have fallen a thousand feet. You're a lucky man. When you didn't return to the hotel for dinner, the staff went looking for you. They managed to find you just before sunset, and I might add, just before you would have bled to death or died from hypothermia."

The doctor's face became hazy.

Savage strained to clear his vision. "Fell off . . . ? But that's not . . ." In panicked confusion, he knew, he sensed, that wasn't the truth, that something far more terrible had happened to him. Blood. In his murky memory, he saw blood.

The glint of razor-sharp metal. Something falling.

As he now fell toward blackness.

15

Kamichi's severed body toppled in two directions. Akira's decapitated body spouted blood. The head thunked onto the floor and rolled to a halt in front of Savage.

Akira's eyes blinked.

Savage woke up screaming.

His entire body, even the skin beneath his bandages and

casts, was clammy with sweat. He hyperventilated despite the lancing pain in his ribs each time his chest heaved.

A nurse rushed into the room. *"Mr. Forsyth? Are you all right?"* She hurried to check his pulse and blood pressure. "You've upset yourself. I'll get more Demerol."

"No."

"What?"

"I don't want to be sedated."

"But it's Dr. Hamilton's orders." She looked flustered. "I have to give you the Demerol."

"No. Tell him I need my mind clear. Tell him the Demerol blocks my memory. Tell him I've started—"

"Yes, Mr. Forsyth?" The blond-haired doctor entered the room. "You've started to what?"

"Remember."

"About your accident?"

"Yes," Savage lied. His protective instincts warned him: say only what's expected. "The hotel's manager was right. The steps down the cliff were clearly marked that they were dangerous. But I used to be a climber. I hate to say it—I got overconfident. I tried to cross an icy rock. I lost my balance. I . . ."

"Fell."

"It seemed more as if the ledge was rushing toward me."

Dr. Hamilton grimaced. "An unfortunate misjudgment. But at least, you survived."

"He doesn't want the Demerol," the nurse said.

"Oh?" Dr. Hamilton looked perplexed. "It's essential to your comfort, Mr. Forsyth. Without the sedative, your pain—"

"Will be severe. I understand. But the Demerol clouds my thoughts. I'm not sure which is worse."

"I realize it's important for you to reconstruct the days before your accident. But given the extent of your injuries, I don't think you comprehend the degree of pain—"

"When the last of the Demerol wears off?" Savage wanted to add, suffering's my specialty. Instead, his pain increasing, he said, "Let's compromise. Half-doses. We'll see how I do. We can always go back to the amount you recommend."

"A patient negotiating with his physician? I'm not accustomed to . . ." Dr. Hamilton's eyes crinkled. "We'll see how you do. If my guess is right . . ."

"I'm resilient."

"No doubt. Since you're feeling aggressive, perhaps you'd care to try to eat."

"Crackers and chicken broth."

"Exactly what I meant to suggest," the doctor said.

"If I hold it down, the IV isn't necessary."

"Correct. Removing the tube would be my next decision."

"And since Demerol reduces the flow of urine, with less sedation I ought to be able to piss on my own without this damned catheter up my—"

"Too much, Mr. Forsyth. Too soon. If you adjust to a half dose of Demerol, and if you don't throw up the crackers and broth, I'll remove the IV and the catheter. We'll see if, to use your word, you don't need help to"—the doctor's eyes crinkled again— "piss."

16

"More apple juice?"

"Please."

It frustrated Savage that he couldn't use his arms. He sipped slowly from a straw, grateful for the nurse's help.

"I have to say I'm impressed," Dr. Hamilton said. "Since you managed to hold down both lunch and dinner, tomorrow we'll try you on something more solid. Bits of meat. Perhaps pudding."

Savage fought a spasm of pain that seized his entire body.

"Sure. Pudding. Great."

The doctor frowned. "Do you want me to increase the Demerol?"

"No." Savage winced. "I'm fine."

"Of course you are. The gray of concrete is your normal color, and you bite your lip for fun."

"Keep the Demerol to a minimum. I need to have my mind clear." Again, with horrifying vividness, he saw a mental image of the *katana* slicing Kamichi in half, of Akira's head thunking onto the floor, of blood spraying.

So much blood.

I fell from a cliff? Who invented that cover story? What happened to Akira's and Kamichi's bodies?

Need to stay alert. Can't make a mistake and say anything that contradicts the cover story. Have to find out what's going on.

An excruciating surge of pain interrupted his desperate thoughts. He held his breath, resisting an involuntary moan.

The doctor stepped closer, frowning harder.

The pain slackened enough for Savage to breathe. He closed his eyes, then opened them, and told the nurse, "More juice, please."

The doctor relaxed. "You're the most strong-willed patient I've ever had."

"I owe it all to meditation. When do I lose the IV and the catheter?"

"Perhaps tomorrow."

"In the morning?"

"We'll see. In the meantime, I have a surprise for you."

"Oh?" Savage tensed.

"You said you didn't want any of your friends informed about what happened to you. But one of them somehow found out. He arrived a while ago. He's waiting outside. But I didn't want to let him in until I saw how you were adjusting and, of course, until you gave me permission to send in a visitor."

"Friend?"

"Philip Hailey."

"No kidding. Good old Phil." Savage had never heard of him. "Send him in. If you don't mind, though, I'd like to see him in private."

"Of course. However, after you've visited with your friend . . ."

"Is something wrong?"

"Well, it has been several days. You're going to have to move your bowels, and with your arms and legs in casts, you won't be able to do it alone."

"Just great."

The doctor left, amused. The nurse soon left as well. Savage waited apprehensively.

17

The door swung open.

Though Savage had never heard of Philip Hailey, his mind was clear enough to recognize the man who entered the room.

American. Midfifties. Expensively dressed. With the calculating eyes of an upper-echelon businessman or diplomat.

One of the principals at the Medford Gap conference.

Savage had known he'd eventually be approached. It was one of the reasons he'd insisted on keeping his mind as free of Demerol as possible. Even so, Savage's body was imprisoned by casts, tape, and bandages. An expert in defense, he felt powerless. Philip Hailey could kill him with minimal effort. A quick injection. A drop of liquid into Savage's mouth. A spray from a canister shoved close to his nose.

The visitor held roses in one hand, a box of chocolates in the other. Both could be weapons. The man had a mustache, wrinkles around his eyes, and an Ivy League ring that might conceal a pin coated with an instantly deadly and undetectable chemical.

"I hope the scent from these roses won't make you nauseous," the man said.

"If you can live with them, I can," Savage said.

"Suspicious?" The man set the roses and the chocolates on a chair.

"By habit."

"A good one."

"Philip Hailey?"

"It seemed as useful a name as any other. Anonymous. Waspishly American. The same as Roger Forsyth."

"I admit my alias is bland. But as you suggest, that's the point," Savage said.

"Indeed. However, the man who chooses the alias must not be bland. *You* have character."

"Maybe not. Apparently I got careless. I fell," Savage said.

"A terrible tragedy."

"Yeah, I fell all the way to the floor of a hallway in the Medford Gap retreat."

"Not as bad as a fall off a cliff. Still, an equally terrible tragedy."

"For a time, I didn't remember. When I did, I kept my mouth shut about the truth. I stuck to the cover story," Savage said.

"As your reputation led us to expect. All the same, I had to make inquiries. To be sure."

Savage winced again, his pain increasing. "Kamichi and Akira? What happened to their bodies?"

"They were hurried away. Have no doubt—they were treated with respect. Scrupulous Japanese rites were obeyed. The ashes of your principal and his escort rest with their noble ancestors."

"And what about the police? How did you explain—?"

"We didn't," Philip Hailey said.

Savage's skull throbbed. "I don't understand."

"It's simple really. The authorities were never involved."

"But the hotel's staff would have called them."

Philip Hailey shook his head. "Special arrangements were made. So brutal an incident would have destroyed the hotel's reputation. With only the few of us staying there, the staff was at a minimum. Each received handsome compensation in exchange for silence. Now that they've accepted the gratuity, even if they have second thoughts, they don't dare inform the authorities for fear of being charged with concealing a felony. What's more, the police wouldn't find any evidence."

"But the blood. There was so much blood."

"That corridor of the hotel has now been remodeled," Philip Hailey said. "As you know, a talented laboratory team can find blood no matter how thoroughly you think you've cleaned the area, so not only the carpeting but the floor and the walls, the doors, even the ceiling, have been replaced. What was taken out was burned. There's absolutely no trace of blood."

"I guess that leaves only two questions." Savage's voice sounded thick. "Who killed them, damn it, and why?"

"The rest of us share your shock and outrage. But I regret I can't answer your latter question. The motive for the murders obviously relates to the purpose for the conference. But the purpose of the conference is not your business, so I'm not at liberty to discuss why your principal was killed. I *can* tell you this—my associates and I are opposed by several groups. An investigation was begun at once. We expect soon to identify and punish whoever was responsible."

"What are you talking about? Businesses? Intelligence agencies? Terrorists?"

"I won't elaborate."

"The assassins were Japanese."

"I'm aware of that. They were seen escaping. But Japanese assassins *could* be hired by a *non*-Japanese. The nationality of the killers means nothing."

"Except that Kamichi and Akira were also Japanese."

"And Akira had martial arts skills against which corresponding skills perhaps seemed necessary," Philip Hailey said. "That still doesn't prove the employer was Japanese. Consider the topic closed. Please. My purpose in coming here was to express our sympathy for your suffering and to assure you that everything possible was being done to avenge the atrocity."

"In other words, stay out of it."

"Given your injuries, do you have any choice? But later, yes, we feel you ought to decide that your obligation has ended.'' Philip Hailey reached inside his suitcoat and removed a thick envelope. He showed Savage the numerous hundred-dollar bills within it, sealed the flap, and set the envelope beneath Savage's right hand.

"You think I can accept money when I failed to protect my principal?"

"As your injuries proved, you defended him heroically."

"I wasn't good enough."

"Unarmed? Against four men expert with swords? You didn't desert your principal. You behaved with dignity, almost at the cost of your life. My associates commend you. Think of the money as compensation. We've also paid for your medical bills. Incentives. Demonstrations of our good faith. In return, we count on *your* good faith. Don't disappoint us."

Savage stared at the man.

Dr. Hamilton opened the door. "I'm sorry I have to ask you to leave, Mr. Hailey. Your friend's overdue for a procedure."

Philip Hailey straightened. "I was just about to say goodbye." He turned to Savage. "I hope I cheered you up. Enjoy the roses and the chocolates, Roger. I'll come back as soon as I can."

"I look forward to it, Phil."

"When you get better, think about a vacation."

"Message understood. And thanks," Savage said. "I appreciate your concern."

"That's what friends are for." Philip Hailey left.

Dr. Hamilton smiled. "Feel better?"

"Overjoyed. Can you bring me the telephone?"

"You want to talk to *another* friend? Excellent. I was worried about your refusal to depend on social contacts."

"You don't need to worry any longer."

Savage told him which numbers to press. "Please, put the phone under my chin."

Dr. Hamilton obeyed.

"Perfect. If you wouldn't mind, I'd like another minute of privacy," Savage said.

Dr. Hamilton left.

Pulse hammering, Savage listened as the phone rang on the other end.

We count on your good faith. Don't disappoint us, Philip Hailey had said.

And good old Phil hadn't needed to add, *If you don't cooperate, if you don't keep away from our affairs, we'll mix your ashes with Kamichi's and Akira's.*

Through the phone, Savage heard the beep of an answering machine. No announcement preceded it. A tape recorder would now be engaged.

"This is Savage. I'm in a hospital in Harrisburg, Pennsylvania. *Get out here fast.*"

18

The number Savage had called wasn't at Graham's home in Manhattan, was instead at an answering service. Graham employed the service because a client sometimes felt it imprudent to contact him directly. Indeed there were various clients whose enemies were so powerful that Graham refused to deal with those clients on anything but an indirect basis, lest the enemies discover which protection agency had acted against them and decide to seek revenge. Once each day, Graham selected a pay phone and called the number reserved for him at the answering service. He held a remote control against the mouthpiece, pressed buttons, and broadcast a sequence of tones that activated the tape machine, causing it to play back all the messages it had recorded. No one could trace the messages to him.

If Savage had been able to move, he'd have used a pay phone in the hospital's lobby to call Graham not at the answering service but his home. *But Savage couldn't use his arms.* He'd been forced to ask Dr. Hamilton to place the call, and he didn't dare compromise Graham's security by telling the doctor Graham's *private* number.

Time. What if Graham had already called his answering service today? What if, before Graham checked his messages again, Philip Hailey had second thoughts about relying on Savage's silence? What if Graham was out of the country and it took him several days to get here? *Time.*

Sweating from pain, Savage craved more Demerol, but he had to stay alert: Philip Hailey might send a representative who brought death in lieu of chocolates and roses. Besides, what difference did it make if Savage *was* alert? He'd still be paralyzed by the casts on his arms and legs. He wouldn't be able to defend himself.

I can't just give up! I can't just lie here, hoping I won't be killed!

Savage had never been to Harrisburg. He had no contacts there. But Philadelphia was less than a hundred miles away.

When Dr. Hamilton reentered the room to see if Savage had completed his call, Savage asked him to press more numbers on the phone.

"You want to talk to another friend?"

"I suddenly feel social."

After the doctor placed the phone beneath Savage's chin and gave him further privacy, Savage waited anxiously for someone to answer on the other end.

A voice growled, "Hello."

"Tony?"

"Depends."

"A blast from the past, good buddy. I saved your life on Grenada."

"Savage?"

"I need your help, my friend. Protection. I think I'm in serious shit."

"Protection? Since when did you ever need—?"

"Since now. If you're available—"

"For *you?* If I was screwing Raquel Welch, I'd tell her I had even more pressing business." Tony chortled at his joke. "When do you want me?"

"Five minutes ago."

"That bad?"

"Maybe worse." Savage paused, fingering the stuffed envelope that Philip Hailey had shoved beneath his right hand. "I've got what feels like fifteen thousand dollars for your effort."

"Forget it, man. I'd be dead if not for you. I pay my debts. I'll help you for nothing."

"It's not a favor, Tony. This is business. You might have to earn every dollar. Bring a friend. And don't come without equipment."

"Equipment's no problem. But friends are in short supply."

"Aren't they always? *Get here.*"

19

Three hours—*nervous* hours—later, Tony and another Italian came into the room. They both had beard stubble and muscular chests. "Nice, Savage. Love your plaster. You look like *I* did after Grenada. What happened? Who—?"

"No questions. Watch the door. The blond-haired doctor's okay. The nurses keep changing. Check them. Anyone else . . ."

"I get the idea."

Safe, Savage finally permitted Dr. Hamilton—who frowned toward Savage's escorts—to give him more Demerol. He drifted and sank, blessedly released from pain. But even with his bodyguards, and even unconscious, he wasn't free from terror. Akira's severed head rolled toward him and blinked.

Again Savage woke up screaming. Fear pierced his grogginess, making him aware of four things. Tony and his look-alike surged upright. His IV tube had been removed. So had his catheter. And outside his room, an English-accented, indignant voice said, "You want me to stub out a *Cuban* cigar?"

Graham! At last!

The bald, portly, well-dressed mentor entered the room.

"Oh, my," he said, surveying Savage's injuries.

"Yes," Savage said. "It didn't go well."

"Your companions are—?"

"Reliable."

"I came as fast as I could."

"I'm sure," Savage said. "Now get me out of here faster."

20

The cottage, south of Annapolis, stood on a wooded bluff with a magnificent view of Chesapeake Bay. Savage's bed was next to a window, and with his head propped up, he could see the wind-swept, white-capped waves. He loved to watch the sailboats, more of them as April turned into May. Imprisoned by his casts, he fantasized about standing on the tilted deck of one of those boats, his hands on the wheel, his hair blown by the wind. He imagined the salty taste of spray and the raucous cries of sea gulls. Abruptly he'd remember Akira's head rolling toward him. The sailboats would disappear, replaced by a grotesque memory of toppling bodies and spouting blood. Savage's casts would again imprison him.

He had two bodyguards and felt troubled by the irony of being a protector in need of protection. The guards weren't Tony and his companion. Because Savage had needed to use a hospital phone to summon them, there'd be a record of the number he'd called. An enemy could easily learn that number and possibly trace the two men to Savage and this cottage. Graham had arranged for other men to keep watch. At the same time, Graham had changed his answering service, for the hospital would have a record of the number Savage had used to call him.

In addition, Graham had hired a trusted doctor, who checked Savage once a day, and an equally trusted nurse, who remained in constant attendance. Every Friday, Savage was placed in the back of a van and driven to a nearby radiologist to determine if his fractured and broken bones were healing without complication.

Graham came to visit every Saturday. He brought bluepoint oysters or beluga caviar or Maine lobsters. Though he persisted in smoking cigars, he thoughtfully opened a window so the warm May breeze remained sweet.

"This cottage, the staff, they must be costing you a fortune," Savage said.

Graham sipped a glass of chilled Dom Perignon and took another puff on his cigar. "You're worth it. You're the best protector I've ever trained. My expenses are insignificant, a minor investment compared to the agent's fee I'll continue to earn from you. Then, too, it's a matter of loyalty. Teacher to student. Friend to friend. I might even say equal to equal. You've never disappointed me. I don't intent to disappoint *you*."

". . . I might decide to retire."

Graham choked on his Dom Perignon. "You'll ruin a perfect afternoon."

"When these casts come off, there's no guarantee I'll be the man I was. Suppose I'm slower. Or crippled. Or"— Savage hesitated—"don't have the nerve to risk myself anymore."

"That's a *future* problem."

"I wonder. When I saw Kamichi's body cut in half . . ."

"You must have seen worse in the SEALs."

"Yes, friends so blown apart I couldn't recognize them. But we were committed to confronting an enemy. If possible, we defended each other. But that wasn't our ultimate purpose."

"To defend? I understand. For the first time, you failed to save a principal."

"If I'd been more alert . . ."

" 'If' is a word that gamblers use. The fact is, you were overwhelmed by greater force. Even the best protector sometimes fails."

"But I had an obligation."

"And the proof of your commitment is your shattered body. I see the evidence. You did your best."

"Still, Kamichi's dead." Savage's voice dropped. "So is Akira."

"Why should your principal's escort matter to you? His obligation was the same as yours. The moment he pledged himself to Kamichi, he accepted every consequence."

"Why should Akira matter?" Savage brooded. "I guess I felt a kinship."

"Perfectly natural. Honor him. But don't leave your profession because of him."

"I'll have to think about it."

"Thinking's a hazard. Concentrate on healing yourself. Anticipate next Friday. The day after, when I visit again, I'll have the pleasure of seeing your arms and legs without casts."

"Yes. And then, God help me, the *real* pain begins."

21

If Savage had injured only a leg or an arm, he could have kept active, could have exercised the rest of his limbs. But with so much of his body disabled, he continued to be helpless after his casts were removed. His arms and legs had shriveled, their once-hard muscles flabby. He didn't have the strength to raise his limbs. To try to *bend* them was agony. Frustration made him despair.

For an hour each morning and afternoon, the nurse turned his arms and legs, then lifted them slowly till Savage cringed.

His elbows and knees felt wooden. But how could wood transmit so much pain?

When Graham came to visit, he shook his head in commiseration. "I've brought a present."

"Two rubber balls?"

"Keep squeezing them. They'll build up the muscles in your forearms." Graham clamped a board to the foot of the bed. "Press your feet against it. It'll strengthen your calves and your thighs."

Savage sweated from the effort, every exhale a gasp.

"Patience," Graham said.

Through the open window, Savage heard voices. A crash.

"Jesus. What's—?"

"Nothing to become alarmed about. Just another present. I've hired a crew to install a hot tub outside. The men don't know you're here. Even if they did, they've often worked for me. I trust them. The tub has a whirlpool accessory. After your daily exercise, the swirl of hot water will soothe your aching muscles."

Savage—still brooding about Kamichi and Akira—recalled that the Japanese were fond of soaking themselves in almost scalding water. "Thanks, Graham."

"Not to mention, water therapy is good for regaining the use of your limbs."

"You're manipulative as always."

"Just keep squeezing your balls."

Savage laughed.

"Good," Graham said. "You've still got a sense of humor."

"Except that there's very little to laugh about."

"You're referring to your pain, or to Kamichi and Akira?"

"Both."

"I hope you're not still thinking about retiring."

"Who attacked them, Graham? Why? You've always said that a protector's obligation to a client doesn't end if the client's killed."

"But the man who calls himself Philip Hailey has relieved you of that obligation. He promised that his investigators were about to determine who'd ordered Kamichi's death. He guaranteed that your principal *would* be avenged. More, he implied that you'd interfere if you involved yourself.''

''But suppose Hailey isn't successful?''

''The shame becomes his. Your sole concern should be to get well. Rest. Sleep. I hope your dreams are peaceful.''

''Not fucking likely.''

22

Slowly, with torturous discipline, Savage learned to bend his knees and elbows. After days of agony, he was able to raise his legs and arms and even sit. His first attempts to walk with crutches ended pathetically, the nurse catching him as he fell.

He asked a guard to bolt a pair of gymnast's rings to the ceiling and strained his hands upward to reach them, struggling to pull his body off the bed. The increasing strength in his arms gave him better control of his crutches. Eventually his legs felt like flesh instead of wood. He swelled with pride the night he didn't have to summon his nurse to help him hobble to the bathroom and relieve himself.

Always, at the end of each day, he blessed Graham for the gift of the hot tub. Soaking in its swirling steaming water, he concentrated to free his mind of every care, seeking an inner peaceful stillness. But the memory of Kamichi and Akira intruded, and shame spread through him, also anger toward the men who'd killed his principal. The pain he'd endured since the attack at the mountain retreat seemed an insufficient penance for his failure to fulfill his pledge of protection. He resolved to punish his body to the maximum, to increase his pain and work even harder.

Graham visited again, easing his hefty frame into a deck

chair beside the hot tub, putting on Rayban sunglasses, his three-piece suit incongruous in this rural setting. "So your father belonged to the CIA."

Savage jerked his head toward Graham. "I never told you that."

"Correct. The first time we met, you avoided questions about him. But surely you didn't think I'd leave it at that. I had to do a security check before I accepted you as a student."

"For the first time, Graham, you've pissed me off."

"Obviously I didn't have to mention what I'd done. I wouldn't have risked your resentment unless I had a motive."

Savage rose from the tub.

"Wait. I'll hand you your crutches."

"Damn it, don't bother." Savage gripped a railing. His skinny legs wobbled. Taking short, cautious steps, he crossed the deck to a chair next to Graham.

"Impressive. I didn't know you'd made so much progress."

Savage glared at him.

"I mentioned your father because he pertains to your threat to retire. Nineteen sixty-one. Cuba."

"So what?"

"The Bay of Pigs disaster."

"So *what?*"

"Your father, working for the CIA, was one of its organizers. But the Kennedy administration had nervous second thoughts. They changed the plan. The invasion—mired in a swamp—became a catastrophe. The White House couldn't acknowledge its mistakes. Someone had to be blamed. A CIA official. A 'fall guy' so loyal that he wouldn't object, that he wouldn't place blame where it really belonged."

"My father."

"Publicly, he was scorned. Privately, he received a bonus for resigning and accepting ridicule."

"My wonderful father." Savage's voice thickened. "How he loved his country. How he honored his obligations. I was only a kid. I didn't understand why he suddenly stayed at home. He'd always been so busy. Away so much. On so many unexplained trips. Understand, when he *was* at home, he made up for his time away. Ball games. Movies. Pizza. He treated me royally. 'I love your mother,' he said, 'but *you're* the pride of my life.' Then everything changed. More and more, with nowhere to go and nothing to accomplish, all he did was drink beer and watch television. Then the beer became bourbon. Then he didn't watch television. Then he shot himself.''

"I apologize,'' Graham said. "Those memories are painful. But I had no choice. I had to remind you.''

"Had to? Graham, I'm more than pissed off. I'm starting to hate you.''

"I had a reason.''

"It better be fucking good.''

"Your father gave in to defeat. That's not a criticism. No doubt he weighed his options carefully. But despair insisted. In Japan, suicide is a noble solution to seemingly unendurable problems. But in America, it's considered shameful. I intend no disrespect. Still, years ago, when I learned about your background, I was troubled that your response to your father's suicide was eventually to join the most arduous branch of the U.S. military. The extremely demanding SEALs. I asked myself *why*. And I concluded . . . please forgive me . . . that you were trying to compensate for your father's failure to endure, for his acceptance of defeat.''

"I've heard enough.''

"No, you haven't. When I learned about your background, I asked myself, 'Is this candidate, however talented, worthy of being a protector?' And I concluded that your determination to succeed, to cancel your father's defeat, was the strongest motive I'd yet encountered. So I accepted you as a student. And now I say to you, recently I feared you'd follow your father's example and kill yourself because of *your* defeat. I urge you not to despair. Years ago, you told me, 'There's so much pain in the world.' Yes. So many victims. They need your help.''

"What happens if *I* need help?''

"I've given it to you. Next Saturday, I hope to find your attitude greatly improved.''

23

Savage worked even harder, not to alleviate his despair but to punish himself for the cause of his despair: his failure to protect Kamichi. As well, pain and exhaustion helped him to repress all thoughts about his father.

But I didn't join the SEALs and eventually become a protector to compensate for him, Savage thought. I did those things to test myself and make my father proud of me, even if he's dead. I wanted to show the bastards who pushed him into a corner that my father taught me character.

Or maybe that's the same as what Graham meant, that I'm trying to cancel my father's defeat. And like my father, I failed.

Sit-ups. Five to begin with. Then one more each day. The gymnast's rings above his bed had increased the strength in his arms, making it possible for him to do push-ups, again in gradually increased amounts. Using his crutches, he managed to walk down the grassy slope to Chesapeake Bay. The doctor stopped making visits. The nurse—no longer needed—left Savage in the care of his two guards.

By then, it was June, and every Saturday, Graham praised Savage's progress. He still made challenging remarks, but Savage had resolved to conceal his depression and give Graham the reassurances he needed to hear.

On the Fourth of July, Graham brought fireworks. At nightfall, teacher and student laughed, exploding bottlerockets, ladyfingers, and cannoncrackers. From far-off cottages, they saw the dazzle of pinwheels and sparklers. With a deafening *whump*, a skyrocket burst brilliantly over the Bay.

Graham restrained his laughter, popped open a fresh bottle of Dom Pérignon, and sat on the lawn, ignoring the dew that soiled the pants of his suit. "I'm delighted."

"Why?" Savage asked. "Because these fireworks weren't just a gift but a test?"

Graham frowned. "I don't know what you mean."

"The fireworks sound like gunshots. You wanted to check my nerves."

Graham laughed again. "I taught you well."

"And *you're* still being manipulative."

"What's the harm?"

"None. As long as we understand each other."

"I had to make sure."

"Of course. A teacher has to test his student. But you also tested our friendship."

"Friends *always* test each other. They just don't admit it."

"You needn't have bothered. Didn't my guards report to you that I've been practicing my marksmanship?"

"Yes. At a nearby shooting range."

"Then you've also been told I'm almost as accurate as I used to be."

"*Almost?* Not good enough."

"I'll get better."

"Are you still worried that Kamichi's killers or Hailey's men might come after you?"

Savage shook his head. "They'd have attacked when I was helpless."

"*If* they'd found you. Maybe they're still looking."

Savage shrugged. "The point is, I've recovered enough to defend myself."

"That remains to be seen. I'm flying to Europe tomorrow. Our weekly visits have to conclude for a time. And I'm afraid your guards are needed elsewhere. Specifically with me in Europe. You're on your own, I'm sorry to say."

"I'll manage."

"You'll have to." Graham stood from the lawn and brushed his pants. "I hope you won't be lonely."

"Exhaustion cancels loneliness. Besides, in summer the Chesapeake Bay's supposed to be so lovely it's all a person needs. I'm looking forward to it. Peace."

"If everyone felt that way, I'd be out of business."

"Peace. It's something to think about."
"I warn you. Don't think too hard."

24

By mid-July, Savage was able to walk ten miles every morning. By August, he could jog. He did a hundred sit-ups and push-ups. His muscles acquired their former lithe hardness. He swam in the Bay, fighting its currents. He bought a rowboat and stretched his arms and legs. Each evening, he perfected his marksmanship.

Only one thing remained—to reacquire his skills in the martial arts. Spiritual discipline became as important as physical strength. His initial sessions ended in disappointment. Shame and anger interfered with the clarity of his soul. Emotion was destructive, thoughts distracting. He had to compose his spirit and merge it with his body. Instinct, not intellect, would then propel him. In combat, to think was to die. To act reflexively was to survive.

He chopped the sides of his hands against concrete blocks to regain his calluses. By the third week of September, he was ready.

25

He was rowing along the Bay, luxuriating in his exertion, smelling a hint of rain from approaching gray clouds, when he noticed a speedboat bobbing a hundred yards away, two men watching him.

The following morning, as he ran through woods, he saw the same blue Pontiac he'd noticed the day before parked on a nearby country road, another two men watching him.

That evening, he kept to his regular routine, turned off the lights at ten-thirty . . .

And crept from the cottage.

Clouds obscured the sky. The absence of stars made the night unusually dark. Dressed in black, with camouflage grease on his hands and face, Savage crawled from the porch, past the hot tub, across the lawn, toward murky trees.

Concealed among bushes, he waited. Crickets screeched. Waves splashed onto the shore. A breeze scraped branches together.

One of the branches snapped. But not on a tree. On the ground. To Savage's left.

Bushes rustled. Out of rhythm with the gusts of the breeze. To the right.

Two men emerged from the trees. They joined two others who appeared past the cottage.

They opened the cottage's door.

Ten minutes later, three of the men came out and blended with the night and the trees.

Savage clutched his handgun and waited.

At dawn, a man in a three-piece suit came out, sat on a chair beside the hot tub, and lit a cigar.

Graham.

You bastard, Savage thought.

He rose from cover and approached the cottage.

"What a pleasant morning," Graham said.

"You set me up."

"Regrettably."

"For Christ's sake, to find out if I spotted those jerks in the boat and the car?"

"I had to make sure you'd recovered."

"They were *obvious.*"

"Only to someone with skill."

"And you didn't think . . . ?"

"You'd retained your skill? I repeat I *had* to make sure."

"Thanks for the confidence."

"But do you *have* confidence? Are you ready for another assignment?"

THE STALKER

1

Savage struggled to control the yacht in the storm. The heavy rain, combined with the night, made it almost impossible for him to see the harbor's exit. Only periodic flashes of lightning guided him. Glancing urgently behind him, he frowned toward the gale-shrouded white buildings of Mykonos and the murky arc light at the end of the village's dock. The guards who'd chased him and Rachel from Papadropolis's estate continued to stare, helpless, enraged, toward the yacht escaping through the turbulent water, afraid of shooting lest they hit their master's wife.

Despite the gloomy distance, one guard in particular attracted Savage's full attention. Handsome, wiry, brown-skinned, his eyes the saddest Savage had ever seen. *The Japanese*.

"Savage?" the man had shouted, racing to a halt at the end of the dock.

"Akira?"

Impossible!

The guards charged back along the dock. The Japanese lingered, glaring toward Savage, then rushed to follow the guards. Darkness enveloped them.

The yacht tilted, shoved by the wind. Waves spewed over the side.

Lying on the deck, Rachel peered up. "You *know* that man?" A flash of lightning revealed her bruised, swollen face. Her drenched jeans and sweater clung to her angular body.

Savage studied the yacht's illuminated controls. Thunder shook the overhang. He felt sick. But not because of the churning sea. Akira's image haunted him. "Know him? God help me, yes."

"The wind! I can't hear you!"

"I saw him die six months ago!" A wave thrust his shout down his throat.

"I still can't—!" Rachel crawled toward him, grabbed the console, and struggled to stand. "It sounded like you said—!"

"I don't have time to explain!" Savage shivered, but not from the cold. "I'm not sure I *can* explain! Go below! Put on dry clothes!"

A huge wave smashed against the yacht, nearly toppling them.

"Secure every hatch down there! Make sure nothing's loose to fly around! Strap yourself into a chair!"

Another wave slammed the yacht.

"But what about *you*?"

"I can't leave the bridge! Do what I say! Go below!"

He stared through the rain-swept window above the controls.

Straining for a glimpse of something, anything, he felt motion beside him, glanced to the right, and saw Rachel disappearing below.

Rain kept lashing the window. A fierce blaze of lightning

suddenly revealed that he'd passed the harbor's exit. Ahead, all he saw was black, angry sea. Thunder rattled the window. Night abruptly cloaked him.

Port and starboard were meaningless bearings. Forward and aft had no significance in the rage of confusion around him. He felt totally disoriented.

Now what? he thought. *Where* are you going? He checked the console but couldn't find the yacht's navigation charts. He didn't dare leave the controls to search for them and suddenly realized that even if he found them, he couldn't distract himself and study them.

With no other recourse, he had to depend on his research. The nearest island was Delos, he remembered: to the south, where he'd arranged for a helicopter to wait in case his primary evacuation plan had failed and he and Rachel needed an airlift from Mykonos.

Delos was close. Six miles. But the island was also small, only one and a half square miles. He might easily miss it and risk being swamped before he reached the next southern island twenty-five miles away. The alternative was to aim southwest toward an island flanking Delos. That island, Rhineia, was larger than Delos and only a quarter-mile farther. It seemed the wiser choice.

But if I miss it? Unless the weather improves, we'll sink and drown.

He studied the illuminated dial on the compass and swung the wheel, fighting waves, heading southwest through chaos.

The yacht tipped over a crest and plummeted toward a trough. The force of the impact nearly yanked Savage's hands from the wheel and threw him onto the deck. He resisted and straightened, at the same time seeing a light pierce the dark to his right.

A hatch opened. Rachel climbed stairs from the underdeck cabin. She wore a yellow slicker. Presumably she'd obeyed Savage and also put on dry clothes. Ignoring his own risk, he'd worried that the cold rain would drain her body heat and put her in danger of hypothermia. Her shoulder-length auburn hair clung drenched to her cheeks.

"I told you to stay below!"

"Shut up and take this!" She handed him a slicker.

In the glow from the instrument panel, Savage saw the determined blaze in her eyes.

"And put on this dry shirt and sweater! You stubborn . . . ! I know about hypothermia!"

Savage squinted at the clothes and the slicker, then peered up toward her bruised, intense face. "All right, you've got a deal."

"No argument? What a surprise!"

"Well, *I'm* surprised. By you. Can you take the wheel? Have you piloted a yacht before?"

"Just watch me." She grabbed the wheel.

He hesitated, but a bone-deep chill forced him to relinquish his grip. "Keep the compass positioned as is. Our bearing's southwest."

In a corner beneath the overhang, partly sheltered from the rain and the waves, he rushed to change clothes and at once felt new energy, grateful to be warm and dry. Protected by the slicker, he took the wheel and checked the compass.

Directly on course.

Good. He planned to tell her so, but a wave struck the yacht, cascading over them. Rachel started to fall. Savage gripped her arm, supporting her.

She caught her breath. "What did you mean I surprised you?"

"When I work for the rich, they're usually spoiled. They expect me to be a servant. They don't understand . . ."

"How much their lives depend on you? Hey, my *dignity* depends on you. I'd still be back in that prison, begging my husband not to rape me again. If you hadn't rescued me, I'd still be his punching bag."

As lightning flashed and Savage again saw the swollen bruises on Rachel's face, he shuddered with rage. "I know it doesn't help to hear it, but I'm sorry for what you've been through."

"Just get me away from him."

If I can, Savage thought. He stared toward the convulsing sea.

"My husband's men?"

"I doubt they'll chase us blindly in this storm. In their place, I'd wait till it ended, then use helicopters."

"Where are we going?"

"Delos or Rhineia. Assuming the compass is accurate. Depending on the current."

"And where do we go after—?"

"Quiet."

"What?"

"Let me listen."

"For *what?* All I hear is thunder."

"No," Savage said. "That's not thunder."

She cocked her head and suddenly moaned. "Oh, Jesus."

Ahead, something rumbled.

"Waves," Savage said. "Hitting rocks."

2

The rumble intensified. Closer and closer. A deafening roar. Savage's hands cramped on the wheel. His eyes ached, straining to penetrate the dark. Assaulted by bomblike concussions, his ears rang. He urged the yacht northward, away from the breakers. But the force of the wind and the waves shoved the yacht sideways, relentlessly toward the continuous *boom* he struggled to escape.

The yacht listed, pushed by the eastward-heaving current, tilting westward. Water gushed onto the deck.

"I'm afraid we'll go over!" Savage said. "Brace yourself!"

But Rachel darted toward the underdeck cabin.

"No!" he said.

"You don't understand! I saw life vests!"

"*What*? You should have told me earlier! That's the first thing we should have—!"

Abruptly she emerged from the hatch, handing him a flotation device, strapping on her own.

The yacht tilted sharper, deeper, westward, toward the *boom*. Water cascaded over the portside gunwale, filling the deck, listing it farther westward.

"Hang on to me!" Savage shouted.

The next wave hit like a rocket. Up became down. The yacht went over.

Savage breathed, lost his balance, struck the deck, grabbed Rachel, slid, and tumbled over the side.

A wave engulfed him. He twisted and groaned, gasping water.

Rachel clung to his life vest.

Savage jerked his head up, breathing frantically. "Kick!" he managed to shout before another wave thrust him under.

Have to get away from the yacht. Can't let it slam against us. Can't let it suck us down when it sinks.

"Kick!"

Rachel lost her grip on his arm. He tightened his grasp on her life vest.

Kick! he thought.

He went under again.

Damn it, kick! He forced his head up, inhaled, swallowed water, and coughed convulsively. The darkness around him was absolute, a nightmare of black, raging madness.

Lightning blazed, searing his eyes. In the agonizing brilliance, he saw towering waves that threatened to crush him, and beyond them even taller waves, impossibly huge.

No! he suddenly realized.

Those massive shapes weren't waves!

They were hills!

Clutching Rachel harder, he felt his stomach drop as a wave scooped him up, and at the crest, an instant before the lightning died, he saw boulders at the base of the hills, waves exploding over them.

Darkness blinded him again. The storm gathered force and catapulted him toward the breakers.

Rachel screamed. As Savage slammed past a rock, he started to scream as well, but water strangled him.

He sank.

It seemed he was back at the Harrisburg hospital, enveloped by the darkness of Demerol.

It seemed he was back at the Medford Gap Mountain Retreat, collapsing into darkness after repeated impacts from Japanese wooden swords.

He saw a gleaming steel sword, a razor-edged samurai *katana*, slice Akira's neck.

Saw blood spurt.

Saw Akira's head thunk onto the floor.

Saw it roll and stop upright, eyes blinking.

"Savage?"

"Akira?"

Madness!

Chaos!

The breakers engulfed him.

3

"Hush," Savage whispered. "Quiet."

But Rachel continued moaning.

He pressed a hand across her mouth. She jerked awake, shoving at his hand, her eyes wild as if she feared he was Papadropolis come to beat her again.

Then recognition replaced her terror. She sighed. Stopped struggling. Relaxed.

He took his hand from her mouth but continued to cradle her against his chest. They were slumped against the back wall of a shallow indentation in a cliff. Boulders rimmed the opening. The morning sun was high enough to shine past the boulders, warming Savage, drying his clothes. The sky was almost cloudless. A gentle breeze drifted over them.

"You were having a nightmare," he continued to whisper.

"You started to scream. I had to stop you, couldn't let them hear you."

"*Them?*"

He pointed through a gap in the boulders. A hundred yards down a steep granite slope, waves continued to crash on the shore. The storm had thrown the yacht onto rocks, breaking it apart. Large fragments lay along the waterline. Two burly men—Greeks, wearing fishermen's clothes—stood above the waves, their hands on their hips, scanning the wreckage.

"Jesus, from my husband?"

"I don't think so. The fact that they're dressed as fishermen means nothing, of course. Your husband's men might decide to put on clothes that help them blend with the local population. But I don't see any guns, and just as important, they don't have walkie-talkies to report what they've found." Savage thought about it. "It's never wrong to be cautious. Until I decide what to do, I don't want to advertise ourselves."

"Where are we?"

"No way to tell. A wave pushed us over the rocks. When we hit the shore, you passed out." Savage had fought to keep his grip on her life vest, knowing he'd never find her in the storm if they were separated. The undertow had tried to suck him back. He'd managed to stand. The waves had slammed his hips. He'd lost his balance, gone under, stood again, and struggled, dragging her from the water. "I carried you up here and found this shelter. The storm didn't end till sunrise. You had me worried. I wasn't sure you'd ever wake up."

She raised her head from his chest, tried to sit straight, and groaned.

"Where do you hurt?"

"The question is, what *doesn't* hurt?"

"I checked your arms and legs. I don't think they're broken."

She moved them gently and winced. "They're stiff. But at least they work."

Savage raised a finger and shifted it back and forth, then up and down, in front of her eyes.

Her vision followed his movement.

He held up three fingers. "How many?"

She told him correctly.

"*Now* how many?"

"One."

"Are you sick to your stomach?"

Rachel shook her head. "I don't feel the best, but it's not like I'm going to vomit."

"If you do get sick or your vision starts to blur, tell me at once."

"You're afraid I might have a concussion?"

"You've got one for sure. Otherwise you wouldn't have lost consciousness for so long. We just have to hope it isn't serious."

And that your skull isn't fractured, he thought.

"They're doing something down there," Rachel said.

Savage stared through the gap in the boulders.

The two men were wading into the waves toward a large chunk of wreckage wedged between rocks. But the waves kept forcing them back. The men turned to each other, talking quickly, emphasizing their words with gestures.

One man nodded and ran to the right along the shore. He soon disappeared past a curve in the slope. The remaining man studied the wreckage again, glanced to the left along the shore, then pivoted toward the slope.

"He wonders if there were survivors," Savage said. "Assuming I guessed correctly and they don't work for your husband, the other man probably went to the local village for help. The largest chunk of the yacht is too far out for them to reach by themselves. But it's tempting salvage. Who knows? Maybe they think they'll find a safe full of money and jewels."

"But if the man who left comes back with help—"

"They'll search the area." Savage's pulse quickened. "We have to get out of here."

He rose to a crouch. Rachel winced and knelt beside him.

"Are you sure you can manage?" Savage asked.

"Just tell me what to do."

"As soon as he stops looking in this direction, follow me. Keep your head down. Don't just crawl. Pretend you're a snake."

"I'll imitate everything you do."

"Move slowly. Blend with the slope."

Rachel pointed. "He's turning toward the wreckage."

"Now." Savage sank to the cave's floor and squeezed out between the boulders.

Rachel followed.

"Don't look toward him," Savage whispered. "People can sometimes feel they're being watched."

"The only person I'm watching is *you*."

Savage squirmed up the slope. An inch. Then another. With painful care.

Though the sun warmed his back, his spine felt cold. With every moment, he expected to hear a shout from the man on the shore.

But seconds turned to minutes, and no shout made him cringe. At his feet, he felt Rachel's hands gripping rocks. He crested the slope, slid into a hollow, waited till she crawled beside him, then turned his face to the sky and exhaled in relief.

He allowed himself only a moment's rest. At once he wiped sweat from his eyes and turned toward the ridge, slowly raising his head. Surveying the shore, he heard voices. The man who'd rushed away was hurrying back, followed by women, children, and other fishermen.

They studied the wreckage with a mixture of awe and excitement. While the children scurried to examine shattered boards thrown up on the shore, the women chattered. Several men had brought ropes and poles. Tying the ropes around their waists, they waded into the surf, shoving the poles at chunks of the yacht to try to free them from the rocks, while others held the opposite end of the ropes, prepared to pull their companions back to shore if the waves knocked them underwater.

The man who'd stayed while his partner went for help gave orders to the women and children, pointing toward the slope behind him. The women and children quickly spread out, searched behind boulders, and climbed.

"They'll soon find where we were hiding."

Squirming backward, Savage suddenly stopped.

"What's wrong?" Rachel asked.

Savage pointed across the water. From the limited perspective of the cave, he hadn't been able to see the full horizon. Now, from the crest of the hill, he saw a small island a quarter-mile to the east. "I know where we are now. Rhineia. Just to the west of Delos."

"Is that good or bad?"

"There's a helicopter on Delos. I hired it to pick us up if we couldn't leave Mykonos by boat. The storm was too severe for it to take off. If we can cross the channel . . ."

"But suppose the pilot doesn't wait."

"His orders were to stay on Delos for forty-eight hours, in case I had trouble getting in contact. I lost my equipment on the yacht. I can't radio to tell him we're coming. But we have to get over there by tomorrow."

"How?"

"The only way we can. Delos is too far to swim. We have to steal a boat."

Again, as he squirmed back from the crest, something stopped him.

A far-off drone.

Savage winced.

The drone became louder. He concentrated, trying to determine which direction the sound was coming from. It increased to a *whump-whump-whumping* roar. A speck appeared above the water, grew rapidly, and assumed the shape of a grotesque dragonfly. Sunlight glinted off spinning rotors.

The helicopter swooped toward the island.

"We don't need to wonder who *that* is," Savage said. "They'll check the coastline. When they see all those people . . . When they find the wreckage . . . *Hurry.*"

They crawled away, standing to run only when the crest of the hill prevented the chopper from seeing them. The island was almost barren. Except for occasional stretches of scrub grass and stunted flowers, Savage saw only eroded ridges of granite. Scrambling over rocks, he strained to recall his research, but his information was limited. Mykonos had been his target, after all, its neighboring islands of secondary importance.

This much he knew, but it didn't console him. Rhineia was small: five square miles. Few people lived here. Tourists seldom visited. The sole attraction was the island's reputation for having been a cemetery in antiquity, but the many sarcophagi, ancient tombs, and funerary altars couldn't compare to the size and splendor of the ruins on Delos.

The men in the chopper will see the villagers and find the wreckage, Savage thought, racing. They'll send for help and search the island. But the island's so small it won't take them long to cover it!

He glanced at Rachel to make sure her pace matched his.

But what if her concussion makes her faint?

And where the hell are we going to hide?

4

When Rachel stumbled, Savage whirled and grabbed her before she fell.

Her breasts heaved against him. "I'm fine. I just snagged my foot."

"The truth?"

"Even *you* tripped a while ago." Sweat streamed down her bruised face. She glanced behind her, terrified. *"Let's go."*

The chopper's whumping roar had stopped five minutes ago, the whine of its rotors echoing above the crest of the hill near the shore. The pilot must have found a level spot near the wreckage, Savage thought. Boats and other choppers will soon bring reinforcements.

The sun angled higher, blazing. Hills stretched before him.

Rachel sprawled.

Jesus.

Savage scrambled back to her.

She'd thrust her hands out, breaking her fall. Even so, she gasped from exhaustion. "You were right."

"You didn't just trip a while ago?"

"Dizzy."

"It might not be the concussion. A few minutes' rest might—"

"No. So dizzy."

Shit, Savage thought.

"I want to throw up."

"You're sick from fear. You have to trust me. *Depend* on me. I'll get you out of this."

"How I hope."

"Catch your breath. They'll need time to organize. They won't start searching for a while."

"But after that?"

Savage wished he had an answer.

"I'm sorry," she said.

"For falling? Hey, it happens."

"No. For getting you into this."

"*You* didn't get me into this. No one forced me. I knew the risks." Savage helped her to stand. "Just don't give up. Your husband hasn't won yet."

Rachel grinned, encouraged, her bruised face pathetic.

Savage glanced ahead.

What are you going to do?

Chest heaving, he scanned the terrain for somewhere to hide.

Small ruins dotted the granite hills. They were circular, made of flat stones. Their roofs had collapsed, but the shapes of surviving walls suggested that the structures had once looked like beehives.

Tombs.

Maybe we can hide in . . .

No, they're obvious! That's the first place someone would look!

But we can't just stand here!
Rachel squeezed his hand. "I'm ready."
Supporting her, Savage stepped forward.

5

Abruptly the ground heaved. His feet slid out from under him. His hip struck granite. He plummeted.

The shock of landing was so unexpected he didn't have a chance to roll and absorb the impact. He lay on his back in darkness, gasping for breath. Rachel struck next to him, groaning. Dust settled, coating Savage's lips, stinging his eyes. He focused his vision.

They were in a pit.

Six feet above them, sunlight gleamed through a slanted opening.

Savage coughed and leaned toward Rachel. "Are you all right?"

"I think so. Wait till I try . . ." She managed to sit. "Yes. I . . . What happened?"

"We're in a shaft grave."

"What?"

He paused for breath, explaining. The ancient Greeks had used various types of burial. The ruins above were called *tholos* tombs, the adjective describing their beehive shape. But sometimes a pit was used, its walls supported by rocks, the opening covered by a granite slab. The corpse sat with its knees up and its head down in a marble container at the bottom of the shaft. Weapons, food, jewelry, and clothing were placed around the sarcophagus. When possible, the morticians filled the shaft with earth. However, Rhineia was mostly stone, and the shaft had not been filled. As Savage studied it, he sensed that the gravesite had been chosen because of a cleft in the granite surface. Only near the top, where the fissure widened, had flat stones been wedged to support the slab that covered the pit.

Or *once* had covered it.

"Grave robbers," Savage said. "They must have raised the slab, stolen the valuables, and replaced the lid so no one would suspect what they'd done. But it looks like they hurried and did a poor job. The corner we stepped on wasn't supported."

Savage pointed toward the lid slanting downward.

"Our weight made it tilt. Its edge gripped the sides of the pit. When it swung, it opened like a trapdoor."

Rachel crouched nervously. "It might have tilted farther. If its edge had slipped . . ."

"The lid would have dropped down the shaft and crushed us." Savage glanced around, his vision adjusting to the murky shaft, helped by a narrow beam of sunlight. "Or maybe the sarcophagus would have stopped it."

They'd landed next to a marble container. Its base obscured by dirt, it was three feet square and tall, set in the middle of the shaft with room around it for mourners to set the corpse's valuables. Chiseled images of soldiers and horses decorated the sides.

Savage peered again toward the shaft's slanted lid. "I think we've found our hiding place."

"Hiding place? It's more like a *trap*. They'll notice the opening and see us down here."

"But what if there isn't an opening?"

Savage stood and tested the lid.

It moved, as if on hinges.

"Be *careful*." Rachel stumbled back.

Crouching beneath it, Savage lifted the lower end. The lid began to close, the beam of sunlight getting smaller. Heart cramping, he heard a helicopter through the gap. Then the lid scraped shut, and in darkness, the only sound was Rachel's strained breathing.

6

"I hope you're not claustrophobic." Savage's whisper echoed.

"After everything I've been through, you think it bothers me to be sealed in a tomb?"

Savage had to grin. "At least you can rest now. Sit beside me." He put his arm around her. "Still dizzy?"

"No." Rachel rested her head on his shoulder.

"Still sick to your stomach?"

"Yes. But I think . . . Maybe the reason I'm queasy is I haven't eaten."

"That I can fix."

He unzipped a pocket on the thigh of his pants and took out a packet sealed in plastic.

"What is it?" Rachel asked.

"Beef jerky. Dehydrated fruit."

She bit off a piece of the jerky. "I *must* be hungry. It tastes wonderful. Not at all what I expected."

"You've never eaten jerky before?"

"I'm rich and spoiled."

He laughed and chewed on his own piece of jerky. "I'm sure you're thirsty, but there's nothing we can do about that."

"How long can we go without water?"

"No exertion? A couple of days. That isn't to say you won't feel parched. But we'll be out of here by tonight."

He lied to reassure her. With no ventilation, the shaft felt warm. Sweat trickled down his cheeks. They might soon need water badly.

The air smelled close and stale.

"I have to . . ."

"What?"

"Have to pee," Rachel said.

"You're not the only one."

"But I'm embarrassed."

"No need. Crawl over beyond the sarcophagus. By the time this is over, we'll have no secrets."

She hesitated, then crawled away.

In the dark, Savage made himself ignore the intimate sounds she made. Chest cramping, he analyzed the problems ahead.

Papadropolis's men would have to stop searching at nightfall. Unless they used flashlights and flares to guide them. Or spotlights from helicopters.

But even before night, they'd have managed to cover an island this small. They'll either decide they missed us, suspect we drowned, or fear we escaped.

So what do you expect? Savage thought.

They're afraid of Papadropolis. *They won't give up*.

And Akira?

If he *was* Akira.

But Savage had no doubt that he *was*.

Akira—

Who'd stared with sadness and shock toward Savage escaping in the yacht—

Who'd shouted Savage's name on the dock—

Whose severed head had rolled to a stop in front of Savage six months ago—

And blinked.

Akira would come. He'd never stop hunting.

Because I've got the feeling this means more to him than retrieving Rachel.

He died. Now he's chasing me.

Something happened six months ago. But Jesus, *what?*

7

Sweating, Savage glanced at the luminous hands on his diver's watch. Nine forty-seven. The sun would have set by now. The searchers would have regrouped to discuss their options. His mouth felt dry, his brain clouded by the foul air in the shaft. Nudging Rachel, he stood, wavered, then steadied himself. "It's time."

Except for their brief conversation after he'd closed the lid on the shaft, they'd maintained almost constant silence, exchanging hushed comments only when he needed to know if she continued to feel all right. Even those few remarks had been risky, since he had no way of telling whether the shaft would amplify sounds that might filter out to warn someone searching nearby.

Mostly they'd drowsed. Now Rachel didn't want to wake up.

Savage nudged her again, less gently, reassured when she responded, though her movements were listless. It worried him that her concussion might be getting worse.

"Come on," he said. "You'll feel better when you breathe fresh air."

That prospect encouraged her. She managed to stand.

Savage groped beneath the lid, reached the far end, and pushed upward.

The lid wouldn't budge.

He pushed harder, straining.

A fist seemed to squeeze his heart.

What if the lid slipped when I closed it? What if it isn't balanced anymore?

Christ, if it shifted so it's flat, even both of us can't lift that much weight! We'll suffocate!

Arms trembling, Savage pushed up with all his strength.

Sweat gushed from his pores. Frantic, he said a silent prayer of thanks when he heard a scrape.

The lid moved a quarter-inch, its edge pivoting on the sides of the shaft.

He kept thrusting, and at once the lid tilted with the same forceful rush that had dropped them into the tomb.

A three-foot gap showed him moonlight and stars. More important, a breeze swept through the opening, cooling his face. He inhaled greedily.

Rachel pressed next to him, filling her lungs. "That feels so—"

Savage capped a hand across her mouth, stared toward the night, and listened intensely.

Had anyone heard?

The night remained silent. No urgent whispers, no furtive footsteps.

Savage reached along the rim, found a rock, and wedged it against the lid so the slab wouldn't fall back onto them as they squirmed out. He boosted Rachel through the opening, waited till she was free, and watched to make sure she stayed low. Then he grabbed the rim of the shaft and pulled himself out, worming past the heavy slab tilted over him.

Flat on his stomach, he scanned his surroundings. No unnatural silhouettes. No shadows moving.

With a nod of satisfaction, he withdrew the rock he'd used to prop the lid above the shaft and pushed the slab back into place. If the searchers came back tomorrow, there was no point in showing them that their quarry had been here all along and weren't far ahead of them.

If we get ahead of them.

Turning to Rachel, he pointed toward the route they'd followed yesterday. They were going to backtrack. She nodded, understanding.

He didn't crawl far before he stopped. His hand groped ahead and felt water that yesterday's storm had left in a basin of granite. When he licked his fingers, the water tasted tepid but fit to drink. He signaled Rachel by dipping his fingers back in the pool and touching her lips.

Her head jerked away. At once she realized what she'd

tasted, and as quickly as she'd recoiled, her lips sought his fingers. She sucked them, stiffened, understood where the water had come from, and scurried past him to dip her face in the pool.

When Savage feared she'd drink so much she'd get sick, he gently pulled her away. She frowned, then complied. He took his turn, lapping gritty water. Wiping his mouth, he scanned the dark hills and urged her forward.

8

A half hour later, they stopped on a crest that revealed the sea. Moonlight reflected off waves. The shore, where the yacht had foundered and the fishermen had gathered, was now deserted.

Savage edged to the right. Yesterday, the villagers had come from that direction. Their homes, he assumed, were also in that direction. A short while later, he discovered his assumption was correct.

Lights glinted from windows in a clump of a few dozen rock-walled huts. To Savage's right, two helicopters rested on a level stretch of shore, safely above the waves. Muscular men, wearing nylon jackets, holding automatic weapons, strode from building to building, patrolling. Some raised walkie-talkies, speaking insistently.

Savage kept scanning the village. On its left, a primitive dock was flanked by six powerboats, each large enough to carry a dozen men. *Farther* left, eight single-masted fishing boats rested on a pebbly beach. Those fishing boats are tempting, Savage thought.

And that's the point, he decided.

The choppers have guards.

The fishing boats don't.

The fishing boats are the trap.

Then how do we get off the island?

Five minutes later, he decided. Using gestures, he tried to tell Rachel what to do, but she didn't understand. After several attempts, he was forced to risk the softest of whispers.

"Follow this bluff toward the right. When you're past the village—fifty yards—wait for me. I might be quite a while. You'll hear shooting. Don't panic."

"But . . ."

"You promised to do what you're told."

She looked frightened,

He stared with disapproval, pointing insistently.

Hesitant, she crawled toward the right.

He felt sorry for her, knowing how frightened she was to be alone.

But he didn't have a choice. He couldn't let her stay with him. Given what he had to do, she'd not only be in the way; she might get both of them killed.

He waited till she disappeared into the dark, then concentrated on the village. To the left, the fishing boats beckoned. The trap was so obvious he had no doubt that hidden sentries guarded them.

The instant I show myself to try to reach a boat, I'll be shot. Maybe searchlights'll suddenly blaze to help the guards aim.

Let's find out.

He squirmed down the hill.

"I might be quite a while," he'd told Rachel, but the need for silence had prevented him from elaborating. "Quite a while" might be hours. He had to move as slowly as shadows cast by the shifting moon.

After thirty minutes, during which he progressed no more than fifty yards, he stiffened.

A faint sound primed his reflexes. The subtle scratch of cloth against rock. Directly before him. Past a wall of boulders.

Savage gingerly raised his head.

A sentry sat hidden from the top of the slope, his rifle directed toward the fishing boats.

Savage thrust his hands down. Jerked the man's head back.

Twisted.

The brittle snap was too faint to cause an alert. The dead man slumped.

Savage eased over the boulders, collecting a .30-06 bolt-action rifle with a telescopic sight. As well, he found a .357 Magnum revolver. The corpse's pockets held plenty of ammunition.

He grasped the weapons and veered around the boulders, returning up the slope. Other snipers hid nearby. He took that for granted. But the route he'd used to get here was safe, so he allowed himself to crawl a little faster.

At the top, he paused to verify that nothing had alarmed the village. The men down there weren't ducking toward cover or racing up the slope as if they'd been warned about an intruder. The first part of the plan had worked. And now? The second part was so risky he almost didn't proceed.

If it fails, you won't get another chance, he thought. But we can't stay here and hope they don't search the island again. The longer we hide, the more we'll lose strength without food. And maybe the next time they search, they'll find us.

Or Rachel might crack from the strain. She's almost at her limit.

It has to be *now*.

He'd told Rachel, "Wait for me. You'll hear shots. Don't panic."

Damn it, Rachel, keep control.

He fired the .30-06 and darted inland. The rifle's report echoed fiercely.

Hearing shouts from the village, he pulled the trigger on the .357 and continued running. More shouts. He fired the rifle again. Two seconds later, the revolver.

The night became filled with commotion. Boots dislodged rocks as the guards charged up the slope from the village. He fired the revolver twice more, the rifle once, and altered his course, no longer racing inland, instead angling toward the left.

The shouts became louder, closer, the men about to crest

the hill. Abruptly Savage stooped. Running in a crouch, he angled farther left.

The men scurried over the hill. A flare burst in the sky, lighting the area where he'd been shooting.

Savage stooped lower, racing harder, escaping the light.

He anticipated what would happen. The men—having heard reports from two different weapons—would assume that the shots had been exchanged between Savage and a sentry. They'd spread out, searching warily, proceeding inland.

In the meantime, Savage had to take advantage of their distraction. He rushed through the night toward the opposite side of the village, reached the hill, and looked for Rachel. Couldn't find her.

Moved farther along the ridge.

And recoiled as a shadow lunged.

He almost chopped with his callused fingers before he realized that the figure was Rachel. She trembled in his arms, but he didn't have time to comfort her.

On the shore below him, a helicopter's engine began to whine. Its rotors turned slowly.

Simultaneously, another flare burst in the sky, lighting the ridge on the opposite side of the village.

The search had become more intense, Savage concluded with satisfaction. The guards are spreading, progressing farther inland. They've ordered a chopper up. They want its searchlights to add to the flares.

Rachel hugged him closer.

Savage pressed his lips to her ear. "Don't *panic*," he murmured. "Not *now*. Five more minutes, and we'll be out of here."

He tugged her down the slope.

The chopper's blades spun faster, the whine more intense. Moonlight and the glow of instruments revealed the pilot through the cockpit's Plexiglas. A copilot ran toward the chopper.

Savage tugged Rachel harder.

The copilot opened a hatch on the chopper. About to climb in, he jolted back, then collapsed from the impact of Savage's rifle butt against his jaw.

Savage pushed him aside, dropped the rifle, and aimed the Magnum revolver into the cockpit, telling the startled pilot, "Get the hell out, or die."

The pilot fumbled at his seat belt, pawed at the hatch, and dove toward the ground.

Savage scrambled inside, yanking Rachel after him.

But she didn't need encouragement. Breathing frantically, she shoved him. "Go!"

He slammed the hatch, ignored his seat belt, and pressed his feet on pedals while grasping levers. His training in the SEALs had not included choppers, but Graham had insisted that a protector ought to be skilled with aircraft. Not jets. They were too sophisticated to be mastered without lengthy intensive instruction. But prop planes—and basic choppers—could be learned during leisure hours in a matter of months.

Thank God, Savage thought, this isn't a military chopper. Their consoles bewildered him. But *this* chopper was designed so civilians could shuttle tourists. Its controls were no frills, do-this-by-the-book-and-*that*-by-the-book, so simple they were elegant.

The whine of the engines changed to a roar. The rotors spun so fast they seemed stationary.

"Go!" Rachel screamed.

Savage pressed pedals, worked levers, and the chopper lifted. His stomach sank from the force. At once, his stomach soared, from excitement. They were *free*.

He guided the chopper up and forward, speeding above the moonlit waves. With a tense glance backward, he saw tiny figures rush down the slope, others out of the village, converging angrily on the shore. They raised rifles.

Swiftly gaining more distance, Savage saw their muzzles flash.

Too late, he thought.

He buckled his seat belt, turning to Rachel. "Get yours on."

"I already have."

"You're something else." Savage grinned. "I have to tell you, I'm impressed. Not many . . ."

When she screamed, he couldn't help it. He flinched. Turning, he saw a pistol aimed at his head.

And beyond the pistol, he saw Akira.

9

"Let's not forget where we are." Akira's eyes were as melancholy as Savage remembered, his English as perfect. "No, don't reach for your weapon. I'll shoot. You'll die. A helicopter needs constant guidance. Before I could yank you aside to grab the pedals and sticks, we'd crash. Then I'd die as well. But so would your principal."

"How did—?"

"I thought to myself, the yacht broke apart on the rocks, but did anyone survive? And if they did, and since *you* once belonged to the SEALs—an expert in survival—what would *I* do in your place? Assuming I found an adequate spot in which to hide, I'd want to get off the island as soon as possible before I lost energy from thirst and hunger. No doubt you had a rescue team nearby. Probably on Delos. I found that helicopter by the way. So I reasoned further and decided you'd feel compelled to get to Delos before the rescue team gave up and left. In *that* case, what were your choices? To steal a fishing boat was obvious, and my principal's men dispersed themselves accordingly. Snipers were everywhere. But your reputation is based on adaptability. A diversion? A skyjacking? I balanced your options and hid in this helicopter. After all, what did I have to lose? A few hours of lying here motionless? I could do so for days. And here you are."

"You weren't this talkative when we worked together at the Medford Gap Mountain Retreat." Savage squinted back toward Akira's pistol. Shivering, he squinted farther back toward Akira's brooding eyes. The eyes of a man he'd seen beheaded.

"The mountain retreat? Yes, that's why I'm here," Akira said. "It's why I stalked you. It's why I hid. I need to ask you a question. *Why* are you still alive? Six months ago, I saw you die."

Shocked, Savage lost control of the helicopter. It tilted sharply toward the sea. Urgently he readjusted its pedals and levers. The chopper regained altitude. His chest relaxed. But his mind felt bludgeoned by Akira's startling words. "Saw *me*? But I saw—!"

"They're after us," Rachel said.

With renewed shock, Savage twisted to stare behind him. So did Akira.

Now, Savage thought. I can grab his gun.

But his instincts warned him that Akira would never allow himself to be totally distracted.

"Good," Akira said. "You defeated temptation."

"How did you know I wouldn't try?"

"I counted on your common sense. But it's better if we all assume trust. As a gesture of my intentions . . ." Akira put the gun in a holster beneath his windbreaker.

At once the cockpit seemed less crowded.

Savage concentrated on the night behind them. "I don't see anything chasing us."

"There." Rachel pointed back to her left. "Lights."

"From the powerboats?"

"The other helicopter," Akira said.

"Jesus. Is it *armed*?"

"The men inside I'm sure have automatic weapons, but the helicopter's a twin to this one. It has no aggressive capabilities."

"If it catches us," Rachel said, "the men can open a hatch and fire."

"But they won't."

"How can you be sure?"

Savage interrupted. "The same reason they didn't shoot when we escaped from the mansion. They're afraid of hitting *you* instead of me."

"That didn't stop them from shooting when we stole the helicopter."

"I think they were so surprised they overreacted. Now they've had a chance to realize how foolish they were. If this helicopter crashes because of them, Papadropolis would cut off their . . ."

"Yes." Rachel winced. "My husband's capable of anything."

"So you're our protection," Akira said.

"*Our?* But you're on their side," Savage said.

"Not any longer. I arrived at the mansion the day before last. A substitute for a guard who was ill." Akira turned to Rachel. "The moment I realized why I'd been hired—to keep you a prisoner so your husband could beat and rape you—I knew I couldn't in conscience remain. In fact, I had plans to rescue you myself. Since Papadropolis misrepresented the assignment to me—he told me he'd been threatened and needed a protector—I consider my agreement with him to be void."

"Then why did you point the gun at me?" Savage asked.

"To prevent you from attacking. I needed your attention while I explained."

"The lights are gaining," Rachel said.

"They might try to force us to land. There's an island to the right." Savage pointed at a hulking mass. Avoiding it, he increased speed. The engine roared so hard the fuselage began to vibrate.

The fuel gauge dipped toward the half-level mark. Savage shook his head. "This fast, we'll use too much gas."

"At the rate they're chasing us, they're wasting as much fuel as you are," Akira said. "I wouldn't worry. Their tanks were low to begin with. They'll soon need to head for land. Be calm. No doubt the two of you are thirsty and hungry." Akira reached toward the floor. With a smile that didn't relieve the sadness in his eyes, he handed Rachel a canteen and a packet of sandwiches.

Rachel fumbled to untwist the canteen's cap and took several large swallows. She suddenly lowered the canteen and frowned at both men. "You're avoiding the issue."

Savage knew what she meant.

Akira's sad eyes narrowed. "Yes."

"What the two of you said sounded crazy. What did you mean?"

Savage and Akira didn't answer. Just stared at each other.

" 'I saw you,' " Rachel quoted. "At the dock, when we left the harbor, that's what you shouted," she told Akira, bewildered.

She turned toward Savage. "And you yelled the same thing back to him . . . but the emphasis was different. 'I saw *you*.' Then it thundered, and I couldn't hear the next few words, except for 'die.' I remember I asked if you knew this man. You wouldn't talk about it. Then a short while later, you said, 'God help me, yes.' You sounded terrified. 'I saw him die six months ago.' But the wind was so loud I wasn't sure I heard correctly. It didn't make sense. Now this man says he saw you—"

"*Beheaded*. Savage, how did you survive?"

"How did *you* survive?" Savage asked.

"The sword sliced your head off. It rolled across the floor."

"Your head stopped upright," Savage said. "Your eyes blinked."

"*Yours* blinked."

"Oh, Jesus," Rachel said, "I was right. The two of you are crazy."

"No," Savage said. "But since both of us are alive, it's obvious something's horribly wrong." An unnerving rush of adrenaline scorched his stomach and made his knees shake.

Rachel turned pale and shook her head. "For God's sake, it's impossible. If neither of you is crazy, someone's lying!" The way she stared at Akira made it obvious she suspected the stranger.

Akira shrugged, dismissing her objection, his sad gaze riveted on Savage.

"Once more," Rachel said. "*Listen* to yourself. You claim you saw him beheaded?"

"That's absolutely correct," Akira said, squinting at Savage.

"And you saw *him* beheaded?" Rachel asked Savage.

Savage nodded. A chill swept through him, as if he shared the cockpit with a ghost.

Rachel jerked her hands up. "I'll say it again. Since this can't have happened, it's a lie."

"Do you trust me?" Savage asked.

"You know I do. How many times do I have to prove it? I swore I'd follow you to hell."

"Well, that's where I feel I am. Because what you insist is impossible is what I'm staring at. I was *there*. I know what happened. I saw it. And Rachel, I'm telling you . . . think I'm crazy, I don't care . . . I'm telling you I saw a Japanese assassin cut this man's head off. It's been haunting me for the past six months."

"Just as I've been haunted by you," Akira said.

"What you say doesn't count," Savage said. "Rachel and I can trust each other. But can I trust *you*?"

"A perfectly professional attitude. I feel the same way. I'd be disappointed if you weren't suspicious. What's more, I'd have to be suspicious if you readily believed."

"Both of you are starting to scare me," Rachel said.

"*Starting* to? I was scared from the moment I saw Akira at the mansion."

"Imagine my own shock," Akira said, "my refusal to accept what I saw, when you passed me in the car . . . when I chased you through the village . . . when I yelled at you on the dock."

"None of that matters," Savage said. "All that does is what I saw six months ago. *That's* what I'm sure of. It's not like you were shot in the chest and you *seemed* to be dead but afterwards a doctor managed to revive you."

"So why am I here? How can I be talking to you?"

"Damn it, I don't know!"

"Stop it," Rachel said. "I'm really frightened."

"No more than I am," Akira said. "How can I make you understand? Savage, for the past six months, you've been in my nightmares. While I convalesced . . ."

"From . . . ?"

"*Bokken*."

Rachel squirmed. "Speak English!"

"Wooden swords," Akira said. "They broke my arms and legs, my ribs, my spleen, my appendix, and my skull. It took me six months to recover."

"And the same thing happened to me," Savage said. "So we're back to where we started. Either both of us are crazy. Or you've been lying. Or . . ."

"*You've* been lying," Akira said. "I know what I saw. How did you survive?"

Savage realized that behind the melancholy in Akira's eyes, there lurked a desperate confusion.

"All right," Savage said. "I'll agree with you. Let's assume we saw each other die. But it's impossible." Desperately he reassessed the explanations. "If we're not crazy . . . and if no one's lying . . ."

"Yes?" Akira leaned forward.

"Your mind's as logical as mine. There is a third option."

"The unknown." Akira nodded. "And since you're alive and I'm alive . . ."

"When you shouldn't be."

"Nor should you."

Savage's mind swirled. "What the hell happened?"

"I suggest we help each other find out."

10

"The lights behind us don't seem as close," Rachel said.

Savage looked. The pursuing helicopter veered and descended toward an island on the right. "It must be almost out of fuel."

"Thank God. At least that's one less thing to worry about." Rachel closed her eyes, exhausted.

"What about our own fuel?" Akira asked.

Savage checked the gauge. "A quarter full."

Rachel's eyes snapped open. "Enough to reach the mainland?"

"Yes. If we follow this course."

"If? Why wouldn't we stay on course?"

"What Savage means is that we have to take for granted the pilot who was chasing us radioed ahead for other helicopters to intercept us," Akira said. "They'll know which direction we're coming from. If we stay on this route, they'll find us."

"So we go where we're not expected." Savage changed course from northwest to west. "Eventually we'll head north."

"But this way, it's farther to Athens. We'll use more fuel," Rachel said.

"And at maximum speed, the engine can't burn it efficiently. I need to go slower to conserve it," Savage said.

"Does that mean we'll still have enough to get there?"

Savage didn't answer.

". . . Oh, shit," Rachel said.

11

The engine sputtered, the gauge disturbingly near empty, when Savage finally reached the mainland. In predawn twilight, he touched down on an isolated clearing, where the chopper that had waited on Delos would have landed if Savage had used it for the escape. He ran with Rachel and Akira toward shadowy bushes at the edge of the clearing. For a nervous instant, he feared that Akira would draw his weapon and confess he'd lied to gain Savage's trust, but Akira kept his hands at his sides and in fact seemed concerned that Savage might draw his own gun.

"There's a dirt road beyond these bushes," Savage said. "A hundred yards to the left, we'll reach a barn."

"Which contains a car?"

Savage nodded, starting to run.

"But what if we couldn't reach here?"

"I arranged for two other landing sites. I also had a choice of ports if we came by boat. You know the rule. If something *can* go wrong, it *will* go wrong. Arrange for as many backup plans as possible."

"Whoever trained you did it thoroughly."

They reached the road and rushed to the left.

"Of course, the authorities will find the helicopter," Akira said. "If Papadropolis decides to report it stolen, a lab crew will dust for fingerprints."

"Are yours on file?"

"I've never been fingerprinted."

"*I* have," Savage said.

"Then Papadropolis will use his power to identify your prints. He'll send men to kill you for taking his wife."

"I wiped what I'd touched before I left the chopper. Still, Papadropolis knows your name."

"Not correct. All he knows is my pseudonym."

"Yes, that's one of the first things my trainer taught me," Savage said. "Be anonymous. Prevent an angry opponent from coming after you."

"A wise instructor."

"He can also be a bastard."

"All wise instructors are."

"I . . ." Rachel's chest heaved, her breathing strident. "I can't keep up with . . ."

Both men turned and grabbed Rachel's arms. Carrying her between them, they rushed toward a barn that the gray light of dawn silhouetted. A dark Fiat waited. Five minutes later, they drove along the road, Rachel on the front seat between them.

Steering, Savage felt her sweat-soaked clothes next to him. "The worst is over. You're safe now. Go to sleep. You'll soon have hot food, fresh clothes, and a very soft bed. I tested it myself."

"What I want"—Rachel sighed—"is a bath.'

"I figured," Savage said. "It's been arranged. And lots of warm water."

"*Hot* water."

"You sound like a Japanese." Akira watched the gray sky become brilliantly blue in the fullness of dawn. "Where are we going?"

"A farm to the east of Athens." Savage's eyes burned from exhaustion. "I rented an abandoned house. 'I'm a writer,' I told the owner. 'I need privacy. I'm doing research for a new biography of Aristotle.' "

"And what did the owner say?"

"He thought I meant Aristotle *Onassis*. He made me promise to tell him all the dirt about Ari and Jackie."

"Did you?"

"According to me, Ari rivaled the pope for holiness. The farmer's eyes glazed over. 'You professors,' he said and took my money. He thinks I'm a fool. He won't come to visit."

Akira chuckled. Rachel snored.

12

They hid the car behind the farmhouse. Grapevines crowded the sunlit fields. Though the house looked dilapidated, its interior was clean and comfortably furnished. Several days earlier, Savage had supervised the arrangements.

En route, Savage and Akira had persistently discussed their nightmare, but once at the farmhouse, Rachel became their priority. What did she want? they asked. Food? More sleep? The *bath*, she insisted. Savage had made sure the house would have electricity. The water heater was set on high. She stayed in the bathroom an hour, and when she came out, wearing a St. Laurent dress that Rachel's sister had chosen for her, she looked beautiful despite the bruises on her face.

Akira frowned at the sight of them. "In the helicopter, I thought your face was merely covered with dirt from two nights and a day of running. I had no idea that what looked like dirt was actually . . . I knew your husband abused you but . . . What kind of monster would . . . ?"

Rachel raised a hand to conceal the worst bruises.

"I apologize," Akira said. "I meant to be sympathetic, not to make you self-conscious. Please remember, the bruises are temporary."

"Those on my body, you mean," Rachel said.

"But no one can bruise your soul."

Rachel lowered her hand and smiled. "Thank you. I needed reminding."

Savage couldn't help being impressed. Her eyes, so splendidly blue, accentuated by the burgundy of her cotton dress, glowed with strength and dignity. She'd combed her wet auburn hair behind her ears, emphasizing the elegance of her jaw and cheekbones, which had started to be prominent now that the swelling from her bruises had begun to recede.

"No, even if your husband had killed you, he wouldn't have harmed your soul," Akira said. "I believe in Shinto."

Rachel shook her head.

"It's the oldest Japanese religion."

"I still don't . . . I've never been religious."

"According to Shinto, when we die, our souls merge with the world around us. Life doesn't end. It only changes. It becomes absorbed. But it still has identity. It accepts. It goes with the flow. Your husband couldn't have defeated your soul, because it's invulnerable. It would have another life."

"*This* life is what I'm concerned about," Rachel said.

"By all means." Akira shrugged. "Shinto doesn't insist that you give up a present form of existence you prefer."

"And in *this* life, I need food."

"We've got it cooking," Savage said. "Lamb stew."

"Sounds delicious."

It was.

But midway through the meal, Savage turned to Akira. "Tell me once more."

"I've told you five times."

"Make it six. Both of us died, but *neither* did. And every time I look at you, I shiver. I'm seeing a . . ."

"*Kami.*"

"What?"

"A ghost. All right, I've been straining to understand. With no success. So if you want to hear yet again . . ."

"In *more* detail. There's *always* something more. You just haven't thought of it yet."

"Very well. I was hired by . . ."

Muto Kamichi.

Savage listened intensely as Akira described the man.

Late fifties. Slightly stooped. Protruding stomach. Streaks of gray in his black hair. Sagging brown cheeks.

"That's exactly how I remember him," Savage said. "Where did he hire you?"

"Tokyo."

"What was his occupation?"

"I don't know."

"You must have had some idea. Describe his office."

"I already told you, we met in neutral territory. A park."

"Yes," Savage said, "and then his limousine picked both of you up."

"Correct."

"Describe the driver."

"A trim man who did his job well. The clouded-glass partition was closed. I didn't get a close look."

"Could Kamichi have been a politician?"

"Perhaps, though he might have been a businessman. My main impression was he looked weary."

"A weary executive. That was *my* impression," Savage said. "But 'executive' can mean many things. Tell me about his hands."

"The tips of his fingers had calluses. So did the sides of his palms."

"Like yours and mine. From karate training."

"That was my conclusion," Akira said. "But in Japan, where martial arts are traditional, many executives practice them."

"What was your assignment?"

"To accompany Kamichi-san to America. He was scheduled to attend a conference, he said. He expected no danger, but he felt it prudent to have an escort."

"That troubles me. Since he had a chauffeur, he must have had other men on his staff who could act as guards."

"He explained that," Akira said. "He wanted a protector who was used to American customs."

"You've worked for Americans?"

"I've worked for *many* nationalities. But my fluency in English makes me a favorite of wealthy Americans who come to Japan. And for wealthy *Japanese* who travel to America."

"Did he tell you he planned to hire an American escort as well?"

"Yes. I saw no problem. I needed someone to substitute for me while I ate and slept, and it's practical to have an associate who's a citizen of the country I'm working in," Akira said.

"So you flew from Tokyo to . . . ?"

"Dallas."

"Did anything happen there?"

"My master spoke with other Japanese who'd been on the plane. Then he met with several Americans."

"The meeting was in the airport?"

"And brief. I didn't hear what they discussed. We proceeded to New York."

"Where we met," Savage said. "Then we drove for an hour and stopped."

"My master said you'd been given instructions. In Japanese, he told me to add refinements you did not know."

"We stopped at a Howard Johnson's. Briefcases . . ."

"Were exchanged. That surprised me."

"I felt the same. Then we reached . . ."

"After many hours and in the dark, a most unusual building that resembled *several* buildings, some made of brick, others of stone, others of wood. They varied in height: five stories, three, four. Each had a different style: a town house, a pagoda, a castle, a chalet. Some had straight walls. Others were rounded. Chimneys, turrets, gables, and balconies added to the"—Akira hesitated—"architectural confusion."

"Yes. Confusion."

"I was worried about security in such an unprotected setting."

"No, *I* was nervous, but you said not to concern myself, that precautions had been taken."

Akira shook his head. "I was merely repeating my master's reassurances. I knew nothing about the arrangements."

"There were guards on the bluffs. And the three other principals at the conference each had two escorts, the same as Kamichi."

"What nationality were the other principals?" Akira asked.

"American, Spanish, and Italian."

Rachel set down her spoon. "I don't know anything about your business."

Savage and Akira looked at her.

"I'm just a civilian, and maybe I ought to keep quiet, but while I listened, one thing occurred to me."

"Oh?" Savage waited.

"It's probably not important, but . . ."

"Tell us," Akira said.

"Well, how did Kamichi get in touch with you?"

Akira looked puzzled.

"The two of you seem obsessed about being anonymous. I doubt very much that you advertise."

Savage laughed. "Certainly not."

"Then how did you and Akira get chosen for the job?"

Akira shrugged. "Standard procedure. My agent found the job."

"Same with me," Savage said. "That detail's not important."

"Five minutes ago, you insisted *everything's* important."

"She's right," Akira said. "We have to consider everything."

"But my agent knows nothing about Kamichi," Savage said. "He couldn't even tell me if I'd be protecting a businessman or a politician. Kamichi simply contacted him with an offer to pay an escort well for five days' work."

"My agent knew nothing about him either," Akira said, then turned to Rachel, explaining, "A businessman requires different security techniques than a politician because they usually face different threats—abduction versus assassination. I remember feeling frustrated by the lack of information."

"Well, since you keep asking each other to repeat what happened," Rachel said, "why not ask your agents, too? Maybe they'll remember something that didn't seem relevant before."

Savage raised his eyebrows.

"I suppose," Akira said.

"Why not? It's worth a try. We're not solving anything on our own."

Savage suddenly looked discouraged. "But your agent's in Japan and mine's in America, and we can't talk about this on a long-distance line."

"So we travel," Akira said. "But only half the distance you think. I don't need to go to Japan. When I work in America, I use an American agent."

"What's his name?"

Akira hesitated, frowning at Rachel, as if debating how much to reveal before an outsider. He stiffened, apparently compelled by his urgent need for answers. "Graham Barker-Smythe."

"Jesus."

13

Savage stood so abruptly his chair fell, clattering. "That's the name of mine. The son of a bitch."

"*Graham's your agent?*" The shock on Savage's face made Akira surge to his feet as well. "There's some mistake. I said 'an American.' He's actually—"

"English. Close to sixty. Overweight. Bald. Smokes cigars. Always wears three-piece suits."

"And only the best," Akira said. "Loves champagne and caviar."

"Beluga and Dom Pérignon. That's Graham. The bastard."

Rachel jerked her hands up. "Would somebody please . . . ? *Both* of you used the same agent, and neither of you realized?"

"We *couldn't* have," Savage said. "The profession is secretive by definition. The work we do makes us a target."

"We guarantee loyalty to our masters," Akira said. "Never to betray a confidence. Never to reveal indiscretions. But we can't always depend on our masters being loyal to us, so we hide our identities, in case our masters decide to come after us to insure our silence. Or in case our masters' enemies decide to punish us."

"You talk like you live in another century," Rachel said.

"If you understand that, then you understand everything," Akira said. "How I wish. If I could be alive three hundred years ago."

Savage stared toward Akira in puzzlement and abruptly swung his gaze toward Rachel. "The point is, we have to be paranoid. Not just for our clients. But for ourselves. A protector trusts his agent completely. Because the agent's the common link among the enemy, the client, the assignment, and—"

"You, the protector," Rachel said, then turned to Akira. "And you. So Graham, as the agent, *also* has to be paranoid."

"And totally reliable. He must never betray his client's confidence," Savage said.

"Or betray the anonymity of the protectors he represents?" Rachel asked.

"Exactly. That's why Savage and I would never have known we had the same agent. If Graham had told me the name of another protector he represented, I'd have instantly distrusted him and looked for another agent."

Savage rounded the table. "So was Graham being ethical by refusing to tell us we had common nightmares?"

"You spent six months recovering. *So did I.* Did he visit you?"

"Every Saturday," Savage said. "On Chesapeake Bay."

"He came to me every Thursday. At Martha's Vineyard."

"And all the time, he knew I thought you'd been killed."

"As I thought *you'd* been killed."

"This isn't an agent being justifiably paranoid. He should have told us!"

"You think he was *part* of it?"

"It sure as hell seems that way," Savage said.

Akira's face hardened.

Rachel gripped their hands. "Not to seem nervous, friends, but . . ."

"We won't catch the next plane to the States and leave you, if that's what you're afraid of," Savage said. "You're still our priority."

"In that case . . ." Rachel's shoulders sagged. Her eyelids flickered. "I need to . . ." Her head drooped. "Awfully tired."

"Go in the bedroom. Get some sleep."

Rachel yawned. "But what about you?"

"Don't worry. Akira and I will sleep in shifts. One of us will guard you day and night."

Her head sank toward the table.

Savage carried her into the bedroom.

14

When Savage came back to the kitchen, Akira was gone. A quick check showed him the other rooms were empty. Frowning, he opened the door in front and found Akira, his brown face raised toward the sun, sitting on rickety steps.

"Trouble?" Savage asked.

"It was time to look around."

"And?"

Akira gestured toward the fields of grapevines. "Everything seems normal. The grapes have been harvested. I can see between the rows. No one's in the fields. You did a good job of selecting this house."

"Thanks." Savage sat next to him. "Given your skills, that's quite a compliment."

"A statement of fact."

Savage grinned. "I'll try like hell to stay humble."

Akira grinned in return, though his eyes remained melancholy.

"Your English is perfect," Savage said. "Where did you learn . . . ?"

"Sometime I'll tell you."

"Provided you're in the mood. *Omote* and *ura*. Right?"

Akira turned to him. "Public thoughts and private thoughts? You're familiar with Japanese logic?"

"I'm doing my best."

"Commendable. A pity, though. You'll never succeed."

"So I've decided."

"The woman?" Akira asked.

"She held up well. Impressive, really. She deserves to be exhausted. She didn't move when I covered her with a blanket. She'll probably sleep till dark."

"So." Akira made the word sound like an affirmative.

"But we need sleep, too. If you like, I'll take the first watch. You can bathe and . . ."

"You've exerted yourself more than I have," Akira said. "And longer. You must be more tired. You go first."

"We could debate this all morning." Savage picked up two pebbles, shook them between closed palms, closed a hand around each of them, and held out his fists. "Small pebble goes first."

"A child's game?"

"Why not? It's as good a way to decide as any."

Akira looked amused and chose the left fist. Savage opened it, comparing the pebble with the one in his right.

"Looks like you'll soon be taking a nap," Savage said.

Akira bowed, then laughed. *"Hai."*

"Does that mean 'yes' in Japanese?"

"Among other things. 'Of course.' 'Indeed.' 'By all means.' It depends on the inflection." Akira studied him. "You're what we call a man of sincerity. Well-intentioned. Serious."

"And with a terrifying problem."

"Two," Akira said. "First, your principal has to be returned to your employer."

"I've made arrangements."

"So far, I admit your work has been excellent. But to expedite the process, I suggest we collaborate on returning her."

"I'd be honored." Savage pressed his palms together and lowered his head.

"Then we go to New York."

Savage straightened. "And force answers out of Graham."

"But there's something I haven't discussed with you. This isn't just about what happened to you and me."

"I know," Savage said. "Kamichi."

Akira looked surprised.

"The forty-seven *ronin*," Savage added.

"You're *aware* of them?"

"It took them two years, but they finally avenged their master's death."

"Kamichi was the only principal I've ever lost." Akira's voice rasped.

"And the only principal *I've* ever lost. If Graham had something to do with it . . ." Savage scowled. "More than Rachel . . . more than our common nightmare . . . what happened to Kamichi . . ."

"Has to be avenged." Akira stood. "If we agree on that ultimate, we . . ."

"Might be friends," Savage said.

Akira squinted. "Friends?"

I assumed too much, Savage thought.

"Temporary partners," Akira said. "To show my respect for *your* respect, I'll use your Western custom."

They shook hands. Akira's grip was as strong as a samurai clutching a sword.

That comparison reminded Savage of the sword that had sliced Kamichi's torso in half and cut off Akira's head.

He tightened his own grip.

And thought of Graham.

TWO

TIME OUT OF MIND

OBSTACLE RACE, SCAVENGER HUNT

1

They couldn't use the Athens airport. That was the obvious place for Papadropolis's men to look. The only other international airports were Salonica, several hundred kilometers to the north, and Corfu, equally far to the northwest. No doubt, those sites would be watched as well. Papadropolis —chronically impatient—would automatically consider the most rapid form of travel, even if reaching the latter two airports was time-consuming.

The subsequent option was to *drive* from Greece, but that would be an ordeal. To reach safety, Savage, Akira, and Rachel would first have to drive north to Yugoslavia, a country four times as large as Greece, then west through the extensive mountains of northern Italy, and finally south through France to the island principality, controlled by Rachel's sister, off the Côte d'Azur.

The best way seemed by boat. Even someone with Papadropolis's wealth couldn't arrange to put every Grecian port under surveillance, though he *would* have his men check those near Athens, of course, as well as the motorrail terminals in the area. So Savage, Akira, and Rachel drove toward Patrai, four hours away, on the western coast of Greece. There, they briefly considered bribing a fisherman to smuggle them across to Italy. But could the fisherman be trusted to violate international boundaries rather than report them to the authorities? Legal transportation seemed safest.

"All the same, I'm skeptical," Akira said. It was nine o'clock at night. He stood with Savage and Rachel in a murky alley, scanning traffic and pedestrians outside a ticket office next to a ferry on a brightly lit pier. "Granted it's faster than driving, but it's not as fast as flying."

"Which we've agreed isn't smart," Savage said.

"That ticket office could be as risky as an airline terminal."

"No question. I'll check it out. They know I'm Caucasian and possibly guess I'm American, but I can pass for a European. A Japanese, though. They'd spot you at once."

Ten minutes later, Savage came back. "I didn't see any surveillance."

"That doesn't mean there isn't any."

Savage shrugged in agreement, handing Akira and Rachel their tickets. "My assumption is they'd watch the ferry as well as the ticket office."

"Or watch *on* the ferry," Akira said. "A limited area. A captive group."

"That works the other way around. We'd have a better chance of spotting *them*."

Akira thought about it. "Yes."

"How long till we reach Italy?" Rachel asked.

"Nineteen hours."

"*What?*"

"The ferry makes two stops up the coast before it cuts across the Adriatic," Savage said. "The fact that it's slow appeals to me. Papadropolis won't expect us to choose a method that takes us so long to escape. We leave in fifty minutes. We'd better get back to the car.''

2

Savage and Rachel drove to the pier, joining a line of cars and small trucks waiting to pass through customs and onto the ferry. In Italy, there'd be customs officials as well, but the Greeks inspected luggage leaving the country to insure that ancient artifacts weren't being smuggled out. Though a customs station wasn't as stringent as immigration, passports would have to be shown.

Passports. Savage had retrieved his from a safe-deposit box in Athens. Akira never went anywhere without his own, in a water-proof pouch.

But Rachel's passport had been kept by Papadropolis, another way for him to exert control.

The usual solution to the problem would have been for Rachel to go to the U.S. embassy, explain that she'd lost her passport, and apply for a new one. But the process might take days, and Rachel didn't have other documents to prove she was a U.S. citizen. More to the point, Papadropolis would assume that she'd need a passport and order the U.S. embassy watched.

An alternative solution was for Savage to arrange to get Rachel a bogus passport. The trouble was that Rachel's face had a multitude of bruises; even cosmetics couldn't disguise them. When an official compared the photograph on the passport to the woman standing before him, her bruises would so nearly match those in the picture it would be obvious that the photograph had been taken less than a day ago, that the passport was forged.

Savage hadn't known about Rachel's bruises before he went in to rescue her. But his professional habits had prompted him to establish a contingency plan, in case she couldn't get her hands on her passport. Joyce Stone had shown him photographs of her sister. Savage had been struck by the eerie resemblance between the two women, as if they weren't just sisters but twins, though Rachel was ten years younger.

So he'd told Joyce Stone to return to her island empire and to use her authority to insist that her passport not be stamped when she arrived. A messenger had then brought Joyce Stone's passport back to Savage in Athens. As a consequence, there wasn't any evidence that Joyce Stone had ever left Greece.

Comparing the photograph in the passport to the younger sister's face, Savage had once again been struck by the eerie resemblance. With two exceptions. Joyce Stone was blond whereas Rachel's hair was auburn. And Joyce Stone continued to look like a movie star whereas Rachel looked like a battered wife.

I can take advantage of those contrasts, Savage had thought. At the farmhouse near Athens, he'd given Rachel dye to change her hair from auburn to blond. And now that he drove the car toward the customs official in the ferry depot, he glanced toward Rachel, shaking his head in wonder. The blond hair made Rachel look amazingly like her sister, and paradoxically the bruises contributed to the illusion, making her look older.

The customs official searched the car. "No suitcases?"

"Just these handbags," Rachel said in keeping with Savage's instructions.

"Passports, please."

Savage and Rachel handed them over. Akira would soon board the ferry separately on foot, so the three of them wouldn't be conspicuous together.

"*Joyce Stone?*" The official glanced up from the passport, staring at Rachel, surprised. "I apologize. I didn't recognize . . . I'm a fan of your movies, but . . ."

"My bruises, you mean?"

"They look so painful. They've ruined perfection. What terrible . . . ?"

"A traffic accident near Athens."

"My deep regrets. My countrymen are clumsy drivers."

"No, it was *my* fault. Thank heaven, neither he nor I was seriously hurt. I reimbursed the man for repairs to his car and paid his medical bills."

The official straightened. "Your Majesty is extremely kind. Even with your injuries, you're as beautiful as in your movies. And as noble."

"May I ask a favor?"

"I'm your humble fan."

She reached for his hand. "Don't tell anyone I'm aboard. Normally I appreciate the attention of admirers. I've retired, but I haven't forgotten my responsibilities to those with memories long enough to recall my career."

"Your magnificence will always be remembered."

"But not when I look like this. People will say I'm ugly."

"Beautiful."

"You're very kind." Rachel continued to grasp his hand. "But there might be photographers on board. If you enjoyed my films . . ."

"I worshiped them."

"Then please don't destroy their memory." Rachel gave his hand a squeeze and released it.

The official stepped back. "Obviously you're not smuggling ancient artifacts. By all means, instruct your driver to proceed aboard."

"Thank you." Rachel rewarded him with a gracious smile.

Savage drove toward the ferry. "You're a better actress than your sister," he murmured. "Very *very* good."

"Hey, I always envied my sister," she said, her lips barely moving. "She always did better. But now when I'm scared, I've got the guts to prove I'm better."

"You'll get no argument." Savage parked the car on the ferry. "Now we wait for Akira."

3

But twenty minutes later, Akira still hadn't joined them as the ferry left the dock.

"Stay in the car," Savage told Rachel.

Shoulders tensing, he got out and scanned the shadowy spaces between the rows of cars. The hold stank of oil and exhaust fumes. The other vehicles were deserted, their passengers having climbed to the upper decks to sleep or to buy refreshments and admire the moonlit water and the lights along the coast. The hold's metal floor vibrated from the muted rumble of the ferry's engines.

Still no sign of Akira.

"I've changed my mind," Savage said. "Get out. Stand next to me. If anything happens, run. There'll be security guards upstairs. Stay close to them."

Rachel hurried toward him. "Is something wrong?"

"I'm not sure yet." Savage kept scanning the hold. "But Akira should have joined us by now."

"Unless he's being extra-cautious checking the passengers."

"Maybe . . . Or else he found trouble."

Despite the surrounding cars, Savage's spine tensed from feeling exposed.

He made it a rule never to try to cross an international border with a firearm. True, the checkpoints in many countries had lax procedures, and handguns made mostly from plastic didn't register on an X-ray machine, especially when disassembled. But Savage's weapon had been an all-metal .357 Magnum revolver, and it couldn't be taken apart, except for its cylinder. More, though Greece and Italy had attempted a conciliatory attitude toward terrorists, the fanatics had taken advantage of their hosts' goodwill and committed further atrocities. Greece and Italy had strengthened security at their borders. Accordingly, Savage and Akira had dropped their handguns down a sewer before they reached the ferry depot.

But now Savage dearly wished he hadn't done so. Footsteps echoed on metal. A man emerged down a stairway. Savage hoped it would be Akira.

No! The man was *Caucasian!*

Savage felt as if arms crushed his chest. Abruptly he exhaled.

The man wore a uniform. A member of the ferry's crew, he studied the cars in the hold, then focused on Savage and Rachel. "I'm sorry, sir. No passengers are permitted down here."

"Right. My wife forgot her purse. We had to come back for it."

The crewman waited until Savage and Rachel passed him. As the man walked across the hold, Savage concentrated on the top of the stairs.

"There's supposed to be safety in numbers, isn't there?" Rachel said, trying to sound confident, not succeeding. "So let's join the crowd."

"And find Akira. Just remember," Savage said, "your husband's men don't know what I look like. And they're searching for a woman whose hair is auburn, not blond."

"But I can't disguise these bruises."

"If you lean on the railing, prop your chin in your hands, and study the water, in the dark no one will notice your face. Ready?"

She trembled for a second, then nodded. "Just hold my hand."

4

The ferry was large, capable of transporting six hundred passengers. Above the hold, a B and an A deck contained cabins and rows of reclining seats. Savage had rented one of the cabins, but until he discovered what had happened to Akira, he couldn't risk using it and being trapped.

Continuing to climb the stairs, approaching the main deck, he heard numerous voices, a babble of accents and languages. A sea breeze cooled his clammy forehead. He squeezed Rachel's shaky hand and stepped through a hatch. At once a swarm of passengers passed him, bumping, jostling.

Rachel flinched.

Savage put an arm around her, guiding her away from lights toward the night-shrouded railing. The moment she leaned on her elbows, resting her face in her hands, he pivoted toward the crowd.

Where was Akira?

The ferry had a promenade area that rimmed a mid-deck restaurant and a bar. Through windows, Savage saw passengers clustered at tables.

Akira.

Where the hell was Akira?

Five minutes. Ten. Savage's stomach writhed. But though desperate to search, he didn't dare abandon Rachel, not even in the cabin he'd rented.

From the mass of Caucasians, an Oriental proceeded along the deck.

Akira!

"Two of them," he whispered, approaching.

Savage glanced toward the restaurant, then turned toward the sea, apparently oblivious to the Japanese who passed him. "Lead them around once again," Savage murmured.

When he turned from the railing, Akira had disappeared into the crowd.

Two men followed, their suitcoats too small for their muscular chests, their expressions grim.

Savage wondered if they were decoys intended to make their quarry realize he was being followed while other members of the surveillance team watched Akira's reaction. That was possible. But the two men weren't clumsy, and Akira wasn't the target. *Rachel* was, and as long as Akira ignored the men behind him, they couldn't be sure they'd found the Japanese they were looking for. So unless they captured Akira and questioned him, they'd have to wait to see if Akira rendezvoused with a Caucasian man and woman. Then, regardless of Rachel's change in hair color, they'd know they'd found their targets.

So what do we do? Savage wondered. *Play hide-and-seek all over the ferry?*

Pulse speeding, he scanned the crowd, alert for anyone who showed interest in Rachel and him. When Akira strolled past the second time and the same two men followed at a careful distance, Savage concluded that they were alone.

But that still didn't solve the problem.

Jesus, how do we deal with them?

The simplest method would be to let Akira keep leading them around until the promenade was deserted, the passengers asleep. Then Savage could try to stalk the stalkers, incapacitate them, and throw them over the side.

But was the surveillance pair under orders to use the ferry's sea-to-shore telephones to call their superiors and make reports at regular intervals, even if they'd found nothing? In the SEALs, that was basic strategy. If a team failed to check in at its scheduled time, their commander would first conclude that the team had logistical problems and been forced to rush toward a safe location. If the team persisted in not reporting, the commander would then conclude that the team had been captured or else been killed.

Maybe preventing these men from checking in would tell Papadropolis where to focus his search.

As Savage analyzed the problem, a corollary disturbed

him. Suppose they'd *already* made their report? What if they'd told their superiors that they'd spotted a Japanese who might be Akira? In that case, Papadropolis would order additional men to board the ferry tomorrow morning when it made its first stop farther up the Greek coast at Igoumenitsa.

Too many unknowns.

But the present situation couldn't be allowed to continue. Something had to be done.

Through a window, Savage saw Akira in the restaurant, sitting at a table, dipping a tea bag into a cup. The two men watched unobtrusively from a distant table. One of the men said something. The other nodded. The first man got up, leaving the restaurant through a door on the opposite side of the ferry.

Savage straightened. "Rachel, let's go."

"But where are . . . ?"

"I don't have time to explain." He led her through the crowded smoke-filled bar beside the restaurant, peered out toward the promenade on the opposite side of the ferry, and saw the man standing at a row of phones. The man inserted a credit card into one of them and pressed a sequence of numbers.

"Rachel, lean against this railing, the same as before."

Savage quickly walked toward the man, stopped next to him, and picked up a phone.

"We don't know yet," the man was saying. He sensed Savage beside him, turned, and scowled.

Savage pretended not to notice, going through the motions of making a call.

"Yes, *Japanese*," the man said. "He fits the description, but we weren't given many specifics. Age, height, and build aren't enough to be sure."

"Hi, dear," Savage said to the phone he held. He'd pressed numbers at random and was getting a busy signal. "I just wanted to let you know I managed to catch the ferry out of Patrai."

"Then *make* sure?" the man asked. "How the—?"

"Yeah, we dock in Italy tomorrow afternoon at five," Savage said.

"*Question* him?" The man scowled again at Savage, unable to speak as freely as he wanted. "But if it is him, I thought the point was to see if he contacted his associates. From what I've heard about this man, the two of us won't be enough to persuade him to cooperate."

"I'm looking forward to seeing you, dear," Savage said to the phone.

"Yeah, that idea's a whole lot better. Send more negotiators."

"No, everything went fine. I saw every client on my list," Savage said to the phone. "They gave me some very large orders."

"Corfu?" The man sounded baffled. "But that's the *second* stop. Why can't they board at Igoumenitsa? Yeah, okay, I see that. If the team's already at Corfu's dock and the airport, they might as well stay in place. Besides, there's no way for them to get off the island at this hour. They'd never be able to cross the channel from Corfu to Igoumenitsa in time to meet the ferry."

"I love you, too, dear," Savage said to the phone.

"Right. I'll see you at nine tomorrow morning," the man said. "If anything develops in the meantime, I'll let you know."

The man hung up and returned to the restaurant.

Savage replaced his phone and walked toward Rachel in the darkness along the railing.

"Change of plans," he said.

"I don't understand," she said.

"I'm not sure I do either." Savage frowned. "I'm still working out the details."

5

At one A.M., the promenade was almost deserted. Most of the passengers had gone to the sleeping areas on the lower decks, though a few still remained in the bar and the restaurant.

One of those in the restaurant was Akira. He'd ordered a meal and taken so long to savor every mouthful that his two watchdogs, still sitting at a corner table, had begun to look conspicuous—and looked as if they *knew* they looked conspicuous.

Any moment, they might decide to find a less exposed vantage point from which to study their prey.

"It's time," Savage told Rachel. While she'd been standing out of sight from the restaurant window, he'd periodically glanced inside. For all he knew, *he* had begun to look conspicuous. Yes, he thought. Definitely time.

"You're sure this'll work?" Rachel's voice shook.

"No. But it's the only plan I can think of."

"That doesn't exactly fill me with confidence."

"You'll do fine. Keep telling yourself, it's another chance to prove you're a better actress than your sister."

"I'm too terrified to care."

"Hey, impress me. Get in there."

Savage smiled and nudged her.

She studied him, returned his smile, breathed deeply, and entered the restaurant.

From the darkness at the railing, Savage watched the two men. They glanced toward Rachel and almost dropped their coffee cups. In contrast, Akira kept eating with deliberate calm.

Rachel sat beside him. Akira put down his knife and fork as if she was exactly the person he'd expected to see. He said something, then said something else, leaning toward her. She responded, elaborated, and gestured toward the lower decks. He shrugged and nodded.

In the background, the man who'd made the earlier phone call stood and left the restaurant.

Savage was waiting in shadows when the man, his eyes bright with victory, veered toward the row of phones.

A quick glance right and left showed Savage that there weren't other passengers on the promenade. He grabbed the man's left arm, thrust his right leg upward, and threw him overboard.

The fall was five stories. The water would have felt like concrete. The man was too surprised to scream.

Savage spun toward the window, remaining in darkness. In the restaurant, Akira stood, paid his bill, and left with Rachel on the opposite side of the ferry.

The watchdog hesitated, seeming to wonder how soon his partner would return from making the phone call. But the watchdog couldn't allow Akira and Rachel to get out of his sight, Savage knew. As expected, the man rose hurriedly, threw money on the table, and followed.

Savage proceeded along the deserted promenade. It wasn't necessary for him to get to the other side of the ferry and track the stalker. After all, he knew where the man was going.

Taking his time, he descended the stairs to the A deck. *Had* to take his time. It was imperative that Akira and Rachel reach the cabin Savage had rented, imperative that the watchdog see them go in, hear the lock shut, and realize he had to rush to tell his partner where their master's wife was hiding.

As Savage pretended to stumble drunkenly toward the bottom of the stairs, he groped in his pockets, apparently unable to find the key to his cabin. The watchdog darted toward him, frantic to return to the main deck and locate his partner. Savage punched him in the stomach, chopped the side of his callused hand across the man's jaw, and lugged the unconscious (to all appearances intoxicated) man along the deserted corridor, knocking three times on the door of the cabin.

The door inched open.

"Room service," Savage said.

6

The cabin was small, starkly furnished with a bureau, a top and bottom bunk, a tiny closet, and a washroom. Designed for two occupants, it provided little room for the four of them to move around. While Rachel locked the door, Akira helped Savage set the unconscious man on the bottom bunk. Working quickly, they used the man's belt to secure his hands behind his back and bound his ankles together with his tie. They searched him and satisfied themselves that he hadn't risked bringing a weapon through customs.

"He's awfully pale," Rachel said. "His jaw . . . it's so *swollen*."

The stress in her voice made Savage turn. He suddenly realized that this was the first time she'd seen the effects of violence on someone other than herself.

"And his breathing sounds . . ."

"Don't worry," Savage said. "I didn't hit him hard enough to really hurt him. He ought to wake up soon."

"Let's see if we can encourage him." Akira brought a glass of water from the bathroom and dribbled it onto the man's face.

The man's eyes flickered and slowly focused. When he saw Savage, Akira, and Rachel staring down at him, he struggled to stand, only to realize in panic that his hands and feet were tied.

"Lie still," Savage said. "Don't be stupid and shout for help. Your friend isn't able to hear you."

"Where's . . . ?"

"He fell overboard," Savage said.

"You son of a bitch," the man said.

"We have a proposition," Akira said. "We'd like you to enjoy a good night's sleep and in the morning make a phone call for us."

"You're not going to kill me?"

"That's always a possibility." Akira's eyes expressed greater melancholy. "We'd appreciate your cooperation so you don't join your ancestors needlessly."

"Ancestors? Is that some kind of Japanese thing?"

"If you wish to call it that. Yes." Akira's lips formed a thin, bitter smile. "A Japanese thing."

"What kind of phone call?"

"The ferry reaches Igoumenitsa at seven tomorrow morning. After it continues to Corfu, you'll call your superiors and tell them we spotted you and your partner. You'll tell them we panicked and drove from the ferry at Igoumenitsa. We're escaping eastward, inland, toward Ioannina, on route nineteen."

"But all of us will really be on the ferry on its way to Corfu?" the man asked.

"Precisely. The reinforcements that would have boarded the ferry at Corfu will then be diverted."

The man became suspicious. "And then what? What happens when we get to Corfu? We continue toward Italy?"

"Our plans aren't your concern."

"I mean what the hell happens to *me?* Why should I make the call? You killed my partner. What stops you from killing me?"

"You have our word you won't be harmed," Akira said.

The man laughed. "Your word? Hey, give me a break. Your word means shit. As soon as I'm no use to you, I'm dead. You can't afford to let me live to tell Papadropolis where you've really gone."

Akira's eyes blazed. "My word does not, as you put it, mean shit."

The man swung his head toward Savage. "Look, you and I are both Americans. That ought to count for something. Damn it, don't you understand my problem?"

Savage sat beside him on the bunk. "Of course. On the one hand, you're worried that we'll kill you after you make the phone call and we don't have further use for you. On the other hand, you're worried that Papadropolis will kill you if he discovers you helped us escape. He won't care if you acted practically in order to save your life. From his point of view, you betrayed him. He'll punish you. Severely. So you've got a problem. I agree. But the issue you have to face is whether you prefer to die now instead of later.''

"And have no doubt, if you refuse, you'll join your partner in the sea,'' Akira said. "We do have other ways to escape the trap.''

"Then for Christ's sake, use them.''

"But what would we do with *you?*'' Savage asked. "Right now, Papadropolis isn't our worry. *You* are. So what are you going to do about that?''

The man darted his frightened eyes from Savage toward Akira, back toward Savage, and finally stared at Rachel. "Mrs. Papadropolis, don't let them—''

"I hate that name,'' she said. "Don't call me that. I'll never use it. I never want to hear it again. My last name is Stone.''

"Miss Stone, please, don't let them kill me. You turned pale when you found out this man''—a nod toward Savage —"killed my partner. You'll feel worse if you let him kill me. You've seen me up close. You've talked to me. My name's Paul Farris. I'm thirty-four. I'm a security specialist, not an assassin. I've got a wife and daughter. We live in Switzerland. If you let these men murder me, even if you don't see them do it, you'll feel guilty for the rest of your life.''

Rachel's brow furrowed. She swallowed.

"Nice try, but we searched you before you woke up,'' Savage said. "We went through your wallet. Your name's not Paul Farris. It's Harold Trask. The only true thing in what you said is your age. Rachel, don't get sentimental about him.''

"You think I'm dumb enough to carry *real* ID when I'm working?'' the man asked. "The people I investigate, if they knew who was after them, they might hunt down my wife and kid to get even. It's a sure bet the two of *you* don't use real ID either.''

"Convincing," Akira said. "But beside the point. You still didn't solve your problem. Even if Rachel told us not to kill you, it wouldn't matter. Her life isn't at risk. If Papadropolis found her or she decided to return to him—"

"Never!" Rachel said. "I'd never go back to him."

"—her husband would beat her, no doubt with increased viciousness, but he wouldn't kill her. He *would* kill *us* if we knew who we were and managed to catch us. So to silence you would be self-defense."

"Make up your mind," Savage said. "Will you cooperate?"

"I call my superiors? Then you let me walk away?"

"We already promised that."

The man debated. "Apparently I'm forced to."

"A reasonable man," Akira said.

The man's eyes became calculating. "Even so . . ."

"I'm getting impatient."

"I'll need an extra incentive."

"Money? Don't press your luck," Savage said.

Rachel interrupted. "Pay him."

Savage turned to her, frowning.

"He's taking a risk," she said. "My husband will be furious if he thinks this man lied."

"That's right, Miss Stone. I'll have to take my wife and daughter and disappear for a while. It'll be expensive."

"If you even *have* a wife and daughter," Savage said. "How much?"

"A quarter million."

"You're dreaming."

"Then make it two hundred thousand," the man said.

"I'll make it *fifty* thousand, and you'll be grateful."

"But how do I know you have it?"

Savage shook his head in disgust. "Do you have a choice?"

The man paled.

"Don't make me impatient," Savage said.

"All right." The man swallowed. "You've got a deal. There's just one other matter."

"You're impossible," Akira said.

"No, listen. I need you to help me think of a way to stop Papadropolis from coming for me."

"We'll sleep on it," Savage said.

"The least you can do is untie my feet and hands."

"No, what I'd like to do is gag your mouth," Akira said.

"I have to go to the bathroom."

Akira raised his hands in exasperation. "I don't think I can tolerate this man till tomorrow morning."

"The look on your face." Rachel started laughing.

7

It was ten after seven the following morning. As the ferry left the small town of Igoumenitsa, heading west toward the island of Corfu, Savage, Akira, and Rachel stood tensely beside the man while he made the phone call. Savage kept a tight grip on his arm, listening to what he told his superiors.

"Hey, I know it's a mess. You don't need to tell me. But damn it, it's not my fault. My partner followed too close. The Japanese spotted him. Just before we docked at Igoumenitsa. The Japanese ran. It took us a while to find him. By then, the American and Mrs. Papadropolis were with him. They must have been sleeping in one of the cabins. Hey, what was I going to do, knock on every door and say, 'Mrs. Papadropolis, are you in there?' The Japanese was obviously the decoy—to check if the ferry was being watched. If everything looked safe, they'd have continued to Corfu."

The man stopped talking. Savage heard someone shouting from the other end of the phone.

"No, we couldn't stop them before they drove off the ferry," the man continued.

More shouting from the other end.

"Hey, I'm telling you it's not my fault. My partner's so scared about fucking up he ran. He figures Papadropolis will kill him."

The man winced, the shouts so loud he held the phone away from his ear.

"Well, it's his ass, not mine. I'm still on the job, but it's damned hard chasing them on my own. I barely caught up to them before they left Igoumenitsa. Heading east on route nineteen. Why didn't I phone you sooner? How was I going to do that and not lose sight of them? I wouldn't even be calling now if they hadn't stopped for gas. I'm in a restaurant down the street. I can see them through the window. They don't realize I'm . . . Wait a minute. Shit, they're about to leave. Look, I think they're headed for Ioannina. The Yugoslavian border's less than an hour's drive north from there. Tell everybody to watch the border crossings. Christ, they're driving away! Can't talk anymore! I'll check in later!"

Sounding breathless, the man slammed down the phone.

Savage released his arm.

The prisoner wiped his sweaty brow. He leaned against the phone and trembled. "Okay?"

"Extremely believable," Akira said.

"And now?" The man looked apprehensive, as if Savage and Akira might kill him after all.

"We relax and enjoy the cruise," Akira said.

"You mean it?"

"You fulfilled your part of the bargain."

The man exhaled and straightened. "I think I got Papadropolis off my back. They'll be looking for my partner."

"Whom they'll never find," Akira said. "Yes, it seems your worries are over."

"And ours," Rachel said. "No one will be waiting for us at Corfu. They'll try to intercept us on the way to Yugoslavia."

"Where we have no intention of going." Savage turned

to the man. "Just make sure you get back to the mainland as soon as possible. You'll have to pretend you're chasing us. Phone in. Keep giving them false reports."

"You bet I will. If I don't rendezvous with a team at one of the border crossings, they won't believe my story. But by then I'll have lost you."

"Exactly."

"There's just one thing," the man said.

"Oh? What's that?"

"You forgot to give me my money."

8

Ninety minutes later, when the ferry reached Corfu, they watched the man drive onto the dock and disappear among traffic.

"He might still betray us," Akira said.

"I don't think so," Savage said. "Rachel's instincts were right about paying him. He knows if he tells them where we really are, we'll implicate him. Papadropolis would kill him for taking a bribe."

"So now we cross to Italy?" Rachel asked.

"Why bother?" Savage smiled. "The Corfu airport won't be under surveillance now. Let's catch the next plane to France. By tonight, you'll be with your sister."

But Rachel looked troubled.

Why? Savage wondered.

"Then you and I catch another plane to New York," Akira told Savage, the sadness in his eyes intensified with anger. "To force answers from Graham. To make him tell us why we saw each other die."

9

"Excited? Of course, I am. Why wouldn't I be?" Rachel said.

They'd left their car at Corfu's airport, then taken an Alitalia flight to Rome, where they transfered to an Air France jet bound for Nice.

Midafternoon. The weather was magnificent. Rachel had the window seat, and as she spoke, she peered toward Corsica to the west, then down toward sunlight glinting off the Mediterranean.

But Savage sensed she was motivated less by attraction to the scenery than by the need to hide her expression when she answered his question.

"Because back at the ferry you weren't overjoyed when I mentioned you'd be with your sister tonight," Savage said.

Rachel kept her face turned toward the window. "You expected me to jump up and down? After everything that's happened, I'm drained. Shell-shocked. Numb. I still can't believe I escaped."

Savage glanced at her hand in her lap. Its fingers were clenched, their knuckles white.

"Rachel . . ."

Her fist became tighter.

"I want you to look at me."

She peered closer to the window. "Eager to see my sister? Naturally. She's *more* than my sister. She's my closest friend. If it weren't for her . . . and you . . . I'd never have gotten off Mykonos. My husband would have kept beating me."

She trembled.

"Rachel, please, I'm asking you to look at me."

She stiffened, then slowly turned in Savage's direction. Her bruises emphasized her somber expression.

Savage reached for her fist, unclasped its fingers, and encircled them with his own. "What's wrong?"

"I keep trying to imagine what's ahead of me. My sister. A happy reunion. A chance to rest and heal. Oh, for sure, I'll be pampered. The best of everything. But then what? A cage is a cage, gilded or not. I'll still be a prisoner."

Savage waited for Rachel to continue, all the while conscious of Akira, who sat at the rear of the plane, assessing the other passengers.

"My husband won't be satisfied until he gets me back. When he learns where I am, he'll put my sister's estate under constant watch. I'll never be able to leave."

"Yes and no. There are ways to sneak out."

"'Sneak.' Exactly. But away from my sister's estate, I'd never feel safe. Wherever I went, I'd have to use another name, disguise my appearance, try not to be conspicuous. Sneak. For the rest of my life."

"It's not as bad as that."

"It *is*." Rachel jerked her head toward the passengers across the aisle and behind her, embarrassed for having raised her voice. She whispered, her words intense, "I'm terrified. What happens to other people you've rescued?"

Savage was forced to lie. Anytime someone needed a protector with Savage's expertise, he knew that their problems were only temporarily solved. He didn't cancel danger; he merely postponed it. "They get on with their lives."

"Bullshit. Predators don't give up."

Savage didn't respond.

"I'm right?"

Savage glanced toward the aisle.

"Hey, damn it, I looked at you. Now you look at *me*," Rachel said.

"Okay. If you want my opinion, your husband's too arrogant to admit defeat. Yes, you'll have to be careful."

"Oh, that's just fucking swell." She yanked her hand from his.

"You wanted the truth."

"And I sure got it."

"The usual option is to negotiate."

"Don't talk to me like a lawyer."

"So what do you want?"

"For the past couple days, as horrible as they've been, I've never felt safer—better—than being with you. You made me feel . . . important, comforted, respected. You treated me like I meant everything to you."

"You did."

"As a client," Rachel said. "And if you deliver me to my sister, you'll be paid."

"You don't know anything about me," Savage said. "I don't risk my life just for the money. I do this because people need me. But I can't stay forever with . . ."

"Everyone who needs you?"

"Sooner or later, I have to let go. Your sister's waiting for you."

"And then you forget me?"

"Never," Savage said.

"Then take me with you."

"What? To New York?"

"I won't feel safe without you."

"Rachel, three weeks from now, sipping champagne at the pool on your sister's estate, you won't remember me."

"For the right kind of man, I'm stubbornly loyal."

"I've had this conversation before," Savage said. "Many times. The man who taught me . . ."

"Graham."

"Yes. He always insisted, 'Never involve yourself with a client.' And he was right. Because emotion causes mistakes. And mistakes are fatal."

"I'd do anything for you."

"Like follow me to hell?"

"I promised that."

"And you survived. But Akira and I have our own kind of hell, and we need to understand why it happened. Believe me, you'd interfere. Enjoy your sister's pool . . . And think of two men trying to solve a nightmare."

"Hold still for a minute."

"Why?"

Rachel leaned toward him, gripping the sides of his face.

Savage squirmed.

"No," Rachel said, "hold still."

"But . . ."

"Quiet." Rachel kissed him. Her lips barely touched his, making them tingle. She gradually increased pressure, her mouth fully on him. Her tongue probed, sliding, darting.

Savage didn't resist, but despite his erection, he didn't encourage her, either.

She slowly pulled away.

"Rachel, you're beautiful."

Rachel looked proud.

Savage traced a finger along her cheek.

She shivered.

"I can't," Savage said, "betray the rules. I'll take you to your sister. Then Akira and I will go to New York."

She jerked away from him. "I can't wait to see my sister."

10

They landed outside Nice shortly after four P.M. Savage had phoned Joyce Stone before he, Akira, and Rachel had flown from Corfu. Now, as they entered the airport's customs-immigration area, a slender man wearing an impeccably tailored gray suit stepped past other arriving passengers toward them. He had an identification pin in his lapel, though Savage didn't know what the pin's striped colors signified. A uniformed guard walked behind him.

"Monsieur Savage?" the distinguished-looking man asked.

"Yes."

"Would the three of you come with us, please?"

Akira showed no sign of tension, except for a brief frown toward Savage, who nodded reassuringly and held Rachel's hand.

They entered a room to the side. The guard shut the door. The distinguished-looking man sat behind a desk.

"Monsieur, as you're aware, visitors to France are required to present not only a passport but an immigration visa."

"Yes. I'm sure you'll find these in order." Savage placed his passport and visa on the table. Before the assignment, knowing he'd have to take Rachel to France, he'd instructed Joyce Stone to obtain visas for the two of them.

The official glanced through the documents.

"And this is Miss Stone's passport," Savage said. Because Rachel had been forced to use her sister's passport instead of her own, and because her sister had become a French citizen, it wasn't necessary to present her immigration visa.

The official examined the passport. "Excellent." He didn't seem at all impressed that he was theoretically talking to a woman of fame and power.

Savage gestured toward Akira. "My friend has his passport, but I'm afraid he neglected to obtain a visa."

"Yes, so an influential acquaintance of yours has explained to me. However, while you were en route, that oversight was corrected." The official placed a visa on the table and held out his hand for Akira's passport.

After flipping through it, he stamped all the documents and returned them. "Have you anything to declare to customs?"

"Nothing."

"Please come with me."

They left the office, passed crowded immigration and customs checkpoints, and reached an exit from the airport.

"Enjoy your stay," the man said.

"We appreciate your cooperation," Savage said.

The official shrugged. "Your influential acquaintance was most insistent. Charmingly so, of course. When possible, I'm pleased to accommodate her wishes. She instructed me to tell you she's arranged for your transportation. Through that door."

Curious, Savage stepped outside, followed by Rachel and Akira. In brilliant sunshine, on a street with a grass divider, a parking lot, and a background of palm trees, what he saw at the curb appalled him.

Joyce Stone—ignoring Savage's advice in Athens to use an inconspicuous car—had sent a Rolls-Royce. And behind the steering wheel sat one of the burly escorts that Savage had met at Joyce Stone's hotel suite near the Acropolis.

"I don't like this," Akira said.

Rachel tensed. "Why?"

"This isn't the way it's done," Savage said. "All that's missing is a sign on the side of the car. 'Important people inside.' We might as well put up a target."

The burly driver got out of the car, squared his shoulders, and grinned at Savage. "So you actually made it. Hey, when I heard, I was sure impressed."

Savage felt more dismayed. "You were *told?* You *knew* we'd be your passengers?"

"The boss has been biting her nails for the last three days. She couldn't wait to tell me." The man kept grinning.

"Shit."

"Hey, everything's cool," the man said.

"No," Akira said, "it isn't."

The man stopped grinning. "Who the hell are *you?*"

Akira ignored him, turning to Savage. "Should we get another car?"

"What's wrong with this one?" the burly man said.

"You wouldn't understand."

"Come on, it's fully loaded."

"At the moment, stereo and air-conditioning aren't our priorities," Akira said.

"No, I mean *fully* loaded."

The stream of passing cars and pedestrians leaving the airport made Savage uneasy. It took him a moment to register what the man had said. "Loaded?"

"A shotgun under each front fender. Automatic. Double-ought buck. Flash-bang ejectors under each side. Smoke canisters in the rear. Bulletproof. Armored fuel tank. But just in case, if the fuel tank gets hit by a rocket grenade, a steel plate flips up in the trunk and keeps the flames from spreading inside. Just what I said. Fucking loaded. With all this terrorist stuff, the boss believes in precautions.''

Akira frowned at Savage. "It's possible."

"Except the car's so damned ostentatious," Savage said.

"But perhaps not here in southern France. I saw five equally vulgar cars drive past while we talked."

"You've got a point. I'm tempted," Savage said.

"Vulgar?" the burly man said. "This car isn't vulgar. It's a dream."

"That depends on what kind of dreams you have," Savage said.

Rachel fidgeted. "I don't like standing out here."

"Okay," Savage said. "We use it." He shielded Rachel while he opened the rear door and she quickly got in. "Akira, sit beside her." He pivoted toward the burly escort. "I drive."

"But . . ."

"Sit in the passenger seat, or walk."

The man's feelings looked hurt. "You'll have to promise I'm not responsible."

"That's a given."

"What?"

"You're not responsible. *Get in the car.*" As Savage scrambled behind the steering wheel, the man scurried next to him, slamming his door.

"Controls," Savage said. "Where are they?"

"It's just an automatic."

"I mean the flash-bangs, the smoke, the shotguns."

"Lift the console to the right of the gearshift."

Savage saw clearly marked buttons. He twisted the ignition key and hurried from the airport.

Despite the airport's name, Savage's destination wasn't eastward toward Nice. Instead he drove west on N 98, a coastal road that curved along the Côte d'Azur and would lead him toward Antibes, Cap d'Antibes, and a few kilometers later, Cannes. Among the islands off that glamorous city was Joyce Stone's equally glamorous principality, which she ruled in the name of her infirm husband.

"Yeah," the burly man said, "just stay on this road until—"

"I've been in southern France before."

A year and a half ago, Savage had escorted an American film producer to the festival at Cannes. At that time, terrorists had threatened to attack what they called "the purveyors of imperialistic racist oppression." Given the tense political climate, Savage had approved of his principal's choice to use a hotel in one of the nearby villages instead of Cannes. While the principal slept, he'd be safely away from the site of the threatened violence. Preparing for that assignment, Savage had arrived a few days early and scouted both Cannes and the surrounding area, learning traffic patterns, major and minor streets, in case he had to rush his principal away from an incident.

"Yes, I've been in southern France before," Savage said. "I'm sure I can find the way to your boss."

The farther he drove from the airport at Nice, the more traffic dwindled, most of it having turned onto a superhighway to the north. That superhighway ran parallel to this road and would have taken Savage to Cannes sooner, but he didn't intend to enter the city. His instructions to Joyce Stone had been to have a powerboat waiting at a beach along this road a half-kilometer before he reached the city. The powerboat would take them to a yacht, which in turn would take them to Joyce Stone's island—an efficient, surreptitious way to deliver Rachel to her sister.

"I hate to tell you this," Akira said. "I think we've got company."

Savage glanced toward his rearview mirror. "The van?"

"It's been following us since we left the airport."

"Maybe it's headed toward one of the resorts along this road."

"But it keeps passing cars to stay behind us. If it's in a hurry, it ought to pass *us* as well."

"Let's find out."

Savage slowed. The van reduced speed.

A Porsche veered around both of them.

Savage sped up. So did the van.

Savage glared toward the burly man beside him. "Is it too much to hope you brought handguns?"

"It didn't seem necessary."

"If we survive this, I'm going to beat the shit out of you." Rachel looked terrified. *"How did they find us?"*

"Your husband must have guessed your sister arranged for the rescue."

"But he thinks we drove into Yugoslavia."

"Right. Most of his men are searching there," Savage said, increasing speed. "But he must have kept a team in southern France in case we managed to get this far. The airport was being watched."

"I didn't notice surveillance," Akira said.

"Not *in* the airport. Outside. And when this idiot showed up in the Rolls—"

"Hey, watch who you're calling an idiot," the burly man said.

"—they activated the trap. They won't be alone. Somewhere ahead, there'll be another vehicle in radio contact with them. And"— Savage glared at the burly man—"if you don't shut your mouth, I'll tell Akira to strangle you."

Savage swerved past a slowly moving truck filled with chickens. The van did the same.

To the left, down a slope, Savage saw Antibes stretched along the sea. The resort had extensive flower gardens, an impressive Romanesque cathedral, and ancient narrow streets. To the right, picturesque villas dotted a hillside.

Savage reached a curve and halfway around it pressed the accelerator. The transmission changed gears sluggishly, finally responding.

"An automatic," Savage said. "I can't believe this." Again he glared at the burly man. "Don't you know a standard's more efficient if you're being chased?"

"Yeah, but an automatic's smoother in stop-and-go traffic, and the streets in these towns are an obstacle course. With a standard, it's a pain to keep using the gearshift."

Savage cursed and rounded another curve. Now opposite the rising slope of villas, a descending slope was cluttered with hotels that almost obscured the sea.

The pursuing van sped closer.

"There might be another explanation," Akira said.

"For their spotting us?" Savage urged the Rolls from the curve.

"Your phone call. Before we left Corfu. The incompetent man beside you admitted that your employer talked openly about the rescue."

"Hey, what do you mean 'incompetent'?"

"If you persist in speaking," Akira told the man, "perhaps I will indeed strangle you."

Savage frowned at another curve.

"I suspect your employer's phones have been tapped," Akira said. "And I also suspect there are spies in the household."

"I warned her," Savage said. "Before I went in, I told her Rachel's safety depended on absolute secrecy."

"Before you went. Afterward, she felt free to reveal her concerns."

Savage scowled toward the rearview mirror. The van was closer. "I think you're right. Someone on Joyce Stone's staff is a spy for Papadropolis. That's why his team was ready."

"So what are we going to do?" the burly man asked.

"What I'd *like* to do," Savage said, "is throw you out."

"Ahead," Akira barked.

Savage's chest constricted as a van appeared.

The interceptor skidded, turning, blocking the narrow road.

"Rachel, make sure your seat belt's tight."

The pursuing van loomed closer.

Savage eased his left foot onto the brake, kept his other foot on the accelerator, and spun the steering wheel. The maneuver was difficult. If he pressed too hard on the brake, he'd lock the rear wheels. He had to balance the pressure between braking and accelerating so the car's rear wheels spun while skidding. The consequent tension of forces gave the car torque. As Savage twisted the steering wheel, the car snapped around. The 180-degree pivot made the tires squeal, rubber smoking. Savage's seat belt gripped him.

The van that blocked the road was now behind him, the pursuing van ahead. Savage jerked his foot off the brake and stomped the accelerator. The Rolls surged toward the approaching van. Its driver veered. Savage rocketed past. In his rearview mirror, he saw the van skid to a stop. Farther back, the van that had blocked the road was in motion again, passing the van that had stopped, resuming the chase.

"At least they're both behind us," Savage said. "If we can get back to—*into*—Antibes, we might be able to lose them."

His stomach turned cold when a third van emerged from a curve ahead.

"Jesus," the burly man said. "The team had backup."

The van turned sideways, blocking the road. In his rearview mirror, Savage saw one of the other vans block the road behind him while the remaining van sped toward him.

"We're boxed," Savage said.

The road was too narrow for Savage to veer around the obstructing vehicle. Now the steep upward slope was on his left, the steeper downward slope on his right.

He tensely reached toward the buttons on the console. "These weapons better work."

The system had been invented by drug lords in South America. He pressed a button. A section of metal rose from above each headlight. He pressed another button and felt the Rolls tremble from the concussion of shotguns firing. Mounted beneath each fender, the guns sprayed double-ought buckshot through a vent above each headlight.

Ahead, the van that blocked the road jolted from the fusillade's repeated impacts. As the shotguns kept firing, the van's windows imploded. Pellets punched metal, causing clusters of holes, three-foot circular patterns that narrowed as the Rolls sped nearer. The continuous shotgun blasts chewed the van to pieces.

Savage released the button and stomped on the brake. The Rolls fishtailed, skidding, barely stopping in time to avoid smashing against the wrecked vehicle.

He swung to stare behind him. While one of the remaining vans continued to block the road, the other rushed nearer and braked. Men scrambled out, weapons drawn.

"Rachel, close your eyes. Cover your ears."

Savage pressed two more buttons on the console and instantly obeyed his own directive, scrunching his eyes shut, squeezing his palms against his ears. Despite these precautions, he winced. Chaos assaulted him.

The buttons he'd pressed had caused flash-bang devices to catapult from each side of the Rolls and detonate when they hit the ground. The devices were deceptively named. "Flash-bang" suggested a firecracker. But the blaze and the blast produced by these matchbox-shaped metal objects were extreme enough to temporarily blind and deafen. Even one could be powerfully disorienting. Several dozen had awesome results.

In the Rolls, Savage saw sudden fierce glares through his tightly closed eyes. Peristent staccato roars forced their way past the hands he pressed to his ears. He heard muffled screams, the hunters collapsing outside the car. Or perhaps the screams were *inside* the car. Possibly from himself. The Rolls shook. His ears rang.

And suddenly the chaos ended.

"Out of the car!" Savage shouted.

He scrambled from the driver's side and found himself enveloped by dense swirling smoke. Not from the flash-bangs, instead from pressurized canisters beneath the car's rear bumper. One of the buttons he'd pressed had triggered the release of their contents.

Both the flash-bangs and the smoke were designed to confuse assailants and allow potential victims to escape amid the confusion, though the flash-bangs *could* be lethal if they detonated directly beside an enemy. In the smoke, Savage had no way to tell if any of Papadropolis's men had accidentally been killed. But he was sure that for the next half-minute they'd be lying on the road, squirming in pain.

His sight impaired, he felt his way hurriedly around the Rolls, bumped into the burly man, pushed him aside, and found Akira guarding Rachel. No conversation was necessary. Both he and Akira knew the only practical escape was down the slope toward the hotels that rimmed the sea.

Concealed by the smoke, they scurried from the road, each holding Rachel between them. Over rocks and grass, they felt their way down the slope. At once they emerged into eye-stabbing sunlight.

"Run," Savage said.

Rachel didn't need encouragement. She darted ahead of them, jumped from a ledge, and landed on the continuation of the slope four feet below. The impact threw her off balance. She rolled, slid on her back, and pushed herself upright, continuing to run.

Savage and Akira lunged after her. Any moment, their hunters would recover from the stunning barrage to their senses. They'd struggle to orient themselves, emerge from the smoke, see their quarry, and continue pursuing.

Rachel's pace faltered. Savage and Akira caught up to her. Charging lower, they passed tennis courts perched on the slope. Players had stopped their games, staring toward the smoke on the road above them. Several noticed Savage, Akira, and Rachel race past, then redirected their attention toward the smoke.

As the slope leveled off, the hotels seemed larger, taller. Savage paused with Akira and Rachel behind a maintenance building near palm trees and a swimming pool. No hunters scurried down the slope.

But Savage was dismayed to see the burly man, breathing heavily, stumble toward them.

"Jesus, I almost lost you. Thanks for waiting till I caught up."

"We didn't wait so you could join us," Akira said. "We're trying to decide what to do. But *one* choice is very clear."

The man wiped his sweaty face. "Yeah? Quick, tell me. What is it?"

"We don't want you with us. Whichever way *we* go, *you* take the opposite direction."

"Come on, quit joking. We're in this together."

"No," Akira said.

"The top of the slope," Savage said.

Akira followed Savage's gaze toward the hunters scurrying downward.

"No, we're *not* in this together." Akira grabbed the man's neck and pressed a finger behind his left ear.

In pain, the man sagged. He groaned and squirmed, struggling to release Akira's grip.

Akira pressed harder. "You *will* not follow us."

The man's face turned pale from the power of Akira's grip. "Okay, I'm out of here."

"Go." Akira pushed him.

The man took a last frightened look at Akira and stumbled toward the opposite hotel.

In the distance, sirens wailed.

"And *we'd* better go," Savage said. He pointed toward the hunters a quarter way down the slope, then grabbed Rachel's arm and ran with her.

"*Where?*" Rachel gasped.

They passed between two hotels and reached a noisy street that flanked the sea. Savage waved his arms toward a taxi. It pulled to a stop. They hurried inside.

Savage echoed Rachel's question. "Where? I worked in this area a year and a half ago. A man I met owes me a favor."

He turned to the driver and gave him directions in French. "We're late for a party. I'll double your fare if you get us there in five minutes."

"*Bien entendu, monsieur.*" As the driver sped toward Antibes, he pointed toward the smoke on the upper road. "*Qu'est ce que c'est?*"

"*Un accident d'automobile.*"

"*Sérieux?*"

"*Je pense.*"

"*Quel dommage.*"

"*Trop de gens ne regardent pas la route.*"

"*C'est vrai, monsieur. C'est vrai.*" The driver turned from Savage, flinched, and jerked the steering wheel, avoiding a truck.

In the backseat, Savage stared behind him. The hunters had not yet rushed from between the hotels onto the palmlined street. When they finally did, they wouldn't be able to read the license plate on this taxi.

Antibes had a population of more than sixty thousand. Though October was past the height of the tourist season, there were still sufficient visitors to congest the narrow streets. When the taxi began to move with frustrating slowness, Savage told the driver to stop, paid him the promised bonus, and left with Rachel and Akira.

They disappeared into an alley above which laundry dangled from ropes. To his right, Savage heard waves crashing onto the beach. To his left, above the alley, he caught a glimpse of a centuries-old, towering château.

Rachel hurried past the alley's narrow walls made even more narrow by garbage. She frowned toward Savage. "But you gave the driver an address. If my husband's men question the driver, they'll know where we're going."

"The address was fake," Savage said.

"Standard practice," Akira said.

They reached the end of the alley.

Rachel stopped and caught her breath. "So *everything's* a lie?"

"No," Savage said. "Our promise to protect you isn't."

"As long as I'm worth money."

"I told you before, the money isn't important. *You* are." Savage tugged her toward an opposite alley.

"Your husband has spies on your sister's island," Akira said. "If we try to take you there, we'll face another trap, and then another. Eventually you'll be captured."

"Which means it's hopeless," Rachel said.

"No," Savage said. "You've got to keep trusting me."

They crossed a street, blended with the crowd, and entered another alley.

"A year and a half ago," Savage said, "when I worked in this district, I needed special additions to a car. I found a man in Antibes who could do the job. But he didn't care how much I paid him. Money, he said, meant nothing if he couldn't buy what he wanted. He needed extra benefits. What kind? I asked. Guess what he wanted? He saw some movie posters my client had left in the car and took for granted I had something to do with the festival at Cannes. So he wanted to meet his greatest idol, Arnold Schwarzenegger. Yes, I said, that might be possible. But *if* it happens, you won't get to talk to him, except to shake his hand. Then one day I'll come back to you and ask a favor. Of course, he said. One favor deserves another. And it'll be worth it, he said.''

"So now you'll demand the favor," Akira said.

"A car."

"And *then* what?" Rachel asked.

"Force of circumstance," Savage said. *"We've* got our nightmare, but *you're* our obligation. So it looks like you get your wish, what you tried to get me to agree to on the plane.''

"You're taking me with you?" Rachel breathed. "To New York?"

"And Graham," Akira said. "But I have to qualify my approval."

"Why?" Savage asked.

"Because we're no longer protecting only this woman," Akira said. "We're also protecting *ourselves.* Solving our common nightmare. *Your* death and mine. If this woman gets in the way . . ."

"You'll defend her," Savage said.

"But of course," Akira said, his eyes tinged with sadness. *"Arigato* for reminding me. The three of us are bound. But our paths conflict."

"We don't have a choice," Savage said.

VANISHING ACT

1

Thirty-six hours later, they arrived at New York's Kennedy Airport. During the intervening time, they'd driven to Marseilles and flown to Paris, where Savage decided that Rachel's bruises had faded enough that, with the use of cosmetics, she could pose for an acceptable passport photograph. She no longer dared risk attracting attention by pretending to be her sister. Using a trusted contact in Paris, Savage arranged for her to obtain a complete set of first-rate counterfeit documents, all in the name of Susan Porter. If anyone—especially an immigration official—commented on her likeness to Joyce Stone, Rachel merely had to say, "Thanks for the compliment." As it happened, she and Savage passed through the checkpoints at Kennedy without incident.

Akira, who stood farther back in line so he wouldn't seem

to be traveling with them, joined them shortly afterward. "I studied the crowd. No one showed interest in us."

"Just as we hoped. Papadropolis has no way to guess where Rachel went. He probably figures we're still in southern France, trying to get onto her sister's island."

They walked through the noisy, crowded concourse.

"Then I'm *free?*" Rachel asked.

"Let's call it 'reprieved,' " Savage said. "I have to be honest. Your problem's been postponed, not canceled."

"I'll settle for what I can get. For now, it's a relief not to have to keep watching behind me."

"Ahead, though," Akira said. "We have to deal with Graham."

"I understand. I'm holding you back. I'm sorry. But if it weren't for the two of you . . . I don't know how to . . . It sounds so inadequate. *Thanks.*"

She hugged them.

2

They took a taxi to Grand Central Station, entered on Forty-second Street, came out on Lexington Avenue, and took another taxi to Central Park, from where they walked two blocks to a hotel on a side street off Fifth Avenue.

The suite that Savage had phoned ahead to reserve was spacious.

"Rachel, the bedroom's yours," Savage said. "Akira and I will take turns using the sofa."

They unpacked the travel bags they'd bought before leaving Paris.

"Anybody hungry?" Savage took their requests and ordered smoked-salmon sandwiches, salads, fruit, and bottled water from room service.

For the next few hours, they rested, bathed, and ate.

Though they'd slept on the plane, they still felt jet lag. A further call to room service brought coffee and tea. The stimulants helped, as did a change of clothes. Just before five, Savage went to a nearby store to buy coats and gloves, a TV news announcer having warned that the night would be chilly and damp.

They waited till nine.

"Ready?" Savage asked.

"Not yet," Akira said. "There are still some things we need to discuss. I know the answer already, but the question can't be ignored. Would it not be better to leave Rachel here?"

"We *think* we weren't followed, but we can't be totally sure," Savage said. "If we leave her unprotected, she might be in danger."

"Might be."

"An unacceptable risk."

"I agree," Akira said.

"So what's the trouble?"

"Something I should have realized. Something I suddenly thought of. Your assignment to rescue Rachel," Akira said.

"What about it?"

"My assignment was to protect her husband. I arrived on Mykonos a day before you did. Graham negotiated my fee. And Graham sent you to get Rachel. Doesn't it strike you as curious that the man who arranged for both of us to protect Kamichi also arranged for both of us to go to Mykonos, our first assignment after we recovered from our injuries?"

"We were meant to meet?" Savage's spine froze.

"There was no guarantee we'd see each other. But I'd have chased you."

"Just as I'd have chased *you* if our roles had been reversed," Savage said. "Graham knew he could count on our sense of obligation."

"And on my skill. No matter how long it took, eventually I'd have found you."

"There are few men I'd admit this to, but yes, you're good enough, eventually you'd have found me. We were meant to come face-to-face," Savage said.

"And confront each other's nightmare."

"A nightmare that didn't happen. But why do we think it did? *Why did Graham arrange for us to meet six months ago and then meet again?*"

"That's why I have to ask. Since we don't know what we're facing, should Rachel be part of it? We might be putting her in worse danger than she already is."

"Then what do we do? Stay here?"

"I have to know why I see a dead man before me."

"So do I," Savage said.

"Then you're going," Rachel said.

They turned, surprised.

"And I'm going with you."

3

The weather forecast had been accurate. A cold, damp wind gusted along Fifth Avenue, bringing tears to Savage's eyes. He rubbed them, closed the top button of his overcoat, and watched the taillights of the taxi he'd left recede toward Greenwich Village.

Rachel stood next to him, flanked by Akira.

"One more time," Savage said. "If there's any trouble, run. Don't worry about Akira and me. Go back to the hotel. If we're not in touch by noon, check out. Leave town. I gave you ten thousand dollars. That'll help you get started. I've told you how to contact your parents and your sister and get money without your husband being able to trace it. Pick a city at random. Begin a new life."

"At random? But how would you find me?"

"We wouldn't, and no one else would either. That's the point. As long as you stay away from anyone or anything related to your former life, your husband can't track you. You'll be safe."

"It sounds so"—Rachel shivered—"lonely."

"The alternative's worse."

The three of them walked down Fifth Avenue.

Three blocks later, near Washington Square, they reached a lane between streets. A wrought-iron gate blocked the entrance, its bars topped with spikes. The gate had a keyhole beneath a handle. When Savage twisted the handle and pushed, he discovered that the gate was locked. That didn't surprise him.

He studied the bars. They were tall. The many passing cars and pedestrians were bound to see two men and a woman climb over.

Despite the myth that New Yorkers minded their own business, it was more than likely that someone would call the police.

"Do the honors, Akira."

On the way here, they'd stopped at an East Side tavern, where the owner—one of Savage's contacts—had sold them a set of lockpicks.

Akira freed the lock as easily as if he'd possessed a key. From their frequent visits here, both men knew that the gate was not equipped with intrusion sensors. Akira pushed the gate open, waited for Savage and Rachel to follow, then shoved the gate back into place. In case they needed to leave here quickly, he didn't relock it. Anyone who lived along this lane and found the gate unlocked would merely be disgusted that one of the neighbors had been irresponsible.

They faced the lane. A century earlier, stables and carriage houses had flanked it. The exteriors of the buildings had been carefully modified, their historical appearance preserved. Narrow entrances alternated with quaint double doors that had long ago provided access to barns. The surface of the lane remained cobblestoned. Electric lights, shaped like lanterns, reinforced the impression that time had been suspended.

An exclusive expensive location.

The lane was wide. Intended for horse-drawn buggies, it now permitted residents to steer cars into renovated garages. Lights gleamed from windows. But the only lights Savage cared about were those that shone from the fourth town house on his left.

He walked with Rachel and Akira toward it. Pausing at the entrance, he pressed a button beneath an intercom.

The oak door was lined with steel, Savage knew. Even so, he heard a bell ring faintly behind it. Ten seconds later, he rang the bell again, and ten seconds later again. He waited to hear Graham's voice from the intercom.

No response.

"Asleep?" Savage wondered.

"At ten P.M.? With the lights on?"

"Then he doesn't want to be interrupted, or else he's gone out."

"There's one way to tell," Akira said. "If he's home, he'll have wedged a bar against the door in addition to locking it."

The door had two dead-bolt locks. Akira picked them in rapid succession. He tested the door. It opened.

Savage hurried through. He'd been here so often that he knew the specifics of Graham's defenses. Not only were the windows barred; they had intrusion sensors. So did the doors to Graham's garage. And *this* door. As soon as its locks were freed, anyone entering had to open a closet on the left and press a series of buttons on a console to prevent an alarm from shrieking throughout the neighborhood and, more important, to prevent the local police from sending a squad car in response to a flashing light on their precinct's monitor. This had to be done within fifteen seconds.

Savage yanked the closet door open. A year ago, after several tries, due to professional habit, he'd managed to catch a glimpse of the numbers Graham had pressed.

He pressed those numbers now. A red light stopped glowing.

No siren wailed.

Savage leaned against the closet's wall.

Akira's silhouette filled the doorway. "I've checked this floor. No sign of him."

Savage had been so preoccupied he hadn't paid attention

to the harsh throbbing music he'd heard when he entered. "Heavy metal?"

"The radio," Akira said. "Graham must have left it on when he went out. If someone tried to break in, the intruder would hear the music, decide the house was occupied, and look for another target."

"But why would Graham bother? If someone tripped a sensor, the sirens would scare an intruder a lot more than the music would. Besides, when we stood outside, I barely heard the doorbell and didn't hear the music at all. The radio's hardly a deterrent."

"It's not like Graham to go out and forget to turn it off. *Heavy metal?* Graham hates electric music. He's strictly classical."

"Something's wrong. Check the top floors. I'll take the basement. Rachel, stay here."

As Akira crept up a stairway to the left, Savage's bowels contracted. He crossed the large room that occupied this level. The room was Graham's office, though the glass-and-chrome desk at the rear was the only detail that indicated its purpose. Otherwise, it seemed a living room. To the right, bookshelves flanked a fireplace. To the left, stereo equipment filled a cabinet, Boston Acoustics speakers on either side, the source of the throbbing music. In the middle, a coffee table—its glass and chrome a match to Graham's desk—separated two leather sofas. Beneath them, an Afghan rug covered most of the floor, the border brightly waxed hardwood. Large pots of ferns occupied each corner. The brilliant white walls— upon which hung only a few paintings, all by Monet—reinforced the feeling of spaciousness created by the sparse furnishings.

A stranger could not have known, as Savage did, that Graham hid business documents in alcoves behind the bookshelves, and that the stereo's purpose was to assure those few clients he trusted enough to come here that the swelling cadences of Beethoven's glorious *Eroica* prevented their subdued conversation from being picked up by undetected microphones.

While Savage passed the coffee table, he noticed three empty bottles of champagne. Approaching the desk in the rear, he saw an ashtray filled with cigar butts and a tall-stemmed glass, the bottom of which contained a remnant of liquid.

To the left of the desk, he reached a door and cautiously opened it. Shadowy steps descended to a murky basement. He opened his overcoat and withdrew a .45 pistol that the owner of the East Side bar had sold him along with the lockpicks. Akira had bought one as well.

Gripping the pistol with his leather-gloved right hand, Savage pawed with his other hand, found a light switch, and illuminated the basement. Sweating, he took one step down. Another. Then another.

He held his breath, sprang to the bottom, and tensely aimed.

Three tables. Neat piles of wires, batteries, and disc-shaped objects covered them, various sophisticated eavesdropping devices in progressive stages of assembly.

A furnace. Ready with the .45, Savage peered behind it, seeing no one. Moisture dripped from his forehead. There weren't any other hiding places. He climbed the stairs.

But he wasn't relieved.

4

When Akira joined him, having searched the upper floors and reporting nothing unusual, Savage still didn't feel at ease.

Rachel slumped on a sofa.

Akira holstered his pistol. Electric guitars kept wailing.

"Maybe we're overreacting. There might be a simple explanation for Graham's uncharacteristic choice of music."

"You don't sound convinced."

Rachel pressed her hands to her ears. "Maybe he likes to torture himself."

"Let's do ourselves a favor." Savage pushed a button on the stereo's tuner, and the heavy-metal radio station became mercifully silent.

"Thank God," Rachel said. She studied the coffee table. "Did you notice these empty bottles?"

Akira nodded. "Champagne. Graham loves it."

"So much? Three bottles in one evening?"

"Graham's large enough to tolerate a great deal of alcohol," Savage said. "But you're right, it does seem strange. I've never seen him overindulge."

"Perhaps he had company," Akira said.

"There's only one glass," Rachel said. "If he did have guests and he put away their glasses, why didn't he put away his own glass and the empty bottles as well? And something else. Have you read the labels on the bottles?"

"No," Savage said. "What about them?"

"At the farmhouse outside Athens, when the two of you talked about Graham, you said he drank Dom Pérignon."

"It's the only brand he'll accept," Akira said.

"Well, *two* of these labels say Dom Pérignon. But the third is Asti Spumante."

"*What?*" Savage straightened.

"And what's that noise?" Rachel asked.

Savage glanced around sharply. His ears had been slow to adjust to the silence after the throbbing music. But now he heard a muted drone.

"Yes," Akira said. "A faint vibration. What's causing it?"

"A refrigerator?" Savage said.

"Graham's kitchen's on the second floor," Akira said. "We wouldn't hear the refrigerator this far away."

"Maybe the furnace turned on," Savage said.

Akira lowered his hand toward a vent. "No rush of air."

"Then what . . . ?"

"It seems to come from"—Rachel frowned, passing Savage— "this door beside the bookshelf."

She opened the door and lurched back as thick gray smoke enveloped her. The faint drone became a rumble. Rachel coughed from the acrid stench of the smoke.

Except that it wasn't smoke, Savage realized.

Graham's garage! Savage hurried through the doorway. The garage was dark, but the lights in the living room managed to pierce the dense exhaust rushing past him. He saw Graham's Cadillac, its engine running, a bald, overweight figure slumped behind the steering wheel.

He rushed to lean through the car's open window and twisted the ignition key. The engine stopped. Straining not to breathe, he yanked the driver's door open, clutched Graham, and dragged him across the garage's concrete floor into the living room.

Rachel shoved the door closed, preventing more exhaust from spewing in, but enough had already entered the living room that when Savage finally breathed, he bent over, coughing.

Akira knelt beside Graham, feeling for a pulse.

"His face is deep red," Rachel said.

"Carbon monoxide." Akira listened to Graham's chest. "His heart isn't beating."

Savage knelt opposite Akira, Graham between them. "Give him mouth-to-mouth. I'll work on his heart."

As Akira opened Graham's mouth and breathed into it, Savage pounded Graham's chest once, then placed both palms over his heart, applying and releasing pressure.

"Rachel, call nine eleven," Savage blurted, pressing again on Graham's chest, leaning back, pressing once more.

Rachel scrambled toward the phone on Graham's desk. She picked it up and began to press numbers.

"No, Rachel." Akira sounded sick. "Never mind." He stared at Graham and slowly stood.

"Keep trying!" Savage said.

Akira shook his head in despair. "Feel how cold he is. Look at his legs. When you set him on the floor, they stayed bent—as if he's still sitting in the car. He's been dead for quite a while. Nothing's going to revive him."

Savage squinted at Graham's bent knees, swallowed, and stopped pressing Graham's chest.

Rachel set down the phone.

For several seconds, they didn't move.

"Jesus." Savage's hands shook. He had trouble standing. Akira's neck muscles were so taut they resembled ropes.

Rachel approached, trying not to look at Graham's corpse.

Savage suddenly noticed how pale she was. He reached her just in time before her legs gave out. He helped her toward a sofa, choosing the one that allowed her to sit with her back to Graham. "Put your head between your knees."

"I just lost my balance for a second."

"Sure."

"I feel better now."

"Of course. I'll get you some water," Akira said.

"No, really, I think I'm okay." Her color was returning. "For a moment there, the room seemed blurry. Now . . . Yes." She mustered strength. "I'll be fine. You don't need to worry. I'm not going to faint. I promised myself I wouldn't get in the way. I won't hold you back." Her blue eyes glinted, stubborn, proud.

"Get in the way? The opposite," Savage said. "If it hadn't been for you, we probably wouldn't have discovered . . ." He bit his lower lip and turned toward Graham's body. "The poor bastard. I came here ready to strangle him. Now I'd hug him if he were alive. God, I'll miss him." He pressed downward with his hands, as if repressing emotion. "So what the hell happened?"

"You mean what *appears* to have happened," Akira said.

"Exactly."

Rachel looked confused.

"Three empty wine bottles," Akira said.

"Right. A drunken man decides to go out for the evening. He starts his car, but before he can open the garage, he passes out. The exhaust fumes kill him."

"A coroner will reject that explanation."

"Of course," Savage said.

"I don't understand," Rachel said.

"The garage was dark, and the door from the living room was shut," Akira said. "Even a drunk would realize that the garage wasn't open when he found himself blundering around in the dark. His first instinct would be to open the outside door."

"Unless he had an automatic garage-door opener, and he figured he could press the remote control in his car while he started the engine."

"But Graham's garage actually has *two* doors. Like the stable doors they're supposed to resemble, they open out on each side, and it has to be done by hand."

"So the garage was left closed deliberately."

"I'm missing something," Rachel said. "It sounds like . . . *Graham committed suicide?*"

"He sits here alone, the stereo blaring while he smokes and drinks and broods. When he's drunk enough to work up his nerve, he goes out to his car. Doesn't bother to shut off the stereo. Why worry about it? Makes sure the living room door is closed to keep the garage sealed. Turns the ignition key. The exhaust smells terrible, but after several deep breaths, his eyes feel heavy. He drifts. He dies. No muss, no fuss. Yeah," Savage said, "the coroner will buy it."

"And that's the way Graham would do it. He's too fastidious about his appearance to put a bullet through his head. All the blood would ruin his three-piece suit," Akira said.

Rachel looked disturbed.

"He'd need a reason to kill himself," Savage said.

"Problems with his health?"

Savage shrugged. "The last time I saw him, three weeks ago, there didn't seem anything wrong. Overweight, of course, but robust as ever. Even if he suddenly learned he had cancer, he's the type that would pamper himself till every medical option proved useless and he was terminal. *Then* he might kill himself. But not before."

"Then *business* problems."

"Better," Savage said.

"You're still confusing me," Rachel said.

"It wouldn't have anything to do with money," Akira said. "Graham was wealthy. He invested shrewdly. So it has to be a client that turned against him, or a client's enemy who discovered that Graham arranged an attack against him.''

Savage thought about it. "Good. It'll work. In his prime, when Graham belonged to the British commandos, a challenge excited him. But after he retired, once he put on weight and got soft from too much champagne and caviar, he'd have realized that he'd lost his ability to tolerate pain. He trained me, but his own skills were memories from his youth. He once admitted to me that these days, one-on-one, he wouldn't have a chance against a practiced opponent. If he knew he was being stalked, if he was certain his death would be painful, he might have chosen a peaceful suicide.''

"Especially if *we* were stalking him," Akira said.

"Except that when Graham sent us to Mykonos, he had to assume we'd eventually come here demanding answers, and he knew us well enough to assume that no matter how angry we were, we'd never kill him. Besides, the coroner isn't aware of us. I don't think he's *supposed* to be aware of us, either.''

"I agree," Akira said. "Still, the coroner will have to believe that *someone* was stalking Graham, or else the scenario isn't valid. Somewhere—probably behind those bookshelves, in Graham's hidden files—the police will find evidence that Graham feared for his life.''

"And knew he would suffer.''

"And chose the dignity of a self-inflicted death." Akira raised his eyebrows. "Very Japanese.''

"Would the two of you please explain?" Rachel asked.

"Graham didn't kill himself," Akira said.

"But the way you've been talking . . .''

"We're pretending to be the coroner," Savage said. "The verdict is suicide. But the coroner doesn't know that Graham would never have chosen a heavy-metal radio station. And the coroner doesn't know that Graham would never have mixed Dom Pérignon with Asti Spumante. Graham was murdered. He was forced—I assume by several men—to drink the champagne he had in stock. But two bottles weren't enough. So they sent a man to buy another. He came back with his choice, not Graham's. When Graham passed out,

they put him in the car, turned it on, shut the living room
door, waited till he was dead, then left.''

"But not before they played the radio to pass the time,"
Akira said. "Again *their* choice of stations. They probably
figured the music would be a realistic touch, so they didn't
switch it off before they activated the alarm on the outside
entrance and left.''

"Almost perfect," Savage said. "The bastards. I'll . . .''

"Make them pay?" Akira's sad eyes blazed. "That goes
without saying.''

5

Savage raised Graham's arms while Akira lifted his legs.
Rachel opened the living room door, turning from the cloud
of exhaust spewing in while the two men carried the corpse
to the garage.

They positioned the body behind the Cadillac's steering
wheel. The poisonous fumes were still so dense that Savage
held his breath while making sure that Graham slumped on
the seat exactly as before. After all, as soon as Graham's
blood had stopped circulating, gravity would have made the
blood settle toward various pockets in his abdomen, hips,
and legs, causing purplish-red discolorations in those areas.
If the corpse had discolorations in higher areas, a coroner
would know that the corpse had been moved.

The corpse *had* been moved, but Graham's body had not
lain in the living room long enough for the blood to be re-
distributed and thus discolor the back. The coroner would not
become suspicious.

Savage twisted the ignition key, hearing the Cadillac's
engine rumble. He slammed the driver's door and ran with
Akira into the living room.

The room was filled with haze. Savage coughed, hearing Rachel shut the door.

"The windows," Akira said.

They hurried toward opposite ends of the room, pressed buttons that shut off intruder-detection alarms, raised panes, and gulped fresh air.

A cold wind billowed drapes, attacking the fumes. Gray wisps swirled toward the ceiling, dispersed, and flowed out the tops of the open windows.

In the wind's subtle hiss, Savage listened to the muffled drone of the Cadillac's engine. He turned toward the living room door, the garage beyond it. "I'm sorry, friend."

"But *was* he a friend?" Akira asked. "A friend wouldn't have deceived us. *Why did he do it?*"

Anger conflicted with grief and made Savage hoarse. "Let's find out." He crossed the room and tugged at the bookshelves.

The wall swung outward, revealing further shelves. Metal containers. Graham's documents.

Savage and Akira sorted urgently through them.

Rachel stood in the background. "You said you didn't think the coroner was supposed to know about you. What did you mean?"

"Too coincidental. Graham's murder. Our coming here to question him. They're related." Savage scanned pages.

"You can't *prove* that."

"Yes," Akira said, "we can." He sorted through another box of files. "Graham keeps these documents for one reason only—to explain his income to the IRS. If it weren't for taxes, his passion for secrecy would never have allowed him to keep business records. Of course, he took the precaution of using pseudonyms for his operatives and his clients, so an enemy wouldn't learn anything vital if he found these files. The code for the pseudonyms is in a safe-deposit box. The arrangement with the bank is that both Graham *and* his lawyer have to be present to open it, so we know the code is secure. But Savage and I don't need the code to tell us which pseudonyms Graham used for us. We chose our pseudonyms ourselves. In fact, the names by which you know us *are* our pseudonyms."

They searched through other boxes.

"What are you looking for?" Rachel asked.

"Graham kept two sets of documents, cross-referenced, one for his operatives and the jobs they did, the other for the clients who commissioned the jobs. Did you find them?"

Akira checked the final box. "No."

"I didn't either."

"Find *what?*" Rachel asked.

"Our files," Savage said. "They're gone."

"We don't know the pseudonym Graham gave Kamichi, or the ones he gave your sister and your husband," Akira said. "But since *our* files aren't here, I assume the others are gone as well. That's the proof I referred to. Whoever killed Graham must have taken the files. The coroner isn't supposed to be aware of us, not even of our pseudonyms. Graham was killed to keep him from telling us why we saw each other die."

"And here's the suicide note Akira predicted we'd find. Typed, of course. Because Graham didn't compose it."

"Left by his killers. All right," Rachel said. "I'm convinced. But how could they be sure the police would look behind these bookshelves?"

"The shelves weren't closed completely."

"We'd better get out," Akira said. "The neighbor on the other side of Graham's garage might wonder about the faint rumble he hears through the wall and call the police."

They replaced the files and arranged the metal containers in their original positions.

Savage shut the bookshelves, leaving a slight gap just as Graham's killers had done.

Akira turned on the radio. Guitars throbbed and wailed.

"The room's aired out. I don't smell exhaust fumes." Rachel closed the windows.

Savage glanced around. "Is everything the way we found it? We all wore gloves. There'll be no fingerprints. Okay."

Akira went outside, checked the lane, and motioned for Rachel to follow.

Savage activated the intrusion alarm in the closet, shut the closet's door, stepped outside, shut the front door, and waited for Akira to use his lockpicks to secure the two dead-bolt locks on the entrance.

Savage held Rachel's arm as they walked along the lane. She trembled. "Don't forget to lock the gate behind us."

"Don't worry. We wouldn't have. But thanks for reminding us," Akira said. "I'm impressed. You're learning, Rachel."

"The way this is going, when it's finally over—assuming it ever is—I've got a terrible feeling I'll be an expert."

6

In the night, they walked down Fifth Avenue, passing streetlights, approaching the shadows of Washington Square. The cold, damp wind continued gusting and again brought tears to Savage's eyes. "Would the killers have left the area?"

"I assume so. Their work was completed," Akira said.

"But *was* it completed? If the point was to silence Graham, they must have guessed we'd be coming here."

"How would they know about us?"

"The only explanation I can think of . . ."

"Say it."

". . . is that Graham worked with and possibly *for* the men who killed him," Savage said.

"But why would he have helped them in the first place? He didn't need money. He valued loyalty. Why did he turn against us?"

"Hey," Rachel said. "Let me understand this. You're saying we're being watched by Graham's killers?" She stared behind her. "And they'll try to kill *us* as well?"

"They'll follow us," Akira said. "But try to kill us? I

don't think so. Someone went to a lot of trouble to convince Savage and me that we saw each other die. Why, I don't know. But we're very important to somebody. Whoever it is will want to protect his investment.''

Savage hailed an approaching taxi. They scrambled inside. "Times Square," Savage said.

For the next hour, they shifted from taxi to taxi, switched to a subway, went back to a taxi, and ended with a stroll through Central Park.

Rachel was surprised to see so many joggers. "I thought the park wasn't safe at night."

"They run in groups. The junkies don't bother them."

She looked doubly surprised when she noticed that Akira wasn't next to her. "Where . . . ?"

"Among the trees, above the rocks, going back the way we came. If we're being followed, he'll deal with them."

"But he didn't explain what he was doing."

"He didn't have to," Savage said.

"The two of you read each other's mind?"

"We know what needs to be done."

Ten minutes later, Akira emerged from bushes. "If we *were* being followed, they're not foolish enough to trail us through Central Park at midnight."

The shadowy path forked.

"This way, Rachel." Savage guided her toward the right. "It's safe to go back to the hotel."

7

The fourth man swung his katana. Its blade hissed, struck Kamichi's waist, kept speeding as if through air, and sliced him in half. Kamichi's upper and lower torso fell in opposite directions.

Blood gushed. Severed organs spilled over the floor.

Akira wailed in outrage, rushing to chop the man's windpipe before the assassin could swing again.

Too late. The assassin reversed his aim, both hands gripping the katana.

From Savage's agonized perspective on the floor, it seemed that Akira jumped backward in time to avoid the blade. But the swordsman didn't swing a third time. Instead he watched indifferently as Akira's head fell off his shoulders.

As blood spewed from Akira's severed neck.

As Akira's torso remained standing for three grotesque seconds before it toppled.

Akira's head hit the floor with the thunk of a pumpkin, rolled, and stopped in front of Savage. The head rested on its stump, its eyes on a level with Savage's.

The eyes were open.

They blinked.

Savage screamed.

Frantic, he struggled to overcome the pain of his broken arms and legs, to force them to move, to raise himself from the floor. He'd failed to protect Kamichi and assist Akira. But he still had an obligation to avenge their deaths before the assassins killed *him*.

He compelled his anguished limbs to respond, lurched upward, felt hands press against him, and fought. The hands became arms encircling him. They pinned his own arms, squeezing against his back, thrusting air from his lungs.

"No," Akira said.

Savage thrashed.

"No," Akira repeated.

Abruptly Savage stopped. He blinked. In contrast with the sweat trickling off his brow, his skin felt terribly cold. He shivered.

Akira—

Impossible!

—hugged him fiercely.

No! You're dead!

Akira's face loomed inches away, his sad eyes narrowed

with alarm, eyes that Savage had just seen blink from a severed head resting upright on the floor.

Akira again repeated, this time whispering, "No." Savage slowly peered around. The image of the blood-spattered hallway in the Medford Gap Mountain Retreat blurred and dissolved, replaced by the tasteful furnishings in a room, in a suite, in a hotel off Fifth Avenue.

The room was mostly dark, except for a dim light next to a chair in a corner to the left of the door to the hallway. Akira, having slept while Savage kept watch, had taken his turn on guard.

Savage breathed. "Okay." He relaxed.

"You're sure?" Akira kept holding him.

"A nightmare."

"No doubt the same as mine. Brace your legs."

Savage nodded.

Akira released his grip.

Savage sank onto the sofa.

The bedroom door jerked open. Rachel appeared, focused on Savage and Akira, inhaled, and quickly approached. She wore a thigh-length blue nightshirt. Her breasts swelled the cotton garment. Her urgent strides raised its hem.

She showed no embarrassment. Savage and Akira paid no attention. She was part of the team.

"You screamed," Rachel said. "What happened?"

"A nightmare," Savage said.

"*The* nightmare?"

Savage nodded, then turned and peered up at Akira.

"I have it, too," Akira said. "Every night."

Savage studied Akira in pained confusion. "I thought, once we'd met for a second time, it would finally go away."

"I thought mine would, too. But it hasn't."

"I've been trying not to talk about it." Savage gestured in frustration. "I still can't get over the certainty that I saw you killed. I *see* you before me! I *hear* your voice! I can *touch* you! But it makes no difference. We've been together for several days. *Yet I'm still sure I saw you die.*"

"As I saw *you* die," Akira said. "Every time I doubt myself, I think of my six months of agony while I convalesced. I've got the scars on my arms and legs to remind me.''

Savage unbuttoned his shirt and revealed two surgical scars, one below his left rib cage, the other near his right pelvic bone. "Where my spleen and appendix had to be removed because they'd been ruptured by the beating I received.''

"Mine were removed as well." Akira exposed his muscular chest and abdomen, showing two scars identical to Savage's.

"So we know . . . we can prove . . . that you both were beaten," Rachel said. "But obviously your 'deaths'—that part of your nightmare—are exactly that: a nightmare.''

"Don't you understand it doesn't matter?" Savage said. "The fact that Akira's alive doesn't change what I know I saw. This is worse than *déjà vu*, worse than the eerie feeling that I've lived through this before. It's more like the opposite. I don't know what to call it. *Jamais vu*, the sense that what I saw never happened. And yet it did, and what I'm seeing now isn't possible. I've got to find out why I'm facing a ghost.''

"We *both* do," Akira said.

"But Graham's dead. Who else could explain what happened? How do we find the answer? Where do we start?''

"Why don't you . . . ?" Rachel's voice dropped.

"Yes? Go on," Savage said.

"This is just a suggestion.''

"Your suggestions have been good so far," Akira said.

"It's probably obvious." Rachel shrugged. "For all I know, the two of you have already thought of it and dismissed it.''

"What?" Akira asked.

"You start where your problem started. Six months ago. At this place you keep talking about.''

"The Medford Gap Mountain Retreat.''

8

They ate a room-service breakfast and checked out shortly after seven. Using evasion procedures, they reached a car rental agency when it opened an hour later. Savage had considered asking one of his contacts to supply a car, but he felt nervously convinced that the fewer people who knew he was in town, the better. Especially now that Graham was dead.

Rachel confessed that she'd had a nightmare of her own, seeing Graham propped behind the steering wheel of his Cadillac, enveloped by exhaust fumes, driving into eternity. But the Cadillac would eventually use up its fuel, she explained. If a neighbor didn't hear the engine's faint rumble before then, it was possible that Graham would sit in the car for several days, bloating, decomposing, riddled with maggots, until the stench from his garage finally made someone call the police. Graham's nostrils, filled with maggots, had climaxed her nightmare, startling her awake.

"Why couldn't we have phoned the police and pretended to be a neighbor concerned about the sound in Graham's garage?" she asked.

"Because the police have an automatic computerized trace on incoming calls. In case someone reports an emergency and hangs up without giving a number. If we phoned from Graham's house or a pay phone, it would have told the police a neighbor wasn't calling. Since we don't know what Graham's killers are up to, it's better to let the scenario play out the way they intended."

As Savage drove the rented Taurus from the city, Rachel lapsed into brooding silence. Akira slept in the back.

Attempting to recreate his previous journey, Savage left Manhattan via the George Washington Bridge and entered

New Jersey, heading along Interstate 80. Twenty minutes later, he started scanning the motels near the exit ramps.

Holiday Inn. Best Western.

"There," Savage said. "Howard Johnson's. That's where Kamichi changed briefcases. It puzzled me."

The October day was splendidly clear, the sun dispersing the chill of the night before. As they left New Jersey and progressed into Pennsylvania, cliffs rimmed Interstate 80. After half an hour, the cliffs were mountains.

Rachel began to relax. "I've always loved autumn. The leaves turning colors."

"The last time I drove here, the trees hadn't budded yet. There were patches of snow. *Dirt-covered* snow. It was dusk. The clouds looked like coal dust. Akira, wake up. We'll soon be leaving the highway."

Savage steered toward an exit ramp. He followed the directions he'd memorized six months ago, found his way through a maze of narrow roads, and finally saw a road sign: MEDFORD GAP.

The town was small. Impoverished. Almost no traffic. Few pedestrians. Boards on many store windows.

"Akira, is this the way you remember it?"

"We came here after dark. Except for the streetlights, I saw almost nothing. We turned to the left at the town's main intersection."

"This stop-street ahead." Savage braked and turned, proceeding up a tree-lined mountain road. It curved, bringing him back to Medford Gap.

"Obviously not the main intersection." He drove farther. "Here. Yes. This is it."

He turned left at a traffic light and angled up a steep winding road. Six months ago, mud and snow on the shoulders had made him worry about descending cars he might have to avoid. The road had been so narrow that he couldn't have passed approaching headlights and would have been forced to risk getting stuck in the ditch near the trees.

But now, as before, no cars descended. Thank God, unlike earlier, the dirt road was dry and firm. And in daylight, he could see where to swerve if a vehicle did approach.

He steered through a hairpin curve, driving higher past isolated cabins flanked by dense forest. "Wait'll you see this, Rachel. It's the strangest building. So many styles. The whole thing's a fifth of a mile long."

He crested the peak, veered past a rock, and braked, his seat belt squeezing his chest. The Taurus skidded.

He stared in disbelief.

Ahead, the road stopped. Beyond, there was nothing. Except boulders and brilliantly colored trees.

"What?"

"You took another wrong road," Akira said.

"No. *This* was the road."

"Day versus night. You can't be certain. Try it again."

Savage did.

And when he'd eliminated every left road up from Medford Gap, he stopped outside a tavern.

A group of men stood next to the entrance, adjusting their caps, spitting tobacco juice.

"The Medford Gap Mountain Retreat. How do I get there?" Savage asked.

"Mountain Retreat?" A gaunt man squinted. "Never heard of the fucking thing."

9

Savage drove faster, unable to control his urge to flee. With tunnel vision, he stared at the broken line down the middle of the narrow road, oblivious to the glorious orange, red, and yellow of the trees on the flanking towering slopes.

"But it was there!" Savage drove even faster. "Akira and I both saw it. We *slept* there. We *ate* there. We guarded Kamichi along every corridor! Three nights! Three days!"

"So *old*," Akira said. "The wagon-wheel chandeliers. The

ancient staircase. I can still smell the must in the lobby. And the smoke from the logs in the parlor's fireplace.''

"But it isn't there," Rachel said.

The Taurus squealed around a bend. Struggling with the steering wheel, Savage suddenly realized he was doing seventy. He eased his foot from the gas pedal. Beyond a bare ridge—a sign said BEWARE OF FALLING ROCKS—he saw an abandoned service station, its sign dangling, its windows broken, and pulled off the road, stopping at the concrete slabs where fuel pumps once had stood.

"We asked a dozen different people." Though Savage no longer drove, he continued to clutch the steering wheel. "None of them had the faintest idea what we were talking about."

He felt smothered. Jerking the driver's door open, he lunged from the car, filling his lungs with fresh air.

Akira and Rachel joined him.

"This isn't some small hotel so far from Medford Gap that the locals might not have heard of it." Savage stared toward the bluffs beyond the service station but was too preoccupied to notice them. "It's a major tourist attraction, so close that Medford Gap's part of its name."

"And we checked every road that led to the top of the mountain," Akira said.

"We even drove back up the road that you're sure is the one you used six months ago," Rachel said. "We searched the trees in case there'd been a fire. But there wasn't any charred wreckage. A half-year isn't enough time for the forest to hide evidence of the building."

"No," Savage said. "The forest couldn't have hidden a burnt-out cabin, let alone a massive hotel. And the fire would have been spectacular. The local population couldn't possibly forget it so fast. Even if there *had* been a fire, it wouldn't have destroyed the lake beside the hotel. But the lake's not there either!"

"And yet we're certain both the hotel and the lake were there," Akira said.

"Certain?" Savage asked. "Just as we're certain we saw each other die? But we *didn't*."

''And''—Akira hesitated—''the Mountain Retreat never existed.''

Savage exhaled, nodding. ''I feel like . . . What I described last night in the hotel. *Jamais vu.* Nothing seems real. I can't trust my senses. It's as if I'm losing my mind.''

''What happened to us?'' Akira asked.

''And where?'' Savage scowled. ''And why?''

''Keep retracing your steps,'' Rachel said. ''Where did you go from here?''

''A hospital,'' Savage said.

''Mine was in Harrisburg,'' Akira said. ''A hundred miles south. I had to be flown by helicopter.''

''Harrisburg?'' Savage's hands and feet became numb. ''You never mentioned . . .''

''It didn't occur to me. The look in your eyes. Don't tell me *you* were flown there as well.''

''Did your doctor have blond hair?''

''Yes.''

''And freckles?''

''And glasses?''

''And his name was . . . ?''

''Hamilton.''

''Shit,'' Savage said.

They raced toward the car.

10

''What's keeping her?'' Akira asked.

''It's been only ten minutes.'' Savage had let Rachel out when he couldn't find a parking space. He'd been driving repeatedly around the block. Still, despite his assurance to Akira, Savage's need to protect her—coupled with his growing affection for her—made him nervous by her absence.

Midafternoon. Traffic accumulated. Savage reached an intersection, turned right, and sat straighter, pointing.

"Yes," Akira said. "Good. There she is."

Relieved, Savage watched her hurry from the Harrisburg public library, glimpse the Taurus, and quickly get in. He drove on.

"I checked the phone book," she said. "Here's a photocopy of the city map. And a list of the hospitals in the area. But this'll take longer than you expected. There are several. You're sure you don't remember the name of the hospital?"

"No one ever mentioned it," Akira said.

"But the name must have been stenciled on the sheets and the gowns."

"I was groggy from Demerol," Savage said. "If the name was on the sheets, I didn't notice."

Akira studied the list and read it to Savage. "Community General Osteopathic Hospital. Harrisburg Hospital. Harrisburg State Hospital."

"Osteopathic?" Savage said. "Isn't that something like chiropractic?"

"No, osteopathic medicine's a theory that most illness is caused by pressure from injured muscles and displaced bones," Akira said.

Savage thought about it and shook his head. "Let's try . . ."

11

"I'm sorry, sir," the elderly woman at the Harrisburg Hospital information desk said. "There's no Dr. Hamilton on our staff."

"Please," Akira said tensely, "check again."

"But I checked three times already. The computer shows no reference to a Dr. Hamilton."

"Maybe he's *not* on the staff," Akira said. "He might be in private practice and sends his patients here."

"Well, of course that's possible," the woman said behind the desk.

"No," Rachel said.

Savage and Akira turned to her.

"When I checked the phone book, I looked under private physicians. He isn't listed."

"Then he works for another hospital," Akira said.

They crossed the crowded lobby toward the exit.

"What troubles me," Rachel said, "is there was no Dr. Hamilton in the white pages either."

"An unlisted number."

"What kind of physician has an unlisted private number?"

The lobby's door hissed open.

12

The overweight man behind the information desk at the Harrisburg State Hospital shook his head, tapped more buttons on the keyboard, watched the computer screen, and pursed his lips.

"Nope. No Dr. Hamilton. Sorry."

"But that's impossible," Savage said.

"After Medford Gap, *nothing's* impossible," Akira said.

"There's got to be an explanation." Savage suddenly thought of one. "This happened six months ago. For all we know, he resigned and moved to another city to work for another institution."

"Then how would we find that information?" Rachel asked the man behind the desk.

"You'd have to talk to Personnel. The computer lists only current staff members."

"And where—?"

The man gave directions to Personnel. "But you'd better hurry. It's almost five. They'll soon be closing."

"I'll do it," Akira said quickly. "Savage, phone the personnel office at the other hospital."

Akira hurried down a corridor.

Trying not to bump into visitors, Savage rushed toward a row of pay phones at the side of the lobby.

"I'll meet you back here," Rachel said.

"Where are—?"

"I've got an idea."

Continuing toward the phones, Savage heard her urgently ask the man at the information desk, "How do I find the business office?" Savage wondered why she wanted to know. But at once all he cared about was that every phone was being used. He glanced at his watch. Six minutes to five. Anxious, he pulled coins from his pocket, scanned the list of hospitals, addresses, and phone numbers Rachel had given him, saw a woman leave a phone, and darted toward it. As the call went through, he glanced across the lobby. Rachel was gone.

13

They sat in the hospital's coffee shop, staring at their Styrofoam cups.

"The personnel office has no listing for a Dr. Hamilton in the past five years," Akira said.

"The other hospital *did* have a Dr. Hamilton," Savage said.

Akira straightened.

"Three years ago," Savage said. "Female. Elderly. She died from a stroke."

Akira slumped back in his chair.

"It's beginning to look as if our Dr. Hamilton didn't exist

any more than the Medford Gap Mountain Retreat did,"
Savage said.

"And that's not all that didn't exist," Rachel said. "The
two of you may think you're real, but you're not."

"What are you talking about?" Akira asked.

"At least as far as the Harrisburg hospitals are concerned.
I went to the business office. While they found out what I
needed, I went to a phone to call the other hospital and get
its business office before it closed. I asked for the same
information."

"*What* information?" Akira asked.

"The business office is the place that sends patients their
bills. Earlier you told me the names you'd used when you
stayed in the hospital. I pretended to be an insurance agent.
I said my company had paid for your treatment several months
ago. Now I was getting complaints from you. I asked each
hospital why it was sending you notices about overdue bills.
The people I spoke to were quite sympathetic. It was easy
to solve the problem, they said. They checked their computers. You'll never guess what. The computers came up
blank. There's no record that you stayed in *either* hospital."

Savage squeezed his Styrofoam cup, almost breaking it.
"Then where the hell were we?"

"Maybe the Osteopathic Hospital," Rachel said. "But
when we go there during business hours tomorrow, I strongly
suspect . . ."

"We'll get the same answers," Akira said. "There's
no such place as the Medford Gap Mountain Retreat. We
didn't see each other die. We never met Dr. Hamilton.
We weren't in a Harrisburg hospital. What *else* didn't
happen?"

Savage stood forcefully and walked away.

"Where are you going?" Rachel hurried to follow, joined
by Akira.

"The information desk."

"But why?" Rachel tried to keep pace as Savage stalked
into the lobby. "We've asked everything we can think of."

"No. There's one thing we *haven't* asked. The way to the
goddamn Emergency Ward."

14

In a brightly lit vestibule, a weary nurse peered up from behind a counter. "Yes, sir? May I . . . ?"

She suddenly frowned, seeing the tension on Savage's face. She shifted her troubled gaze toward Rachel and Akira.

"I want to see a doctor," Savage said.

"Has there been an accident?" She stood. "You don't look injured. Is it someone else who needs . . . ?"

"I said I want to see a doctor."

The nurse blinked, startled. "Of course, sir." She stepped back nervously. "Please wait right here." She disappeared down a corridor.

"Be calm," Akira said.

"I'm trying, but it's not doing any good. I have to *know*."

Abruptly the nurse returned, accompanied by a tall man wearing hospital greens.

"Yes, sir?" The young man slowed, approaching Savage cautiously. "I'm Dr. Reynolds. The senior resident on this ward. Is there something—"

"I need an X ray."

"Why?" The resident studied him. "Are you in pain?"

"You bet I'm in pain."

"But *where?* Your chest? An arm?"

"Everywhere."

"What?"

"I want . . . What I need . . . is a full-body X ray."

"A full-body . . . ? Why would you . . . ? Describe your symptoms."

"I ache from head to foot. I can't bear the pain anymore. I *have* to know what's wrong. Just give me the X rays."

"But we can't just . . ."

"I'll pay."

"We still can't . . . Does your family doctor know about your pain?"

"I travel a lot. I don't have a family doctor."

"But without a diagnosis . . ."

"I said I'm willing to pay."

"Money's not the issue. We can't give X rays needlessly. If your pain's as severe as you indicate, you'd better come into the ward. Let me examine you."

"Your name, please," a young woman said.

Savage turned toward a civilian, who'd replaced the nurse at the counter.

"And the name of your insurance company."

"I changed my mind," Savage said.

The resident frowned. "You don't want to be examined?"

Savage shook his head. The resident's suspicious gaze bothered him. "I thought if I asked . . . My friend here was right. Be calm."

"But something *is* wrong with you."

"You're right about that. The question is *what*. Don't worry, though. I'll take your advice. I need a family doctor."

15

The elderly physician, who had a gray mustache, wore suspenders, and didn't mind ordering full-body X rays for anyone willing to pay him five thousand dollars, came out of a door marked TECHNICIANS ONLY. Instead of sending his patients to one of the hospitals, he'd chosen a private facility called the Radiology Clinic. As he crossed the waiting room, Savage, Akira, and Rachel stood.

"Well?" Savage asked.

"The films are excellent. We won't need to take a second set. I've studied them carefully."

Savage couldn't keep the anxiety out of his voice. "But what did you find?"

"You paid so handsomely to have your pictures taken, why don't you come along and see for yourselves?"

The doctor led them through the door. They quickly entered a dimly lit room. To the right was a counter with cupboards above and below. To the left was a wall upon which a row of X-ray films hung from clips, illuminated by fluorescent lights behind them.

Various skeletal segments were revealed in shades of gray.

"These are yours," the doctor said, gesturing to Savage. "And these farther over are yours," he told Akira.

They leaned toward the films. After thirty seconds, Akira shook his head and faced the doctor. "I don't know how to read them."

"You asked me to determine how well your injuries had mended. My response is, *what* injuries?"

"Jesus," Savage said. "I was right."

"I'm not sure what you mean, but I'm sure of this." The doctor traced a pencil along bones on the various films. "I'll save you the medical terminology. This is your upper right leg. Your lower. Your *left* leg, upper and lower. Right ribs. Left ribs. Various views of the skull."

The doctor shifted toward Akira's X rays and used the pencil to draw attention to the images of his bones as well. "Completely intact. No sign of calcium deposits where the bones would have mended. Why would you tell me that *each* of you had suffered broken legs, broken arms, broken ribs, and a fractured skull, when *none* of those injuries obviously ever happened?"

"We *thought* they did," Akira said.

"*Thought?* Traumas that extensive wouldn't leave you in doubt. Your suffering would have been *enormous*."

"It was," Savage said.

He trembled. Rachel gripped his arm.

"How *could* you have suffered?" the doctor asked. "If the injuries didn't occur?"

"That's a damned good question. Believe me, I intend to find out."

"Well, while you're at it, find out something else," the doctor said. "I don't like coincidence. Both of you claim identical injuries, though they never occurred. But both of you *do* have signs of surgery"—he gestured with his pencil toward two X-ray films—"which weren't the result of broken bones."

"Yes, each of us had our spleen and appendix removed," Akira said.

"You showed me those scars," the doctor said. "They're exactly as they should look if those organs were in fact removed. Your X rays aren't detailed enough to verify my conclusion, of course. Only further surgery would prove it. But that's not my point. The surgery I'm referring to wasn't on your chests and your lower torsos. *It was on your skulls.*"

"What?" Savage said.

"Of course. Because of the fractures," Akira said.

"*No.*" The doctor kept gesturing toward separate X-ray films. "These tiny circles? One above each left ear? They're unmistakable evidence."

"Of?"

"Intrusions into the left temporal lobe of each brain." The doctor pivoted toward Savage, then Akira. "And neither of you is aware of the surgery?"

Savage hesitated.

"I asked you a question."

"No," Savage said, "we weren't aware."

"That's hard to believe."

"It wouldn't be if you'd been with us for the past few days. Please." Savage swallowed bile. "Help us."

"How? I've done what I could."

"No, where do we go? Who do we ask from here?"

"All I can tell you"—the doctor turned to the films—"is the surgeon was a genius. I'm merely a Pennsylvania general practitioner about to retire. But I haven't ignored the latest medical texts. And I know of nothing this sophisticated. The juncture between detached skull segments and each skull itself is almost perfectly disguised. The procedure was magnificent. Where do you go from here? Where money buys superstars. The best neurosurgeons at the biggest institutions.''

JAMAIS VU

1

The neurosurgeon's name was Anthony Santizo. He had thick dark hair, swarthy skin, and extremely intelligent eyes. His handsome features were somewhat haggard—the consequence of fatigue, Savage guessed, since the doctor had just completed seven hours of surgery. In contrast, his body was trim—the consequence of addiction to racquetball games, one of which Santizo had explained he was scheduled to play in an hour.

"I know you're busy," Savage said. "We're grateful you made time for us."

Santizo raised his shoulders. "I normally wouldn't have. But the neurosurgeon your physician spoke to in Harrisburg happens to know a former classmate of mine, a good friend from Harvard Medical School. Harrisburg has excellent physicians, of course, but the way your problem was described to me, I think my friend was right to send you here."

Here was Philadelphia, the hospital of the University of Pennsylvania. A hundred miles east of Harrisburg, it was quicker to get to than Pennsylvania's other major university hospital, twice as far to the west, in Pittsburgh.

"I'm intrigued by mysteries," Santizo said. "Sherlock Holmes. Agatha Christie. The wonderful clues. The delicious riddles. But the brain is the *greatest* mystery. The key to the door to the secret of what makes us human. That's why I chose my specialty."

A secretary entered the immaculate office, bringing in cups and a pot on a tray.

"Excellent," Santizo said. "On time. My herbal tea. Would you care for . . . ?"

"Yes," Akira said. "I'd like some."

"I'm afraid it's less strong than you're used to in Japan."

Akira bowed. "I'm sure it's refreshing."

Santizo bowed in return. "I went to Harvard with one of your countrymen. I'll never forget what he said to me. We were both just starting our internships. The long, brutal hours wore me down. I didn't think I'd survive. Your countryman said, 'When you're not on duty, you must find an exercise you enjoy.' I told him I didn't understand. 'If I'm already tired, why would I want to exercise?' You know what his answer was? 'Your fatigue is caused by your mind. You must combat that fatigue by *physical* fatigue. The latter will cancel your former.' That made no sense to me. I told him so. He responded with one word."

"*Wa*," Akira said.

Santizo laughed. "Yes! By God, you remind me of your countryman!"

"'*Wa*'?" Rachel asked, assessed the word, and frowned. As everyone looked at her, she reached self-consciously for a cup.

"It means 'balance,'" Akira said. "Mental fatigue is neutralized by . . ."

"Exercise," Santizo said. "How right your countryman was. It's tough to find time, and after the days and nights I put in, I'm usually so exhausted I hate to do it. But I *have* to do it. Because racquetball makes me a *better* neurosurgeon.'' Preoccupied, he glanced at his watch. ''And in fifty minutes, I'm due at the court. So show me these supposedly baffling X rays.''

He took the oversize folder. ''Hey, don't look depressed. Remember '*wa*.' Racquetball and neurosurgery. Sherlock Holmes.''

2

''Mmmmm.''

Santizo stood in a corner of his office, glancing back and forth at two X-ray films of skull profiles that he'd clipped onto a fluorescent screen.

He'd been studying the films for several minutes, his arms crossed, listening to Savage's explanation of the events that had brought them here.

''Executive protectors?'' Santizo continued to assess the films. ''It sounds like the two of you have a fascinating profession. Even so . . .''

He turned toward Savage and Akira, took a penlight from his shirt pocket, and examined the left side of each man's head.

''Mmmmm.''

He sat behind his desk, sipped his herbal tea, and thought a moment.

''The surgeon did an excellent job. State of the art. Mind you, I'm referring only to the cosmetic aspects of the procedure. The skillful concealment of the fact of the surgery. The minimal calcification around the portion of each skull that was taken out and then replaced. You see, the standard method is to drill holes in the skull, at the corners of the area to be removed. These holes are carefully calculated so the drill doesn't enter the brain. A thin, very strong, very sharp wire is then inserted into one of the holes and guided along the edge of the brain until the wire comes out another hole. The surgeon grips each end of the wire and pulls, sawing outward through the skull. He repeats the process from one pair of holes to another until the segment of skull can be removed. The wire is thin, as I explained, but nonetheless not thin enough to prevent the demarcation between the skull and the segment that's been removed and later replaced from developing obvious calcification. Even without that calcification, the holes in the skull would be impossible to miss on an X ray. In this case"—Santizo rubbed his chin—"there *aren't* any holes, only this small circle as if a plug of bone had been removed and then replaced. The demarcation between the plug and the skull is so fine that calcification is negligible. I'm surprised the general practitioner you went to detected the evidence. Someone not prepared to look for it might not have seen it."

"But if a standard technique wasn't used, what *was*?" Savage asked.

"Now that's the question, isn't it?" Santizo said. "The surgeon could have used a drill with a five millimeter bit to make a hole the same size as this plug. But he wanted a technique that wouldn't leave obvious signs. The only solution that occurs to me is . . . The plug was removed from the skull by a laser beam. Lasers are already being used in such delicate procedures as repairing arteries and retinas. It's only a matter of time before they become common procedure in other types of surgery. I've experimented with them myself. That's what I meant—this was state of the art. There's no doubt—in terms of getting in and out, whoever did this was impressively skilled and knowledgeable. Not uniquely so, I should add. Among the top neurosurgeons, I know at least a dozen, including myself, who could have concealed the evidence of the procedure equally well. But that's a superficial test of excellence. The ultimate criterion is whether the surgeon accomplished his purpose, and because we're not aware of *why* the surgery was required, I can't fully judge the quality of the work."

"But"—Akira hesitated—"could the surgery explain . . . ?"

"Your dilemma? Perhaps," Santizo said. "And then again maybe not. What was the term you used? The opposite of *déjà vu?*"

"*Jamais vu,*" Savage said.

"Yes. Something you *think* you've seen, but you've *never* seen. I'm not familiar with the concept. But I enjoy being educated. I'll remember the phrase. You realize"—Santizo set down his teacup—"that if it weren't for these X rays, I'd dismiss you as cranks."

"I admit what I told you sounds bizarre," Savage said. "But we had to take the risk that you wouldn't believe us. Like you, we're pragmatists. It's our business to deal with facts. *Physical* problems. How to get our principal safely to his or her destination. How to anticipate an assassin's bullet. How to avoid an intercepting car. But suddenly the physical facts don't match reality. Or our perception of it. We're so confused, we're not just nervous—and it's normal for us to be nervous. We're scared."

"That's obvious," Santizo said. "I see it in your eyes. So let me be honest. My schedule's so crowded the only reason I agreed to see you was that my former classmate asked me. He thought I'd be intrigued. He was right. I am."

Santizo glanced at his watch. "A half hour till I'm due for my racquetball game. After that, I need to make rounds. Meet me back here in"—he calculated—"two and a half hours. I'll try to arrange for a colleague to join us. Meanwhile, I want you to go to Radiology." He picked up his phone.

"More X rays? To make sure the first sets are accurate?" Savage asked.

"No. I'm ordering magnetic resonance images."

3

A frail-looking man with a salt-and-pepper beard, wearing a sportcoat slightly too large for him, was sitting across from Santizo when they returned. "This is Dr. Weinberg," Santizo said.

They all shook hands.

"Dr. Weinberg is a psychiatrist," Santizo said.

"Oh?" Savage's back became rigid against his chair.

"Does that trouble you?" Weinberg asked pleasantly.

"No, of course not," Akira said. "We have a problem. We're eager to solve it."

"By whatever means necessary," Savage said.

"Excellent." Weinberg pulled a notebook and a pen from his sportcoat. "You don't mind?"

Savage felt ill at ease. He tried never to have his conversations documented but was forced to say, "Make all the notes you want."

"Good." Weinberg scrawled several words. From Savage's perspective, they looked like the time and date.

"Your MRI scans are being sent up to me," Santizo said. "I thought, while we wait, Dr. Weinberg could ask you some questions."

Savage gestured for Weinberg to start.

"*Jamais vu.* The term is your invention, I'm told."

"That's right. It was all I could think of to describe my confusion."

"Please elaborate."

Savage did. On occasion, Akira added a detail. Rachel listened intently.

Weinberg scribbled. "So to summarize. You both thought you saw each other die? You failed to find the hotel where the deaths supposedly occurred? And you can't find the hospital where you were treated or the physician in charge of your case?''

"Correct," Savage said.

"And the original traumatizing events took place six months ago."

"Yes," Akira said.

Weinberg sighed. "For the moment . . ." He set down his pen. "I'm treating your dilemma as hypothetical."

"Treat it any way you want," Savage said.

"My statement was not antagonistic."

"I didn't say it was."

"I'll explain." Weinberg leaned back in his chair. "As a rule, my patients are referred to me. I'm given corroborating documents. Case histories. If necessary, I can interview their families, their employers. But in this instance, I really know nothing about you. I have only your word about your unusual—to put it mildly—background. No way to confirm what you claim. No reason to believe you. For all I'm aware, you're pathological liars desperate for attention or even reporters testing the gullibility of what the public calls 'shrinks.' ''

Santizo's eyes glinted. "Max, I told you their story—and their *X rays*—intrigue me. Give us a theory."

"As an exercise in logic," Weinberg said. "Purely for the sake of discussion."

"Hey, what else?" Santizo said.

Weinberg sighed again, then spread his hands. "The most likely explanation is that you both experienced, you're suffering from, a mutual delusion caused by the nearly fatal beatings you received."

"How? The X rays show we weren't beaten," Savage said.

"I disagree. What the X rays show is that your arms, legs, and ribs weren't broken, that your skulls weren't fractured as you believed. That doesn't mean you weren't beaten. I'll reconstruct what conceivably happened. You both were assigned to protect a man."

"Yes."

"He went to a conference at a rural hotel. And while he

was there, he was killed. In a graphically brutal manner. With a sword that severed his torso.''

Akira nodded.

''In the process of defending him, the two of you were beaten to the point of unconsciousness,'' Weinberg said. ''On the verge of passing out, you each were tricked by your failing vision into thinking mistakenly that the other was killed. Inasmuch as neither of you died, *something* caused the hallucination, and the combination of pain and disorientation is a logical explanation.''

''But why would they both have the same hallucination?'' Rachel asked.

''Guilt.''

''I don't follow.'' Savage frowned.

''If I understand correctly, your profession means more to you than just a job. Obviously your *identity* is based on protecting, on saving lives. It's a moral commitment. In that respect, you're comparable to devoted physicians.''

''True,'' Akira said.

''But *un*like physicians, who inevitably lose patients and are consequently forced to put a shell around their emotions, I gather that both of you have had remarkable success. You've never lost a client. Your success rate has been an impressive one hundred percent.''

''Except for . . .''

''The events in the rural hotel six months ago,'' Weinberg said. ''For the first—the *only*—time, you lost a client. A major threat to your identity. With no experience in dealing with failure, you weren't prepared for the shock. A shock that was reinforced by the vividly gruesome manner of your client's death. The natural reaction is guilt. Because you survived and your client didn't. Because your client's safety meant everything to you, to the point where you'd have sacrificed yourself to save him. But it didn't turn out that way. *He* died. *You're* still alive. So your guilt becomes unendurable. Your subconscious struggles to compensate. It seizes on your murky impression that your fellow bodyguard died as well. It insists, it demands, that your client couldn't possibly have been defended if both he and your counterpart were killed and *you*, too, nearly died in your heroic but demonstrably futile effort to fulfill your vocation. Given your similar personalities, your mutual hallucinations are understandable, even predictable.''

"Then why can't we find the hotel?" Savage asked.

"Because deep in your mind you're struggling to deny that your failure ever took place. What better way than to convince yourselves that the hotel, where your failure occurred, doesn't exist? Or the doctor who treated you? Or the hospital where you recovered? They do exist, at least if your account is authentic. But they don't exist where your urge for denial compels you to search."

Savage and Akira glanced at each other. As one, they shook their heads.

"Why"—Akira sounded skeptical—"did we both know where the hotel ought to be? And the doctor? And the hospital?"

"That's the easiest to explain. You reinforced each other. What one of you said, the other grasped at. To perpetuate the delusion and relieve your guilt."

"No," Savage said.

Weinberg shrugged. "I told you, this was all hypothetical."

"Why," Akira asked, "if our arms and legs weren't broken, were we put in casts? Why did we endure the agony of rebuilding our muscles for so many terrible months?"

"Casts?" Weinberg asked. "Or were they immobilizers required to help repair ligaments detached from your arms and legs? Were the casts on your chests actually thick, tightly wound tape that protected bruised—but not broken—ribs? And possibly your bandaged skulls indeed had fractures, hairlines that healed so perfectly an X ray wouldn't detect them. You admit you were given Demerol. It affects one's sense of reality."

"Certainly," Rachel said. "And of course I wasn't there. I didn't experience their pain. I grant I'm fond of these two men. We've been through a lot together. But I'm not a fool, and of the three of us, I'm the one with the best claim to be objective. My friends have *not* been reinforcing each other's delusions."

"Well, of course you've heard of the Stockholm principle," Weinberg said. "People under stress tend to identify with those they depend on for their safety."

"And of course you've heard of the ostrich principle," Rachel said. "A psychiatrist who puts his head in the sand because he can't acknowledge a problem he's never heard of before."

Weinberg leaned forward, scowled, and abruptly laughed.

"You were right," he told Santizo. "This *is* amusing."

"You're sublimating, Max. Admit it. She made you angry."

"Only hypothetically."

Now Santizo laughed. "Hey, of course. Let's write a hypothetical article. About the phenomenon of being hypothetically angry."

"What's going on?" Savage asked.

Santizo stopped laughing. "A test. To determine if you were cranks. I had no choice. And Max is wonderful. A gifted man with a marvelous mind and a talent for acting."

"I wasn't acting," Weinberg said. "What I've heard is so bewildering I want to hear more."

Someone knocked on the door.

Santizo pivoted. "Come."

A secretary, who'd brought in the teacups, now brought a large brown folder.

"The MRIs." Santizo stood.

Two minutes later, he turned from the films. "Thanks, Max. I'll take it from here."

"You're sure?"

"Yes. I owe you a dinner." Santizo faced the MRIs. "But the problem's back to me. Because psychiatry won't explain *this*."

4

Savage stood next to Akira and Rachel, studying the dusky films. Each had twelve images, arranged in four rows and three columns. They made little sense to him, harder to read than the earlier single-image X rays.

"Beautiful," Santizo said. "I couldn't ask for clearer pictures."

"You could have fooled *me*," Akira said. "They look like ink blots."

Santizo chuckled. "I can see where you'd get that impression." He studied the films again. "That's why, to help you understand, I have to begin with some basics, though I'm afraid the basics will still sound technical. . . . An MRI scan is an advanced technique of photography, based on magnetic resonance, that allows us to see past your skull and into your brain. It used to be that the only way we could get pictures of your brain was with a CAT scan. But a CAT scan isn't detailed enough, whereas *these* are the next best thing to actually opening up your skull and having a look. We take so many pictures from so many different angles, the combined result provides the illusion of 3-D."

"But what have you learned?" Akira asked.

"Just bear with me a little longer," Santizo said. "The brain has many parts." He gestured toward portions of the MRIs. "The right hemisphere. The left hemisphere. Paradoxically the right hemisphere controls the left side of the body, and vice versa. Our ability to think spatially comes from the right hemisphere, our verbal skills from the left. The hemispheres are divided into parts. The frontal lobe. The parietal lobe. The occipital lobe. The temporal lobe. And these in turn contain numerous subparts. The visual cortex. The olfactory tract. The somatic sensory area. The pituitary gland. Et cetera. What makes this awesomely complex organ work is the presence of billions of interconnecting nerves that transmit energy and information. These nerves are called neurons. They're analogous to electrical wires and telephone cables, but that's a simplification. No analogy can truly describe them. . . . By the way, have you ever had epilepsy?"

The question was so unexpected that Savage blinked.

"Epilepsy? No. Why? *What makes you ask?*"

"I'm trying to account for something." Santizo pointed toward a dark speck on a light portion of one of the images. The speck was on the left, near the middle. "This is a view of your brain from the rear. That speck is in your mesial temporal lobe—the amygdala hippocampal area. It's in line with the plug of bone that was taken out and then replaced in your skull."

Savage felt as if he'd swallowed ice. "Speck? Jesus, what—?"

"A lesion. That's why I asked about epilepsy. An abnormality in this area sometimes causes that condition."

"You're telling me something's growing in my brain?"

"No." Santizo turned to Akira, then pointed toward another film. "There's an identical speck in the same area of *your* brain. The coincidence leads me to conclude that whatever it is, it's not a growth."

"What *is* it then?" Akira asked.

"An educated guess? Scar tissue. From whatever was done to your brain."

5

Savage listened in shock as Santizo returned to his desk.

"More basics," Santizo said. "First rule. Eliminate the obvious. The purpose for the operation performed on each of you was *not* to excise a tumor. That type of surgery requires a major invasion of the brain. Hence a major portion of the skull would have to be removed.''

"But not," Rachel said, "a five-millimeter plug of bone."

"Correct. The only reason to create so small an access to the brain would be"—Santizo debated—"to allow an electrode to be inserted."

"*Why?*" Savage had trouble breathing.

"Assuming familiar but serious circumstances? *Many* reasons. I mentioned epilepsy. An electrode inserted into the brain can measure electrical impulses from various clusters of neurons. In an epileptic, different levels of the brain transmit normal and *non*normal current. If we can determine the source of the nonnormal current, we can operate in a specific location to try to correct the abnormality.''

"But we're not epileptics," Savage said.

"I was offering an example," Santizo said. "I'll give you another. A patient with impairments of sight or hearing or smell—impairments due to the brain and not external receptors—can sometimes have their impairments corrected if *internal* receptors, those in the brain, are stimulated by electrodes.''

"But we can see and hear and smell," Akira said.

"And yet you think you saw each other die. You can't find a hotel where you were beaten. Or a hospital where you were treated. Or a doctor who supervised your case. Someone has interfered with your brain functions. Specifically your ability to . . .''

"Remember," Savage said.

"Or more interesting, has someone caused you to remember what never happened? *Jamais vu*. The phrase you invented is fascinating.''

"To remember what never happened? I didn't mean it literally. I never believed . . .''

"I can take you down to Pathology," Santizo said. "I can dissect a corpse's brain and show you each component. I can tell you why you see and hear, why you taste, touch, and smell, why you feel pain—though the brain itself *cannot* feel pain. But what I can't do is show you a thought. And I certainly can't find a specific site in your brain that enables you to remember. I've been doing research on memory for the past ten years, and the more I learn, the more I'm baffled. . . . Describe what happens when you remember a past event."

Savage and Akira hesitated.

Rachel gestured. "Well, it's sort of like seeing a movie inside my head."

"That's how most people describe it. We experience an event, and it seems as though our brain works like a camera, retaining a series of images of that event. The more we experience, the more films we store in our brain. When circumstances require, when we need to review the past to understand the present, we select an appropriate reel and view it on a mental screen. Of course, we take for granted that the films are permanent records, as immutable as a movie."

Rachel nodded.

"But a movie *isn't* permanent. It cracks. It discolors. Scenes can be eliminated. What's more, we're explaining memory by means of analogy. There *aren't* films in our brain. There *isn't* a screen. We merely imagine there are. And memory becomes even harder to explain when we pass from concrete events to learned abstractions. When I think of the mathematical principle of pi, I don't see a film in my head. I somehow, intuitively, understand what pi signifies. And when I think of an abstract word such as 'honor,' I don't see a film. I just *know* what 'honor' means. Why am I able to recall and understand these abstractions?"

"Do you have an answer?" Savage's chest ached.

"The prevailing theory is that memories are somehow encoded throughout the brain in the neurons. These billions of nerves—the theory goes—not only transmit electricity and information but also retain the information they transmit. The analogy of a computer is frequently used to illustrate the process, but again, as with the illusion that we have a movie screen in our heads, an analogy is not an explanation. Our memory system is infinitely more complex than any computer. For one thing, the neurons seem capable of transferring information from one network to another, thus protecting certain memories if a portion of the brain is damaged. For another, there are two types of memory—short term and long term—and their relationship is paradoxical. 'Short term' refers to temporary memories of recently acquired but unimportant information. The telephone number of my dentist, for example. If I need to make an appointment, I look up the number, remember it long enough to call his office, and immediately forget it until the next time I need an appointment and repeat the process. 'Long term' refers to lasting memories of necessary information: the telephone number for my home. What physical mechanism causes my dentist's number to be easily forgotten but not my own? And why, in certain types of amnesia, is a patient unable to remember any recent event, whether trivial or important, while at the same time he can recall in vivid detail minor long-forgotten events from forty years ago? No one understands the process.''

''What do *you* believe?'' Akira asked.

''A musical by Lerner and Loewe.''

''I don't . . .''

''*Gigi*. Maurice Chevalier and Hermione Gingold sing a wonderful song, 'I Remember It Well.' Their characters are former lovers recalling when they met. 'We went *here*.' 'No, we went *there*.' 'You wore *this* dress.' 'No, I wore *that*.' 'Ah, yes, I remember it well.' But they *don't*. Sure, the point of the song is that old age has made them forget. The trouble is, I'm not sure the rest of us don't forget also. A *lot* of specifics. And sooner than we realize. Dr. Weinberg and I have a sentimental tradition. Every Saturday night, when Max and I aren't on call, we and our wives see a movie and then go to dinner. After the stress of the week, we look forward to the distraction. Yesterday, Max fondly remembered a film the four of us had seen together. 'But Max,' I said, 'I saw that movie on cable television, not in a theater.' 'No,' Max insisted, 'the four of us saw it downtown.' 'No,' I told him, 'I was at a conference that weekend. You, your wife, and mine went to see the film without me.' We questioned our wives, who didn't remember the circumstances. We still don't know the truth.''

"Of course," Savage said. "You just explained short-term memory doesn't last."

"But where does short term end and *long* term begin? And how can we be sure that long-term memory truly endures? The basic issue is the limitation of consciousness. We're capable of knowing we remember only *if* we remember. We can't be aware of something we've forgotten. . . . Describe the future."

"I can't. The future doesn't exist," Savage said.

"No more than the past, though memory gives us the illusion the past does exist—in our minds. It's my opinion that our memories don't remain permanent after they're encoded. I believe our memories are constantly changing, details being altered, added, and subtracted. In effect, we each create a version of the past. The discrepancies are usually insignificant. After all, what difference does it make if Max and I saw that movie together or separately? But on occasion, the discrepancies are critical. Max once had a neurotic female patient who as a child had repeatedly been abused by her father. She'd sublimated her nightmarish memories and imagined an idyllic youth with a gentle, loving father. To cure her neuroses, Max had to teach her to discard her false memory and recognize the horrors she'd experienced."

"False memory," Savage said. "*Jamais vu*. But *our* false memory isn't caused by psychological problems. Our brain scans suggest someone surgically altered our ability to remember. Is that possible?"

"If you mean, would *I* be able to do it, the answer is no, and I'm not aware of any other neurosurgeon who could do it, either. But is it *possible*? Yes. Theoretically. Though even if I *knew* how to do it, I wouldn't. It's called psychosurgery. It alters your personality, and except for a few procedures— an excision of brain tissue to prevent an epileptic from having seizures, or a lobotomy to stop self-destructive impulses—it isn't ethical."

"*But how, in theory, would you do it?*" Rachel asked.

Santizo looked reluctant.

"*Please.*"

"I pride myself on being curious, but sometimes, against my nature, I've refused to investigate intriguing cerebral phenomena. When necessary, I've inserted electrodes into the brains of my patients. I've asked them to describe what they sensed."

"Wait," Akira said. "How could they describe the effects if their brains were exposed? They'd be unconscious."

"Ah," Santizo said. "I take too much for granted. I skip too many steps. I'm too used to dealing with fellow neurosurgeons. Obviously you think exposing the brain is the same as exposing the heart. I'll emphasize a former remark. The brain—our sense receptor—does not *itself* have a sense receptor. It doesn't feel pain. Using a local anesthetic to prevent the skull from transmitting pain, I can remove a portion of bone and expose the great mystery. Inserting an electrode into the brain, I can make the patient smell oranges that don't exist. I can make the patient hear music from his childhood. I can make him taste apples. I can make him have an orgasm. I can manipulate his sense receptors until he's convinced he's on a sailboat, the sun on his face, the wind in his hair, hearing waves crash, skirting Australia's Great Barrier Reef—a vacation he experienced years before."

"But would he remember the illusions you caused?" Rachel asked.

"Of course. Just as he'd remember the true vivid event, the operation."

"So that explains what happened," Savage said.

"To you and your friend? Not at all," Santizo said. "What I've just described is an activation of the patient's memory by means of an electronic stimulation to various neurons. But *you* have memories of events that apparently . . . ."

"Never happened," Akira said. "So why do we remember them?"

"I told you, it's only a theory," Santizo said. "But if I expose the left temporal lobe of your brain . . . and if I stimulate your neurons with electrodes . . . if I describe in detail what you're supposed to remember, perhaps show you films or even have actors dramatize the fictional events . . . if I administer amphetamines to encourage the learning process . . . and when I'm finished, if I use the electrode to scar selected neurons, to impair your memory of the operation . . . you'll remember what never happened and forget what *did* happen.''

''We've been *brainwashed*?''

''No,'' Santizo said. '' 'Brainwashed' is a crude expression that originated during the Korean War and is used to describe the process by which a prisoner can be forced to surrender deeply held political convictions. The methodology originated in the USSR, based upon Pavlov's theories of stimulus and response. Subject a prisoner to relentless pain, break his spirit, then offer him a reward if he'll agree to denounce the country he loves. Well, as we know, a few soldiers did succumb. The miracle is that more did not. Especially when psychosuggestive drugs are added to Pavlov's theory of conditioning. But if you've seen newsreels from the fifties, you know that prisoners who were conditioned always *looked* as if they'd been conditioned. Gaunt features. Shaky hands. Glazed eyes. Their confession of war crimes wasn't convincing. You two show none of those symptoms. You're frightened, yes. But you're functional. What's more, no attitudinal changes seem to have occurred. Your identity remains intact. You're still determined to protect. No, you haven't been conditioned. Your problem isn't directed toward the future. It's not anything you might have been programmed to do. It's what happened to you in the *past*. Or what *didn't* happen. And what *really* happened that you don't recall.''

''Then why was this done to us?'' Savage asked.

''Why? The only answer I can suggest—''

The phone rang. Santizo picked it up. ''Hello?'' He suddenly listened intensely, his face becoming more grave. ''I'll be there at once.''

He set down the phone. ''An emergency. I'm due in OR right away.'' Standing, he turned toward a wall of bookshelves. ''Here. Some standard texts. Young's *Programs of the Brain*, Baddeley's *The Psychology of Memory*, Horn's *Memory, Imprinting, and the Brain*. Study them. Call my secretary tomorrow. She'll arrange a time for us to meet again. I really have to go.''

As Santizo hurried toward the door, Akira surged from his chair. "But you started to tell us why you thought—"

"You were given false memories?" Santizo pivoted. "No. I can't imagine. What I meant to say was the only person who'd know is whoever performed the procedure."

6

They managed to get a room in a hotel near the hospital. The setting sun was obscured by smog. After ordering room service—fish and rice for Akira, steak and fries for Savage and Rachel—they each took a book and read in silence.

When their food arrived, they used the distraction of what Savage called "refueling" to talk.

"The medical terms are difficult for me to interpret," Akira said. "My knowledge of English, I'm embarrassed to confess, has limitations."

"No," Rachel said, "your English is perfect. For what it's worth, these medical terms might as well be Japanese to me."

"I appreciate the compliment. You're very gracious. *Arigato*," Akira said.

"That means . . . ?"

"Thank you."

"And what should I say in return? What's the equivalent of . . . ?"

" 'You're welcome'? I'll make it simple. *Domo arigato*. A rough translation—'thank *you* very much.' "

"Exactly," Rachel said. *"Domo arigato."*

Akira smiled, despite his melancholy eyes.

"Well," Savage said, "while the two of you are having a cultural exchange—"

"Don't get grumpy," Rachel told him.

Savage studied her, *admired* her, and couldn't help smiling. "I guess that's how I sound. But I *think* I understand a part of this book, and it scares me."

Rachel and Akira came to attention.

"Memory's more complicated than I realized. Not just that no one's really sure how the neurons in our brain store information. But what about the implication of what it *means* to be able to remember? *That's* what scares me." Savage's head throbbed. "We think of memory as a mental record of the past. The trouble is the past, by definition, doesn't exist. It's a phantom of what used to be the present. And it isn't just what happened a year ago, last month, or yesterday. It's twenty minutes ago. It's an *instant* ago. What I'm saying is already in the past, in our memories."

Rachel and Akira waited.

"This book has a theory that when we see an apple fall from a tree, when we hear it land, when we pick it up, smell it, and taste it, we're not experiencing those sensations simultaneously with the events. There's a time lag—let's say a millionth of a second—before the sense impulses reach the brain. By the time we register the taste of the apple, what we think is the present is actually the past. That lag would explain *déjà vu*. We enter a room and feel eerily convinced we've been there before, though we haven't. Why? Because of the millionth of a second it takes the brain to receive a transmission from the eyes and tell us what we're seeing. If the two hemispheres of the brain are temporarily out of sync, one side of the brain receives the transmission slightly before the other. We see the room *twice*. We think the sensation happened before *because it did*. Not in the distant past, however. Instead, a fraction of an instant before, one side of the brain received what the other side later received."

"But our problem isn't *déjà vu*—it's *jamais vu*," Akira said. "Why are you disturbed by what you just read?"

"Because I can't be sure of the present, let alone the past. Because there is no present, at least as far as my brain's concerned. Everything it tells me is a delayed reaction."

"That may be true," Rachel said. "But for practical purposes, even with the time lag, what we perceive might as well be the present. You've got a big enough problem without exaggerating it.''

"*Am* I exaggerating? I'm scared because I thought I was struggling with false memories someone implanted in my brain six months ago. But *was* it six months ago? How do I know the operation didn't happen much more recently? How can I be sure of what occurred yesterday or even this morning?" Savage turned to Rachel. "In France, when you learned about our pseudonyms and the cover stories we had to invent, you said it seemed that everything about us was a lie. In a way I never imagined, maybe you're right. How many false memories do I have? How do I know who I am? How can I be sure that you and Akira are what you seem? Suppose you're actors hired to trick me and reinforce my delusions.''

"But obviously we're not," Akira said. "We've been through too much together. Rachel's rescue. The escape in the helicopter. The ferry out of Greece. The vans that tried to intercept us in France.''

"My point is maybe *none* of it happened. My false memories might have begun *today*. My entire background—everything about me—might be a lie I'm not aware of! Did I ever meet Rachel's sister? *Is Graham really dead?*''

"Keep thinking like that," Akira said, "and you'll go crazy.''

"Right," Savage said. "That's what I mean—I'm scared. I feel like I'm seeing through a haze, like the floor's unsteady, like I'm in an elevator that's falling. Total disorientation. I've based my identity on protecting people. But how can I protect *myself* from my *mind*?''

Rachel put an arm around him. "You've got to believe we're not actors. We're all you have. Trust us.''

"Trust you? I don't even trust myself.''

7

That night, as Savage slept fitfully, assaulted by nightmares, he woke abruptly from a hand that caressed his cheek. Startled, he grabbed the hand and lunged upright on the sofa, prepared to defend himself.

He restrained his impulse. In the soft light from a lamp in a corner, he saw Rachel's worried face beside him. She was kneeling.

"What?" Savage scanned the room. "Where's Akira?"

"In the hallway. I asked him to leave us alone."

"Why would—?"

"Because I asked him," she repeated, her blond hair silhouetted by the dim light in the corner.

"No, why did you ask him to leave?"

"Because I need to be with you."

"That still doesn't answer my—"

"Hush." Rachel touched his lips. "You think too much. You ask too many questions."

"It's *impossible* to ask too many questions."

"But sometimes it's wiser not to ask any."

Savage smelled her perfume. "I can't imagine—"

"Yes," she said, "I know you can't. You've been a protector so long you're automatically suspicious. Questions are precautions. Answers are safety. And safety's your absolute value." She touched his cheek. "It's been too many years since I told this to anyone."

"Told?"

"I love you."

Savage squirmed and brushed her hand away. "Don't be absurd."

"That's what Kierkegaard says in *Fear and Trembling*. 'Abraham believed in God by virtue of the absurd.' Faith is absurd. *So is love*. Because neither faith nor love makes sense. God might not exist and the person you love might betray you.''

"Say what you mean."

"Since you entered my bedroom on Mykonos, you've treated me as if I meant everything to you. It's a rare experience. I can't help loving you, though I realize we're together only because you were hired to protect me. I ought to be smarter. I *shouldn't* love you. But I do. . . . By virtue of the absurd."

"Pay attention to what Weinberg said. People under stress tend to identify with those they depend on for their safety."

"Yes, I depend on you," Rachel said. "And I identify with you. But more than anything, I want to make love with you."

"No, I—"

"Yes."

"But—"

"Damn it, hold still."

As she kissed him, she released his belt.

And to Savage's surprise, he let her.

8

In his dream, he made love to Rachel's sister, and the dream was identical to the most famous scene in Joyce Stone's most famous movie, *Cat's Claw*. The actress had portrayed a wealthy American on the French Riviera. A charismatic jewel thief had tried persistently to seduce her. Eventually, to gain his trust and obtain information, *she'd* seduced *him*. The thief had been confident he had sufficient control not to fall in love with her. He was wrong, and in the end she stole his soul.

Joyce Stone and *Rachel* Stone. In Savage's dream, one sister merged with the other. He made love not only to a legendary movie star but to a client he'd pledged himself to protect. Even as he stroked her hard-nippled breasts, her smooth, lithe arms and slender, supple stomach, reaching lower, grazing her silken pubic hair, he told himself this was wrong, unprofessional, twisted, almost incestuous. In all his years of being a protector, he'd never succumbed to the temptations his female clients had on occasion forced upon him. Graham had insisted—Never allow yourself to be sexually involved with a client. It destroys your objectivity. It'll make you careless. It's liable to get her killed.

But as Savage dreamed, as he reexperienced entering Rachel's exquisite body, as he lengthened and thrust, he couldn't stop himself. Guilt fought with need. Confusion blurred the rules. Fear required reassurance. When he came and Rachel moaned, rising against him, grasping his hair, repeating, "I love you," Savage felt empty, self-betrayed, racked by a bottom-of-the spirit melancholy. No! he wanted to scream. I shouldn't have! I had an obligation to resist! *Why wasn't I stronger?*

At once his dream changed. His ejaculation exploded from him with the startling crack of a Colt .45, and he wakened, scrambling to stand, a child who sensed that something had been wrong in the house for days, who'd been sleeping in nervous turmoil, who stumbled from his room and lurched downstairs to his father's study but not before his mother rushed to intervene, too late to prevent his apprehensive gaze from focusing through the open door. The blood. There'd been so much blood. And his father's body on the study's hardwood floor—a towel wrapped around the left side of his head, the *exit* wound side to minimize the blood, though the thrust of the bullet had been too powerful for the towel to do its work—had looked like an obscene clump of rags.

Tears streaming down his cheeks, Savage had wailed, his language shocking from someone so young, "You bastard, you promised you'd never go away again. God damn you."

And his mother had slapped his face.

9

For a moment, Savage didn't understand why he wasn't outside his father's study, peering toward the horror. For another moment, he expected to see the elegant suite in the French Riviera hotel where Joyce Stone had seduced the jewel thief. In confusion, what he saw instead, blinking, was Akira in a chair in a corner of the Philadelphia hotel suite, setting down a magazine, rising, glancing toward the locked door, frowning, approaching.

"Your sleep wasn't restful. I'm sorry."

Savage wiped his eyes. "And did you think if Rachel screwed me, I *would* have a restful sleep?"

"I thought nothing." Akira hunkered beside him. "She asked me to watch the hallway. She insisted she needed a private conversation."

"Oh, it was private, all right."

"I don't want details."

"Why *would* you? Since she already told you."

"She told me nothing. Except to ask me to return from the hallway. After that, she went to her bedroom. As far as I know, she's asleep."

"Which is more than *I* am."

"Whatever happened between you is not my concern. Your conduct has been impeccable."

"Yeah, right, yeah, sure."

"Our principal is clearly attracted to you. And if I may say, *you* are attracted to her."

"And what happened tonight is the proof. It's *wrong*."

"Under ordinary circumstances," Akira said. "But these aren't ordinary circumstances. You're being too critical of yourself. You feel threatened and . . ."

"That doesn't excuse my behavior. *You* feel threatened, but you're still in control."

"My culture taught me to hide distressing emotions . . . Let me tell you a story." Akira paused. "My father was a pilot during the Great East Asian War."

Savage was confused by the reference.

"What you call World War II," Akira said. "After my country's surrender, my father returned to his home to discover it no longer existed. The city was Hiroshima. His parents, his wife, and his two children had been destroyed by your country's atomic bomb. For years, he brooded, obsessed by his loss. His only solace was the satisfaction he took in helping Japan rebuild itself. A skilled mechanic, he converted warplanes for civilian use and managed to achieve financial success. Eventually he remarried. I was the only product of their union, for his second wife—my mother—had been near Hiroshima when the bomb went off. Her left arm was scarred by radiation burns, and the delayed effects of that radiation caused her to die from bone cancer. My father's grief was almost more than he could bear. He surmounted it only by devoting himself to *me*."

Akira closed his eyes a moment. "Japan has been ravaged so often by typhoons, tidal waves, and earthquakes that fatalism is a national mood and security a national obsession. My father told me that if we couldn't control the disasters that the world inflicted upon us, we *could* control the discipline and dignity with which we faced those disasters. Thus he sent me to the most demanding *sensei* at the most demanding *dojo* he could find. I learned judo, jujitsu, aikido, various Japanese forms of karate, and of course the way of the sword. In time, I decided to use my skills and respond to a hostile universe by becoming a protector, though I've come to realize that even discipline and dignity are no defense against fate, that nothing ultimately can protect us. My father was fatally injured by a car while he walked across a street."

"I'm sorry," Savage said. "Your family suffered more than its share. I'm beginning to understand why you seldom smile and even then your eyes remain sad."

"My *sensei* used to call me 'the man with no joy.' " Akira shrugged. "But my family's hardships are only part of the reason I seldom smile. One day I'll explain. For *now*, my purpose in allowing you a glimpse of my private self is I want you to know that like you I feel threatened. What's been done to our memories makes me question everything I am. Maybe none of what I've told you is true. And that possibility not only threatens me but makes me angry. Have I grieved for a father, a mother, and ancestors that never existed? I must find out."

"Yes," Savage said, "I want to know how much of what made me what I am didn't happen."

"Suppose that isn't possible."

"It has to be."

"But how do—?"

"Tomorrow we leave for Baltimore. There's someone I have to see. I can't explain. Don't make me talk about it."

"But you did say, '*We* leave for Baltimore.' " Rachel's voice was unexpected. "Does that mean you've decided to trust us again?"

Savage turned toward where she stood in the open bedroom door. She wore a blue nightshirt that conformed to her breasts. His body retained the sensation of having made love to her. Though she looked as if her sleep had been as troubled as Savage's, she was beautiful.

"Let's put it this way," Savage said. "I *want* to trust you."

10

Baltimore was southwest of Philadelphia: a ninety-minute urgent drive. When Savage stopped the Taurus in front of a two-story house in a well-maintained subdivision on the city's outskirts, he stared at the sculpted evergreen bushes surrounding the meticulously landscaped property and finally shut off the engine. Despite the chill of October, his brow exuded sweat.

"Who lives here?" Rachel asked.

"That's a damned good question," Savage said. He stepped from the car and shuddered.

"Do you need any help?" Akira reached for his door.

"No." Savage gestured firmly. "I have to find out by myself."

"Find out?" Rachel asked.

"If I told you, you *would* think I'm crazy. If this works out, I'll wave for you to come in. Whatever the answer, it won't take long."

Savage braced himself and walked up the sidewalk, passing fallow flower beds, reaching the porch, crossing it, his footsteps echoing, approaching the front door.

For an instant, he almost knocked but decided to behave as naturally as possible, to do what he always did. Simply go in.

The hallway—in shadow—smelled musty. Cutting through the must was the stomach-growling aroma of pot roast flavored with garlic and wine. To Savage's right, a living room had too much furniture, all of it covered with plastic sheets, protection from the ravaging claws of several aggressive cats.

Down the hall, from the kitchen, Savage heard melodramatic actors intoning TV-soap-opera dialogue. As well, he heard the unmistakable rhythmic clink and thunk of a wooden spoon against a metal bowl: batter being mixed.

Unlike the shadowy hallway, the kitchen was bright. Savage entered and saw a wrinkled, stoop-shouldered, grayhaired woman staring toward a ten-inch color TV next to a microwave while she stirred the batter.

As Savage approached the butcher-block table where she worked, he grinned. "Surprise, Mom."

She jerked her head in his direction and dropped her spoon. "You . . ."

"I know I don't come to visit as often as I should, but my work keeps me busy. At least I send you money each month.

You've been taking care of the house, I see. It looks wonderful.'' Savage kept grinning.

"What are you doing here?"

"I told you. I haven't come to visit often enough. I'm sorry, Mom. I'll try to do better."

"Answer my question. What are you doing here?"

"I'm not in any trouble if that's what you're thinking. You won't have to hide me and send for a doctor like you did the last time. I just felt like dropping in. To talk about the old days. About Dad." Savage stepped closer to hug her.

She backed away.

"Come on, Mom. Don't be angry. I said I was sorry for—"

"Stay away from me. Who *are* you?"

In that instant, Savage knew that everything he'd feared had come true. A sickening dizziness seized him. His legs felt weak.

He managed to take another step. "Your son."

She screamed.

"No, please, don't—"

Her scream became more intense, fierce, shrill, desperate.

Footsteps thundered up the basement stairs. A husky elderly man, his sleeves rolled up, his forearms sinewy, charged into the kitchen. His hair was white and wispy. He had liver spots on his face. Despite his age, he exuded strength. "Gladys, what's wrong?"

The woman's face had become as pale as the dough she'd been beating. Backed against a counter by the sink, she stopped screaming, had trouble breathing, and pointed at Savage, her bony finger trembling.

"Who the hell are you?" the man growled.

"Frank, he says . . ." The woman gasped. "He opened the door and walked right in. Scared me half to death. Called me . . . He thinks he's our *son*."

The man's cheeks turned red. He spun toward a counter, yanked open a drawer, and pulled out a hammer. "In the first place, buddy, the only son we had died twenty years ago from cystic fibrosis." The man raised the hammer and stalked toward Savage. "In the second place, you've got seven seconds to get your ass out of here before I beat your skull in and call the cops."

Savage held up his hands in surrender. His stomach felt swollen with writhing snakes. He couldn't control his terror. "No, listen. Something terrible has happened. You don't understand. You've got to let me explain."

"Something terrible's happened, all right. You barged in my house and scared my wife. And something *really* terrible's about to happen to you if you don't get the hell out of here."

The woman lunged for a phone on the wall beside the refrigerator.

"Wait!" Savage said.

She pressed three numbers.

"Please! You've got to listen!" Savage said.

"Officer, this is an emergency!"

"Get out!" the man told Savage.

As the man raised the hammer, Savage bumped backward against a doorjamb. He suddenly couldn't move, paralyzed with shock.

With *horror*.

Because the husky elderly man confronting him with the hammer was Savage's father, not as he remembered his father from their last conversation a few hours before his father had shot himself, but as his father would have looked if he'd had the chance to age. Savage recognized the dimple on the man's square jaw, the narrow gap in his bottom row of teeth, the scar across the back of his left hand.

The woman trembled, blurting an address to the phone.

"No!" Savage said. "You're my parents! *I'm your son!*"

"You're nuts is what you are!" the man said. "Maybe this hammer across your head will—"

"Why don't you remember me?"

Savage ducked from the blur of the hammer. With a hissing rush, it walloped against the doorjamb. The bang was so loud, so close, it made his ears ring.

"Stop!"

The man swung again.

Savage stumbled in retreat down the hall. He passed the study where his father had shot himself. A cat sprang from nowhere and clawed up Savage's leg.

"No!" The man kept coming, swinging the hammer.

"If you're not my father, who *are* you?" Savage reached behind him, frantic to open the outside door. The cat kept clawing his leg. Savage shook his leg and thrust the cat away. "For God's sake, who am *I*?"

He spun, rushing from the house, racing across the porch, almost losing his balance, leaping down the steps.

At the curb, staring from the Taurus, Akira and Rachel looked startled.

Savage scrambled inside.

"You bastard!" The man kept chasing him, abruptly throwing the hammer. It whacked against the car door.

Savage stomped the car's accelerator. Tires screeching, the Taurus sped away. In the distance, a siren wailed.

"What *happened*?" Akira asked.

"I just saw a dead man." Savage reached toward his throat, massaging it, sounding hoarse as if he'd been strangled.

"You're not making sense," Rachel said

"That's the point. *Nothing* makes sense. Jesus help me. What did they do to us?"

11

"I imagined it might be true, but I never believed it." Savage drove with fury, passing every car he could, ignoring billboards that cluttered the wooded countryside. "A logical extension of *jamais vu*. A terrifying possibility. So I had to convince myself that my fears were only that—fears, not reality. I had to prove that all my false memories were restricted to the Medford Gap Mountain Retreat and the Harrisburg hospital. But now? Damn it, that man and woman *are* my mother and father. I was *raised* in that house. I saw my mother a *year* ago. She looked exactly the same as that woman. And my father, if he'd lived, would have looked exactly like that man!''

Rachel and Akira stayed silent.

"You don't believe me?'' Savage asked. "You think I picked a house at random and simply walked in?''

"No,'' Akira said. "I believe you. It's just that . . .''

"What? You know we saw each other die. You have to believe the rest of it.''

"I think what Akira means,'' Rachel said, "is that he doesn't *want* to believe you. What you said last night . . . I assumed you were overtired, under too much stress. I finally understand. No—more than that—I *feel*. If your memories *have* been completely reconstructed, you don't have anything to depend on. Everything you're sure of is called into doubt.''

"That's why we're going to Little Creek, Virginia,'' Savage said. "To find out what *else* I can't be sure of.''

The woodland dwindled, giving way to marshes, then beaches.

At the southern lip of the mouth to Chesapeake Bay, Savage turned west from Route 60 and two miles later reached the Little Creek Naval Amphibious Base.

"My God, it's huge,'' Rachel said.

From beyond the base's perimeter, they saw clusters of administration buildings and living quarters, an eighteen-hole golf course, twenty tennis courts, two picnic areas, an indoor recreation center, a marina, an outdoor pool, and a lake with canoes and paddleboats. The impression of the base's size was reinforced by the swarm of personnel and the thirty-two ships in the harbor.

"How many sailors are stationed here?'' Rachel asked, amazed.

"Nine thousand. Three thousand dependents live here as well,'' Savage said. "But 'sailors' is too broad a term. Most of them belong to traditional units. A few, though, are part of special operations. This is the eastern seaboard training area for the Navy SEALs."

He scanned the base with pride. "It's just the way I remember it." His voice had a tremor of fear. "I rushed to get here. Now I don't want to . . ."

He forced himself to step out of the car and approach the guards at the gate. The sun was low in the sky. His heart pounded.

"Yes, sir?" A guard stood rigidly.

"I'd like to see Captain James MacIntosh."

"What reason, sir?"

"We're friends. I haven't seen him in several years. I happened to be in the area. I thought I'd say hello."

The guard squinted.

"I don't want to enter the base," Savage said. "I won't breach security. Tell him I'm here. If he doesn't want to see me, fine."

"What unit, sir?"

Savage's pulse quickened. "He *is* still stationed here?"

"I'm not able to tell you that, sir, unless I know his unit."

"The SEAL training team."

Again the guard squinted. "Just a moment, sir." He entered a building beside the gate. Through an open door, Savage saw him pick up a phone. A minute later, the sentry returned. "Sir, Captain MacIntosh left the base. He's got a twenty-four-hour pass."

"Did they tell you where he went?"

The guard stood more rigidly. "No, sir."

"Of course not. Thanks anyhow. I'll try again tomorrow." Despondent, Savage walked back to the car, explaining to Akira and Rachel.

"I'm in no mood to wait. I think I know where to find him." Brooding, Savage drove from the base, heading toward Virginia Beach.

12

The Ship-to-Shore Tavern was a block from the sea. Savage smelled salt in the air and heard sea gulls over the beach. At once he smelled cigarette smoke and heard Elvis's version of "Johnny B. Goode" as he left the sunset-tinted street and entered the murky bar with Rachel and Akira.

When his eyes adjusted, Savage saw tables crowded with young, trim men looking unaccustomed to civilian clothes, talking and drinking energetically. Glassed-in cases along the walls held models of aircraft carriers, battleships, destroyers, submarines, minesweepers, landing vessels, and patrol boats. There were models of the *Merrimac* and the *Monitor*, the first armored American gunships to engage in combat, ironically against each other, during the War Between the States.

"The man who owns this place is a former SEAL," Savage said, guiding Rachel and Akira past an arm-wrestling competition toward a narrow open space at the crowded bar. "After he retired, he couldn't let go of the team, so he started the Ship-to-Shore Tavern. A lot of Navy personnel, especially SEALs, come in here."

A bartender walked over. He was in his fifties, had a brush cut, was built like a football player, and wore a short-sleeved white shirt, similar to Navy issue, that showed a tattoo of a seal on his right forearm. "What'll it be, folks?"

"Seltzer water."

Rachel and Akira ordered the same.

The bartender shrugged.

"Harold, do you remember me?" Savage asked.

"Can't say I do." The bartender concentrated. "Should I?"

"I used to come here often, when I was on leave."

"A lot of sailors pass through. How long has it been since—?"

"October, nineteen eighty-three."

"No offense. Over the years everybody looks the same. My memory's not what it used to be."

"I know what you mean."

The bartender squinted at Akira and went for the seltzer water.

"It doesn't prove anything that he doesn't remember me," Savage said. "But it must mean *something* that I remember him, that I knew about this bar."

Rachel looked uncertain.

"Just like I knew where my mother lived?" Savage asked. "Is that what you're thinking?"

She didn't have a chance to answer. The bartender came back with their drinks. "That's three seventy-five."

Savage gave him a five. "Keep the change."

"Thanks, buddy."

"Does Captain MacIntosh still come in here?"

"Mac? Sure, I see him a couple times a month."

"Did he come in here this evening?"

"Not that I know of. If he did, one of the waitresses must have served him." The bartender squinted at Akira again and walked toward the cash register.

"I don't think he likes Japanese," Akira said.

"Or maybe no Japanese has ever been in here. He's not the only one staring at you," Rachel said.

"I noticed."

"Maybe *you're* the attraction," Savage told Rachel. "If you were by yourself, a hundred sailors would be asking to buy you a drink."

"I don't know whether that's a compliment or a threat." Rachel's eyes crinkled.

"Tell us about this Captain MacIntosh," Akira said.

"I served with him in the SEALs. After Grenada, I resigned. He was promoted and put on the training team." Savage shook his head. "We were close. I remember him vividly. Training together. Shipping into combat together.

Coming here, drinking, raising hell together. He *can't* be another false memory. . . . In fact"—Savage's shoulders cramped—"there he is."

A well-built sandy-haired man in his middle thirties came into the tavern. He was tall, with tanned, chiseled features, dressed in sneakers, jeans, and a denim shirt, the three top buttons of which were open, revealing light-brown chest hair. He wore a diver's watch.

As he waved toward a group of men at a table, grinned, and walked toward them, Savage pushed away from the bar and veered through the crowd to intercept him. "Mac!"

The man paused, turning in puzzlement, trying to determine the source of the voice.

"Mac," Savage said and reached him. "How are you?"

Mac stared, his expression impossible to read.

Savage quelled his unease, struggling to flash his best good-buddy smile. "What's the matter? After everything we've been through, don't you remember me?"

"Remember you?" Mac kept staring, his forehead deeply furrowed.

No! Savage thought. Not again! He felt as if he plummeted, dizzy, stomach hollow, arms and legs numb.

Mac pursed his lips, turning to walk away.

Savage dodged in front of him. "Wait. *Please*. You really don't . . .?"

"I told you I was good for the money. Damn it, here's your twenty bucks. Stop hounding me. Get out of here."

Savage frowned at the money shoved into his hand. His mind reeled. "But . . ."

Mac started to walk away again.

"You didn't owe me . . ." Stunned, Savage followed him. "What's this all about?"

Mac stopped, leaning close, his voice a tense whisper. "That's a damned good question. What are you doing here? Have you gone nuts, Doyle? You know we're not supposed to be seen together."

"What?"

"Get out."

"But . . ."

Mac's voice was barely audible. "In the alley. Fifteen minutes."

As Savage blinked, Mac continued toward his friends at a corner table.

"The guy lends me twenty bucks, then thinks I won't pay him. That's what I get for playing cards with civilians," Savage heard Mac tell his friends.

The din of the tavern abruptly seemed louder, the smoke filled air more unbreathable. Savage felt trapped, constricted, smothered. Chest cramping, he glanced toward Rachel and Akira, gesturing for them to meet him outside.

Dusk had turned to darkness. On the noisy, crowded street, Savage shook his head, so astonished he could hardly speak. "He called me Doyle."

Rachel studied him. "Then he *does* remember you?"

"No, you don't understand," Savage said. "My real name isn't Doyle. Why would he—? Jesus, did they steal my name and teach me another?" His temples throbbed. "Who the hell *am* I?"

13

The alley was rimmed by a clutter of boxes, garbage cans, and a Dumpster bin. Halfway along, a dim bulb above a door on the right fought to dispel the gloom.

"The tavern's rear exit," Savage said. With Rachel and Akira, he stood on a quiet side street, surveying his destination. "I must have been here before if I know that."

"Unless . . ."

Savage realized what Akira meant to say. "Another false memory? *Something* has to be real. Mac did recognize me. I'm sure of it, *even if he called me by a name I don't remember having.*" Savage inhaled. "Fifteen minutes, he said. It'll soon be time. I want *answers.*"

Savage entered the alley.

"Wait," Akira said.

Savage glanced back, nervous. "What's wrong?"

"I can't let you meet him alone."

"But Rachel . . ."

"Yes. She can't stay here unprotected," Akira said. "But if she comes with me down the alley, if there's trouble, she'll get in the way. Since New York, when you decided to bring her with us, I knew this moment would come. I can't be your backup and at the same time guard her."

"When *I* decided? You agreed with me."

"Reluctantly."

"I promised I wouldn't make trouble," Rachel said. "Go with him, Akira. I'll be safe here."

"No. As long as you're with us, we're responsible for you," Akira said.

"My husband can't know where I am. I'll be fine."

"At the moment, it's not your husband I'm worried about. Whatever's happening to us, if this meeting becomes what you Americans call sour . . ."

Even in the night, Savage could see Rachel's eyes flash.

"I'm as concerned about Savage's safety as you are," she said. "More than my own. If it bothers you to leave me here, we'll *both* go with him. There isn't another alternative."

"I'm afraid she's right," Savage said.

"If there's trouble?" Akira said.

"I stay out of the way. I hide," Rachel said.

"And if we're separated?"

"We need a prearranged rendezvous. For starters, where we parked the car. If we can't reach it, I'll get a room in a Holiday Inn in this area. I know the pseudonyms on your credit cards. You know mine: Susan Porter. We phone the other Holiday Inns till we make contact. If—after two days—we fail to make contact, we know it's a worst-case scenario. We give up and proceed on our own."

"Not bad," Savage said.

Akira raised his eyebrows in reluctant respect.

"I had good teachers," Rachel said. "Your fifteen minutes are almost up," she told Savage. "Any moment, your friend'll come through that door."

Savage glanced toward Akira, waiting for his reaction.

Akira squinted. "Very well." He sighed and stayed close to Rachel as he followed Savage down the alley. "Here," he told Rachel. "We hide in this alcove."

Savage proceeded toward the tavern's rear exit.

14

The door came open, filling the alley with the sounds of loud conversations and the Everly Brothers' "Bye Bye Love." From where Savage stood at the rim of the faint bulb's illumination, he saw Mac appear and scan the alley. Behind Mac, a narrow corridor led toward the tavern's main section. A door labeled MEN'S ROOM was on the corridor's left.

Mac finished scanning the alley, stared at Savage, and stepped out, shutting the door, muffling the voices and music.

"The guys I'm with think I'm taking a leak. I can't stay away long. What *is* this, Doyle? For Christ's sake, why did you show up here? If anybody recognized you . . ."

"This is difficult to explain. We need to talk. About a *lot* of things. It'll take quite a while. We can't do it here."

"I just told you I can't stay away long. Suppose somebody sees us out here."

"Why *shouldn't* they?"

"Damn it, Doyle, you know the rules. You're the one who wanted it this way. To get together again, we have to use the codes and safe houses you insisted on."

"What are you *talking* about?"

"Doyle, are you all right?"

"I asked you in there—do you remember me?"

"Make sense."

"What's all this about you owing me money?"

"It's all I could think of to explain the way you were acting. Except for punching you out. I could have done that. It fits your cover story. But someone would have called the MPs and the cops and . . . Wait a minute, Doyle. Is *that* what you wanted? Was I supposed to fight with you again?"

"Jesus, I don't understand what you're saying. Why are you calling me 'Doyle'?"

Mac tensed, bracing his shoulders, swelling his chest. His eyes became wary, his voice a growl. "Okay, where are they?"

"Who?"

"The blonde and the Japanese who followed you out of the bar. It's obvious they're with you. What's the point? To advertise? To make everybody notice you? Damn it, if you had a plan, why didn't you let me know beforehand? I can't help you if I don't know. . . . I said, *where are they*?"

Savage gestured. Across the alley, halfway between Savage and the alley's entrance, Akira and Rachel stepped out of the alcove's darkness into the shadows cast by the light above the door.

"Sure," Mac said, his anger contorting his rugged features. "Watching. Listening. A test, right? To find out if I still obey the rules. What happens now? You got me to say more than I should have. What's my punishment? Shit duty? Forced retirement? You bastard, Doyle. Even if we're supposed to be enemies, I thought we were friends."

"I don't know what you're talking about! Listen, Mac, someone did something to me! I told you it's hard to explain! I *remember things that never happened*. I don't know what *did* happen. I don't know why you call me 'Doyle'! I don't know why —!"

Savage stiffened, pivoting in alarm. Hearing a powerful engine's roar, he saw a huge vehicle steer into the alley, coming from the same direction he had. The vehicle's shape was grotesque. Its headlights blinded him. Startled, he raised a hand to shield his eyes, saw Akira and Rachel duck back to the darkness of the alcove across from him, and suddenly realized that he himself had no place to hide. Crouching, fighting the urge to run, he shifted toward Mac, his hand on the .45 tucked under his belt at his spine beneath his jacket. At once, he recognized the vehicle lumbering noisily toward him.

"It's only a Dumpster truck," Mac said. "Something *must* have happened to you, Doyle. Your nerves are shot. Is that why they gave you an escort? To watch how you behave? What did you say? You remember what never happened? What *did* happen? Too many missions? Too much stress? You had a breakdown? *Tell* me, Doyle. I want to help you."

The truck rumbled closer. Steady, Savage told himself. Hang on. Be cool. There's no way in fifteen minutes anyone could have set this trap. No one knew I'd be here in this alley. Except for Mac.

Savage glanced warily toward the man he remembered as a friend. *Did Mac make a call from the bar while I waited outside?*

No! I have to trust my instincts! I have to believe he was—*is*—my friend! Even if Mac *did* phone—why *would* he?—there still wasn't time to get this truck here.

As the truck moved clumsily nearer, Savage saw a driver, and *only* a driver, in the cab. The weary-looking man peered toward the Dumpster bin, pressed a button on the dash, and lowered the massive metal forks that had sat on the roof of the truck, aiming them toward a slot on each side of the bulky steel bin.

The truck came abreast of Savage. He pressed his back against the alley's grimy brick wall.

Mac squeezed next to him, his voice indistinct as the truck's roar increased. "You worry me, friend. Who *are* those people? The blonde and the Japanese, are they watchdogs? From the agency?"

Savage felt smothered by the noise and fumes of the truck.

He pressed his back harder against the wall. "Agency? *The CIA*?"

"What other agency is there? Doyle, are you serious? Someone actually screwed with your memory?"

"Why do you call me 'Doyle'? That's not my name."

"It is! Your first name's Robert. We had two Bobs on our team. So we used your last names to avoid confusion. Don't you remember?"

"No! Tell me why we're supposed to pretend we're enemies!"

"Because of your cover story."

"What?"

The truck's roar intensified, deafening. Its forks strained, raising the bin, dumping garbage into the top of the truck. The stench made Savage gag. With a reverberating thunk, the truck set the bin down. It made another roar, its forks rising, the truck rumbling down the alley.

"Cover story?" Savage asked.

"Shit!" Mac pointed.

Savage spun, the truck no longer obscuring his vision. In front of the alcove where Akira had hidden with Rachel . . .

Akira and a tall Caucasian kicked and jabbed at each other, circling, lunging. Farther along the alley, two other Caucasians dragged Rachel—squirming and screaming—toward a car that blocked the alley's exit.

The attackers had stalked behind the truck, Savage realized. They'd used its noise and its bulk to conceal their approach. Out of sight from Savage, they'd taken Akira by surprise.

The two men tugged Rachel closer to the car. She screamed harder.

Dodging a blow, Akira whirled with the speed of a dervish. In a blur of hands and feet, he slammed his opponent's nose, rammed his rib cage, and smashed his larynx. The man fell, dying.

From the moment Savage had seen the commotion, he'd started running. Not toward Akira. He took for granted that Akira wouldn't need help. But even if Akira *had* needed help, Savage would have assisted him only if their prime objective wasn't jeopardized.

Rachel. *She* was what mattered. Their principal. *The client they'd pledged themselves to protect.*

As Savage raced to help her, Akira joined him. At the end of the alley, the car's driver revved its engine. The two men—one on each side of Rachel—yanked her toward an open rear door.

Savage was too far away to reach her in time. No option. He knew what had to be done.

Halting abruptly, he drew his pistol. Akira halted simultaneously next to him, drawing his own. As if they'd trained together, as if they'd practiced coordinated maneuvers, each cocked his weapon precisely when the other did, the sharp clicks merging, echoing. They braced themselves identically, each turning slightly to the right, their feet apart, one foot angled away from the other for balance. They each used two hands to grip their weapons. Raising them, they each kept their left arm straight, their right arm slightly bent, their elbows locked for a steady aim.

Keeping both eyes open, lining up the front and rear sights, focusing on the *front* sight, the target beyond it slightly blurred, they fired. The simultaneous blasts reverberated along the alley. Ears rang, concussed. Though each man's bullet struck its target's chest, Savage and Akira fired again to make sure. The bullets walloped foreheads. Blood spurting, the targets fell.

Rachel stopped screaming. She knew enough, had learned enough, not to scramble around in confusion. Instead she dove to the alley's pavement, hugging it, removing herself from the line of fire.

The driver jerked up an arm.

Even at a distance, Savage recognized the shape of a pistol in his hand.

Savage aimed.

The driver shot first. His bullet buzzed past Savage's scalp as Savage dove to the left, Akira to the right.

Hitting the pavement, landing on their stomachs, they instantly propped their elbows to shoot from a prone position.

Too late. The driver stomped his foot on the throttle. Engine roaring, he sped from the alley's entrance. A cloud of exhaust replaced the car.

Savage thrust to his feet, charging toward Rachel. "Are you all right?"

"They almost wrenched my arms from their sockets." She rubbed them. "Otherwise . . . Yes, I . . . What about *you*?"

Savage and Akira looked at each other. Trembling, breathing heavily, they exchanged reassuring nods.

"And what about—?" Rachel's incomplete question became a moan.

Mac lay beside the tavern's exit, the dim bulb above it glinting off a spreading pool of blood.

"No!" Savage raced toward him.

Mac's eyes were open, unblinking.

"Oh, Christ," Savage said. He felt Mac's wrist, put an ear against Mac's chest, rested a finger against Mac's unmoving nostrils. "No."

"Please," Akira said. "There's nothing we can do for him. I'm sorry, but we have to leave."

The tavern's back door banged open.

Savage pivoted, aiming.

A man with a brush cut, who was built like a football player, with a tattoo of a seal on a forearm, glared toward Mac's body, toward Savage, Akira, and Rachel, toward the *other* bodies.

Harold. The Ship-to-Shore's owner.

Savage lowered his aim.

"I knew you were trouble when you came in," Harold said.

He scowled at Akira. "You bastards killed my father on Iwo Jima."

He raised his arms. "It took me a while. But Doyle, at last I remember. Go ahead, shoot me, you son of a bitch. I'll die a hero. Along with Mac. You're a fucking disgrace. You don't deserve to have been a SEAL."

Harold lunged.

Savage felt paralyzed.

Akira intercepted the attack, kicked Harold's groin, and grabbed Savage, urging him away.

As Harold fell toward the alley, Rachel helped Akira, tugging Savage.

Discipline insisted. Savage twisted his arms, freeing the hands that gripped him.

"Okay," he said. *"Let's go."*

15

Sirens wailed in the night. Despite his anxiety, Savage forced himself to maintain the speed limit, driving unobtrusively, blending with traffic. Rachel sat, her knees bent, her head hunched, on the floor in front of the passenger seat. Akira lay on the floor in back.

"I don't think anyone saw us reach the car," Savage said. "So they don't know our license number. They won't be looking for a Taurus."

"But two men and a woman. A blonde and a Japanese," Rachel said. "Harold will tell the police who to look for. If a cop pulls up next to us, he might see us hiding in here."

"In daylight maybe," Savage said. "But at night? Unless the cop used a flashlight, he wouldn't notice you."

Savage tried to sound reassuring. The truth was, the headlights and streetlights he drove past sometimes illuminated her. He kept his eyes straight ahead, barely moving his lips when he spoke, doing his best not to attract attention by seeming to talk to himself or to make a passing motorist guess he was talking to someone hidden in the car.

"Harold indeed will tell the police." Akira's voice came muffled from the floor in back. "I could have killed him. I think now I should have."

"No," Savage said. "You did the right thing. We're protectors, not assassins! We were forced to kill to save Rachel. We made an ethical, necessary choice. But killing Harold would have been . . ."

"Needless?" Akira asked. "Gratuitous? What he saw— what he tells the police—*threatens* us. If we were justified in killing those men to save Rachel, I'd have been equally justified in killing Harold to save *ourselves*."

"It's not the same," Savage said. "I can't tell you why I'm sure of that. But I *am* sure. Harold must have heard the shots. Why didn't anyone else? Who knows? Maybe Harold was coming out of the men's room in the corridor. So he opened the outside door and found us. His timing, by accident, was terrible. A hit man for the mob would have killed him. But I'll say it again. We're not assassins. We don't kill innocent people because their timing's bad."

"Evidently I agree. Because I *didn't* kill him."

"And I thank you for that."

"This is *my* fault," Rachel said. She sounded cramped in the narrow space. "If I hadn't begged to come with you . . ."

"We accepted you," Savage said. "We *agreed*. That topic's settled."

"Let me finish," Rachel said. "If I hadn't come along, if I hadn't been in that alley, my husband's men wouldn't have tried to grab me. You wouldn't have killed them. A misaimed bullet wouldn't have killed your friend. He'd have told you what you needed to know. You wouldn't be grieving. You wouldn't be trying to escape the police. Everything—all of it—is *my* fault."

"If? My God," Savage said, "is *that* what you've been thinking? Blaming yourself? Don't you understand what happened? The men who attacked you had nothing to do with your husband."

"*What?*"

"Your husband couldn't have known where you were," Akira said from behind the front seat. "We concealed your trail impeccably. From the attempt on you in southern France, we used every strategy we could think of to elude your husband. His men could *not* have followed us here."

"Maybe they're better than you imagine," Rachel said.

"If so, they'd have chosen an earlier moment to try to abduct you. At the various hotels where we stayed. Outside the various hospitals where we sought help. I can think of a dozen perfect intervention sites. If your husband's men *did* decide to grab you, why did they wait so long? And in such a complicated situation?''

''To take advantage of that complication, hoping you'd be distracted,'' Rachel said.

Savage interrupted. ''But your husband's men *couldn't* have known that I'd agreed to meet Mac in that alley! To support your theory, we'd have to assume that these presumably clever professionals decided all at once, with no plan, just for the hell of it, to take advantage of the Dumpster truck that entered the alley, to depend on luck and make a grab for you.''

''They did very well,'' Rachel said. ''They got me away from Akira.''

''That's something else that troubles me,'' Akira said. ''They should have killed me before they grabbed you. They had the chance. Instead one man distracted me while the others dragged you away. I didn't have a chance to draw my pistol. I was forced to fight hand to hand.''

''They responded to the confusion of the moment,'' Rachel said.

''*What* confusion? If the Dumpster truck was part of the plan, Savage and I would have been confused. But not your husband's men. They'd have been ready. To do what was necessary. To kill me.''

''But they didn't,'' Savage said. ''Which suggests they didn't *want* to kill Akira, hadn't been ordered to.''

''And your husband's so arrogant he'd have insisted that Savage and I be killed. For humiliating the great man's pride,'' Akira said. ''The tactics were wrong. They should have killed *us* before they abducted *you*.''

''Easier. Safer,'' Savage said. ''Instead *Mac* died. God help him. I didn't just happen to duck so the bullet hit him. If the driver wanted to hit me, he could have. He shot *before* I ducked. The target was Mac. Whatever's happening, he couldn't be allowed to talk. And Rachel, *you* were in the way, not part of the plan. You're not supposed to be with us. But you are. So whoever managed to predict where we'd be, decided to solve both problems at once. To take you away from us. To stop Mac from telling what he knew. And in the bargain, to continue confusing Akira and me.''

"But *why?*" Rachel asked.

11

The North Carolina motel room was small and drab. But at least it was clean, and its entrance was in a corridor at the rear of the building, where Rachel and Akira had a good chance of slipping in unnoticed. Late at night, the only take-out restaurant Savage found open served pizza. Sitting on the motel room's floor, they chewed unenthusiastically on a thickly crusted, five-ingredient ''supreme,'' not hungry but knowing they had to maintain their strength. A six-pack of Coke helped them swallow the overspiced, undercooked dough. Akira, who retained his culture's preference for vegetables, rice, and fish, picked off the sausage on his pizza slices.

"Let's analyze the conversation one more time," Akira said. "Mac assumed you knew things you don't, so he didn't elaborate, didn't explain. As a consequence, what he said seemed cryptic. Even so, is there anything you feel sure of?"

"Mac did know me," Savage said.

"Even though he called you 'Doyle,' which isn't your name."

"Or maybe it is," Savage said. "False memory. How do I know what's true? Whoever operated on my brain might have taught me to forget my *real* name and convinced me that one of my pseudonyms isn't a lie but the name I was born with."

"Everything's a lie," Rachel said. Disgusted, she dropped a half-eaten slice of pizza into the box.

Savage studied her, then continued. "What doesn't seem a false memory is that Mac and I in fact were friends. He mentioned that several times. But he *also* said that we were enemies, or *supposed* to be enemies. There were rules, he said. If we wanted to see each other, we had to use codes and meet at safe houses."

"That's an expression used by intelligence operatives," Akira said.

"Yes, and Mac thought you and Rachel were what he called my 'watchdogs,' assessing me because I was under stress. How would I behave when I tried to make unscheduled contact with him? How would *he* behave? He kept talking about rules and whether he still obeyed them. He seemed afraid that you were testing him."

"But who did he think we worked for?" Rachel asked.

Savage hesitated. "The CIA."

"What?"

"He got angry, as if he thought he'd be punished for breaking the rules and talking to me in the alley."

Akira straightened. "Mac was CIA?"

"I can't be certain. It doesn't make sense for a SEAL to be a civilian intelligence operative. *Navy* intelligence maybe. But not a *Langley* operative. No," Savage said, "the impression I got was that Mac thought I reported to you, that I worked for the agency."

"My God," Rachel said, "is that possible?"

"The last few days have proved that anything's possible. But if you're asking me, 'Do I remember being an operative?' the answer is no. Of course, you might suspect I'm lying."

Akira shook his head. "In Philadelphia, you talked about being so unsure of what was real that you felt afraid to trust Rachel and me. Maybe we weren't what we seemed, you said. Maybe we'd been sent to trick you. We insisted you had to trust us. Because the alternative was paralysis. Now I take my own advice. My friend, as a necessary act of faith, I trust you. I refuse to suspect you're lying."

" 'Abraham believed by virtue of the absurd,' " Rachel said.

Akira looked puzzled.

"It's something I said to Savage last night in Philadelphia." Rachel stood. "An act of faith."

"So we have to question whether I'm remembering correctly," Savage said. "In Philadelphia, Dr. Santizo explained that a false memory required the cancellation of a *true* one. Otherwise I wouldn't behave consistently. So maybe I did—do—belong to the CIA, and I'm not aware of it."

" 'Maybe'? 'Perhaps'? This is getting us nowhere," Akira said.

Savage rubbed his aching forehead. "Mac told me something else. 'Was I supposed to fight with you again?' That's what he said. It didn't make sense. Fight with him again? The implication is I fought with him before. But why—if we were friends? He said when I spoke to him in the bar, he pretended he owed me money because it was the only way he could think of to explain our conversation. 'Except for punching you out. I could have done that. It fits your cover story,' he said."

"Cover story?" Akira frowned.

"Mac used that phrase a lot."

"Friends supposed to be enemies. Cover story. CIA," Rachel said. "I'm beginning . . . When Harold found us in the alley, he suddenly remembered you. He said you disgraced the SEALs. He went so berserk he didn't care about your pistol. He said he'd die a hero if he attacked you. Cover story."

"I don't understand," Savage said.

"Theory. Assumptions. If you did work for the CIA, you'd need a cover story to convince the opposition that you weren't still loyal to America. So the agency recruits you. You resign from the SEALs. You become a protector. While guarding your clients— important clients, *influential* clients, wealthy enough to afford your fee—you gather information about them. Because they're *powerful*. Because their secrets have strategic value or are so incriminating that the agency can blackmail your clients into working for them."

Savage stared at the floor, his forehead persistently throbbing no matter how hard he rubbed it.

"But how to convince your clients that you're a free agent?" Rachel continued. "By disowning your government. Why?"

"Because I was part of the first wave of U.S. soldiers that invaded Grenada," Savage said. "And what I saw there convinced me the Marxist government on the island—as crazy as they were—didn't threaten America. The invasion was a public relations ploy, to distract America from the two hundred and thirty U.S. marines that died in Beirut because of a terrorist bomb. Grenada was the president's scheme to increase his popularity ratings. Too many of my comrades died needlessly. I resigned in disgust."

"And fought with a fellow SEAL who disagreed with you, who thought you'd betrayed your team?" Akira asked. "A fight in public? Two friends become enemies? A convincing cover story."

Savage raised his head but continued to rub his temples. "Especially if my father committed suicide because his country betrayed him, because the White House needed a scapegoat to explain the Bay of Pigs catastrophe. God damn it." Savage glared. "That invasion failed because U.S. politicians lost their nerve and changed the Cuban invasion site from a town to a goddamn swamp."

"But your background's consistent," Rachel said. "Cuba. Grenada. Two invasions. One seems necessary but isn't successful. The second *isn't* necessary."

"But *is* successful," Savage said. "And both invasions are based on—"

"Lies?"

"Disinformation. Graham was fascinated with the concept. Events that never happened but changed the world. Hitler sending German soldiers into Poland, having them dress in Polish uniforms and fire toward the German lines, so the Germans could justify invading. The United States sending a destroyer too close to North Vietnam's Gulf of Tonkin, daring the North Vietnamese to fire, then claiming that the North Vietnamese attacked without provocation, and using that incident to justify increasing America's presence in South Vietnam. Convincing deception. Plausible deniability."

"False memory," Akira said. "Entire nations remembering what never happened. But right now *your* false memory is what matters. Let's assume your father—not the man you met in Baltimore but your real father—did kill himself. That makes it believable that you'd resign from the SEALs because the Grenada invasion wasn't necessary and you were furious about the needless deaths of fellow SEALs. You'd seem to be a true free agent, uninvolved with your government," Akira said.

"False memory. Cover story. Lies. We don't know—we can't be sure of—"

"Anything," Rachel said. "That pizza . . . It's making me sick. My head's . . . I'm too exhausted to think." She reached for a package Savage had bought at an all-night convenience store. "But one thing I'm sure of. I have to dye my hair. So I'll be auburn again. Instead of blond. And *not* my sister. After that . . ." She pointed toward the narrow bed.

"One of us will stand guard while the other sleeps on the floor," Akira said.

"No way," Rachel said. "Decide who takes the first watch. Whoever's off duty shares the space next to me. I don't want someone with a stiff back trying to protect me. I'll put a pillow between us, so I don't interfere with anyone's peace of mind. We're a family, right? We're comfortable sharing space together. But Akira, when it's Savage's turn, I hope you don't object if in my sleep I squirm around and hug him."

17

The North Carolina morning was fresh and clear. After assessing the motel's parking lot, Savage left the corridor's rear exit and crossed the street to get take-out breakfasts from

McDonald's. Coming back, he bought several newspapers from vending machines on the sidewalk.

Akira locked the door behind him and examined the styrofoam containers of food that Savage arranged on the bureau beside the bolted-down television set. "Hash browns? Sausage? Scrambled eggs? And English muffins?"

"Plus strawberry jam. I grant it's not quite your usual diet, but it's the best I could find," Savage said. "Frankly, those hash browns look damned appealing."

"Speak for yourself." Akira pried off the lids on steaming containers of liquid. "Coffee? *No tea?*"

"Here, my friend." Savage handed Akira a tea bag and opened a plastic cup of hot water.

"Arigato." After sipping the tea and nibbling a hash brown, Akira added, "May my ancestors forgive me. I've been corrupted. This tastes delicious."

"Starch," Savage said. "It gives you strength to face the day."

"You'll need it," Rachel said.

Akira frowned. "What do you mean?"

Her hair a brilliant auburn but her eyes extremely somber, Rachel sat on the bed, a newspaper spread open next to her, a plastic forkful of egg suspended in front of her mouth. "You're not going to like this." In despair, she set down the fork.

Savage and Akira crossed the room to stand behind her.

She pointed toward the front page. "Virginia Beach. Four men killed behind the Ship-to-Shore tavern, three of them by gunshots, one by a blow to the throat."

"We assumed," Savage said. "So many deaths. It's a major story."

Rachel kept pointing toward the article. "Yes, and Harold identified you as someone called Robert Doyle. He refers to you and Mac as having been friends, as having argued, having fought in public, and having turned into enemies. Back in nineteen eighty-three. Because you disagreed with the U.S. invasion of Grenada. Because you insisted that the deaths of your fellow SEALs had been needless. Harold mentions me—a blonde—and *you*, Akira, a Japanese. Even with my hair darkened, the three of us—an American couple and a Japanese—are bound to attract suspicion.''

Savage tensely glanced at his watch and spun to turn on the television. ''It's almost twenty-five after seven. Maybe the morning news has an update.''

He managed to find a Virginia Beach station. The first segment of *Good Morning America* was ending. Joan Lunden smiled at the camera. ''And in our next half hour, Tony Bennett will be here, not as a singer but a painter.''

A toothpaste commercial about grinning kids bragging to their parents that they had no cavities seemed interminable.

Savage's shoulders ached. He realized he wasn't breathing.

The local news came on: films of police cars and ambulances, their lights flashing; attendants wheeling sheet-covered corpses from the alley; an announcer grimly explaining what had happened, describing Savage, Rachel, and Akira.

The story took ninety seconds.

''Graphic but short, and nothing we didn't read in the newspaper,'' Akira said. With relief, he moved to shut off the television.

''Wait,'' Savage said. ''Let's see if we're on the national news when the network program comes back on the air.''

''At least they didn't have police-artist sketches based on Harold's descriptions of us,'' Rachel said.

''The police will be working on that.'' Savage reached for his suitcase. ''Let's get our stuff together. After the network news, we need to leave here fast.''

''But what about after that?'' Rachel asked. ''Even if we get out of here without being noticed, we haven't solved our problems. The police will still be looking for us.''

''Us. Yes, that's the trouble,'' Savage said. ''Rachel, you're not responsible for any of this. But if you stay with us, if we're caught, you'll be charged as an accomplice. When you leave this building, keep walking. Don't look back. Find a bus station. Get as far away as fast as you can. Start a new life.''

''No! Why can't I make you understand? I love you!''

Savage was speechless.

''And I'm not leaving you,'' she said. ''The odds are I'd

never see you again. So I'll ask it one more time—if we manage to get away from here, what do we do after that? How do we . . . ? I just thought of something. Suppose Mac was right. Suppose you did belong to the CIA. Can't *they* help us?''

Savage shook his head. ''If it's true that I am involved with the agency, I've got no way to get in touch. I don't know who my contacts are supposed to be. I don't know where or how to leave a written message for them or what number to phone. I can't just call the agency's headquarters in Langley and tell the switchboard operator that I'm wanted for several murders and it's possible I work for the government and this is the name I was told I used to have and would someone please help me out. Whoever I spoke to would figure I was nuts. Even if the agency knew who I was, it would have to deny ever having heard of me. Hell, now that I think about it, everything's so twisted around, someone in the agency might be behind all this. No,'' he insisted, ''we're on our own.''

''The network program is coming back on,'' Akira said.

Savage spun toward the television. Joan Lunden beamed. She and her cohost chorused, ''Good morning, America!'' Sean Connery would join them in this half hour, along with Tony Bennett and his paintings, a special report on high school athletic injuries, and a controversy about whether trick-or-treating on Halloween amounted to devil worship. But first the news.

A devastating hurricane in Central America. A massive defense-contract scandal. A skyscraper fire in New York City.

Savage checked his watch. ''Their news segment lasts five minutes. Just another minute to go. It looks like the killings aren't being treated as national news.''

''Thank God,'' Rachel said. ''If we can get farther down the seaboard, to South Carolina or even Georgia . . .''

''Yes,'' Savage said. ''The police down there might not be looking for us as hard.''

Akira abruptly pointed toward the television. His brown skin seemed to turn pale. He spoke in Japanese—a sharp, quick outburst of surprise and shock.

When Savage saw what Akira was pointing at, his body went cold. His heartbeat skipped several times, making him fear he'd pass out. He slumped onto a chair, all the while continuing to stare at the nightmare on the television screen.

The story was from Tokyo. It showed a Japanese diplomat inciting thousands of Japanese students, who angrily chanted anti-American slogans, holding up anti-American placards outside the U.S. embassy. The diplomat was in his fifties, with salt-and-pepper hair and haggard features; of moderate height, slightly overweight. His name was Kunio Shirai, the announcer said. Despite Shirai's traditional businessman's appearance, he was the radical leader of an anti-American faction, the power of which was growing so fast that it threatened to splinter Japan's main political group, the Liberal Democratic Party. What made the story so unusual wasn't the ferocity of the students, who periodically demonstrated with equal ferocity about other causes, though it had to be admitted that they hadn't shown such outrage since the seventies. Instead the story was unique because Japanese politicians were traditionally models of decorum in public, impassive, composed. In mustering hostility toward America, Kunio Shirai was behaving more like an American than a Japanese.

A moment later, Joan Lunden introduced the program's weatherman, who pointed at lines and arrows on a map.

As if hypnotized, Savage and Akira kept staring at the screen.

"What is it?" Rachel asked.

"Kunio Shirai," Savage said.

"But that's not his name." Akira breathed.

"Or at least not the name we were given." Savage turned to Rachel. "Muto Kamichi. *That's* his name. The Medford Gap Mountain Retreat. The man we were hired to protect. The man we saw cut in half."

"*We* survived, though we saw each other die," Akira said. "But I never doubted that *Kamichi* died. It never occurred to me. In my nightmares, I still see the sword slice through him."

"And the halves of his body fall. And the blood. So much blood."

Akira's features hardened. "We know what to do now."

"Yes," Savage growled. "And where to go."

"I don't understand," Rachel said.

"Japan."

THREE

ⵎⵎⵎⵎ

THE LAND OF
THE GODS

ARTS OF PEACE
AND WAR

1

Savage drove from the motel, hoping no one had seen them get into the car.

Again Akira hid on the floor in back, though Rachel sat next to Savage, her auburn hair making it safe for her to show herself. She studied a road map. "The nearest major airport is in Raleigh. That's a hundred and fifty miles west."

"No, Raleigh won't do," Savage said. "There'd be so few Japanese flying out of that airport—probably none—Akira would be sure to attract attention." Reaching a highway, he headed northwest. "Will this route take us around Virginia Beach?"

Rachel checked the map. "No problem. But where are we going?"

"Washington. Dulles International Airport. We can count

on a lot of Japanese flying in and out of there. Akira won't be noticed."

A few miles later, Savage pulled into a truckstop. He took care to park well away from other vehicles so no one could see into the back of the Taurus. Referring to the directory in a pay phone's booth, he called the toll-free numbers for several airlines. Though it would have been easier to phone from the motel, he didn't want to leave a record of his calls.

"We're in luck," he said, getting back in the car. "I managed to get three seats on an American Airlines flight."

"What time does it leave?" Akira asked.

"Tomorrow morning. Ten to eight."

"But Dulles Airport must be—"

"Four hundred miles away, given the roundabout route we're forced to take to avoid the eastern part of Virginia," Savage said. "The airport's security inspection takes longer on an overseas flight. All our luggage is carry-on. That'll save time. Even so, to pick up our tickets and guarantee we're on the plane, we need to be at the airport by five A.M. at the latest."

"Can we do that?" Rachel asked.

Savage glanced at his watch. "Twenty-one hours to drive four hundred miles? Sure. Even if traffic's bad, we'll be in Washington tonight."

Despite his confident tone, Savage reflexively increased speed. At once he thought better and strictly obeyed the limit. They didn't dare get stopped by a traffic cop. "There's plenty of time."

"Then we should use it," Akira said. "You have much to learn."

"What about?" Savage asked.

"I gather that neither of you has been to Japan."

Savage and Rachel agreed.

"Yes," Akira said. "You have much to learn."

"I've read books about Japan," Savage said.

"But I can't assume that the books were accurate or that you retain the essentials," Akira said. "And Rachel apparently knows almost nothing about Japan."

"True," Rachel said.

"You must be prepared. Soon you will enter a culture completely alien to you. Behavior you take for granted might be interpreted as rudeness. And what you think of as an insult might be a sign of respect. In the West, I've taught myself to behave as a Westerner, to adjust to your values, to accept your ways of thinking. Perhaps, then, you've concluded that the only differences between Americans and Japanese are the food we prefer to eat and the color of our skin, not to mention our language. The differences are much greater. Profound. If you are to survive the dangers we face, you must learn *my* ways just as I learned yours. Or try to learn—because I don't have much time to teach you."

2

The 747 cruised over the glinting Pacific at forty thousand feet. As Savage assessed everything Akira had told him, he wished there'd been a chance for Akira to continue explaining during the long flight. There was so much to know, to absorb. But the only seats available had been widely separated, in three different sections of the plane, and Savage couldn't even see Akira, let alone talk with him.

Not only Akira but Rachel.

Savage felt nervously isolated from her. His instincts as a protector made him squirm at being distanced from his principal. More, despite his professional's need to be objective about a client, he reluctantly admitted that another need had grown within him. Accustomed to fearing for others, he'd never feared for his own safety—till now. Suffering a nightmare in which the dead came back to life, how could he be sure of anything? How could he trust his sense of reality? He had to depend on *something*. Love gave him hope.

He glanced out his window. Below, for many hours, there'd been nothing but ocean, and he understood why Akira had said that east of Japan there was only west. It was obvious why Japan identified so strongly with the sun. In ancient times, the blazing globe that seemed to rise each day from the infinite expanse of the sea must have exerted a powerful force. The land of the rising sun. The symbol on the nation's flag. As Akira had said, "Japan is the only country whose tradition maintains its citizens are descendants of gods. One deity in particular. Amaterasu. The goddess of the sun."

Savage felt pressure on his ears and didn't need the pilot's announcement to make him aware that the jet had begun to descend. He opened his mouth wide, hearing a pop behind his eardrums, and leaned close to the window. The sky was cloudless, except for a haze along the horizon. As the 747 continued its gradual descent, he saw a coastline amid the haze. He noticed specks of ships on the ocean and, fifteen minutes later, saw buildings crammed along the shore.

"Japan has a population of one hundred and twenty-five million," Akira had said. "That makes it the sixth most populous nation in the world. Its combined square miles make it equivalent in mass to your state of Montana, but three-fourths of the country is mountainous and most of my people are forced to live along the coast, so the actual usable living space for those one hundred and twenty-five million people is smaller than your state of Connecticut."

The jet sped lower, closer. Staring at the congested buildings along the enlarging shore, Savage marveled. More than three hundred years ago, Akira had explained, the Japanese had decided to solve the problem of overcrowding by extending their boundaries. Using massive landfill projects, they'd expanded the coast, a process that still continued with the result that more than forty percent of the shore, including part of Tokyo, was land claimed from the sea.

The haze toward which the jet descended wasn't mist or low clouds but smog, Savage realized. Despite it, he managed to see the vague shapes of the rugged inland mountains and the overwhelming sprawl of cities merging with cities. He couldn't ignore the irony: a people renowned for savoring nature lived among urban blight. Narita International Airport toward which the jet descended provided a good example.

In 1966 when Japan's rapid economic development had necessitated a new and larger international airport, the Japanese government had chosen a site on irreplaceable farmland east of Tokyo. Instead of negotiating with the reluctant farmers, the government had annexed the land for an unfair price. The farmers demonstrated angrily, as did farmers on nearby land whose tranquillity would be destroyed by the roar of jets. Students and antigovernment groups joined in the protests, producing such chaos that after Narita Airport was completed it couldn't be opened for seven years. Still the protests continued. Numerous bombings and armed assaults injured more than eight thousand and killed at least thirteen. For their safety, visiting heads of state had been compelled to land at the old Haneda Airport in Tokyo. Even now, Savage noted as the 747 landed, police patrolled the steel barricades, watchtowers, and several rows of tall fences around Narita. He saw water cannons and armored vehicles. Beyond, more buildings were being constructed, further despoiling what once had been idyllic countryside. Progress.

After the seventeen-hour flight, Savage's legs ached. The local time was 4:05 P.M., but his body clock told him it was one in the morning. Bumped and jostled by the swarm of departing passengers, he left the aircraft, exhausted. Akira and Rachel—both looking haggard—waited for him in the concourse, and before Savage realized what he was doing, he embraced her.

"God, I'm tired," she said. "I feel like I've gained ten pounds. Every time I fell asleep, they woke me for another meal."

Akira smiled, though his eyes remained sad. "Immigration and customs are this way."

The process was lengthy but uneventful. At last proceeding through the noisy, crowded terminal toward an exit, Savage felt more and more self-conscious. Surrounded by thousands of Japanese, he'd never felt so out of place, so awkwardly aware of being Caucasian. His skin seemed unnaturally pale, his body too large, his movements clumsy. Though the Japanese were fascinated by his appearance, they also seemed repelled, doing their best not to let their shoulders touch him.

Does Akira feel this self-conscious in the West, surrounded by Caucasians? he wondered.

"I'll arrange for a taxi," Akira said.

"Then where will we be going?" Rachel asked.

For a moment, pride replaced the sadness in Akira's eyes. "The most special place in the world."

3

The leather-coated taxi driver steered this way and that through a maze of narrow, traffic-jammed streets in northern Tokyo. The noise and commotion were awesome, even for someone accustomed to New York City. Exhaust fumes flared Savage's nostrils. During the forty-minute drive into the city, he'd noted the cultural schizophrenia of the buildings along the highway: Western-style hotels and office buildings adjacent to temples and cherry orchards. But within the city, Western architecture dominated: skyscrapers, shopping centers, apartment buildings that looked like concrete capsules stacked on top of each other, a steel-girder spire that resembled the Eiffel Tower.

"During the final months of the Great East Asian War" —Akira corrected himself—"what you call World War Two, American aerial cluster-bomb attacks and the consequent fire storms left most of Tokyo in ruins. Almost one hundred thousand civilians were killed. The chaos was so severe, the necessity to rebuild so urgent, that no one had time to reconstruct the city in an orderly fashion. Survival mattered, not logic. Tokyo's baffling labyrinth of streets is the legacy. Instead of traditional architecture, Western architecture became the norm, the influence of America's seven-year military occupation here after the war."

Savage studied the crowded sidewalks. Every pedestrian wore Western clothes. A Kentucky Fried Chicken restaurant stood next to a sushi bar. Signs written in Japanese ideograms often included the equivalent of their message in the Western alphabet.

Akira gave more instructions to the driver. The taxi rounded a corner, passed several American-style shops and apartment buildings, and stopped before a tall stone wall in the middle of which stood a polished wooden door.

As Akira paid, Savage wondered why Akira had brought them here. He almost reached for the handle on the taxi's door, then remembered the unique device in Japanese taxis and waited for the driver to pull a lever that automatically opened the door for his passengers. Politeness combined with efficiency. Savage had to smile.

His smile slowly faded after he got out with Rachel and Akira. They lifted their travel bags from the taxi's trunk, which had also been opened by remote control, and faced the stone wall.

It was double Savage's height. What *is* this place? he wondered, barely aware that the taxi had driven away. He frowned toward Rachel, who shook her head, equally confused.

Akira stepped toward an intercom mounted to the wall beside the wooden door. He pressed a button. Seconds later, a woman's frail voice said something in Japanese. Akira responded. The woman quickly answered, her tone a complex blend of respect and delight.

Akira turned toward Savage and Rachel. "Good. For a moment, I was afraid that I'd brought you to another false memory."

"The most special place in the world?"

Akira nodded.

Behind the door, something scraped and clanked. The door swung inward, and Savage was amazed to find himself before an elderly woman wearing sandals and a brilliantly colored kimono, the first traditional costume he'd so far seen in Japan.

The kimono had an intricate flower design. Its material was smooth gleaming silk. Savage heard Rachel exhale in admiration.

The elderly woman's long gray hair was tucked in a bun

behind her head, secured by an ornate bamboo comb. She leaned a stout wooden bar against the inside of the wall, pressed her palms together, and bowed to Akira.

He bowed in return, said something that made her smile, and gestured for Savage and Rachel to pass through the door.

With wonder, they entered. As the woman shut the door and placed the wooden bar into metal loops on each side to prevent the door from being opened, Savage was so overwhelmed by what he saw that he stopped and set down his bag.

The view was completely harmonious, every detail arranged so that no one thing drew attention any more than anything else. Only gradually was Savage able to analyze his impressions. He stood on a path of white pebbles. To his right and left, golden sand had been carefully raked so that the prong marks formed curving patterns, enhancing volcanic rocks distributed at pleasing intervals. The rocks were of different sizes and shapes, each with intriguing contours, ridges, and cracks, and they in turn were enhanced by two tastefully positioned cedar shrubs on the right and one on the left. The high wall muffled the noises from the street, enough so that Savage heard water trickling. Dusk cast soothing shadows.

At the end of the path, which curved in imitation of the rake patterns in the sand, Savage saw a single-story house. It was plain, rectangular, made of wood, with a tiled roof that sloped past the house to form an overhang on each side. The rim of the roof curved slightly upward, reminding Savage of the curve in the path and the curve marks in the sand. Each corner of the roof was supported by a post, and these existed in perfect symmetry with the front door between them and a window on each side that was equidistant between each post and the door. Bamboo blinds covered the windows, behind each of which a lamp glowed.

Purity, balance, beauty, order.

"Yes," Rachel said, then surveyed the looming oppressive concrete buildings on each side and returned her attention toward the garden and the house. "The most special place in the world."

"I feel like I've stepped through a time warp," Savage said.

"Or *halfway* through. Part of me's still in the present, but another part is in the . . ."

"Past," Akira said, his voice sad. "Out there, the past is the source of our problem. In here, it gives me comfort."

"But how did . . . ? Where . . . ?"

"This house belonged to my father. I once told you, after the war he achieved a modest degree of financial success by converting military planes for civilian use. He used much of his money to purchase this property. That was in nineteen fifty-two when this area was on Tokyo's outskirts. But even then land was expensive, and this was the most he could afford. The street outside wasn't here then, and of course neither were the buildings that hem the property. But he saw the future and longed for the past, for the peace he'd known as a boy on a farm years before the war. So he arranged for this house to be built in the ancient style, and after its completion he shielded it with these walls, and each evening after work, he came home to compose this garden. It took him fifteen years, patiently arranging, *re*arranging, meditating, assessing. Sometimes he'd study it for hours, slowly crouch, and cautiously shift a few pebbles. Before he died in the hospital after being struck by a car, one of the last things he told me was that he regretted not having the chance to complete his garden. I'm still working on it for him."

Rachel touched his arm. "It's beautiful."

"*Arigato.*" Akira swallowed, stood straighter as if repressing emotion, and gestured toward the elderly Japanese woman. "This is Eko. She used to tend house for my father." He spoke in Japanese to her.

Amid the unfamiliar words, Savage heard his name and Rachel's.

Eko bowed.

Savage and Rachel did the same.

Footsteps crunched on the path. Savage saw a slender

young man approach from the house. His face was narrow, his forehead high. He wore sandals, as did Eko, and a beige karate *gi* with a brown belt tied around it.

"This is Churi, Eko's grandson," Akira said. Returning Churi's smile and bow, Akira spoke warmly to him and completed the introductions.

Churi bowed.

Again Savage and Rachel did the same.

"When I'm home," Akira said, "I try to be Churi's *sensei*. He's made excellent progress in the martial arts, though his use of the sword needs improvement. Neither Churi nor Eko speak English, by the way, but I'm sure you'll find that they anticipate your needs."

"We're grateful for your hospitality," Rachel said.

"Your spirit is Japanese." Akira studied her with appreciation, then said something to Eko and Churi, who quickly departed. "I'd be honored," he told Savage and Rachel, "if you'd enter my home."

4

In shadows, on a low porch beneath the roof's overhang, Savage removed his shoes, making a point to do so before Akira removed his own. He wanted to let Akira know he remembered what Akira had told him prior to leaving Dulles Airport. Rachel followed his example. Akira nodded approvingly, set his shoes next to theirs, and opened the door, stepping back to let them enter before him.

The lamps at each window cast a warm glow over the room. Savoring the fragrance of incense, Savage admired the burnished cedar beams across the ceiling, the space between and above them making the small room seem spacious. The walls were white, in latticed sections, made of paper upon which objects from other rooms cast shadows. The floor was covered by rectangular rice-straw mats that Akira had explained were called *tatami*. Their resilient woven fibers had a massaging effect on Savage's stockinged feet.

Rachel approached a pen-and-ink drawing that hung on a wall. With economical vividness, it depicted a dove on a leafless branch. "I don't think I've ever seen anything so . . ." When she turned away, her eyes glistened.

"From the sixteenth century," Akira said. "It's a hobby of mine. Collecting classical Japanese art. An *expensive* hobby, to be sure. But it gives me satisfaction." He reached toward a section of a wall and slid it to the right, creating a door to another room. "Would you care to see others?"

"Please."

For the next twenty minutes, Savage was stunned by beauty. His eerie sensation of having been transported back in time intensified as Akira led them from room to room, opening and closing sections of walls, displaying increasingly impressive artworks. Silk screens, sculptures, ceramics, more pen-and-inks. The elegant simplicity of the images, sometimes of nature, sometimes of soldiers in combat, made Savage frequently hold his breath, as if to breathe would disturb the subtlety of his pleasure.

"Everything I've shown you has a common element," Akira said. "They were all created by samurai."

Rachel looked surprised.

"Men of war devoting themselves to the arts of peace," Akira said.

Savage remembered what Akira had explained. The samurai had come into prominence during the twelfth century when regional warlords, known as *daimyo,* needed fiercely loyal warrior-protectors to control their domains. The following century, Zen Buddhism was introduced to Japan from Korea. That religion's insistence on disciplining both the body and the spirit appealed to the samurai, who realized the practical value of making their sword arms an extension of their souls. To act without thought—to respond instantaneously to instinct—insured victory over an enemy who had to plan before he struck. An extra advantage was that Zen Buddhism encouraged meditation whereby one was purged of emotion and achieved a stillness at one's core. The samurai trained themselves to be neither fearful of death nor hopeful of victory and thus entered combat with a neutral attentiveness, indifferent to—but prepared for—the violent demands of each instant.

"For a time, the ruling class despised the crude warriors they depended on for their safety," Akira said. "The samurai responded by teaching themselves courtly arts and eventually displacing the snobbish elite who ridiculed them. These paintings, sculptures, and ceramics are perfect examples of the samurai's devotion to Zen. All soothe the spirit. All produce peace of mind and soul. But the ultimate samurai artwork is the sword."

Akira slid open another section of wall, leading Savage and Rachel toward scabbarded swords arranged on a wall.

"A samurai meditated before creating the instrument of his profession. After purifying himself, he then purified his workshop, put on a white robe, and began the slow, patient, arduous process of layering steel upon steel, repeatedly heating, folding, and hammering these layers until he achieved an ideal resilience, so the sword would adapt to stress, and an ideal hardness, so the blade would retain its edge: similar to the spirit and the body of the samurai. The long sword was used in battle. And this, the short sword"—Akira removed one from the wall and unsheathed it, turning it this way and that so the polished blade gleamed with reflected light—"was used for ritual suicide. *Seppuku.* If a samurai failed in combat or inadvertently offended his lord, it was his duty to kill himself by disembowelment, the ultimate test of his code of honor." Akira sighed, sheathed the blade, and hung it back on the wall. "I'm behaving like a Westerner. Forgive me for talking too much."

"Not at all. I was fascinated," Rachel said.

"You're very kind." Akira seemed about to say something else but turned as Eko entered, bowed, and spoke to him. "Good. Our bath is ready."

5

They took turns using a gleaming white shower stall at the rear of the house, wrapped towels around themselves, and met on a softly lit porch in back.

"Cleansing oneself is only a preliminary to bathing," Akira said. "To bathe, one must soak."

"A hot tub?" Rachel was amazed.

"Along with electricity and indoor plumbing, one of my compromises with the twentieth century. A useful way to keep the water at the necessary temperature."

The tub was sided with cedar wood, though its interior was made of plastic. It stood on the left end of the porch, the overhang providing privacy. Steam rose off the water.

Rachel mounted steps to a platform, put a foot in the tub, and at once jerked back. "It's scalding!"

"It will seem so at first," Akira said. "Enter slowly. Your body will adjust."

She didn't look convinced.

"A bath must be very warm," Akira assured her. To prove his point, he got in the tub without hesitation and submerged himself to the neck.

Biting her lip, Rachel eased down.

Savage joined them, abruptly thrashed, and almost scrambled out. "My God, it's hot!"

Rachel roared with laughter.

Her outburst made Savage laugh as well. He splashed water at her. That made Akira start laughing, and Savage splashed water at *him*.

As their laughter subsided, Savage realized that the temperature no longer felt oppressive. Indeed it penetrated knotted muscles, loosening cramps in his legs and back, relieving the fatigue of seventeen hours in an airplane. He leaned back on a ledge along the tub, the soothing hot water above his shoulders, and admired Rachel.

Her hair—wet from the shower—was combed back behind her ears. It emphasized the shape of her head, the elegant contours of her face. Steam glistened on her cheeks and gave them color. Her blue eyes were still bright with laughter, reminding him of sapphires. He felt her nudge his foot with her toe. He smiled and glanced past the porch toward the garden at the back of the house.

Though dusk had turned into darkness, the glow from the lamps in the windows and the light on the porch allowed him to see the indistinct shapes of rocks and shrubs among sand.

Beyond, he heard water trickling.

"There's a pool you can't see in the dark," Akira said as if knowing what Savage thought.

"With goldfish and lily pads?"

"It wouldn't be a pool without them."

"Naturally." Savage kept smiling.

"It feels so . . . Why would you ever leave here?" Rachel asked.

"To be useful."

"That's our trouble," Savage said.

"Not our only trouble," Akira added and broke the spell, bringing Savage from the past to the present. "I haven't been in Japan since Muto Kamichi hired me to protect him."

"Since you *think* he hired you to protect him," Savage said.

Akira agreed. "False memory."

"And as we found out, his name's not Muto Kamichi. It's Kunio Shirai."

"A militant neo-nationalist politician. In the months before our nightmare began, when I was still in Japan, or think I was still in Japan, I never heard of him. Granted, there are ultraconservative groups that emphasize anti-Americanism, but they're small, without influence. The man we saw on television, though, was capable of mustering support from thousands of students. The announcer said that Shirai's power base was strong enough to splinter Japan's major party. It doesn't make sense. Who *is* this man? Where did he come from? How did he gain influence so quickly?"

"And what do both of you have to do with him?" Rachel asked. "Who wants you to believe you saw Shirai cut in half six months ago?"

"Tomorrow, we'll find some answers," Akira said.

Savage squinted. "How?"

"By talking to a wise and holy man."

Savage didn't understand, but before he could ask Akira to elaborate, Eko came onto the porch, bowed, and spoke.

"She wants to know if you're hungry," Akira said.

"Lord, no," Rachel said. "I'm still digesting the ton of food I ate on the airplane."

"Me neither," Savage said.

Akira sent Eko away.

"This heat." Rachel yawned. "The water's so soothing. I could fall asleep right here."

"We could *all* use some sleep," Akira said. He climbed from the tub, his wet towel clinging to his muscular hips, and as if on signal, Eko returned with three terry-cloth robes. He put one on and handed the others to Savage and Rachel when they got out. "I'll show you to your rooms."

Inside, along a narrow corridor, Akira slid open two sections of a wall, revealing adjacent rooms. In each, a lamp on a low table cast a golden glimmer. A *futon* mattress, which Akira had explained was rolled up and stored in a closet during the day, had been unfolded and set upon the *tatami* mats, along with a pillow and quilts. Rachel's travel bag was in the room on the left, Savage's on the right.

"My room is across from yours," Akira said. "The house has intrusion detectors, as do the walls around the property. I've arranged for Churi to stand watch. He's dependable, with skills to match. Sleep peacefully. *O-yasumi nasai*, or as you say, 'good night.' "

Akira bowed, stepped into his room, and shut its sliding door.

After bowing to Akira, Savage turned to Rachel.

He felt awkward. "See you in the morning."

Rachel looked equally awkward. "Right."

Savage kissed her. Her breasts were soft yet firm beneath her robe. As his body responded, he wanted to ask her to share his room, but the house had the atmosphere of a temple, and because Akira had assigned them separate rooms, it seemed indelicate to change his arrangements. Then, too, the walls were literally paper thin. Akira might be embarrassed by the sounds of their lovemaking.

Rachel's throat squeezed her voice and made it husky. "Good night, love. *O-yasumi nasai*."

Savage stroked her cheek. With a gentle whisper, he repeated the Japanese expression.

They studied each other.

Reluctantly Savage entered his room and slid the wall shut.

Standing motionless, he waited for his breathing to become subdued, his heart to stop racing. A pair of black pajamas had been laid out on the table. Putting them on, he noticed that a toothbrush and a small tube of paste had been set beside a glass of water and an orange and blue ceramic basin on a shelf.

Considerate down to the smallest detail, Savage thought.

Fatigue insisted. Languidly he brushed his teeth. He'd relieved himself before taking his shower. All that remained was to shut off the lamp and slump onto the *futon*. In the dark, he saw faint light through the wall beside him, Rachel's shadow moving. Then the light was extinguished, and he heard her settling onto her mattress.

He stared at the murky ceiling, preoccupied by what had brought them here, what possibly awaited them tomorrow, and what their chances were of surviving.

No option, he thought. We have to take the risk. We're compelled to go forward. And if we do survive, what will happen between Rachel and me? Does she just need to feel secure, to have someone devoted to her protection?

Or is that a definition of love? Doesn't everyone want to feel secure? And don't forget, she had the chance to leave. She's putting herself at risk to be here, to be with you.

So what's your problem? What's bugging you?

I'm afraid if I fall any harder in love . . . When she realizes her protector's only human, with flaws like anyone else, it might be she'll move on.

He shook his head. Don't think so much. What is it Rachel keeps saying? *Abraham believed by virtue of the absurd. Faith is absurd, and so is love. You've got to trust.*

Don't worry about the future. Now is what matters.

On the *futon,* he turned toward the wall that separated him from Rachel. He suddenly realized that Akira had arranged for Rachel's *futon* to be set directly against the other side of the wall just as Savage's was directly against *this* side. If it weren't for the wall, he'd be able to reach over and touch her.

The wall. His pulse quickened as he understood how truly delicate Akira had been. Rather than raise the indiscreet issue of whether they preferred two rooms or one, he'd left the choice for them to make in private. All Savage had to do was . . .

Reaching over, he slid a section of the wall to one side. He saw the contour of her body beneath the quilt. She was three feet away, and his vision had adjusted to the darkness sufficiently for him to see that she lay on her side, her face to him.

Her eyes were open. She smiled.

His soul ached. He lifted his quilt. She shifted from beneath her own and joined him. When he lowered the quilt to cover their heads, he felt as if they were in a sleeping bag in a tent.

Her mouth found his. His heart pounded faster. They held each other, pressing, squirming. He was on her, then she on him. Their kiss became more insistent. They tugged at each other's pajama bottoms, soft cotton sliding down over thighs, knees, and ankles. He drew his fingers up her leg, stroked her stomach, cupped a breast.

"Please," she murmured.

With his head beneath the quilt, he raised her pajama top, kissing her nipples, their hardness increasing, swelling between his lips.

"Please," she whispered.

When he entered her, she gasped. He shuddered, gently stroking, wanting to slide so deeply within her that he'd be one with her. She dug her fingernails into his back. She clutched his hair. At once she kissed him again, mouth open, tongue probing as if she wanted to enter, to be one with, him.

As they climaxed, their kiss became so full that Akira couldn't possibly have heard them, for they swallowed each other's moans.

6

Savage woke in greater darkness. The lamps in the hallway and in other parts of the house had been turned off, their glow no longer penetrating the paper walls of his room. The house was silent. Rachel lay next to him, an arm across his chest, her head against his. He smelled the scent of her hair, the sweetness of her skin. The memory of their lovemaking made him smile. He felt privileged to have her beside him and more than that, fulfilled.

Stretching his legs, enjoying the comfort of the *futon*, he studied the luminous numbers on his watch. Seventeen minutes after three. He'd slept more than six hours. Normally that would have been sufficient for him, but after the exhausting flight from America and the languor he'd experienced after Rachel and he finished making love, he was surprised that he hadn't slept longer. Maybe his body clock hadn't adjusted to the change in time zones, he thought. Maybe he subconsciously felt it was morning in America instead of the middle of the night in Japan.

Rachel sighed in her sleep and nuzzled against him. He smiled again. Go back to sleep, he told himself. Get all the rest you can. *While* you can. Surrendering to the warmth of the quilt, he yawned and closed his eyes.

But at once he reopened them.

To his left, toward the back of the house, possibly *outside* the house, he heard a muffled cough. Tense, he almost sat up. Then he realized that the cough must have come from Churi, who was standing guard outside the house.

Straining to listen, Savage waited five minutes but didn't hear another cough. Relax, he told himself. But he wondered if Churi, who'd been trained by Akira, would have *allowed* himself to cough or if his body absolutely insisted, to cough with sufficient force to be heard inside the house. Akira would have told him, don't do anything to reveal your position.

Still, Akira had mentioned that Churi wasn't fully trained. It could be that Churi's discipline had momentarily failed.

Savage shrugged off his apprehension and snuggled closer to Rachel, absorbing her warmth. Abruptly he jerked his head up.

The faint dry scrape of rice straw, of something applying gradual pressure to the woven fibers of a *tatami* mat, made him stare toward the wall that led to the corridor.

When he heard a second subtle scrape, he had no doubt —they were footsteps. Carefully placed. Slow and cautious. From bare or stockinged feet. If not for the paper-thin wall, they'd have been undetectable.

Akira going to the bathroom?

No, Savage instantly decided. There'd been no sound of a section of wall being opened.

Churi patrolling the corridor?

Why? The interior was guarded by intrusion sensors. Churi was useful only if he watched from outside.

Eko? Perhaps she'd wakened early, as elderly people often did, and decided to perform some necessary chore, possibly preparations for a special breakfast.

No, Savage thought. Although her room was farther along the corridor, toward the back, he was sure he'd have heard a section of the wall slide open when she entered the corridor.

Besides, the delicate footsteps weren't toward the rear of the house, where the kitchen and the bathroom were, but directly between Akira's room and Savage's.

He almost touched Rachel to wake and warn her. Pulse rushing, he decided not to. Even if he pressed a hand to her mouth, she might make a sound that would alert whoever was in the corridor. Warily, silently, he raised the quilt, doubling it over her. His nervous system quivered. Adrenaline flooded through him. Blood surged from his extremities toward his stomach, burning. He contracted his chest muscles, controlling the reflexive urge to breathe rapidly, and stealthily rose to a crouch.

But he didn't dare move from the *futon*. If he stepped on the mats, he'd make the same subtle noise the intruder had and warn him. He had to stay immobile, his reflexes primed, till circumstances forced him into action.

He didn't have a handgun. Prior to reaching Dulles Airport, Akira and he had thrown their .45s down a sewer because they couldn't hope to get the weapons past the X-ray machines and metal detectors at the airport's security gates. If the intruder entered Savage's room, Savage would have to get close enough to fight with him hand to hand.

His muscles hardened. He stared toward the dark wall, hearing a slight scratch—a section of wall being gingerly opened.

Not Savage's wall. Beyond it. On the other side of the corridor, someone was entering *Akira's* room.

Now. Savage had to act before Akira was taken by surprise.

Stomach on fire, he took a step, and suddenly flinched as the wall to his room burst inward, wood and paper flying, two figures hurtling toward the floor. They landed so hard that the figure on the bottom grunted from the impact, breath knocked out of him.

Two men.

Savage recognized Akira's silhouette on top, chopping the edge of his hand toward the other man's face. The intruder was dressed completely in black, a dark hood over his head. As he grunted again, this time from Akira's blow, he fired a pistol equipped with a silencer. The spitting bullet struck the ceiling, and Savage dove.

But not straight ahead to help Akira. He assumed that Akira could control the threat. Instead he dove to the right, over Rachel, landing beside her, dragging her into the adjacent room. She'd woken, screaming, when the wall burst inward and the men slammed onto the floor. She screamed again as Savage tugged her, desperate to remove her from the intruder's line of fire.

The intruder shot again despite repeated blows from Akira. The bullet struck the wall near Savage and Rachel.

She was too breathless from shock to scream now. Whimpering, she followed Savage's lead and surged to a running crouch. Desperate, disoriented in the blackness of the unfamiliar house, she reached the next wall before she realized, and unable to control her momentum in time to tug at a section of the wall, she crashed through it, sprawling in a frenzy on the mats of a farther room.

Savage dragged her to her feet and pushed. *"Keep going. Get to the front of the house. Stay low."*

The instant she stumbled away from him, he spun to rush back to Akira. As he did, his temples throbbed when he realized where he was—the room in which Akira had shown Rachel and him the samurai swords. Savage charged toward the wall on which they hung, grabbed one, unsheathed it, and surprised by how long it felt, pointed it toward the ceiling lest he cut himself, and hurried through the gap in the wall.

The intruder's pistol spat again. The bullet punctured a wall as Savage rushed through Rachel's room into his own. Desperate, he saw Akira chop the side of his hand against the intruder's face yet again, and the man lay still.

Savage exhaled.

But at once he shouted, "Akira, behind you!"

Another dark figure loomed, filling the hole in the wall, arm extended, aiming.

Akira rolled.

With a muffled whump, the assassin's bullet missed Akira's back and struck the motionless man on the floor.

Savage still held the sword so it was pointed toward the ceiling. Using both hands to grip its handle, mustering the full strength of his arms, he whipped the blade down. At the same time, he released his grip and hurtled the sword toward the man in the corridor.

He'd aimed the blade's tip toward the intruder's chest. In the dark, he couldn't see the sword flying. Hoping to hear cloth tear, flesh being sliced, instead he heard the clang of metal against metal.

The blade had struck the intruder's pistol.

The handgun thumped on the floor.

The intruder pivoted, his murky silhouette disappearing. Footsteps charged along the corridor toward the back of the house.

Savage heard bodies collide, Eko gasping, someone falling. He rushed toward the hole in the wall.

Akira got there before him, stooping, fumbling for something. "Where's the gun?" He barked a Japanese expletive when his pawing hands failed to find it. Cursing again, he grabbed the sword and lunged through the hole in the wall.

Savage followed in time to glimpse the intruder stoop beside a body, pick up another sword, and rush through the open back door.

The body on the floor in the doorway was Churi, who lay on his chest with his legs toward the porch.

With a wail of outrage, Akira, too, leaped over him, landed warily, ready with his sword in case the intruder was hiding in wait for him, then scurried off the porch into the blackness of the garden.

About to race down the corridor and join the pursuit, Savage suddenly paused when his foot struck an object. The handgun Akira had been searching for. He scooped it up and ran.

Eko staggered from her room, shaken by the intruder's impact against her.

Savage pivoted sideways, frantically passed her, saw a dark stain on Churi's back as he leaped over him, and crouched on the porch, aiming the pistol toward the garden.

From the handgun's shape, Savage knew that it was a Beretta 9 mm, the sidearm for NATO and the U.S. armed forces. A silencer projected from its barrel. Its magazine held fifteen rounds.

He shifted nervously toward the shelter of the steps that led to the hot tub and continued staring toward the garden, aiming the Beretta. A three-quarter moon and the spill of streetlights from beyond the garden's wall made the garden less murky than the house's interior. He saw the shadows of rocks and shrubs on the golden sand. He was even able to see the dark curves of the rake marks in the sand.

And two sets of widely spaced footprints that showed where Akira had chased the intruder toward the greater blackness of the rear of the garden.

Though Savage strained his vision, he couldn't see farther than thirty paces beyond the porch. Toward the back, a dark cloud seemed to have settled. He heard traffic beyond the wall, a distant car horn, a faraway squeal of brakes, and abruptly amid the darkness at the rear of the garden, steel clanged against steel, a sharp, hard, high-pitched reverberation: swords colliding.

Another clang instantly followed. And another, fierce and urgent.

Savage sprang from behind the steps. Chest tight, he raced toward the garden. The sand was cold, his bare feet sinking into it as he scrambled past a rock, then a shrub. The closer he sped toward the rear of the garden, the better he could see. Moonlight flashed off swords. The clang of their impacts intensified. He jerked to a stop, startled by a dark figure rushing backward toward him, sword raised, blocking a thrust, darting to the right, striking in return.

The flurry of movement was so unexpected, a blur in the night, that Savage couldn't tell if the figure was Akira or the intruder. He raised the Beretta, prepared to fire the moment he had an unambiguous target. The two figures circled each other, both hands gripping their swords, the blades on an upward angle.

Akira! Savage recognized him.

Akira *had* been the figure who'd abruptly appeared, rushing backward. Savage aimed the Beretta, but before he could shoot Akira's opponent, the two men struck at each other, parried, darted sideways, struck yet again, and rapidly circled.

Savage concentrated, focusing along the Beretta's sights. Sweat streamed off his forehead. His trigger finger was tensely poised. If they'd just stop moving, he thought. Stand still for a second! That's all I need! A second! No more! Just time for one clean shot!

But the figures kept striking, darting, exchanging positions. The intruder lunged into Savage's line of fire. Before there was time to shoot, Akira replaced the intruder.

The swords collided more rapidly.

Savage kept aiming.

"Stay out of this, Savage! He's mine! *For Churi!*"

Reluctant, Savage lowered the handgun. If he shot the intruder, if he denied Akira the chance to maintain his honor by avenging his student, Akira would never forgive him.

Stepping back from the fight, Savage watched in dismay. Helplessness soured his stomach.

Akira's blade flashed toward the intruder's chest. The intruder twisted away and struck at Akira's head. Or seemed to, for the movement was a feint. As Akira thrust to block the sword, the intruder twisted again and swung with stunning speed toward Akira's right thigh.

The force of the blow would have severed Akira's leg. But breathing fiercely, Akira leaped backward. The moment he hit the sand, he dodged to the left, avoiding a further eyeblink-rapid strike. While the blade hissed past him, Akira swung. Lunged. Swung again, forcing his opponent to retreat. Lunged and swung again, anticipating that his opponent would dodge to the left.

The intruder reversed his direction and thrust. Akira veered nimbly, attacking with a flurry of blows—upward, sideways, downward—all the while advancing, his speed and grace astonishing.

Abruptly he pivoted sideways and crooked his left arm in front of his chest. Resting the flat of his blade on his forearm, gripping the sword with his other hand, directing the tip of the blade straight ahead, he took short, smooth, relentless steps toward his opponent.

The opponent backed away.

Akira kept advancing.

The opponent continued his retreat, unexpectedly shifted to the left, and began to circle Akira, who stopped his advance and turned in place, remaining eye to eye with his circling enemy.

The intruder attacked. As Akira dodged, he slipped on the sand, lurched backward, and bumped against a rock. His blink of surprise made Savage moan.

Heart swollen, Savage jerked the Beretta up, aiming.

The intruder slashed toward Akira.

Akira darted sideways. The intruder's sword whacked chips from the rock, and Akira swung upward, slicing his enemy's torso from the lower left to the upper right. With the sound of a zipper being opened, Akira severed the intruder's intestines, stomach, and rib cage.

Blood fountained. Organs cascaded. Wheezing, the intruder dropped his sword, stumbled backward, jerked grotesquely, and toppled into what looked like a black pit behind him.

The pit was a pond. The intruder splashed heavily, water erupting. As the waves subsided, he floated, face up, eyes wide, motionless.

Numb, Savage approached. In the night, he couldn't see the crimson that tainted the water, but he imagined it. Intestines floated. Despite his years of witnessing death, he wanted to vomit.

Akira stared at the corpse. His chest heaved. Swallowing audibly, he turned to Savage. "I thank you for not interfering."

"It took all my self-control."

"But I knew that I could depend on you." Sweat glistened, reflecting moonlight, on Akira's face.

"Listen," Savage said. "In the house. I didn't try to help you right away because—"

"You had to see to our principal's safety first."

"Right. Our principal. The reflex was automatic. It had nothing to do with the way I feel about her."

"And if she *hadn't* been our principal but simply the woman you love?" Akira asked.

Savage didn't know the answer.

"In that case, I think it's fortunate," Akira said, "that the woman you love *is* our principal."

"Yes," Savage said, distressed, at the same time grateful that Akira had absolved him. "Extremely fortunate."

"How did they get in? The top of each wall has intrusion sensors." Akira passed the pond, no longer staring at the corpse that floated there. He reached the back wall and paced along it toward the right.

Savage followed him to a corner, then along another wall. Fifteen seconds later, they came to a rope imbedded in the sand. The rope slanted up toward the top of a four-story building. Akira dug into the sand. In the ground beneath it, he found that the rope was attached to a bolt.

"They fired the bolt from the roof of the building," Akira said. "The device they used to fire it must have had a sound suppressor. Either that or they used an extremely powerful catapult, something silent like a crossbow that Churi wouldn't hear."

"And as soon as the rope was anchored, they slid down, avoiding the top of the wall," Savage said. "But your house has intrusion detectors as well. How did they get inside?"

Akira walked despondently toward the house. "Churi let them."

"What? But I thought you trusted him."

"Without question." They neared the back porch. Akira pointed toward Churi's body. "Note his position. The door is open. He fell, half in, half out of the house. He's on his stomach. His head is within the corridor." They reached the body. "And he has blood on his back. A bullet hole."

"So he was going into the house when he was shot from behind," Savage said.

Akira knelt and touched Churi's shoulder. His voice was thick with grief. "The evidence supports that conclusion. There's a switch hidden near the hot tub that shuts off the sensors. After standing watch for hours, Churi must have felt the need to enter the house, possibly to use the bathroom. When he shut off the sensors and opened the door, he was shot."

And his last frantic breath must have been the cough I heard, Savage thought. The sounds of the door being opened, of Churi falling, must have been what made me wake up, but I wasn't aware I'd heard them. They also woke Akira.

"Handguns are strictly controlled in Japan," Akira said. "That's why Churi had the sword, which the man in the pool grabbed as he ran from the house. Presumably Churi intended to reactivate the intrusion sensors after he entered and locked the door. Note the urine stain around his hips." Akira stroked the back of Churi's head. "My dear friend, how could you have been so foolish? So many times I told you, don't breach the perimeter of what you're guarding. Don't leave your post. Make sure you relieve yourself before you go on duty, and if the needs of your body later insist, urinate in your clothes. Soundlessly. The discomfort you'll feel is nothing compared to the need to fulfill your obligation as a protector. *Why, Churi?* Did I not teach you well enough? Was I not worthy to be your *sensei?*" Akira's shoulders heaved. He sobbed, leaned down, and kissed the back of Churi's neck.

Savage watched helplessly. There was nothing he could think of to say. Every consoling statement that occurred to him seemed pathetically inadequate.

At last, compassion told him what to do. No speeches. No rationalizations. No attempt to minimize the loss or try to make some sense of it. Two heartfelt words would say it all.

"I'm sorry." Savage gripped Akira's heaving shoulders.

Wiping his tears, struggling for breath, Akira said, his voice unsteady, *"Domo arigato."*

A movement in the corridor caught Savage's attention. Glancing up from Akira, he saw Eko standing in front of Churi. Tears streamed down her face. Slowly kneeling, then sitting, she cradled her grandson's head.

Savage felt choked.

But another movement in the corridor attracted his gaze as well. Like someone who'd been hypnotized, Rachel stepped haltingly from the dark. Her face was disturbingly pale, her features slack, her eyes blank with shock.

She stared uncomprehendingly straight ahead, seemingly unaware of Eko sitting before her, of Akira stroking Churi's hair, of Savage gripping Akira's shoulders.

Unfocused, though directed toward the garden, her eyes refused to blink.

My God, Savage thought. He shivered when he studied her arms straight down her sides and realized she held a pistol in her right hand, its silencer pointing toward her right foot. *After we left the house, she must have gone back to my room. She must have found the pistol on the floor beside the first intruder Akira killed.*

I told her to stay in the front of the house.

Why didn't she listen? What's she doing with the gun?

Feeling pressure behind his ears, Savage cautiously straightened. Afraid that he'd startle her, make her flinch and reflexively fire the pistol, he moved slowly, stepped gingerly past Akira, Churi, and Eko, and warily put both hands on hers. As he shifted the weapon so it was pointed toward a wall, he removed her finger from the trigger and pried her fingers off the grip.

"There," he said. His shoulders relaxing, he set the pistol on the floor. "That's better. I know you're scared, but you shouldn't have picked up the gun. You might have shot yourself. Or one of us."

She didn't reply, didn't seem aware that he'd taken the gun, but just kept staring toward the night.

"Before you pick up a pistol again," Savage said, "wait till I teach you how to handle it."

"Know," she whispered.

"Know?"

"How to handle one."

"Of course, you do." Savage hoped he didn't sound as if he humored her.

"Father taught me." Though close to him, Rachel's murmur sounded far away.

Savage waited, his arm around her. Her back was disturbingly rigid.

"Rifles, pistols, shotguns. Skeet shooting every Sunday. He once made me kill a pheasant." She shuddered.

"Long ago," Savage said. "And what happened tonight is over. You're safe now."

"*For* now. It isn't going to end. Others will come. They'll never stop."

"You're wrong," Savage said. "They will stop. We'll make them stop. And I'll protect you."

"Had to . . . Picked up the pistol. Three of them."

"I'm not sure what you . . ."

Then Savage *was* sure what she meant, and he shuddered just as she did. *"Three?"*

She pivoted slowly, an inch at a time. It was almost as if a section of the floor moved instead of her feet. Blank, she faced the murky corridor.

Appalled, Savage picked up the pistol and hurried along the corridor. He found a light switch, turned it on. Blinking from the sudden glare, he stepped through the shattered wall to his room. The dark-clothed corpse on the floor was the first man Akira had killed. Blood soaked his chest, but that had been caused by the other intruder's shooting at Akira, missing, and hitting his partner.

Three of them?

Savage looked into Rachel's room and saw no one. Apprehensive, he entered the room beyond it, turned on a lamp, and found it deserted. For a moment, he studied the samurai swords on a wall and the blank space where the sword he'd taken had hung.

He opened a section of the wall and returned to the corridor. At the far end, Rachel hadn't moved. Trancelike, she faced him, her back to Akira and Eko as they touched Churi's body, grieving.

"Rachel, are you sure?"

Then he saw the empty bullet casings on the mats between Akira's room and his own. Ready with the pistol, he approached the open wall to Akira's room.

Inside, a black-clothed man lay flat on his back, his eyes open wide with surprise, blood all around him, his chest stitched with bullet holes. There were empty casings at his feet.

Savage turned toward the empty casings in the corridor and further casings in his own room. Some of the casings had been ejected from the pistol when the intruder shot, struggling with Akira.

How many times had the intruder fired? Savage wondered.

Four, maybe five. There'd been so much going on that Savage couldn't remember. Dreading what he'd discover, he removed the magazine from the bottom of the pistol's grip.

The magazine was empty.

He pulled back the slide on top of the pistol. The firing chamber was empty. The pistol was designed so that when the last empty casing flipped from the gun the slide would stay back. That's what had fooled him. Rachel must have pressed the release so the slide slid forward as if the pistol were loaded.

Jesus, he thought. He surveyed the trail of casings from his room, across the corridor, into Akira's room. The third intruder must have hidden in the house when their plan went bad. Rachel came into my room, found the pistol, heard or saw the third man.

And shot him until the gun was empty, ten rounds at least, all the time walking toward him into Akira's room, standing above him, continuing to fire.

Jesus, he repeated. She was so damned terrified that she'd completely lost control. No wonder she looks like a zombie. She isn't in shock because they attacked us. She's in shock because . . .

He walked down the corridor and held her tightly. "You didn't have a choice."

Her arms remained at her side, her body rigid.

"Rachel, you had to defend yourself. Think about it. *He'd* have killed *you*. You probably saved Akira's life, Eko's, and mine as well. You did the right thing."

Her chest heaved against him. "Corpses. Everywhere we go, people die. . . . And now I'm a killer, too."

She didn't need to add, because of *you*, because I stayed with you, because I fell in love with you.

What a price to pay for loving someone, Savage thought.

"I didn't just shoot him. I mutilated him," Rachel said.

At last she started to cry. Her tears soaked Savage's pajama top. They stung his skin.

Because I let you stay with me, Savage thought. This is *my* fault. For letting myself get involved. Churi isn't the only one who made mistakes tonight.

Damn it, I broke so many rules.

If Rachel had been just my principal and not my lover, I'd have known what to do! *My responsibility was to stay with her.* Akira knew the risks! But because I didn't know if I was protecting my principal or my lover, I felt guilty for choosing sides, for looking after *my* interests, for deserting Akira.

Akira. That's another rule I broke. Making friends with him. A protector *shouldn't* be friends with another protector! Because then you don't know whom to protect, your friend or your principal!

Christ, what a mess. As soon as Rachel was safe, I shouldn't have run to help Akira. I should have searched the goddamn house to make sure there weren't other intruders. Rachel was forced to kill that man because I fucked up.

Rachel convulsed, sobs racking her.

Savage held her tighter. "I'm sorry, Rachel."

That's twice tonight I said those words, he thought.

And how many *more* times will I have to say them?

"I'd give anything to change what happened," he told her.

He was just about to say *the sooner you get away from me the better it'll be for you* when she surprised him, putting her arms around him.

"Whoever sent those men, whoever made me kill," she said, "God help me, I want him to pay. I'm angry enough to kill again."

Her outburst shocked him. Frowning past her shoulder, Savage saw Akira and Eko touching Churi's body at the end of the corridor.

Akira rose, trembling with grief, and turned toward the garden, his voice deep, strangled with emotion. "For fifteen years, my father concentrated to create this garden. For almost as many years, I continued his efforts. Look at it. Footprints obscure the rake marks. Blood soaks the sand. The pool has been desecrated. The efforts of what amounts to half a lifetime ruined. Whoever hired these cowards to invade my home so lacks nobility that he doesn't deserve to be treated as a worthy adversary. When I find him, I shall kill him with contempt, dismember his body, and dump it into the sea. His spirit will not be at peace with those of his ancestors. I swear to achieve this for what they did to my father's garden.'' Akira exhaled. ''And to Churi.''

Akira's anger, coupled with Rachel's, made Savage's heart plummet. Their vows of revenge chilled his veins. What was it Rachel had said? *Corpses. Everywhere we go, people die.* Yes, so much death, he thought. We're caught in it. Trapped. I once believed what Graham taught me, that vengeance was honorable. Now? The bitterness in Rachel's voice. The ferocity on Akira's face. What we do to survive this nightmare could destroy us.

Feeling Rachel sob against him, Savage held her tighter.

7

They sat on cushions at a low black table in a room that hadn't been despoiled.

''Who sent those men here? How did they know they'd find us?'' Savage asked.

Akira's usually melancholy features were now hard with outrage. ''They didn't just happen to attack us on the night we arrived. They were waiting.''

''Which means that someone assumed we'd eventually come here from America,'' Rachel said. ''. . . Virginia Beach, and now here.''

''I don't think the two attacks are related,'' Savage said. ''In Virginia Beach, the intent seemed to be to kill Mac, so he wouldn't reveal information, and to get you away from Akira and me, so you wouldn't . . . What? Be in the way? Interfere with the reason we'd been given false memories? Evidently you're not supposed to be a part of this.''

"In contrast, tonight's attack was indiscriminate," Akira said. "Only people I totally trust have been invited into my home. Eko would never tell anyone about the arrangements inside. Nor would Churi. The intruders could not have known which bedroom was mine and which were the guest rooms. No single one of us was their objective. If they'd wanted to take Rachel away from us, they'd have chosen a controllable situation in which they had a clear view of her. *But to sneak inside my home?* It appears that they came for, meant to kill, all three of us."

Rachel's eyes narrowed. *"Whoever hired the team in Virginia Beach isn't the same as whoever sent these three men tonight."*

"It looks that way," Savage said. "The two attacks were controlled by different people with different goals. One wants us to continue searching. The *other* wants the search to end. But who? Damn it, what's going on?"

Rachel turned toward Akira. "You mentioned a man you wanted to talk to. You called him 'wise and holy.' "

Akira nodded. "I hoped we could see him this morning. But now I'm afraid we'll have to postpone the visit. . . . Because of Churi." The tendons in Akira's throat bulged like ropes. "Arrangements must be made."

From the rear of the house, Savage heard Eko weeping and imagined her continuing to cradle her grandson's head. The corpse had been brought inside and the door locked.

"If only the three intruders had been killed, I'd be tempted to dispose of their bodies," Akira said. "But I don't own a car to take them away, and by the time I rented one, the streets would be so crowded that we'd be seen carrying the bodies outside, no matter how well we tried to disguise them. An alternative would be to take advantage of the remaining darkness and bury the corpses in the garden. That solution is unacceptable. I refuse to permit a further insult to my father's garden. Besides, the intruders don't matter. *Churi* does. He *must* be given a proper funeral. He *must* be buried with honor. It's essential that Eko and I be able to visit him often, to pray at his grave. My duty is clear. I'm forced to alert the police."

Savage studied him. "Yes."

"When they arrive, you shouldn't be here," Akira said. "If two Americans are implicated in the deaths, the police will conduct a much more rigorous investigation. They'll discover that you entered this country with counterfeit passports. You'll be arrested. Even if the police don't question your passports, the publicity will attract so much attention it'll hurt our search."

"But what will you tell the police?" Rachel asked.

"Three men broke into my house to steal my art collection. They shot Churi in the process. The commotion wakened me and led to a struggle. I killed one in hand-to-hand combat, used his pistol to kill another, emptied the weapon, grabbed a sword and chased the third intruder, who'd also grabbed a sword but failed to defend himself against my attack. That I used a sword will seem heroic and be in my favor."

Savage thought about it. "All the details fit. It ought to work." It better, he silently added.

"But only if I wipe your and Rachel's fingerprints from the pistols you held," Akira said. "After that, because the weapons won't have prints, I'll need to press them against the fingertips of the dead man in your room and the one in the garden. Then too, I'll need to fire a weapon to put traces of burnt gunpowder on my hands, in case the police test my skin to prove that I did indeed discharge a pistol. . . . Can you think of anything else?"

"Yes," Savage said. "My fingerprints are on one of the swords."

"I'll take care of it. You should leave right now. Before the condition of the bodies warns the medical examiner that an undue amount of time passed between the fight and when I phoned the police."

Rachel looked reluctant. *"But where should we go? How do we get in touch with you?* I'm so used to the three of us being together, the thought of being separated . . ."

"I'll join you as soon as possible," Akira said. "I'll give you my phone number, but you shouldn't call here unless it's absolutely necessary. I'll also give you directions to a restaurant I'm fond of. Be there at noon. If I can't meet you, I'll phone. The owner knows me. I trust him.''

"But what if you don't have the chance to call there?" Rachel's voice quavered.

"Return to the restaurant at six in the evening.''

"And if you still don't make contact?''

"Try the restaurant the following morning at nine. If I continue to fail to get in touch with you, call my home. If Eko answers and says *'moshi, moshi,'* which means 'hello,' that'll tell you there's a reasonable explanation for my absence. Call back. But if she says *'hai,'* which is 'yes' and a rude way to answer the phone, something's very wrong. Hang up, and leave Japan as quickly as possible.''

"I can't do that," Savage said.

Akira squinted. "Oh?''

"I've come too far. I've been through too much. With you or without you, I intend to settle this," Savage said.

"By yourselves, with no knowledge of Japanese, you couldn't possibly succeed. Remember what I told you. Japan is an insular tribal society. Among its one hundred and twenty-five million people, less than fifteen thousand Americans live here. Outsiders are suspect. You'd receive no cooperation in your search. And *where* would you search?''

"The same place *you* intended to search," Savage said. "Where would I find this holy man you mentioned?''

"He wouldn't speak with you.''

"Maybe. But I'd have to try, so just in case, how would I find him?''

"Your stubbornness is commendable.'' But Akira looked doubtful as he brought a pen and paper from a narrow lacquered desk and wrote a sequence of numbers along with directions to several places. "The holy man is my *sensei*. He ought to be at this location.'' Akira tapped the piece of paper. "But your priority is to go to the restaurant first.''

Savage took the piece of paper. "Absolutely.'' He stood.

"I'll get dressed as fast as I can," Rachel said.

Savage followed her from the room and along the corridor.

At the far end Eko knelt, stroking her grandson's hair as her tears dripped onto the corpse's face.

God help her, Savage thought.
God help us all.

8

Fifteen minutes later, Savage and Rachel carried their travel bags along the shadowy white-pebbled path. The once peaceful garden felt haunted. At the door, Savage turned and bowed to Akira.

Akira bowed in return. *"Sayonara."*

"Sayonara. Let's hope it isn't for long."

"I'll deal with the police and join you soon." Akira made a motion so unexpected that for several seconds Savage didn't realize what he intended.

Akira's arm was outstretched. In a remarkable lapse from Japanese custom, he wanted to shake Savage's hand.

Savage's chest was warm with emotion as their palms met. Akira's grip felt gentle yet firm, delicate with the implied strength of a swordsman.

A moment later, Akira lifted the wooden bar from the metal hook on each side of the door. Savage cautiously pulled the door open, peered out, and scanned the deserted dark street. Detecting no obvious threat, he proceeded nervously along the sidewalk, making sure his body shielded Rachel. Under his jacket, he carried one of the intruders' pistols, a calculated risk that the police wouldn't question why three intruders carried only two handguns.

Behind him, the door whispered shut. A thunk was the bar being put back in place. As they rounded a corner, despite Rachel's presence Savage felt hollow.

Incomplete.

Lonely.

AMATERASU

1

Making sure they weren't followed, they walked for several miles. By then, the sun was up, the streets bustling, noisy. Crossing intersections, Savage had to keep reminding himself not to check for cars approaching from the left, as he would have in America and most of Europe, but instead to glance toward the right, for here as in England motorists drove on the left side of the street and thus approached from a pedestrian's right.

At first, Savage's impulse had been to hire a taxi, but for the moment he and Rachel had no destination. Even if they *did* have an immediate destination, their lack of familiarity with the Japanese language made it impossible for them to give directions to a driver. Akira had partially solved that problem by writing his instructions—how to reach the restaurant and his *sensei*—in both English and Japanese script. Those instructions didn't help their present circumstance, however, and Savage and Rachel felt totally lost.

Still, they had to go *somewhere*. Wandering wasn't only pointless but fatiguing. Their travel bags became a burden.

"Maybe we should get on a bus," Rachel said. "At least we'd be able to sit."

She soon changed her mind. Every bus was crammed, with no possibility of finding a place even to stand.

Savage paused at the entrance to a subway.

"The trains will be as crowded as the buses," Rachel said.

"That's more than likely, but let's have a look."

They descended into a claustrophobia-producing maze. Travelers jostled past them, almost too urgent to cast curious glances at the two Caucasians among them. Savage's bag was slammed painfully against his leg. Ahead, he heard the echoing roar of a train. Emerging from a passageway, he faced a deafening, throng-filled cavern. At least, in contrast with New York subways, the terminal was clean and bright. A chart hung on a wall, various colored lines intersecting. Beneath Japanese ideograms, Savage saw English lettering.

"It's a map of the subway system," Rachel said.

With effort, they deciphered the map and determined that this branch of the subway was called the Chiyoda line. Its green path led to midtown Tokyo, to the east of which was a black path labeled GINZA.

Savage examined the piece of paper Akira had given him. "The restaurant's in the Ginza district. If we take this train and get off at one of the midtown exits, maybe we'll be close to the rendezvous site."

"Or even more lost than we are."

"Have faith," Savage said. "Isn't that what you keep telling me?"

Travelers lined up at a gate to buy tickets from a machine. Savage imitated them, using Japanese currency he'd obtained at the airport. When a train arrived, the waiting crowd surged toward its opening doors, thrusting Savage and Rachel inside. The sway of the speeding train and the crush of passengers pressed Rachel's breasts against him.

Several stops later, they left the subway, climbing congested stairs to the swelling din of midtown Tokyo. Office buildings and department stores towered before them. The swarm of traffic and pedestrians was overwhelming.

"We can't keep carrying these bags," Rachel said.

They decided to find a hotel, but what they found instead was a massive railway terminal. Inside the busy concourse there were lockers, where they stored their bags, and finally unencumbered, they felt revitalized.

"Only nine o'clock," Savage said. "We're not supposed to be at the restaurant till noon."

"Then let's check out the sights."

Rachel's buoyant mood was forced, Savage sensed, an anxious attempt to distract herself from the traumas of the night before. She managed to seem carefree only until she reached an exit from the station and noticed a vending machine filled with newspapers. Faltering, she pointed. The front page of a newspaper showed a large photograph of the Japanese they'd seen on television in the North Carolina motel.

"Muto Kamichi." Savage exhaled forcefully, unable to repress the false memory of Kamichi's body being cut in half. At once he corrected himself, using the name the television announcer had called the anti-American politician. "Kunio Shirai."

The photograph showed the gray-haired Japanese haranguing an excited group of what looked like students.

Why am I supposed to think I saw him die? Savage thought. An eerie chill swept through him. Does *he* think he saw *us* die?

"Let's get out of here," Savage said, "and find someplace that isn't crowded. I need a chance to think."

2

They headed west from the railway station and reached a large square called Kokyo Gaien. Beyond a moat, the Imperial Palace glinted. As Savage walked with Rachel along a wide gravel path toward the south of the square, he struggled to arrange his thoughts. "It's almost as if Akira and I were manipulated into coming to Japan."

"I don't see how that's possible. Every step of the way, we made our own choices. From Greece to southern France to America to here," Rachel said.

"Yet someone *anticipated* that we'd arrive at Akira's home. The assault team was ready. Someone's thinking *ahead* of us."

"But *how?*"

They came to a street and once again proceeded west. To the left was the Parliament Building, to the right, beyond a moat, the Imperial Gardens, but Savage was too distracted to pay them attention.

He walked for quite a while in troubled silence. "If two men thought they'd seen each other die and then came into contact with each other," he finally said, "what would they do?"

"That's obvious." Rachel shrugged. "The same as you and Akira did. They'd be desperate to know what had really happened."

"And if they discovered that someone they knew had arranged for them to come into contact?"

"They'd go to that person and demand an explanation," Rachel said.

"Logical and predictable. So we went to Graham and discovered that he'd been murdered. No answers. But we *needed* answers. Where else could we look for them?"

"Only one choice," Rachel said. "Where you thought you'd seen each other die. The Medford Gap Mountain Retreat."

"Which we discovered didn't exist. So is it also predictable that our next choice would have been to find out what *else* had never happened?" Savage asked. "To go to the Harrisburg hospital where we thought we'd been treated for our injuries and where we *each* remembered the same doctor?"

"But after that, your theory falls apart," Rachel said. "Because no one could predict that you'd decide to have X rays taken to find out if you'd really been injured. And for certain, no one could predict that eventually you'd talk to Dr. Santizo in Philadelphia."

They passed two institutional-looking buildings. A wooded park attracted them. A Japanese sign at the entrance had English beneath it: INNER GARDEN OF THE MEIJI SHRINE.

"But a surveillance team could have been waiting at the hospital," Savage said. "Or more likely at Medford Gap, where we'd be easier to spot when we showed up to search for the Mountain Retreat. In New York, we made sure we hadn't been followed. But after Medford Gap, we were so distracted we might not have realized we had a tail. When we left the car to go into the Harrisburg hospitals, the surveillance team could have planted a homing device on the car and followed us easily after that, all the way to Virginia Beach where they killed Mac to keep him from talking and tried to get you away from us. Now that I think of it, Mac's death didn't only stop us from getting information. We were blamed for his murder. It put more pressure on us to run."

"And when we saw Kunio Shirai on television, we knew exactly *where* to run," Rachel said. "Japan." She shook her head. "There's a flaw in the logic, though. How could anyone be sure we'd see a picture of Shirai?"

"Because we'd be forced to check the news to learn what the police were saying about the murders. If not on television, then in magazines or newspapers, we'd eventually have found out about him."

". . . I agree."

Savage frowned. "But the team that killed Mac works for

someone different than the team that tried to kill us last night. One wants us to keep searching. The *other* wants us to stop." He gestured, angry, bewildered.

Ahead, a wide path led them through a huge cypress gate, its tall pillars joined near the top by a beam and at the very top by other beams, each beam progressively wider, the entire structure reminding Savage of a massive Japanese ideogram. Trees and shrubs flanked the path and directed Savage's troubled gaze toward a large pagoda, its three stories emphasized by long, low buildings to the right and left: the Meiji Shrine. The pagoda's roof was flat, its sides sloping down, then curving up, creating a link between earth and sky. Savage was struck by the elegance and harmony.

A voice speaking English startled him. Rachel clutched his arm. Nervous, he pivoted and saw something so unexpected he blinked in confusion.

Americans!

Not a few but several dozen, and though Savage had arrived in Japan only yesterday, he'd become so used to seeing crowds composed exclusively of Orientals that for a moment this throng of awkward Caucasians seemed as foreign to him as he and Rachel felt amid the numerous Japanese they'd been following toward the shrine.

But the voice he'd heard speak English belonged to an attractive female Japanese in her twenties. She wore a burgundy skirt and blazer that resembled a uniform. Holding a clipboard with pages attached, she turned her head as she walked and addressed the Americans following her.

A tourist group, Savage realized.

"The Meiji Shrine is one of the most popular pilgrimage sites in Japan," the guide explained, her English diction impressive, though the *l* and *r* in "pilgrimage" gave her trouble.

She paused where the path led into a courtyard. The group formed a semicircle.

"In eighteen sixty-seven," she said, "after more than two and a half centuries in which a *shogun* was absolute ruler of Japan, an emperor again assumed power. The name of His Imperial Highness was Meiji"—she bowed her head—"and the return of authority to the emperor was called the Meiji Restoration, one of the four greatest cultural changes in the history of Japan.''

''What were the other three?'' a man in blue-checkered pants interrupted.

The guide answered automatically. ''Influences from China in the fifth century, the establishment of the Shogunate in sixteen hundred, and the United States occupation reforms after World War II.''

''. . . Didn't MacArthur make the emperor admit he wasn't a god?''

The tour guide's smile hardened. ''Yes, your esteemed general required His Highness to renounce his divinity.'' She smiled even harder, then gestured toward the pagoda. ''When Emperor Meiji died in nineteen twelve, this shrine was created in his honor. The original buildings were destroyed in nineteen forty-five. This replica was constructed in nineteen fifty-eight.'' She tactfully didn't mention that American bombing raids had been what destroyed the original buildings.

Savage watched her lead the group across the courtyard. About to follow toward the shrine, he glanced reflexively behind him and noticed, his stomach hardening, that some Americans hadn't proceeded with the group. They lingered thirty yards back on the tree-rimmed path.

Savage redirected his gaze toward the shrine. ''Come on, let's join the group,'' he told Rachel. He tried to sound casual but couldn't conceal the urgency in his voice.

She turned sharply toward him. ''What's wrong?''

''Just look straight ahead. Match my pace. Pretend you're so fascinated by what the tour guide's saying, you want to keep up with her.''

''But what's . . . ?''

His heart cramped. ''When I tell you, don't look behind us.''

They neared the group. The spacious courtyard was bathed in sunlight. Savage's spine felt cold.

''All right, I won't look behind me,'' Rachel said.

''Five men on the path. For a moment, I thought they were

tourists. But they're wearing suits, and they seem more interested in the shrubs along the path than they are in the shrine. Except for *us*. They're *very* interested in *us*."

"Oh, God."

"I don't know how they found us." Savage's fingers turned numb as adrenaline forced blood toward his muscles. "We were careful. And that subway was too damned crowded for anyone to keep us in sight."

"Then maybe they really are tourists. Businessmen with a few hours off, trying to get over jet lag. Maybe they're less interested in the shrine than they thought they'd be and wish they'd gone to a geisha house."

"No," Savage said, pulse hammering. They reached the tour group. He had to keep his voice low. "*I recognized one of them.*"

Rachel flinched. "You're sure?"

"As sure as I am that I saw Akira beheaded and Kamichi cut in half. *One of those men was at the Medford Gap Mountain Retreat.*"

"But the Medford Gap Mountain Retreat . . ."

"Doesn't exist. I *know* that. I'm telling you I remember him *being* there." Savage's head throbbed. His mind reeled, assaulted again by *jamais vu*.

Though he tried to hide it, the distress in his voice made members of the tour group turn and frown at him. A fiftyish woman with blue-tinted hair told him, "Shush." The Japanese guide hesitated, peering back toward the distraction.

Savage murmured apologies, guiding Rachel around the group, walking anxiously toward the looming shrine. "False memory, *yes*," he told Rachel. "But that doesn't change the fact that it's in my head. It feels real to me. Akira and I both remember Kamichi having a conference with three men. One looked Italian, the other Spanish, or maybe Mexican or . . . The third, though, was American! And I saw him just now behind us on the path!"

"But the conference never happened."

"I saw him one other time."

"What?"

"At the hospital. While I convalesced."

"In *Harrisburg?* But you were never *in* a hospital in Harrisburg. How can you recognize a man you never met?"

"How could Akira and I recognize Kunio Shirai, the man we knew as Kamichi?"

"You never met Kamichi either."

Savage flooded with terror. He needed all his discipline, the effects of all his years of training and hardship under fire, to keep from panicking. Reality—the shrine before him—seemed to waver. False memory insisted that it alone was true. If what I remember isn't true, Savage thought, how can I be sure that *this* is?

They entered the shrine. In a glimmering corridor that stretched to the right and left, Savage saw burnished doors emblazoned with golden suns. Equipped with hinges in the middle, the doors had been folded open, revealing the precinct of what looked like a temple. Railings prevented him from going farther.

"This way," Savage said, urging Rachel to the left, disrupting the concentration of Japanese who gazed toward the shrine's interior in reverence of solemn artifacts that symbolized their noble heritage prior to the U.S. occupation, prior to the Second World War.

Judging the corridor ahead, Savage jerked his eyes furtively to the left, through a doorway that led outside. The five Americans, led by the distinguished-looking, expensively dressed man he remembered from the Mountain Retreat and the Harrisburg hospital, hurried with strained long strides across the crowded courtyard, nearing the shrine. The only reason they didn't break into a run, Savage guessed, was that they knew their skin had attracted too much attention to them already. A commotion here would provoke a rapid police response.

The jasmine-scented corridor veered to the right. Struggling to avoid further groups of meditating Japanese, Savage and Rachel zigzagged, turned sideways, twisted, and veered, desperate to reach an exit on the left.

They burst from the shrine into blinding sunlight, faced

another wide courtyard, heard indignant Japanese voices behind them, American voices apologizing, and started to run.

"I'm certain," Savage said. Past the courtyard, another path—lined with trees—beckoned. "The well-dressed man, the one with the mustache, who seems to be their leader? Midfifties? Sandy hair? Eyes like a politician?"

"Yes, from a door in the shrine I got a look at him," Rachel said, racing.

"In my memory of the Harrisburg hospital, he came to visit me. He said his name was . . ."

Words that were never spoken made Savage shiver.

Philip Hailey. "As useful a name as any other. Anonymous. Waspishly American."

"Kamichi and Akira. What happened to their bodies?"

"They were hurried away."

"The police?"

"Weren't informed."

". . . So much blood."

"That corridor of the hotel has now been remodeled."

"Who killed them, damn it, and why?"

"The motive for the murders relates to the conference, but the purpose of the conference is not your business. We expect to identify whoever was responsible. Consider the topic closed. My purpose in coming here was to express our sympathy for your suffering and to assure you that everything possible is being done to avenge the atrocity."

"In other words, stay out of it."

"Do you have any choice? Think of this money as compensation. We've also paid for your hospital bills. Incentives. Demonstrations of our good faith. In return, we count on your good faith. Don't disappoint us."

And good old Phil hadn't needed to add, *"If you don't cooperate, if you don't keep away from our affairs, we'll mix your ashes with Kamichi's and Akira's."*

Spurred by fear, Savage raced harder. Japanese pilgrims darted to the side, glaring in outrage at this violation of the shrine's peaceful atmosphere. Rachel's low-heeled shoes rapped on the concrete courtyard.

The tree-lined path seemed to widen as Savage charged

toward it. Ten yards. Five. Sweating, he surged into its funnel, hearing Rachel exhale beside him.

He also heard shouts. With a frantic glance backward, he saw the five men led by Philip Hailey lunging out of the temple and across the courtyard.

"Forsyth!" Hailey yelled. "Stop!"

Forsyth? Savage tensed with shocked recognition. *Forsyth was the alias I used in the hospital! Roger Forsyth! But I was never in that hospital! I never met Philip Hailey! So how could he know—?*

"Damn it, Forsyth, stop!"

Again the objects before him seemed to shimmer, as if the path, the trees and bushes along it, weren't *real*. But the urgent footfalls of the men in the courtyard sounded *very* real.

Savage strained to run faster. "Rachel, are you okay? Can you keep up?"

"These shoes"—she breathed—"weren't built for a marathon." She kicked off the shoes and sprinted next to him, her long strides billowing her loose cotton skirt.

"Forsyth!" Hailey yelled. "*Doyle!* For God's sake, stop!"

Doyle? In Virginia Beach, that's what Mac said my name was! Savage thought. *Robert Doyle! And that's who the bartender told the police killed Mac!*

Ahead, the path curved toward the right, but just before the curve, another path intersected with it.

Savage slowed. He couldn't know what lay beyond the curve. Perhaps a barrier. Staring desperately to the right, he saw that the intersecting path formed a straight line for quite a distance. It was almost deserted. *We'll be in the open—easy targets.* He spun toward the left and saw that *this* side of the intersecting path had several tangents along the way.

Tugging Rachel's hand, he sprinted toward the left as Hailey and his men rushed closer.

"Doyle!"

Savage almost drew the Beretta from beneath his jacket. But so far Hailey and his men hadn't shown any weapons. Despite their evident determination to stop Savage from continuing to search for answers—had *they* been responsible for the attack on Akira's home last night?—they weren't foolish enough to start shooting and cause the Japanese pilgrims to panic and the shrine's attendants to alert the authorities. Hailey and his men have to kill us in private, quietly, or they'll never get out of the park before the police block off the exits, Savage thought. If there's shooting, every Caucasian in the area, even blocks away, will be questioned.

Racing past bushes, Savage saw another path to his right and twenty yards farther, one on his left. But the path to his left would lead back toward the shrine. For a startling instant, Savage was reminded of the maze in Mykonos through which he and Rachel had fled her husband's men.

A labyrinth. Assessing the path to his right, he saw that it too had many tangents. Thick shrubs and trees flanked them. "Come on!" he told Rachel, veering right.

"Doyle!"

Another intersection. Which way? Savage wondered. To the right—other paths. Straight ahead—a sharp angle that also led right. To the left—nothing. Dead end. A barrier of trees and bushes.

Can't get trapped, Savage thought and almost charged straight ahead before he realized that Hailey would think as he did. Have to keep moving. Can't get cornered.

But why should the trees and bushes be a trap?

Abruptly Savage corrected his direction and dodged to the left, pulling Rachel with him. The path was short. The dead end threatened. Spotting a gap between shrubs, Savage gripped Rachel and urged her through it, stooping, squirming after her. He squeezed past trees, crawled under branches, struggled up a slope, snaked around boulders, and crouched in a thicket, his shoes sinking into a deep, moist, unpleasant mulch. Bushes surrounded them. The park was a perfect blend of artifice and chaos, the meticulously tended paths in contrast with the formlessness of nature. A wilderness in downtown Tokyo.

Canopied by leaves, tickled by ferns, Savage inhaled the mulch's loamy fragrance and drew his Beretta. Rachel's breasts heaved, sweat trickling off her forehead, her eyes wide with apprehension. He motioned for her not to speak. She nodded rapidly, emphatically. Ready with the pistol, he stared down the slope, the woods so thick he couldn't see the path.

The cloying leaves buffered sound. Hurried footsteps, urgent breathing, frustrated curses, seemed to come from far away.

But Savage's hunters couldn't have been more than twenty yards below.

"Which fucking—"

"—way. How do I know where they—"

"—must have gone—"

"—over here. No—"

"—there. They wouldn't—"

"—choose a trap. This other path—"

"—heads toward that *other* path which—"

"—heads toward the western exit. Damn it, give me the radio. Christ." The labored voice belonged to Hailey, Savage realized. But with frightening clarity, he remembered the voice not from the shouts that had chased him out of the shrine, instead from the cultivated, threatening, oh-so-confident, imperious aristocrat who'd tried to bribe him in the hospital and implied a death sentence if Savage didn't back off.

False memory. Yes! But it made no difference. I didn't back off, you son of a bitch, Savage thought. And if it's death you want to talk about—Savage clutched the Beretta —let's debate.

Below him, past the dense tangle of trees and shrubs, he heard Hailey say, "Beta, this is Alpha!" Hailey evidently spoke to the radio he'd told one of his men to give him. "We've lost them! Instruct all units! Block all exits from the park!"

In the distance, sirens wailed, the distinctive alternating high-low blares of police cars approaching. Had the disturbance at the shrine been sufficient for attendants to phone the authorities?

"Christ!" Hailey said. "Beta, fall back! Avoid all contact with—!"

The sirens reached a crescendo, their wail diminishing.

"Wait!" Hailey said.

The wails receded, farther, fainter.

"Beta, disregard fallback order! Maintain surveillance on exits! Assume camouflage status! Out!" His tone changed, less loud, as if he addressed the men beside him. "Let's *go*."

"Which way?" a man on the path asked.

"How the hell do I know? Split up! Check *all* the paths! Maybe they've doubled back! One thing we're sure of—they can't get out, and they're bound to attract attention!"

Footsteps scurried from the area, veering down various lanes.

"What if they're in the woods?" a receding voice said.

"Hope to God they're not!" Hailey's voice diminished. "A hundred and eighty acres! We'd need fucking Tonto and Rin Tin Tin to find them! . . . No, they'll feel trapped! They'll want to get out of here as quick as they can! Before we block off the exits!"

A breeze rustled branches. Birds sang. This section of the park became silent.

Savage exhaled softly, slowly, and lowered his Beretta. When he turned toward Rachel hunkered behind him in the bushes, he saw her open her mouth to speak. Quickly he put a hand to her lips and forcefully shook his head. He pointed toward the unseen path below and shrugged as if to indicate that one of the men might have stayed behind.

She flicked her eyes in acknowledgment. He removed his hand and eased his hips to the ground, straining to be quiet. Sweat trickled down his face. The shadows of trees cooled his brow.

But fear still churned his stomach. How long will they search? he thought. Besides the men who chased us, how many others does Hailey have? Who *is* he? *Why am I a threat to him? How did he find us?*

The nagging questions made Savage's temples throb.

Forsyth. He called me Forsyth, then Doyle. *But why both names?* And why *last* names? Why *didn't* he call me Roger or Bob?

Because a first name is used for a friend. But a last name's for someone you hate or . . .

Yes? Or what? Or control. During SEAL special warfare training, the instructors always chose our last names and always made them sound as if they were calling us shitheads.

But this isn't the SEALs. Hailey looks like a corporate executive or a politician, and for whatever reasons, he sure wants me out of the way.

Savage frowned, suddenly hearing voices on a path. He didn't understand what they were saying, suspected that the bushes muffled their words, then realized that the words were Japanese. The speakers didn't sound frantic or angry but rather seemed entranced by the gardens. He relaxed his tight grip on his handgun.

A further glance toward Rachel forced him to smile. She was tugging at her cotton top, trying to fan the sweat that had trickled onto her breasts. He averted his gaze from the dark stains that emphasized her nipples, pulled his own damp shirt from his chest, flicked a bug off his arm, and pretended disgust. It did the trick. Her blue eyes brightened, tension slowly draining from her.

But at once she seemed to remember something, scrunched her forehead, and pointed toward her Rolex watch. Savage knew what she meant. It was almost eleven o'clock. They were due to be at the restaurant in the Ginza district at noon, ready for Akira's phone call.

If Akira had a chance to phone. Maybe the police hadn't believed his story about defending himself against the three intruders. Maybe they'd taken Akira to headquarters for intensive questioning.

Maybe.

But maybe not. If Akira phoned the restaurant at the scheduled time and Savage and Rachel weren't there, he'd . . .

Phone again at six P.M. as they'd agreed. That was the point of a backup plan—to allow for contigencies.

But what if we can't get out of here by six? Savage thought. The next contact time was nine in the morning, and if *that* didn't work, if Savage and Rachel still couldn't get away from Hailey by then . . .

Akira would assume the worst. He might go to ground.

The only chance for contact was the further backup plan of Savage's phoning Akira's home. But Eko didn't speak English. Her sole instructions were to answer *"moshi, moshi"*—hello—if Akira was safe, and *"hai"*—a rude tone of "yes"—if Akira was threatened and wanted Savage to run.

Christ, we didn't plan enough, Savage thought. We're professionals, but we're used to protecting others, not ourselves. *We* need protectors. As it is, trying to defend *ourselves,* we're too involved, we've got fools for clients, and we screwed up. We assumed that *Akira* would be the only one in danger. But now . . . !

Get control, Savage told himself. You're safe for the moment, and even if it's impossible to get to the restaurant by noon, six P.M. is a long way off.

Yes, that's what worries me, he thought. Anything can happen. If Hailey and his men are stubborn—and Savage assumed that they *would* be—we won't get out of here till dark.

And then?

We can't just walk out. We'll have to go over a wall. And in a city of *twelve million* Japanese with only a *few thousand* Americans living here, we'll attract as much attention, we'll be as conspicuous, as Godzilla.

Shit! Savage mustered the strength to subdue his increasing distress and turned yet again to Rachel. Leaves on her skirt. Dust on her cheeks. Dangling strands of auburn hair. Despite all those imperfections, she looked as beautiful . . . as spirited, angular, sharply featured, and glowing . . . as only Rachel could look.

I love you, Savage wished he could take the risk of telling her. Instead of violating silence, he leaned close and gently kissed the tip of her nose, tasting her dusty, sweat-salty skin. She closed her eyes, shuddered, reopened her lids, blinked nervously, and stroked his hair.

Remember, Savage told himself. Until this is over, she's your principal, *not your lover*. And Akira's waiting. *Maybe*. And Hailey's men are out there. *Certainly*.

So what are you going to do?

Move!

Savage gripped Rachel's elbows, kissed her . . .

And turned her, pointing toward the thickets beyond them.

She mouthed silent words. It took him a moment before he realized. What she'd silently told him . . . a familiar refrain . . .

Was . . .

I'll follow you to hell.

They squirmed through the mulch through the forest.

3

The park had frequent low hills. On occasion, thickets gave way to stretches of waist-high ferns, which Savage and Rachel avoided, anxious not to crush the ferns and leave a path in case Hailey's men managed to follow them. Staying among the trees, Savage took his bearings from the passage of the sun, imitating its movement, heading westward. He worried that when they reached a path, a sentry would see them rushing across it, but this section of the park was evidently extremely remote, for they never did reach a path. Though the temperature felt like low sixties, comparable to October weather in New England, he and Rachel sweated from exertion. Their dusty clothes snagged on branches. Rachel's skirt tore. Worse, because she'd been forced to kick off her shoes to be able to outrun Hailey and his men from the shrine, her feet—despite the mulch—became scratched and bloody. Savage took off his shoes and gave her his socks. He'd have let her have the shoes as well, but they were much too big for her and would have added blisters to her scratches. As it was, without socks, *he* developed blisters. Sometimes, where the mulch was too deep, he carried her. Their progress slowed. By one P.M., they slumped to the ground, exhausted.

"This park's enormous," Rachel said. "And the Japanese

claim they've run out of space. Not that I'm complaining."
She massaged her feet. "Hailey would have caught us by
now if it weren't for . . ." She cocked her head. "Do I hear
traffic?"

Savage focused his attention. The dense trees around them
buffered sound, but beyond, it did seem . . . A rush of energy
made him stand. "I'll check." He made his way through the
mulch and trees, smiled at what he saw, and quickly came
back. "There's a wall about fifty yards ahead. We've reached
a street."

"Thank God." At once she looked troubled. "But *now*
what? Hailey's men are probably still looking for us. They'll
assume there's a chance we'll go over a wall."

"Whoever Hailey is, his reinforcements have to be limited.
They'd need to be widely spaced to watch every section of
the wall around the park. But you're right—as soon as one
of them saw us, he'd radio for the others to converge. With
your feet hurt, we couldn't outrun them." Savage thought
about it. "Let's follow the wall."

With no basis for choosing one direction instead of another,
he arbitrarily decided on north. The wall was high enough
to conceal them, low enough for them to climb over if they
needed to. As they moved along it, weaving past bushes,
Rachel limping, Savage imagined Akira's unease if he'd been
able to call the restaurant at noon. Failing to make contact,
what would Akira fear had gone wrong? How would he react?
What would he do until the next scheduled call at six?

The wall angled east, then north again. After sixty yards,
Savage heard Japanese voices, tensed, crouched, peered beneath low concealing branches, and saw an east-west path.
Traffic was louder. To the left, a gap in the wall formed an
exit from the park, cars and pedestrians swarming past beyond
it.

Savage scanned the exhaust-hazed street and squirmed
backward through shrubs until he and Rachel could talk without being overheard. Overhanging boughs cloaked them with
shadows.

"I didn't see any Americans," he said. "Not that it matters. They wouldn't be in the open. For all we know, they're

directly behind the wall at each side of the exit. Or in a van across the street. Or . . ."

"In other words, nothing's changed. We *still* can't get out of here."

Savage hesitated. "Yes."

"Then what do we—?"

"Wait for dark."

Rachel's eyes widened. "Then we'll miss Akira's next call at the restaurant."

"If we try to leave now, the odds are against us. Hailey's men . . . We'd be stopped. We'd never reach the restaurant," Savage said. "I don't know why Hailey wants us so bad, but I'd sooner depend on Akira's patience than on Hailey's *losing* patience."

"I feel so . . . Is this the way you normally live?"

"Normally? If you can call it that."

"I've been with you for less than two weeks, and already I feel like I've been through several wars. How do you *stand* it?"

"Right now, after having fallen in love with you"—Savage swallowed—"I'm beginning to wonder. What I wish, what makes me want to keep going, is . . ."

"Tell me."

"It's foolish to think about. A beach near Cancun. I'd like to take off your swimsuit. I'd like to make love in the surf in the moonlight."

"Don't stop. Describe the feel of the waves."

"I can't. What I mean is, I don't dare."

"Make love to me?"

"Don't dare distract myself," Savage said. "My love for you could make me so careless it kills you."

"At the moment . . . How long did you say we had to wait?"

"Till dark."

"Then there's plenty of time. When I close my eyes, I can hear the surf."

She reached for him.

And she was right. When he closed his eyes, as they tenderly, languidly embraced, Savage *could* hear the surf.

4

Rachel slept while Savage watched over her. The shadows thickened. Near sunset, she wakened, beautiful despite puffy aftersleep.

"Now it's your turn," she said.

"No, I have to . . ."

"Sleep," she said. "You're no good to me if you're exhausted." Her blue eyes twinkled.

"But suppose Hailey's men . . ."

Rachel gently removed the Beretta from his hand, and Savage—recalling last night—was well aware that she could use it. At the same time, he was also aware of the trauma she repressed. Her hand shook on the pistol's grip. With determination, she held the gun firmly.

"You're sure?" he asked.

"How else will we get to Cancun?"

"If something makes you afraid . . ."

"I'll wake you. Provided there's time and the target isn't obvious."

Savage squinted.

"You're thinking I'll lose control again . . . shoot . . . keep shooting . . . and maybe for no reason."

"No," Savage said. "I'm thinking you don't deserve to belong in my world."

"To hell with your world. I want to belong with *you*. Put your head down," she said.

He resisted.

"Do it," she said. "On my lap. If you're tired, you'll make mistakes. Don't fight me. There. Yes, there. That's right. Oh, yes. That feels so good." She shivered. "Right there."

"It's after six. We've missed Akira's next call. He'll . . ."

"Be nervous, yes, but he'll call again at nine tomorrow."

"Unless *he* has problems in the meantime. We should never have separated."

"There wasn't an option," Rachel said. "The way you talk about him . . . the bond between you . . . it almost makes me jealous."

Savage chuckled. "Remember where my head is."

"Just close your eyes and keep it there."

"I doubt I'll sleep."

"You might if you think about that beach near Cancun. Imagine the rhythm of the waves on the shore. Even if you *don't* sleep, relaxing will do you good. R and R. Is that what you call it? So you're ready for what we'll be facing."

"As soon as it's dark . . ."

"I'll wake you," Rachel said. "That's a promise. Believe me, I want to get out of here."

5

Rachel's teeth chattered—less from fear than cold, Savage sensed. In the dark, as the temperature kept dropping, he draped his jacket around her shoulders and guided her farther along the wall. He'd decided that trying to leave through a path from the park was possibly more dangerous during the night than in daylight. Hailey's hidden men would have a safer chance of killing them and escaping under cover of the neon confusion of Tokyo's nightlife.

Reversing their earlier direction, Savage led Rachel southward, reached a western jog in the wall, and followed its angle. Unseen branches tugged at his shirt and threatened his eyes. If not for the halo of dense traffic opposite the wall, he couldn't have found his way. Horns blared. Engines roared.

"Enough," Savage said. "Hailey's pissing me off. This

spot's as good as any. If we go much farther, we'll circle the park. Screw it. Let's go."

Savage raised his arms to grip the top of the wall, pulled himself up so his eyes showed just above the wall, and warily studied the street below him. Headlights surged past. A Japanese man and woman strolled beneath him along a sidewalk. Otherwise there were few pedestrians.

Savage dropped back onto the ground. "I didn't see anything to make me change my mind. Are you ready?"

"As I'll ever be." She mustered resolve. ". . . Better give me a boost."

Savage put his arms around her legs and lifted, feeling her skirt and thighs against his cheek. A moment later, she squirmed upward out of his grasp. As soon as she reached the crest, inching over, he hurriedly climbed after her. Together, they dangled from the opposite side. Heart pounding, Savage landed first and helped her down so her stockinged feet wouldn't be injured if her full weight struck the concrete.

Checking both ways along the sidewalk, Savage barked, "Quickly. *Cross the street.*"

A man had appeared from shadows a hundred yards to his left. Headlights revealed the man's face. A Caucasian. He blurted something to a radio in his hand and raced toward Savage and Rachel, fumbling for an object beneath his suitcoat.

"Do it!" Savage said. *"Cross the street!"*

"But . . . !"

The blazing cars formed a constantly moving barrier.

"We can't stay here!" To Savage's right, opposite the Caucasian running toward them, *another* Caucasian appeared, racing to flank them.

"We'll be . . . !"

"Now!" Savage said. He grabbed Rachel's hand, saw a slight break in traffic, and darted off the sidewalk.

Headlights streaked toward them. Brakes squealed. Savage kept running. He still gripped Rachel's hand, although she no longer needed urging.

In the next lane, another speeding car made Rachel curse. She surged in front of him.

Horns shrilled. The stench of exhaust flared Savage's nostrils. His stride lengthened.

They reached the street's divider. Wind from rushing cars flapped Rachel's skirt. Breathing hard, Savage glanced behind him and saw the two Caucasians rushing along the sidewalk. Assessing traffic, they searched for a break between cars so they could sprint across the street.

Savage waved at drivers in the opposite lanes, warning them that he and Rachel were about to race across. A Toyota slowed. Savage took the chance and bolted, Rachel charging next to him. They dodged another car and reached the far sidewalk.

Storefronts gleamed. Pedestrians gaped. An alley beckoned. As Savage ducked into it, he glanced again behind him, seeing the two Caucasians bolt from the sidewalk. At the same time, he sensed an object looming toward him. Pivoting, startled, he saw a van veer out of traffic. It aimed toward the alley.

He turned to run, but not before the van's windshield starred. Holes stitched it, glass imploding. *Bullet* holes.

The van hit the curb. With a jolt, it heaved above the sidewalk, walloped down, veered, kept surging, and smashed through a storefront to the left of the alley.

Metal scraped. Glass shattered. Despite the explosive impact, Savage thought he heard screams from within the van. For certain, he heard pedestrians scream. And shouts from the men across the street.

Several cars skidded to a stop.

Rachel trembled, frozen with shock.

"Run!" Savage said.

He tugged her.

The compulsion of fear canceled her stunned paralysis. She raced past garbage cans along the dark alley.

But what if the alley's a trap? Savage suddenly thought.

Suppose Hailey's men are *in* here.

No! They can't be *everywhere*!

Who shot at the van? Who was *driving* the van?

Dismay racked Savage's mind. Confusion threatened his sanity.

Someone wants to stop us. Someone else wants us to search.

Who? Why?

What the hell are we going to do?

They reached the next street. An approaching taxi made Savage's chest contract. He flagged it down, shoved Rachel inside, and scrambled after her, saying, "Ginza," hoping the driver would understand that they wanted to go to that district.

The driver, wearing a cap and white gloves, frowned at the disheveled appearance of his harried Caucasian passengers. He seemed uncertain whether he wanted Savage and Rachel to be his customers. But Savage held up several thousand-yen bills.

The driver nodded, pulled away, expertly merging with speeding traffic.

Savage heard the increasing wail of sirens—with no doubt where they were headed. Straining not to show his tension, he could only hope that the driver wouldn't decide that his passengers had something to do with the sirens.

The taxi turned a corner. Police cars swiftly approached in an opposite lane, their sirens louder, flashers blazing.

Then the cruisers were gone, and though the taxi's driver glanced after them, he didn't stop. Savage touched Rachel's hand. Her fingers trembled.

6

Amid dense traffic that somehow kept flowing, they finally reached the Ginza district. Akira had explained that Ginza meant "silver place" and referred to the fact that several hundred years ago the national mint had been located here. Since then, the area had developed into Tokyo's major shopping center, with seemingly endless stores, bars, and restaurants.

The closest equivalent Savage could imagine was New York's Times Square before the junkies, hookers, and porno shops had contaminated its glamour. Neon. Savage had never seen so much of it. Everywhere he looked, brilliant lights turned the night into day. An awesome combination of electrified colors. Some constantly blazed. Others pulsed or flashed messages in a row along buildings like a massive radiant ticker tape. The glare of congested headlights added to the spectacle. Well-dressed pedestrians crowded the exciting streets.

Savage had no intention of showing the driver Akira's note, which in Japanese provided directions to the restaurant where Akira was supposed to call. The authorities might question all taxi drivers who'd picked up Caucasians, and Savage wanted to keep the rendezvous site beyond suspicion. Besides, he and Rachel weren't due there again until Akira's next scheduled call at nine tomorrow morning.

But Savage had *other* motives that compelled him to reach this district. For one thing, the comparatively few Caucasians in the city tended toward the Ginza's glittering nightlife, and he and Rachel needed desperately to blend in. For another, they needed fresh clothes, but having been followed so expertly, they didn't dare return to the railway station, where they'd left their travel bags in a locker. A surveillance team might be waiting, on the chance that Savage and Rachel would retrace their steps and attempt to retrieve their belongings.

"*Arigato*," Savage told the taxi driver, pointing toward the curb. The white-gloved man pulled over, counted the money Savage gave him, and nodded with satisfaction. With a flick of a front-seat lever, he opened the door in back. Savage and Rachel got out.

As the taxi drove away, Savage became more aware of the blazing lights around him. The din of traffic and music from bars overwhelmed him. Exhaust fumes assaulted his lungs. Pungent cooking odors drifted from restaurants.

Wanting to rush, he and Rachel were forced to match the pace of the crowd so they wouldn't attract attention. But despite their efforts to look calm, they did attract attention. Japanese pedestrians kept staring at them. Because Caucasians are unusual, even in the Ginza district? Savage wondered. Or because our faces are dirty, our clothes torn? Rachel's limp and the socks on her feet didn't help.

Savage led her toward gleaming storefronts. "We've got to find—"

He halted abruptly before an electronics shop, stunned by the image on television sets in the window. No sound came through the glass. Not that it mattered. The words that matched the startling scenes would have been incomprehensible to him, the text in Japanese.

But he didn't need an interpreter to make him understand the dismaying significance of what he watched. Heart sinking, again he saw a ghost. Muto Kamichi . . . Kunio Shirai . . . the man he'd seen sliced in half at the nonexistent Medford Gap Mountain Retreat . . . harangued thousands of Japanese protestors holding up anti-American signs outside the gates of a U.S. Air Force base. American soldiers stood nervously on guard beyond the fence.

The news report was similar to the TV footage Savage had watched three days ago in America and the photographs he'd seen this morning on the front page of newspapers in vending machines at Central Station.

With two important differences. The earlier protests had been outside U.S. *civilian* buildings, and the demonstrators —numerous to begin with—had increased dramatically not only in size but intensity.

The grim-eyed faces of American officials appeared on the array of television screens. Savage recognized the U.S. secretary of state, haggard, his brow furrowed, being interviewed by Dan Rather. The image shifted to the President's press secretary tensely answering questions from reporters.

At once, Kamichi—Shirai—was back on the screens, inciting the protestors. Whatever his name, the gray-haired, slack-jowled, slightly overweight, midfiftyish man who resembled a weary executive projected an unexpected charisma when he stepped in front of a crowd. His commanding eyes and powerful gestures transformed him into a spellbinding zealot. With every jab of his karate-callused hands, the crowd reacted with greater fervor, their expressions distorted with outrage.

"This new demonstration must have happened today while Hailey's men trapped us in the park," Savage said. He turned toward Rachel. Her pallor made him frown. "Are you all right?"

She shrugged, impatient, as if the blood that soaked her socks hardly mattered. "What's going on? What *caused* this?"

"Some incident we don't know about?" Savage shook his head. "I think Kamichi"—he quickly added—"*Shirai* doesn't need an incident. I think the point is America . . . *America in Japan.*"

"But America and Japan are friends!"

"Not if you believe those demonstrators." Savage sensed movement behind him and nervously pivoted. Japanese pedestrians crowded toward the television screens.

"Let's get out of here," he said. "I'm awfully self-conscious."

They squirmed through the thickening crowd. Savage's veins chilled. His contracting muscles stopped aching only when he reached the comparative openness of the normally congested sidewalk.

"But all of a sudden," Rachel said. "Why? The demonstrations are larger, more dangerous."

"Catalyzed by Kamichi."

"Shirai."

"I can't get used to calling him that," Savage said. "The man I drove to Pennsylvania."

"To a hotel that doesn't exist."

"In *my* reality, I drove him there. To me, the hotel *does* exist. But all right"—Savage's mind whirled, seized by *jamais vu*—"let's call him Shirai. *He's* the cause of the demonstrations. I don't know *why*. I can't imagine the source of his power. But he, Akira, and I are somehow connected."

A sudden thought made Savage face her. "The former emperor, Hirohito, died in January of 'eighty-nine."

Rachel kept walking. "Yes? And?"

"After Japan's defeat in World War Two, MacArthur insisted on a new Japanese constitution. Even *before* that, when Japan surrendered in 'forty-five, America insisted that Hirohito go on the radio and not only announce the unconditional surrender but renounce his divinity and publicly tell his people that he was human, not a god."

"I remember reading about it," Rachel said. "The announcement shocked Japan."

"And helped MacArthur reconstruct the country. But one of the strictest articles in the new constitution was that church and state *had* to be separated. By law, religion and politics were totally severed."

"What's that got to do with Hirohito's death?"

"His funeral. In violation of the constitution, but with no objection from America, political and *religious* rites were combined. Because of Japan's economic power, every important nation sent its highest representatives. A *Who's Who* of international government. And *all* of them stood passively under wooden shelters in a pouring rain while a Japanese honor guard escorted Hirohito's coffin into a shrine, where behind a screen *Shinto* rites, traditional Japanese *religious* funereal rites, were performed. And no outsider said, 'Wait a minute. This is illegal. This is how the Pacific War got started.' "

"They respected a great man's death," Rachel said.

"Or they almost shit their pants in fear that if they objected to the Shinto rites, Japan would get so angry it would cut off their credit. Hell, Japan finances most of America's budget deficit. No country would dare object if Japan reverted to its former constitution. As long as Japan has the money—and the power—its government can do what it wants."

"That's where your argument falls apart," Rachel said. "Japan's government is responsible."

"While moderates rule it. But what if Kamichi—*Shirai*—takes command? Suppose the old ways come back and a radical party assumes control! Did you know that Japan—supposed to be nonmilitary—spends more on defense than any NATO country except America? And they're suspicious of South Korea! And China's always worried them! And . . . !''

Savage realized he was talking too loud. Japanese pedestrians frowned at him.

Rachel kept limping.

"Come on. We've got to do something about your feet."

A brightly lit sportswear shop attracted Savage's gaze. He and Rachel stepped inside. There were almost no customers. When two clerks—a young man and woman—bowed in greeting, they looked puzzled by Rachel's stockinged feet.

Savage and Rachel bowed quickly in return and proceeded through the store. In addition to athletic clothes, there were jeans, T-shirts, and nylon jackets. Rachel made a stack in her arms and looked questioningly at the female clerk, who seemed to understand that Rachel wanted to know if there was a changing room.

The clerk pointed toward a cubicle in the back, where a drape functioned as a door. Adding thick white running socks and a pair of Reeboks to her pile, Rachel disappeared behind the drape.

In the meantime, Savage chose a pair of brown socks to replace the pair he'd given Rachel. His pants were filthy, his shirt soiled with sweat. He picked up replacements. As soon as Rachel came out of the cubicle, wearing stone-washed jeans, a burgundy top, and a blue nylon jacket that matched the cobalt of her eyes, Savage went in to change, glancing periodically through a corner of the drape to make sure no one who looked threatening entered the store while Rachel was unprotected. Eight minutes later, they paid and left the store, carrying their dirty clothes in a bag, which they dumped in a trash container a few blocks away.

"These shoes make all the difference." Rachel sighed. "It feels so good not to be limping."

"Not to mention we don't look like we slept in a ditch." Savage wore khaki slacks, a yellow shirt, and tan windbreaker. The combination made his chameleon green eyes seem tinged with brown. He'd combed his hair in the changing room, as had Rachel. "A few smudges on our faces. All in all, though, not bad. In fact, you look lovely."

"Blarney, but I never turn down a compliment. The bonus is, now that we've changed clothes, it'll be harder for witnesses at the park to identify us if the police decide to pick us up."

Savage studied her with admiration. "You *are* catching on."

"Given the right teacher and the proper motivation—fear—I learn damned fast." She wrinkled her brow. "That van at the park. It seemed to veer out of traffic and aim toward the alley, toward *us.*"

"Hailey must have had vehicles circling the park, so his men could radio to them if we were spotted. Our bad luck that the van was nearby."

"*Our* bad luck? The unlucky ones were in the van," Rachel said. "The windshield starred as the van headed toward us. Did I see *bullet* holes?"

Savage pursed his lips and nodded. "Someone was determined to stop Hailey's men from catching us."

"But *who,* and *how* did they know where we'd be?"

"For that matter, how were *Hailey's* men able to follow us through the subway? We were careful. I kept checking behind us while we walked from the railway station. But then all at once they showed up at the park. It's like they're thinking the same as us or even *ahead* of us."

"You said earlier . . ." Rachel brooded. "A lot of what we've done is predictable, given the problems we need to solve. But that park had nothing to do with our problems. We just happened to go there."

"Yes," Savage said. "We've been intercepted too many times. I don't understand how they keep doing it."

"My God"—Rachel turned—"I just thought of something. We've been assuming that Hailey's the one who wants to stop us."

"Right."

"But what if we've got it turned around? What if *Hailey* wants to protect us? What if the team in the van belonged to whoever wants to kill us, and it was *Hailey's* men who shot out the windshield, so we'd keep searching?"

For a moment, Savage had trouble understanding, the twist

in assumptions bewildering. Abruptly he felt pressure behind his ears. Something seemed to snap in his brain. His vision paled, his mind attacked by unsettling contradictions. Nothing seemed sure. Everything was false. *Jamais vu* fought with reality. But *something* had to be true! There *had* to be a solution! He couldn't bear . . .

No! Three weeks ago, his single burden had been to prove himself again. Now?

Total confusion!

He wavered.

Rachel grabbed his arm. Her eyes wide, she steadied him. "You turned pale."

"I think . . . For a moment there . . . I'm . . . all right now . . . No . . . Feel dizzy."

"I feel a little off balance myself. We haven't eaten since yesterday." She pointed. "Here. This restaurant. We need to sit down, rest, get something in our stomachs, and try to clear our heads."

Now instead of Savage guiding Rachel, *she* guided him.

And he felt so helpless he didn't resist.

7

The waitress—wearing white makeup, a kimono, and sandals—presented them with a menu. When Savage opened it, he again felt disoriented. The items on the menu weren't printed horizontally, as in the West, but vertically, the contrast reinforcing his sense that everything was inverted, his mind off balance. Mercifully, English script appeared beside Japanese ideograms. Still, Savage was so unfamiliar with un-Americanized Japanese food that all he could do was point toward a column on the left, the restaurant's recommendation for a dinner for two.

"Sake?" the waitress asked with a bow.

Savage shook his throbbing head. Alcohol was the last thing he needed.

"Tea?" he asked, doubting he'd communicate.

"*Hai*. Tea," she said with a smile and left, her short steps emphasized by her tight kimono, which in addition emphasized her hips and thighs.

In the background, at the restaurant's frenetic cocktail lounge, a Japanese country-western singer delivered a flawless version of Hank Williams's "I'm So Lonesome I Could Cry."

Savage wondered if the singer understood the words or had expertly memorized them.

The midnight train is . . .

"If we're in trouble and we thought only *Akira* would be in trouble . . ." Savage shook his head.

"I know. I hate to imagine what's happened to *him* today." Rachel reached across the table. "But there's nothing we can do to help him, not right now. I told you, *rest*. The food will be here soon. You've got to try to relax."

"You realize how turned around this is?"

"Me taking care of you?" Rachel asked. "I love it."

"I don't like feeling . . ."

"Out of control? You'll have plenty of chance to *exert* control. To do what *you* do best. And *soon*. But thank heaven, not right now."

Can't you hear the whippoorwill . . . ?

The restaurant was filled with cigarette smoke and the permeating aroma of sauces. Savage and Rachel sat on cushions at a low table with a cavity beneath it that allowed them to dangle their legs, an architectural concession to long-legged foreigners who wanted to sit according to Japanese tradition but without discomfort.

"Kamichi . . . Shirai . . . We've got to meet him," Savage said. "Akira and I *have* to learn if he saw *us* die as we saw *him* die."

"In *his* place, if I were leading demonstrations against U.S. Air Force bases, I'd have protection that even *you* couldn't breach," Rachel said. "It won't be easy to meet him. And since you're American, I doubt you can simply call him up and arrange an appointment."

"Oh, we'll talk to him, all right," Savage said. "Bet on it."

The waitress brought warm, damp napkins. Then their meal arrived: a clear soup with bits of onions and mushrooms, seasoned with grated ginger; yams in a mixture of soy sauce and sweet wine; rice with curry sauce; and boiled fish with teriyaki vegetables. The various sauces accented each other superbly. Savage hadn't realized how hungry he was. Though the portions were more than ample, he ate everything, so ravenous he was hampered only slightly by his awkwardness with chopsticks.

But throughout, he kept thinking about Akira and how in the eighteen hours they'd been separated so much had changed that their arrangements for getting in touch with each other no longer seemed adequate.

"I can't wait till nine tomorrow morning," Savage said. He gulped the last of his tea, left a generous tip with payment for the bill, and stood. "I saw a pay phone in the lobby."

"What are you—?"

"Calling Akira."

The phone was in a corner away from the restaurant's entrance and the coatcheck area. Partially sheltered by a screen that depicted brilliant sunflowers, Savage put coins in the phone and dialed the number Akira had given him.

The phone rang four times.

Savage waited, his fingers cramping around the phone.

A fifth ring.

A woman suddenly answered. Eko. Savage couldn't fail to recognize her voice.

"*Hai.*" In response to her curt tone, Savage's knees weakened. He'd just heard the signal that Akira was in trouble, that Savage was supposed to leave Japan as quickly as possible.

Heart racing, he desperately wanted to question her, to find out what had happened. But Akira had emphasized—Eko didn't speak English.

I can't just break contact! Savage thought. I have to think of a way to communicate! There's got to be a—!

He heard a rattle on the phone. Another voice spoke abruptly. A *man's* voice. In Japanese.

Savage's heart pounded faster as he listened, dismayed, unable to identify the speaker or to understand his furtive statements.

With equal abruptness, the voice switched to English.

"Doyle? Forsyth? Damn it, whatever you call yourself, listen, buddy! If you know what's good for you, if you want to save your ass, you'd better—"

Savage acted without thinking. Reflexively, in shock, he slammed down the phone. His knees kept shaking.

Madness.

In the background, from the raucous bar, the Japanese country-western singer reprised Hank Williams's song.

So lonesome I could die.

8

"Who was it?" Rachel asked.

They skirted the crowd on the neon-blazing street. Heat from the massive walls of lights felt like sunlamps.

Savage's stomach churned. He feared he'd vomit the enormous meal he'd eaten. "I never heard the voice before. I can't judge his Japanese accent, but his English was perfect. I think—American. No way to know whose side he's on. He was angry, impatient, threatening. I didn't dare stay on the line. If the call was traced, they'd know to search the Ginza district. One thing's sure. Akira wouldn't have permitted strangers in his home, and Eko wouldn't have answered *'hai'* without a reason.''

''The police?''

''Don't have Americans on their staff. And how did he know to call me 'Forsyth' and 'Doyle'? *Akira* wouldn't have told them.''

''Willingly.''

Savage knew how effective certain chemicals were in making reluctant informants cooperate. ''I have to assume Akira's in trouble. But I don't know how to help him.''

A siren made him flinch. Turning, primed to run, he saw an ambulance wail past.

He exhaled.

''We can't keep walking the streets,'' Rachel said.

''But where would we feel safe to spend the night?''

''There's no way I could sleep,'' Rachel said. ''I'm so uptight I—''

''Two choices. Find someplace to hide, wait till morning, and go to the restaurant, hoping Akira will call at nine. But the restaurant might be a trap.''

''So what's the second choice?'' Rachel asked.

''Skip plans. I told Akira that even if Eko gave me the warning signal over the phone, I *wouldn't* leave Japan. *I want answers*.'' Surprised by the growl in his voice, Savage unfolded the note of directions Akira had given him. ''A wise and holy man, Akira said. His *sensei*. The man he wanted to talk to. Well, let's see just how wise this holy man is.''

9

In contrast with the glare of the Ginza district, this section of Tokyo was shadowy, oppressive. A few streetlights and occasional lamps in narrow windows did little to dispel the gloom. After paying the taxi driver, Savage got out with

Rachel and felt conspicuous despite the darkness. His shoulder blades tensed.

"This might not have been such a good idea," Rachel said.

Savage studied the murky street. The murmur of distant traffic emphasized the silence. Though the sidewalk seemed deserted, even in the darkness Savage detected numerous alleys and alcoves, in any of which hidden eyes might be watching, predators waiting to . . . "The taxi's gone. I don't see any others. It's too late to change our minds."

"Swell. . . . How can we be sure the driver even brought us to where we wanted to go?" Rachel asked.

"'Abraham believed by virtue of the absurd,'" Savage said, reminding Rachel of her favorite quotation. "At this point we have to trust."

"Swell," Rachel said again, making the word sound like an expletive.

Savage parted his hands, a gesture of futility. "By the book, the way to do this is to leave the taxi several blocks away and approach the area cautiously, trying to get a sense of whether there's a trap." He glanced around. "But Tokyo has very few street names. Without the driver's help, I'm not sure I could have found this place, even from a few blocks away."

The place he referred to was a five-story, dingy concrete building without windows. It looked like a warehouse, out of place among the numerous tiny-windowed apartment complexes along the street, though those structures too looked dingy.

The building was dark.

"I can't believe anyone lives here," Rachel said. "There's been a mistake."

". . . Just one way to learn." *Yet again* Savage scanned the dark street. He placed his hand on the Beretta beneath his windbreaker and approached the front door.

It was steel.

Savage looked but couldn't find a button for a doorbell or an intercom. He didn't see a lock.

He tried the doorknob. It turned.

"Apparently no one cares if strangers go in," Savage said. He couldn't subdue the puzzlement in his voice. "Stay close."

"Hey, if I was any closer, I'd be in your underwear."

Savage almost grinned.

But her joke didn't ease his tension. He pushed the heavy door open and frowned at a dimly lit corridor. "Quickly," he said, tugging Rachel in before their silhouettes made them easy targets.

As quickly, he shut the door behind them and noticed that there wasn't a lock on this side either. More puzzled, he scanned the corridor.

It ended ten feet before him.

No doors on either side. A staircase led up.

"What kind of—?" Rachel started to ask.

But Savage put a finger to his lips, and she became silent.

He knew what she'd meant to say, though, and nodded with understanding. He'd never seen a warehouse or an apartment building with a layout like this. No sign on the wall to give directions or indicate where they were. No mailboxes with names and buzzers. No further door with a security system that prevented access to the core of the building.

The stairway was concrete. As Savage and Rachel ascended warily, their shoes scraped faintly, echoing.

The next floor was also dimly lit, the corridor short, without doors, a further staircase leading upward.

Again they climbed, Savage's nervousness increasing. Why weren't Akira's instructions complete? he thought. How the hell can I find where someone lives when there aren't any doors or names on—?

At once he realized that Akira's instructions *were* complete.

The absence of doors eliminated the possibility of making a mistake. There was only one continuing direction—upward—and after an identically barren third floor and fourth floor, there was only one destination: the *fifth* floor.

Where the staircase ended.

Like the others, this corridor was short.

But at its end, a steel door beckoned.

Savage hesitated, his hand on the pistol beneath his jacket.

The door seemed larger the closer he came. Again, as with the door through which he and Rachel had entered the building, Savage couldn't find a doorbell or an intercom, and this door too had no lock.

Rachel's eyes narrowed, communicating bewilderment and apprehension.

Savage squeezed her arm to reassure her, then reached for the doorknob. Pulse hammering, he changed his mind and decided that this door—seemingly unprotected—looked too much like the entrance to someone's apartment for him to just walk in.

Holding his breath, he raised his knuckles and rapped.

The steel door responded with muted thunks.

Savage knocked again, this time harder.

Now the steel door reverberated, a hollow echo beyond it.

Five seconds. Ten seconds.

Fifteen. Nothing.

No one's home, Savage thought. Or there's no apartment beyond the door, or Akira's *sensei* is too asleep to hear me, or . . .

Akira's *sensei* would be the best. No professional sleeps that deeply.

Screw it.

Savage turned the doorknob, pushed the door open, and entered.

Though Rachel clutched the back of his jacket, Savage ignored her, finding himself confronted by muted lights in a massive chamber.

No, not muted lights. The recessed bulbs beneath ledges that framed the ceiling glowed so dimly that "muted" wouldn't describe them. Twilight. False dawn. Even those descriptions weren't adequate. The illumination was vaguer than candles but just sufficient to reveal an enormous *dojo*, countless *tatami* mats on the floor, with subtly reflecting polished cypress wood on the beams and panels of the burnished walls and ceiling.

Like moonglow.

With deep dark spaces between each isolated, recessed, barely perceptible light.

Savage felt overwhelmed, awestruck, as if he entered a temple. The *dojo*, though in semidarkness, exuded an aura. Of sanctity. Of solemnity.

It was redolent of the sweat and pain . . . the discipline and humility . . . the mysticism of the Oriental martial arts. Mind and body, soul and sinew, combined as one. A sacred place. And as Savage inhaled its holy fragrance, stepping forward, metal slid against polished metal.

Not a scrape, not a grating sound, not a rasp, but a smooth, oiled, slippery hiss that made Savage's scalp prickle.

Not one hiss, but many. All around him. The dark walls seem to come alive, to swell and give birth. Gleaming objects appeared, reflecting the dim, widely separated bulbs that rimmed the ceiling. Long, curved, glinting blades apparently hung in midair. Then the walls gave birth again, shadows emerging, assuming the shapes of men dressed totally in black, with hoods and masks that covered their faces. They'd been perfectly camouflaged against the walls, and each gripped a sword he'd drawn from a scabbard.

Where Savage stood a third of the way into the *dojo*, he pivoted and saw that he was flanked on every side. His spine froze. He drew his Beretta.

Rachel moaned.

Glancing toward the open door, Savage frantically wondered how he could concentrate on fighting to get Rachel out and at the same time not be distracted by the need to keep Rachel from getting hurt. The Beretta held fifteen rounds. But there were certainly more than fifteen opponents. The shots would be deafening, however, the muzzle flashes a distraction. The swordsmen might hesitate for a couple of seconds, enough time for us to get through the door and start scrambling down the stairs! he thought.

But while he thought, the door was slammed shut. Swordsmen stepped in front of it. Savage's stomach sank. In desperation, he aimed toward the men who blocked the door.

Lights blazed, searing, blinding, the murky *dojo* suddenly as bright as the sun. Savage jerked a hand toward his eyes, frantic to shield them from the stabbing rays. In that instant, his only warning was a swift, subtle brush of air, an unseen swordsman lunging toward him. The Beretta was yanked from Savage's grasp. Powerful fingers paralyzed nerves in his hand, preventing him from firing. Distraught, Savage blinked, fighting to focus his eyes, to erase the white-hot image of multiple suns temporarily imprinted on his vision.

At last his pupils adjusted to the glare. He lowered his hand, his chest cramping, cold despite the heat of the lights, and studied his captors. He understood now that their masks had not only helped to camouflage them in the shadows but that the eyeslits in the masks had guarded the swordsmen's vision from the sudden disorienting glare.

Rachel moaned again, but Savage was forced to ignore her distress, to focus his attention, every instinct, on his captors. Without a weapon, he couldn't hope to fight them with any chance of escaping. He and Rachel would be sliced to pieces!

But the man who yanked the pistol away could have cut me in half while I was blinded, Savage thought. Instead he stepped back to the wall, his sword raised like the others. Does that mean they're not sure what to do with us, whether to kill us or—?

As if on command—but without any perceptible signal passing among them—they abruptly stepped forward. The *dojo* seemed to shrink. Then they lowered their swords, tips aimed toward Savage and Rachel, and the *dojo* shrank even more.

Another step forward, each of the numerous footfalls almost silent on the *tatami* mats, just a faint sibilance as if the woven reeds exhaled from the weight upon them.

Savage pivoted slowly, tensely, judging the room, searching for exits, for the slightest sign of weakness on any flank. But even if I *do* see a possible exit, a corridor, *anything*, he thought, there's no way I can get Rachel past those swords without a weapon!

The masked, hooded figures stepped forward yet again, blades pointing, gleaming, their presence more constricting, and as Savage kept pivoting, his eyes narrowed fiercely toward the wall opposite the one through which he and Rachel had entered. At the same time, another undetectable signal seemed to pass eerily around the room, and the swordsmen stopped their relentless advance. The *dojo*—virtually silent to begin with—became as silent as the dead.

Except for Rachel's repeated moans.

The swordsmen who'd proceeded from the wall at the far end of the *dojo* shifted to the right and left, leaving a gap through which a man who'd been hidden behind them stepped forward. He too gripped a sword and was dressed in black, complete with a hood and mask. Unlike the others, he was short, gaunt as opposed to lithe, his tentative footsteps suggesting fragility. He pulled off his hood and removed his mask, revealing the almost bald skull and wrinkled features of an elderly Japanese, his gray mustache and dark-yet-glowing eyes the only features that prevented his face from looking mummified.

But Savage had the nerve-tingling impression that the tentative footsteps were actually the product of stealth, that his fragility was deceptive, that this old man could be more adept and dangerous than any of the others.

Scowling at Savage and Rachel, the old man gestured with his sword as if he intended to slash.

He suddenly darted, each stride as fast as an eyeblink.

But he didn't slash toward Savage.

Rachel!

Savage lunged in front of her, prepared to sweep with his arms, hoping to deflect the blade, to duck under it, and chop the brittle-looking bones of the old man's throat. He didn't stop to consider what the blade would do to him if he failed. *He* didn't matter. *Rachel* did!

Savage's gesture was reflexive, his instincts making it impossible for him to do anything else but fulfill his profession's mandate—to protect.

In a blur he braced himself, straining to prepare for the greater blur of the old man's lunge, the flashing edge of the speeding blade so fast that Savage could barely see it. He parried with his arm, though he knew before he began, *knew in his soul*, his attempt was futile.

But I can't just give up!

I can't let the sword hit Rachel!

He imagined the blade flicking through his forearm, the stub of his hand and wrist flipping through the air, his arteries pulsing crimson. But he didn't flinch as he misjudged the old man's timing and parried too soon, his arm exposed as his soul had predicted.

He stared defiantly, and the blade stopped with startling abruptness, as if an invisible force had blocked it. The sword's polished, gleaming edge hovered rigidly against the sleeve of Savage's jacket. With fear-intensified vision, everything magnified before him, and he saw severed threads on his sleeve.

Jesus.

Savage exhaled, adrenaline flooding through him, volcanic heat erupting upward toward his chest.

The old man squinted at him, jerked his chin down, a curt nod, and barked an incomprehensible question.

But not to Savage, instead to someone behind him, though how Savage knew this he wasn't sure—because the old man's searing eyes, as searing as the spotlights, never wavered from Savage's defiant gaze.

"*Hai*," someone answered in the background, and Savage's heart swelled, for he recognized the voice.

"Akira?" Savage had never spoken anyone's name more intensely or with greater confusion.

"*Hai*," Akira answered again and appeared through the gap in the swordsmen. Like them he wore black clothing, almost like pajamas but the material rugged. *Un*like them, he had no hood and mask. His handsome rectangular face, seeming all the more rectangular because his short black hair was combed straight from left to right, the part in his hair severe, had a somberness that made Savage frown. The melancholy in Akira's eyes had become more deep, more brooding, more profound.

"*What's going on?*" Savage asked.

Akira pursed his lips, his cheek muscles hardening. When he opened his mouth to respond, however, the old man interrupted, barking another incomprehensible question to Akira.

Akira replied, with equal unintelligibility.

The old man and Akira exchanged two further remarks, quick intense bursts that Savage found impossible to interpret, not just the words but the emotion that charged them.

"Hai." This time the old man, not Akira, used that ambiguous affirmative. He jerked his chin down again, another curt nod, and raised his sword from the severed threads on Savage's sleeve.

The blade gleamed, nearly impossible to track, as with impressive speed the old man slid the sword into a scabbard tucked under a knotted black belt made of canvas. The blade hissed in to the hilt.

Akira came forward, his expression controlled except for his melancholy, his public self severely in charge of his private self. Stopping beside the old man, he bowed to Savage and Rachel.

All day, Savage had felt hollow, incomplete without Akira, but he hadn't realized how *much* he felt incomplete until now, at last rejoined with his friend. In America, Savage would have given in to impulse and reached for Akira's hand, perhaps in less public circumstances have clasped his shoulders to show affection. But he resisted his Western urge. Because Akira was obviously behaving according to the expectations of those around him, Savage conformed to Japanese protocol and bowed in return, as did Rachel.

"It's good to see you again," Savage said, trying to imply strong emotion without embarrassing Akira in front of the others by displaying it. "And to find that you're safe."

"And I, you." Akira swallowed, hestitating. "I wondered if we'd ever meet again."

"Because Eko gave me the signal to run?"

"That," Akira said. ". . . And other reasons."

The cryptic remark invited questions, but Savage restrained them. He needed to learn what had happened to Akira and to tell Akira what had happened to them, but other immediate questions insisted.

"You still haven't answered me." Savage gestured toward the swordsmen. *"What's going on?"*

The old man barked again in Japanese, his voice deep and raspy.

"Permit me to introduce my *sensei*," Akira said. "Sawakawa Taro."

Savage bowed, repeating the name, adding the obligatory term of respect. "Taro-*sensei*." He expected another curt nod in response, surprised when the old man braced his shoulders and imitated Savage's bow.

"He's impressed by your bravery," Akira explained.

"Because we came in here?" Savage shrugged in self-deprecation. "Considering what almost happened, I was stupid, not brave."

"No," Akira said. "He means your attempt to protect your principal from his sword."

"That?" Savage raised his eyebrows. "But you know the rules. It wasn't something I thought about. I just responded to training and did it."

"Exactly," Akira said. "For Taro-*sensei*, bravery means instinctive obedience to duty, regardless of the consequence."

"And that's all that saved us?"

Akira shook his head. "You were never in danger. Or at least only briefly while you entered. After the door was slammed shut and Taro-*sensei* recognized you from my description, he knew you weren't a threat."

"What? You mean . . . ? Those men stalking toward us . . . ? *The son of a bitch was testing me?*"

Taro's aged voice rasped. "Neither a son of a bitch nor a bastard."

Savage gaped, skin shrinking in astonishment.

"You disappoint me," the old man said. Though a foot and a half shorter than Savage, he seemed to tower. "I expected more. Never assume that because a stranger addresses you in his native language he doesn't understand your own." Taro glared.

Savage's face burned. "I apologize. I was foolish and rude."

"And more important, careless," Taro said. "Unprofessional. I was about to compliment whoever trained you. Now . . .''

"Blame the student, not the teacher," Savage said. With distress, he remembered Graham's corpse behind the steering wheel of his Cadillac, acrid exhaust fumes filling his garage, while he drove for all eternity. "The fault is mine. Nothing excuses my behavior. I beg your forgiveness, Taro-*sensei*."

The old man's glare persisted, then slowly dimmed. "Perhaps you redeem yourself. . . . You learned from your instructor to admit mistakes."

"In this case," Savage said, "with regard to information about your country, my instructor was Akira. But again blame the student, not the teacher. He warned me to be careful not to give offense. I'll try harder to behave like a Japanese."

"By all means," Taro said. "Try. But success will elude your grasp. No outsider, no *gaijin*, can ever truly understand . . . and hence behave like . . . a Japanese."

"I don't discourage easily."

Taro's wrinkled lips tightened, possibly in a smile. He addressed Akira in Japanese.

Akira replied.

Taro turned to Savage. "I'm told you're a serious man. What we call 'sincere,' a word that should not be confused to mean your strange Western custom of pretending that your public thoughts and private thoughts are identical." The old man debated. "I may have been hasty. Your offense is forgiven. I invite you to accept my humble hospitality. Perhaps you and your principal would care to enjoy some tea."

"Yes, very much," Savage said. "Fear has a habit of making my mouth dry." He gestured toward Taro's sword and did his best to make his eyes crinkle, trying to sound respectful, humble, and ironic all at once.

"*Hai*." Taro inflected the word so it seemed a laugh. "Please"—he bowed—"come."

As Taro led Savage, Rachel, and Akira toward the swordsmen at the rear of the *dojo,* the old man motioned subtly with his hand. Instantly, in unison, the hooded figures sheathed their blades. The combined slippery sound, the high-pitched metallic *ssss* of polished steel against steel, again made Savage's skin prickle.

"Taro-*sensei,* a question," Savage said. "I'm troubled. But please understand, I mean no offense in asking."

"You have my permission," the old man said.

"When we entered, after you recognized that we weren't enemies . . ." Savage hesitated. "I can understand why you wanted to test us. You needed to know how we'd react when apparently threatened, to determine if you could depend on us. Outsiders. *Gaijin.* But even so . . ." Savage frowned. "There was no guarantee I wouldn't panic. Suppose I'd lost my nerve and started shooting, even though I didn't have an escape plan and hence would have wasted ammunition that I might have needed later. Many of these men would have died."

"Your question is wise," Taro said. "But the test had controls."

"Oh? In what way? I'm sure these men are superbly skilled, their swords unbelievably fast, but not as fast as a bullet."

"If you'd raised your weapon . . ."

Taro didn't need to complete his sentence. As Savage approached the rear of the *dojo,* he saw two men concealed behind the row of swordsmen. . . .

And each man held a tautly strung bamboo bow, a fiercely barbed arrow strung, ready at any instant to be fired.

Yes, Savage thought. If I'd seemed about to shoot, I'd never have had a chance to pull the trigger.

In a rush, another question insisted, but he forced himself not to ask. Cold sweat trickled down his back. Would the archers have shot to disable his gun arm?

Or to kill?

10

"Taro-*sensei*'s building is self-sufficient," Akira explained.

They sat, cross-legged, on cushions at a low cypress table. The small room had latticed paper-thin walls with exquisite pen-and-ink drawings hanging upon them. It reminded Savage of Akira's home.

In an obvious display of deference, Taro dismissed a servant and poured tea into small, thin, beautifully painted ceramic cups, each depicting a colorful scene from nature (a waterfall, a blossoming cherry tree) with a minimum of brush strokes.

Akira continued explaining. "The fifth floor, of course, is the *dojo*. On the other floors, there are dormitories, a shrine, a library, a cooking and eating area, a shooting range . . . everything that Taro-*sensei*'s students need to attempt to perfect their spirits, minds, and bodies, to make them as one."

Akira paused to pick up his cup, placing his left hand under it, using his right hand to support the cup on one side. He sipped the tea and savored it. "Perfect, Taro-*sensei*."

Savage watched Akira carefully and imitated the way he gripped the cup. Prior to their leaving America, Akira had explained the protocol of the tea ceremony. Its sanctified tradition dated as far back as the fourteenth century. Influenced by Zen Buddhism, the ritualistic sharing of tea was intended to produce a condition of purity, tranquillity, and harmony known in Japanese as *wabi*. When strictly performed, the ceremony took several hours and incorporated a minimum of three locations and servings, accompanied by various foods. The tea-master prepared each serving, adding tea to hot water and whipping it with a bamboo whisk. Conversation was limited to gentle, soothing topics. The participants felt freed from time and the turmoil of the outside world.

On this occasion, the ceremony had been starkly abbreviated. Of necessity. But respect for the ritual still applied. Noting the solemnity of Akira and his *sensei*, Savage quelled his urgent questions and raised the gleaming cup to his lips, inhaling the fragrance of the steaming tea, sipping the clear, delicately flavored liquid. "My spirit feels comforted, Taro-*sensei*." Savage bowed.

"This quenches the thirst in my soul," Rachel added. "*Arigato*, Taro-*sensei*."

Taro chuckled. "My not-inadequate student"—he indicated Akira—"taught you well."

Akira's brown face became tinged with a blushing red. He lowered his eyes in humility.

"It's rare to meet a civilized *gaijin*." Taro smiled and lowered his cup. "Akira mentioned a library in this building. Most *sensei* would never allow their students to read. Thought interferes with action. Words contaminate reflex. But ignorance is itself an enemy. Facts can be a weapon. I would never permit my students to read works of fantasy. Novels"—he gestured with disparagement—"though poetry is another matter, and I encourage my students to expand their spirits by composing haiku and studying such classic examples as those by the incomparable Matsuo Basho. But books of information are mostly what my students read. History, in particular that of Japan and America. Manuals of weaponry, both ancient and modern. The principles of locks, intrusion detectors, electronic surveillance equipment, and various other tools of their craft. Also languages. I require each of my students to be skilled in three, apart from Japanese. And one of those languages *must* be English."

Savage glanced surreptitiously at Akira, at last understanding how his counterpart had acquired so impressive a fluency in English. But why the emphasis on English? Savage wondered. Because English was pervasive throughout the world? Or because of America's victory in World War Two? Why did Akira's expression become more melancholy as Taro emphasized that his students had to be expert in America's history and language?

Taro stopped talking and sipped his tea.

Akira kept a close watch on his *sensei*. Apparently concluding that Taro did not intend to say anything further for the moment, that it would not be rude to break the silence, he resumed his explanation.

"When I was ten," Akira said, "my father sent me to Taro-*sensei*, to study martial arts. Until I completed high school, I came here five times a week for two-hour sessions. At home, I religiously practiced what I had been taught. Most male teenagers in Japan supplement their high school classes with intensive private tutoring in order to devote themselves to preparing for university entrance examinations. These occur in February and March and are known as 'examination hell.' To fail to be accepted by a university and especially Tokyo University is a great humiliation. But as my studies with Taro-*sensei* became more demanding and intriguing, I realized that I had no interest in applying to a university, or rather that *he and this institution* would be my university. Despite my unworthiness, Taro-*sensei* graciously accepted me for greater instruction. On my nineteenth birthday, I came here with a few belongings and never stepped outside for the next four years."

Savage tightened his grip on his cup. Turning to Rachel, he saw that the surprise on her face was as strong as what he felt. "Four years?" She was too amazed to blink.

"A moderate amount of time, considering the objective." Akira shrugged. "To attempt to become a samurai. In our corrupt and honorless twentieth century, the only option for a Japanese devoted to the noble traditions of his nation, committed to becoming a samurai, is to join the fifth profession. To make himself the modern equivalent of a samurai. An executive protector. Because now—just as then—a samurai without a master is a warrior without a purpose, a frustrated wanderer, a directionless, unfulfilled *ronin*."

Savage gripped his frail teacup harder, afraid he'd break it but controlled by greater surprise. "And all those men in the *dojo* . . ."

"Are Taro-*sensei*'s advanced students. Many are about to graduate after the privilege of having studied with my master for almost four years," Akira replied. "You might compare them to monks. Or hermits. Except for grocers and other merchants who bring necessary goods, no outsider is permitted to enter."

"But the outside door was unlocked," Savage said. "And so was the door to the *dojo*. In fact, I didn't even *see* a lock. *Anyone could walk in.*"

Akira shook his head. "Each door has a hidden bolt, electronically activated, although tonight the bolts were left open. In case my enemies managed to follow me here. An enticement. So they could be subdued and questioned. The stairway, of course, is a trap once the doors are sealed."

Savage pursed his lips and nodded.

Taro inhaled softly.

Akira turned to him, aware that his master intended to speak.

"Although my students retreat from the world," Taro said, "I do not wish them to be ignorant of it. By means of newspapers, magazines, and television broadcasts, they're instructed in contemporary events. But in these sequestered surroundings, they're trained to study the present with the same detachment that they do the past. They stand apart, watchers, not participants. Because only by being objective can a protector be effective. The essence of a samurai is to be neutral, without expectations, maintaining a stillness at his core."

Taro considered his words, bobbed his wizened head, and sipped his tea, the signal that others could speak.

"My apologies, Taro-*sensei*. But another potentially indelicate question occurs to me," Savage said.

Taro nodded in permission.

"Akira mentioned the corrupt age in which we live," Savage said. "In that case, few young men—even Japanese—would be willing to shut themselves away and commit themselves to such arduous training."

"Yes, few. But sufficient," Taro said. "The way of the samurai is by definition limited to the most determined. You yourself, as I've been told, committed yourself to the severest branch of America's armed forces—the SEALs.''

Savage stiffened. He strained not to frown at Akira. What *else* had Akira revealed about him? Mustering discipline not to look troubled, he replied, "But I wasn't shut off from the world, and the military paid for my instruction. This school . . . four years of isolation . . . surely few candidates could afford the financial expense of . . .''

Taro chuckled. "Indeed. And you warned me. Your question is indelicate. Americans do say what they think." His good-humored tone barely hid his disapproval. He sobered. "None of my students bears any financial expense in coming here. The only criteria for acceptance are ability and determination. Their equipment, meals, and lodging, *everything* they require, is given to them.''

"Then how can you afford . . . ?" Savage held his breath, unable to bring himself to complete his further indelicate question.

Taro didn't help but merely studied him.

The silence lengthened.

Akira broke it. "With your permission, Taro-*sensei*.''

A flick of the eyes signified yes.

"My master is also my agent," Akira said, "as he is for every student with strength and discipline enough to complete the course. Taro-*sensei* arranges for my employment, continues to advise me, and receives a portion of everything I earn—for the rest of my life.''

Savage felt jolted. Thoughts raced through his mind. If Taro was Akira's agent . . .

Taro must have information about Kunio Shirai, the man Savage knew as Muto Kamichi and saw cut in half at the Medford Gap Mountain Retreat.

Akira had said he worked with an American agent when assigned to America. Graham. But Graham had *not* been the primary agent. Taro was. *Taro might have the answers Savage needed.*

But Kamichi—Shirai—was never at the Mountain Retreat. No more than *we* were, Savage thought.

He winced. Lancing, crushing, spinning, and twisting, *jamais vu* yet again assaulted his mind.

If we never met Kamichi, we couldn't have been hired to protect him! Savage thought. So Taro might know nothing about him.

But *someone* set this up. *Someone* arranged for Akira and me to imagine we were hired. *Who? When?* At what point did *jamais vu* intersect with reality?

This much was sure, Savage knew. Akira had held back information. In emphasizing that his agent was Graham, he'd deliberately avoided drawing attention to Taro.

Was Akira an enemy? Savage's former terrible suspicion flooded through him, chilling his soul. His sense of reality had been so jeopardized that he feared he couldn't trust anyone.

Even Rachel? No, I've got to trust! If I can't depend on Rachel, nothing matters!

Again he realized the dilemma of trying to protect himself as well as Rachel, in trying to be his own principal. He needed a protector who wasn't involved, and at the moment, that luxury wasn't possible.

"I'm afraid I *will* be rude," Savage said. "I know that conversation over tea is supposed to be soothing. But I'm too upset to obey the rules. Akira, what the hell happened since we last saw you?"

11

The question hung in the room. Akira, who'd been sipping tea, gave no indication he'd heard it. He took another sip, closed his eyes, seemed to savor the taste, then set down his cup, and looked at Savage.

"The police arrived quickly." Akira sounded oddly detached, as if what he described had happened to someone else. "One car, then two, then three, as word of the situation's gravity spread. The coroner arrived. Police photographers. A forensic team. Senior police officials. At one point, I counted twenty-two investigators in my home. They listened to my account. They made me repeat it several times. Their questions became more detailed, their expressions more grave. I'd rehearsed my story before they arrived. I'd made necessary adjustments so the crime scene would be consistent with the robbery attempt I described and the murderous reaction of the intruders when they were discovered. But this isn't America, where multiple killings seem an everyday occurrence. Here, violent crime involving handguns is rare. The investigators were grim and methodical. In my favor, although I'd fired and killed with one of the intruders' pistols, I'd also used a sword in defending my home, and that—as I anticipated—evoked tradition, making me seem heroic.

"As noon approached, I was still being questioned. I anticipated your concern if I didn't phone the restaurant on schedule, so I asked permission to excuse myself and make a call to break an appointment. Imagine my concern when I learned that you weren't at the restaurant to receive my call. I hid my feelings and answered more questions. By midafternoon, the bodies had been removed. Eko mustered strength despite her grief and accompanied Churi's body to the morgue, to make arrangements for his funeral. In the meantime, the investigators decided they wanted me to go with them to headquarters and dictate a formal statement. On the street, the police cars had attracted a swarm of reporters. Without making it seem I had something to hide, I tried not to face their cameras, but at least one man took my picture."

Akira's voice became somber, and Savage knew why. A protector had to be anonymous. If a photograph was published, Akira's ability to defend a principal would be jeopardized, because an assailant might be able to recognize and attack him before attacking the primary target. In this case, the potential complications were even more serious. A newspaper photo of Akira would draw the attention of his and Savage's hunters and possibly hinder their search.

"It couldn't be helped," Savage said.

"At headquarters while I dictated my statement, the police checked my background. I'd told them I was a security specialist. Several major corporations I'd worked for gave the police a positive assessment of me. But I sensed that the police checked other sources. Whoever they spoke to, the police soon treated me differently. With deference. I didn't understand their reaction, but I certainly didn't argue when they told me I could leave. But not to go far. They made clear they'd want to talk to me again."

"And after that?" Rachel asked, self-conscious, her voice strained, the first time she'd spoken in several minutes.

"An enemy wouldn't have had any trouble following the police car that drove me to headquarters," Akira said. "It turned out the police were so inexplicably deferential that they offered to drive me back to my home. I politely declined, pleading the need to walk and clear my head. Puzzled, I found a side entrance from the building and tried to blend with the crowd on the street. But I soon discovered I had company. Japanese. Skilled, though not skilled enough. For the next two hours, I tried to elude them. Six o'clock loomed quickly. I managed to use a pay phone to call the restaurant on schedule, knowing how distressed you'd be if I didn't report. But *again* you weren't at the restaurant. Something was obviously wrong! *What happened to you?*"

"Soon," Savage said. "Finish your story."

Akira stared at his teacup. "Seeking shelter in a public place, a bar that wasn't so crowded that I wouldn't see my pursuers coming in, I noticed a news report on a television behind the counter. Kunio Shirai. Another demonstration." He shook his head in dismay. "But this one was larger, more intense, almost a riot. Outside a U.S. Air Force base. Whatever Shirai's trying to do, he's turned up the pressure dramatically."

"We saw the same report." Rachel's forehead was knotted.

"And somehow we're connected with him," Savage said. "Or with the man we knew as Muto Kamichi, whom we never met."

"But saw cut in half at the nonexistent Medford Gap Mountain Retreat.'' The veins in Akira's temples throbbed. ''Madness.'' His eyes blazed. ''I knew I had only one option—to seek safety with my mentor.'' He glanced toward Taro. ''I didn't dare return to my home. But I couldn't ignore my responsibility to Eko. On the chance that she'd come back from being with Churi at the morgue and arranging his funeral, I used the phone in the bar to call my home and felt startled when she answered '*hai*,' the warning signal to run. I quickly asked her, '*Why?*' 'Strangers,' she blurted. '*Gaijin.* Guns.' Someone yanked the phone from her hand. An American spoke Japanese. 'We want to help you,' he said. 'Come back.' I slammed down the phone before they could trace the call. Americans with guns? *In my home?* And they claim they want to help? Not likely! The police would have posted guards to restrict reporters from the crime scene. How did *Americans* get inside?'' Akira glared, his emotions finally showing. ''If I could get to Eko and rescue her . . .''

''We called her as well,'' Savage said. ''At eleven tonight. She gave us the warning signal before an American grabbed the phone. They need her. They'll question her, but she knows nothing. They'll scare her, but she's valuable as a hostage. I don't think they'll hurt her.''

'' 'Don't think' isn't good enough,'' Akira snapped. ''She's like a *mother* to me!''

Taro raised his wrinkled hands, motioning for silence. He spoke to Akira in Japanese.

Akira responded. His melancholy tinged with relief, eyes bright, he turned to Savage. ''My *sensei* has vowed to rescue her. His most advanced students will leave a few weeks early. Tonight will be their graduation. And Eko's release.''

I bet, Savage thought. Those guys upstairs looked as if there wasn't *any* obstacle they couldn't overcome. Whoever's in Akira's house, they won't know what hit them.

Savage bowed to Taro. ''For my friend, I thank you.''

Taro frowned. ''You call Akira a friend?''

''We've been through a lot together.''

''But the friendship is impossible,'' Taro said.

''Why? Because I'm a *gaijin?* Call it respect. I *like* this man.''

Taro smiled enigmatically. "And I, as you put it, like you. But *we* will never be friends."

"Your loss." Savage shrugged.

Taro raised his head in confusion.

Akira interrupted, speaking solemnly to Taro.

Taro nodded. "Yes. An irreverent attempt to be humorous. So American. Amusing. But another reason that we'll never be friends."

"Then let's put it this way. I'm a fellow protector. A good one. And I ask for professional courtesy." Savage didn't give Taro a chance to react. Pivoting quickly toward Akira, he asked, "And then you came here?"

"Where I waited in case my enemies arrived. I couldn't imagine why you hadn't gone to the restaurant as we agreed. I feared that you *still* wouldn't be there when I called again in the morning."

"Just as *we* feared for *you* after Eko gave us the warning signal."

"What *happened?*"

Savage focused his thoughts, trying as best he could to restrain emotion, to summarize objectively what they'd been through: the chase at the Meiji Shrine, the escape from the gardens, the attack on the street.

"But we don't know if Hailey's men were in the van or if they shot at the van." Rachel's voice dropped, plummeting toward despair. "More questions. The answers keep getting farther away."

"And maybe that's the point," Akira said. "To keep us confused. Off balance."

"The obstacle race and the scavenger hunt," Savage said.

Akira looked puzzled.

"That was Graham's view of life. It fits. While we search, we try to elude whoever wants to stop us."

"But we don't know which group is which," Akira said. He repeated a word he'd used earlier: "Madness."

"I may be able to help you," Taro said. "With regard to Kunio Shirai."

It took a moment before Savage registered what Taro had

said. Chest contracting, he stared in surprise at the deceptively frail old man.

"Before I explain, I sense," he told Savage, "that you need to be assured. I have no acquaintance with the name by which you knew him . . . or *falsely* remember that you knew him . . . in America. *Jamais vu*, I believe you call it."

Savage frowned. Straightened. Tensed.

"No need to be alarmed. My excellent student"—Taro gestured toward Akira—"earlier described to me the impossible events at the nonexistent Mountain Retreat. You saw each other die. You saw a man called Muto Kamichi, whom you've learned to call Kunio Shirai, cut in half. But none of it happened. *Jamais vu*. Indeed. As good a description as any. I'm a Buddhist. I believe that the world is illusory. But I also believe that earthquakes, tidal waves, and volcanic eruptions are real. So I force myself to distinguish between illusion and truth. Kunio Shirai is real. But at no time did I arrange for my excellent student to accompany him—under *any* name—to America. I've never met the man. I've never dealt with him through intermediaries. I beg you to accept my word on this."

Savage squinted, felt his shoulders relax, and nodded. Trapped in a sickening, wavering assault on his consciousness, he repeated to himself Rachel's favorite quotation. *Abraham believed by virtue of the absurd.*

"Very well," Taro said and turned to Akira. "A great deal has happened in the six months since I last saw you. In Japan. Or at least in the *undercurrents* of Japan." The old man's eyes changed, their pupils expanding, as if he concentrated on an object far away. "In secret, a small force has been gaining power. Even longer ago than six months. It began in January of nineteen eighty-nine. With the death of our esteemed emperor, Hirohito, and with the forbidden Shinto rites involved in his funeral."

Savage felt Rachel flinch beside him and recalled their conversation in the Ginza district about this same subject.

Taro's eyes abruptly contracted as he shifted his attention from the imaginary distant object and steadied them, laserlike, on Savage. "Religion and politics. The postwar constitution demanded their separation, insisting that never again would God's will be used to control this nation's government. But words on a document imposed by a *gaijin* victor don't cancel tradition or suppress a nation's soul. In private, the old ways are bound to persist. In pockets. Among absolute patriots, one of whom is Kunio Shirai. His ancestors descend from the zenith of Japanese culture, the beginning of the Tokugawa Shogunate in sixteen hundred. Wealthy, determined, disgusted by our present corrupt condition, he wants the ancient ways to return. Others share his vision. *Powerful* others. They believe in the gods. They believe that Japan is the *land* of the gods, that every Japanese is *descended* from gods. They believe in Amaterasu."

12

The name, eerily evocative, made Savage tingle. He strained to remember when he'd heard it before—and suddenly recalled that Akira had mentioned it on the way to Dulles Airport while he tried to teach Savage and Rachel about Japan prior to flying here.

"Amaterasu." Savage nodded. "Yes, the goddess of the sun. The ancestress of every emperor. The ultimate mother of every Japanese from the beginning of time."

Taro cocked his ancient head; he clearly hadn't expected Savage to recognize the name. "Few *gaijin* would . . . I compliment you on your knowledge of our culture."

"The credit belongs to Akira. He's as excellent a teacher as he was your student. . . . Amaterasu? What about her?"

The old man spoke with reverence. "She symbolizes the greatness of Japan, our purity and dignity before our glorious ways were contaminated. Kunio Shirai has chosen her as the image of his purpose, the source of his inspiration. In public, he calls his movement the Traditional Japanese Party. In private, however, he and his staunchest followers refer to their group as the Force of Amaterasu.''

Savage straightened sharply. "What are we talking about? Imperialism? Is Shirai trying to recreate what happened in the nineteen thirties? A mix of religion, patriotism, and might to justify trying to dominate the Pacific Rim and . . . ?''

"No," Taro said. "The opposite. He wants Japan to become secluded.''

The statement was so astonishing that Savage leaned forward, trying to repress the force in his voice. "That goes against everything that . . .''

"Japan has accomplished since the end of the American occupation.'' Taro gestured in agreement. "The economic miracle. Japan has become the most financially powerful nation on earth. What it failed to do militarily in the thirties and forties, it achieved industrially in the seventies and eighties. It subdues other countries economically. We bombed Hawaii in nineteen forty-one but failed to capture it. Now we're buying it. And huge chunks of mainland America and other nations as well. But at a cost beyond money, a terrible penalty, the increasing destruction of our culture.''

"I still don't . . .'' Savage squeezed his thighs, frustrated. "What does Shirai want?''

"I mentioned that his ancestors date back to sixteen hundred, the beginning of the Tokugawa Shogunate. Did Akira explain what happened then?'' Taro asked.

"Only briefly. There was too much to know, too little time for him to . . . *You* tell me.''

"I hope you appreciate the value of history.''

"I was trained to believe it's imperative to learn from mistakes, if that's what you mean,'' Savage said.

"Not only mistakes but successes.'' Taro braced his shoulders. Despite his frail body, he seemed to grow in stature. His eyes again assumed a faraway gaze. "History . . . During the middle ages, Japan was inundated by foreign cultures. The Chinese, the Koreans, the Portuguese, the English, the Spanish, the Dutch. To be sure, not all of these influences were bad. The Chinese gave us Buddhism and Confucianism, for example, as well as a system of writing and an administrative system. On the negative side, the Portuguese introduced firearms, which quickly spread throughout Japan and almost destroyed *bushido*, the ancient noble Way of the warrior and the sword. The Spaniards introduced Christianity, which attempted to displace the gods, to deny that Japanese were divinely descended from Amaterasu.

"In sixteen hundred, Tokugawa Iyeyasu defeated various Japanese warlords and gained control of Japan. He and his descendants returned Japan to the Japanese. One by one, he banned foreigners. The English, the Spanish, the Portuguese . . . all were expelled. The only exception was a small Dutch trading post on a southwestern island near Nagasaki. Christianity was exterminated. Travel to foreign countries was forbidden. Ships capable of reaching the Asian mainland were destroyed. Only small fishing boats, their designs restricting them to hugging the coast, were allowed to be built. And the consequence?" Taro smiled. "For more than two hundred years, Japan was shut off from the rest of the world. We experienced—enjoyed—continuous peace and the greatest blossoming of Japanese culture. Paradise."

At once the old man's face darkened. "But all of that ended in eighteen fifty-three when your countryman, Commodore Perry, anchored his squadron of American warships in Yokohama Bay. They are still known by their bleak prophetic color. Perry's *black* ships. He demanded that Japan reopen its borders to foreign trade. Soon the Shogunate fell. The emperor, formerly kept in seclusion in Kyoto, was moved to Edo, which soon changed its name to Tokyo, where the emperor became the figurehead ruler for politicians eager to exercise power. It's called the Meiji Restoration. I believe in the emperor, but because of that restoration, the *gaijin* contamination resumed . . . increased . . . worsened."

Taro paused, assessing the effect on his audience.

Rachel breathed. "And Kunio Shirai wants to return Japan to the quarantine established in the Tokugawa Shogunate?"

"It's easy to understand his intention," Taro replied. "As a tribe, we no longer abide by the ancient ways. Our young people disrespect their elders and treat tradition with irreverence. Abominations surround us. Western clothes. Western music. Western food. Hamburgers. Fried chicken. Heavy metal.'' Taro pursed his lips in disgust. ''Eventually Japan, like a sponge, will absorb the worst of other cultures, and money—not Amaterasu—will be our only god.''

''You sound like you agree with Shirai,'' Savage said.

''With his motive, not his method. This building, the four years of isolation that each of my students submits to . . . *they* are my version of the Tokugawa quarantine. I despise what I see outside these walls.''

''You've joined him?''

Taro squinted. ''As a samurai, a protector, I *must* be objective. I follow events. I don't create them. My destiny is to be distant, to serve present masters without involvement —and without judgment. The Tokugawa Shogunate insisted on that relationship between retainer and principal. But I hope he succeeds. He probably won't, however. The thrust of history moves stronger forward than backward. Shirai can use his wealth, his influence and power, to bribe, to coerce, and entice multitudes of demonstrators. But on television, I've seen the faces, the *eyes*, of those demonstrators. They're not devoted to the glory of their past. They're consumed by hate for outsiders in the present, for those who don't belong to the tribe. Make no mistake. Pride controls them. Long-repressed anger. Because America won the Pacific War. Because atomic bombs were dropped on our cities.''

Chilled, Savage noticed that Akira's eyes had become more melancholy. In despair, with compassion, Savage recalled that Akira's father had lost his first wife . . . and his parents . . . and his brothers and sisters . . . because of the A-bomb that hit Hiroshima. And the father's *second* wife, Akira's *mother*, had died from cancer caused by radiation from the blast.

Taro's brittle voice rasped. ''Make no error. Whenever you speak to a Japanese, no matter his reserve and feigned politeness, he remembers the bombs called Fat Man and Little Boy. And this long-repressed rage is the power behind the multitudes Shirai has gathered. *He* wants retreat, a return to the glorious sacred past. But *they* want a too-long-postponed attack, to the land-of-gods destiny. Domination.''

"It'll never happen," Savage said flatly.

"Not under present circumstances. Greed insists, and if Shirai misjudges, the multitudes he incites will outreach his control. Land, possessions, money. That's what they want. Not peace and balance. Not harmony. Shirai was right to protest America's presence in Japan. Away with you! All of you! But in the vacuum of your absence, the Force of Amaterasu could become not a blessing but a curse.''

Savage's muscles felt drained. Sitting cross-legged on the cushions at the low cypress table, he leaned back on his hips and tried to diffuse his tension. "How do you know this?'' His voice was strained, a whisper.

"I seclude myself. But my many former students remain in contact. And *they* have reliable sources. Kunio Shirai . . . for motives I admire . . . has the potential to cause a disaster. Aggression, not consolidation. All I want is peace. But if Shirai pushes harder, if he finds a way to attract even larger and more zealous followers . . .''

Savage spun toward Akira. "Does what happened . . . or *didn't* happen . . . at the Medford Gap Mountain Retreat have something to do with this?''

Akira raised his increasingly melancholy eyes. "Taro-*sensei* referred to seclusion. At my father's home, which I maintain, I preserve a piece of the past, though I'm seldom there to enjoy it. I wish now I *had* enjoyed it. Because after everything that's happened I no longer believe in protecting others. I want to protect *myself*. To retreat. Like Taro-*sensei*. Like the Tokugawa Shogunate.''

"Then I guess we'd damned well better talk to Shirai," Savage said. "I'm tired of being manipulated." He glanced toward Rachel and put an arm around her. "And I'm *tired*," he added, "of being a follower, a servant, a watchdog, a shield. It's time I took care of what I want." Again he glanced with undisguised love toward Rachel.

"In that case, you'll lose your soul," Taro said. "The

Way of the protector, the fifth profession, is the noblest—''

"Enough," Savage said. "All I want to do is . . . Akira, what do you say? Are you ready to help me finish this?''

BLACK SHIPS

1

"What are they shouting?" Savage asked.

The seething crowd roared louder, some jerking placards, others shaking their fists. Their furious movements reminded Savage of a roiling river. It was ten A.M. Despite smog, the sun was blinding, and Savage raised a hand to shield his eyes from the glare as he studied the enormous mob that filled the street for blocks, their fury directed toward the U.S. embassy. How many? Savage thought. He found it impossible to count. An estimate? Perhaps as many as twenty thousand demonstrators. They chanted rhythmically, repeating the same brief slogan with greater intensity until the din—amplified echoing off buildings—made Savage's temples throb.

"They're shouting 'Black ships,' " Akira said.

In a moment, the translation became needless, the demonstrators changing to English. From last night's conversation with Taro, Savage understood the reference. Black ships. The armada that America's Commodore Perry had anchored in Yokohama Bay in 1853. As a symbol of the demonstrators' antipathy to America's presence in Japan, the image was fraught with emotion. Succinct. Effective.

But lest the message nonetheless fail to make its point, the mob chanted something new. "America *out! Gaijin* out!" The roar became overwhelming. Savage's ears rang, and although he stood with Akira in a doorway at the fringe of the furious demonstrators, he hugged his chest, suffocated, threatened. The self-consciousness he'd felt when he arrived at Narita Airport, one of very few Caucasians among thousands of Japanese, was magnified to the point that his lungs and stomach felt seared by adrenaline.

Jesus, he thought. The TV newscasts show the magnitude of the demonstrations, but they don't communicate the *feeling*, the raw anger, the sense of a critical mass about to explode. Rage radiated from the crowd, redolent of sweat, of ozone before a tornado.

"With this many people, we'll never get close to him," Savage said. *Him* referred to Kunio Shirai, far down the street, on a makeshift platform haranguing the protestors in front of the embassy. Periodically the mob stopped chanting, and Shirai exhorted them to greater outbursts.

"If we keep to the fringes, we can try for a better look," Akira said.

"I just hope they don't turn around. If this crowd sees an American behind them . . .''

"It's all we can do for now. Unless you feel like going back to Taro-*sensei*'s and waiting."

Grim, Savage shook his head. "I've had my fill of waiting. I want to *see* this guy."

During the night, on a *futon* in a dormitory room on the third floor of Taro's building, Savage had tried unsuccessfully to sleep. His brief naps had been shattered by nightmares. Of multiple versions of Kamichi's body being sliced in half, organs spilling knee-deep onto the blood-pooled floor, writhing like snakes. Of a sword repeatedly cutting Akira's head off, his torso standing while the skull rolled across the floor, *many* skulls superimposed upon one another, a hideous multiple exposure, one skull after the other stopping in front of Savage and blinking.

Rachel's sleep had been equally disturbed. Shocked awake, whispering hoarsely in the dark, she'd described the relentless nightmare of her husband persistently beating and raping her. As she and Savage held each other for comfort, Savage had brooded. Apprehensive, he'd worried about how Taro's students were proceeding in their attempt to get Eko away from the men at Akira's home. He'd asked Taro to send a messenger to rouse him when the rescue team returned, but by dawn the team had failed to report, and Taro's gloom during breakfast was manifest, for once his private thoughts intruding on his public thoughts.

"I cannot believe that they were caught," Taro said. "They wouldn't go in unless they knew they'd be successful. So they must be . . ."

"Waiting," Taro decided, just as he, Savage, Akira, and Rachel had waited anxiously throughout the early part of the morning.

"This is pointless," Akira had said. "Those men know their job. When they can, they'll do it. In the meantime, *we* must do *ours.*"

"Locate Kunio Shirai." His stomach rebelling against a supposedly soothing breakfast of noodles and soy sauce, Savage had set down his chopsticks. "Find a way to meet him. Confront him. Question him. *Alone.* Did he see us die just as we saw *him* die?"

But contacting Shirai had proved a frustrating near-impossibility. His home had an unlisted number. A call to his corporation—a conglomerate of real estate and publishing enterprises—had revealed that Shirai was supposed to be at his political headquarters, and a call there had produced the cryptic response that Shirai would not be hard to locate if the caller would go to a certain address. The address, they soon discovered, was near the U.S. embassy.

"Another demonstration?" Akira's features had hardened in an anguished scowl.

"Rachel, stay here." Savage had stood, gesturing for Akira to follow him toward the door.

"But . . ."

"No. The situation's changed. You can't come with me," Savage had insisted. "Till now, my obligation was twofold. To find out what happened to Akira and me . . . and at the same time to protect you." He'd breathed. "But finally you're safe. Here, with Taro-*sensei*, with the students who remained, no one can get to you in this fortress. My attention isn't divided. I can do my work. I won't be distracted."

She'd looked hurt, shut out, abandoned.

"Rachel, I'm doing this for you. All I want are two things. To cancel my nightmare." He'd come back and kissed her, lovingly, tenderly. He'd stroked her chin. "And to spend the rest of my life with you."

Akira and Taro had glanced away, embarrassed by this undisguised show of emotion.

"But I need to do it alone," Savage had said. "No, not exactly alone. What I mean is, with Akira."

Her blue eyes had flashed. With jealousy? Savage had wondered. No. That's crazy.

But Rachel's next statement had made Savage wonder if she was in fact jealous.

"I've helped you so far," she'd said. "I've made suggestions . . . at Graham's . . . at the Harrisburg hospital that . . ."

"Rachel, yes. There's no question. You've *helped*. But what Akira and I are about to do could get us killed . . . and *you* killed if you're *with* us. I want you alive, so if—*when* —I come back, we . . ."

"Go. God damn it," she'd fumed. "But if you come back dead, I'll never speak to you again." She gestured, as if toward the gods. "Listen to what I'm saying. I'm as nuts as *you* are. Get out of here."

One hour later, as the mob kept chanting, "Americans *out*. *Gaijin* out," Savage felt hollow, accustomed to having Rachel with him during stress. But *Akira* was with him, and in this unfamiliar land, the Japanese demonstrators shouting, Savage felt oddly secure, *comitatus* and samurai together, skirting the fringe of the crowd, cautiously approaching Kunio Shirai, two professionals determined to do their work so they could ultimately *abandon* their work and be themselves, not followers, not servants.

The crush of bodies was overwhelming, the backs of protestors pressing hard against Savage, squeezing him against a wall. He squirmed sideways and freed himself, only to be caught by the backward force of other demonstrators. The effect was like waves thrusting him against rocks. *Human* waves, and the pressure thrust air from his lungs. Though he'd never suffered from claustrophobia, his skin became clammy from his effort to breathe and his sudden feeling of helplessness.

He reached Akira, who'd managed to find space in a doorway a few feet ahead of him. "This was a mistake," Savage said.

The nearest protestors, hearing an American, turned angrily.

Akira held up a hand to them, as if to signify he had the American under control.

The rest of the demonstrators continued shouting "*Gaijin* out!" as Kunio Shirai chopped the air with his karate-callused hands. His voice boomed, raucous with fury, louder than their shouts, urging them to a greater fervor.

"We'll never get near him this way," Savage continued. "And if this crowd starts to riot, there's a good chance we'll be crushed."

"Agreed," Akira said. "But we need to have a close look at him. I don't trust newspaper photographs or the shots they show on television. Cameras lie. We *must* see him face-to-face. We have to be sure he *is* Kamichi."

"Not this way. How?"

Down the street, loudspeakers blared, their shrill reverberation intensifying Shirai's impassioned outbursts.

"He certainly sounds like Kamichi. If we can make our way through the crowd for just another block," Akira said, "we might be near enough to—"

"Wait," Savage said. "I think I . . . There might be an easier route."

Akira waited.

"Shirai's taking an enormous risk, exposing himself like this," Savage said. "I assume he has bodyguards in front of the platform, and I've noticed police among the crowd. But he'd need an army to protect him if all these people got out of control and rushed him. Sure, they worship him. But that's a threat. If everyone wanted to touch him or lift him onto their shoulders, he'd be crushed. He couldn't possibly survive."

"So how does he plan to leave?" Akira asked. "I don't see a limousine, but supposing there is one near the platform, he can't be certain he could get inside or that the crowd would part to let the car drive away. What's his escape plan?"

"Exactly," Savage said. "Look at the way the platform's constructed. A railing all around it. No stairs. How did he get up there? And the platform's on the sidewalk, not the street, with the rear against a building."

Eyes gleaming, Akira understood. "That must be where the stairs are, leading up from a door in the building. *That's* how Shirai got here. *That's* how he plans to leave, down the stairs, into the building and . . ."

"*Through* the building?" Savage asked, heart racing with excitement. "If he planned this properly, if he didn't draw attention to himself when he arrived on the other street, there won't be a crowd back there waiting for him. He'll be able to hurry out the opposite door of the building, get into his car while his guards form a cordon, and be gone before these demonstrators realize where he went."

Akira straightened, muscles primed. "Hurry. We don't know how long he'll continue speaking."

With painful effort, they retreated in the direction from which they'd come. Savage glimpsed a photographer and ducked. He avoided a policeman and suddenly flinched, pushed by the crowd, his shoulder banging hard against a wall. A few tortured steps farther, he strained to resist another push that nearly slammed him through a huge window.

Sweating, he imagined his body spewing blood, impaled by shards of glass. He squeezed and thrust, squirming past what felt like a tidal wave of protestors. Six months ago, he knew, before the onslaught of his nightmare, he wouldn't have felt this close to panicking, but then six months ago, he had to admit, he would never have allowed himself to be trapped in such an uncontrollable situation. His sickening sense of *jamais vu* had changed him, impaired his judgment. He'd become a victim, less a protector than someone in *need* of a protector.

Damn it, I have to get out of here. With a final frantic thrust, he stumbled from the crowd, gulping air, concentrating to control his trembling muscles.

2

He barely had a moment to allow himself to recover. Ahead, Akira glanced back to make sure that Savage was with him, then broke into a run, crossing the street. Sweat trickling off his forehead, Savage rushed to follow. They darted through traffic that was stalled by the demonstrators. With everyone's attention directed toward the protest, no one seemed to notice Savage and Akira's frenzied effort. They reached a side street, charging along it, desperate to get to the street that paralleled the street upon which Shirai harangued his followers.

At a corner, Savage swung frantically toward the right, relieved to discover that *this* street had only the normal congestion of cars and pedestrians, not another threatening impervious mass of demonstrators. Even here, though, the chant of "*Gaijin* out!" bellowed distinctly from the other street, rumbling off buildings.

Urgency strengthened Savage's legs. His long, quick strides brought him next to Akira. As one, the *comitatus* and samurai glanced at each other, nodded, tightened their lips in what might have been a smile. Increasing speed, they dodged pedestrians and raced along one block, then another, quickly approaching the building from which they expected Shirai to emerge.

Akira pointed. A half-block before them, a long black limousine was parked at the curb. Muscular Japanese men, wearing sunglasses, double-breasted blue suits, and white ties, clustered on the sidewalk, some watching the exit from the building, others surveying passing cars and pedestrians approaching the limousine.

Savage didn't need to debate with Akira about their next move. He felt as if he'd swallowed ice and abruptly slowed.

Akira imitated, suddenly strolling, just another pedestrian, glancing toward merchandise in windows, blending with the pattern of the street.

"It doesn't look like they saw us coming," Savage said. "Or if they did, they're too well trained to react and warn us we were spotted."

"That family ahead of us shielded us," Akira said. "Nonetheless, for all the guards know, we're merely two businessmen late for an appointment. They don't have cause for concern."

"Except that I'm an American," Savage said. "Conspicuous."

"There's no way to solve that problem. As long as we don't seem a threat, they'll leave us alone. All we want to do is get a close look at Shirai. If we arrange to stroll up at the appropriate time, it shouldn't be difficult. Provided the guards aren't on edge, we might even be able to speak with him."

"Their blue suits look like a uniform," Savage said.

"Double-breasted. And the white ties and the sunglasses. Very much a uniform," Akira said. *"Yakuza."*

"What? But isn't that . . . ?"

"What you'd call the Japanese mafia. In America, you're used to mobsters being outside the system. Here it's common practice for politicians and businessmen to hire gangsters as protectors."

Savage stared. "And the public doesn't object?"

Akira shrugged. "A give-and-take tradition. Even prime ministers have hired *yakuza* as escorts, and at stockholders' meetings for major corporations, gangsters are often employed to discourage questions. They shout. They throw chairs. It's accepted procedure. The authorities tolerate gangsters, and in return, the *yakuza* avoid drug trafficking and crimes involving firearms.''

Savage shook his head, off balance. Like so much he'd learned about Japan, this symbiosis between the establishment and the underworld was bewildering. More, that these *yakuza* protectors would choose to wear what amounted to uniforms was also bewildering, an inversion of one of the most basic rules Graham had taught him—dress to be a chameleon.

At the moment, though, Savage was most disturbed by Akira's reference to firearms. It reminded him that he'd felt compelled, uneasily, to leave his Beretta at Taro's. He couldn't take the risk that, in case of an incident, the police would stop him and discover him carrying a pistol, a major offense at any time in Japan but much more severe and suspicious if someone were found to have a handgun at a political demonstration. ''Does that mean Shirai's guards won't be carrying weapons?''

''Perhaps. Indeed it's highly possible, although Shirai has created such a controversy—become so conspicuous—that they might decide to bend the rules.''

''In other words, we don't know what we're facing.''

''Of course,'' Akira said. ''This, after all, *is* Japan.''

Approaching the guards, frowning toward the roar of the protestors that echoed from the other street, Savage and Akira responded as one. As if sensing each other's thoughts, they veered to step into a flower shop, needing somewhere to linger until Shirai left the demonstration. While Akira pretended to browse along a row of chrysanthemums, Savage stayed close to the door. But even through its glass, the rumbling shouts were easily heard. He listened for a difference in the chant, a change in rhythm or volume, anything to indicate that Shirai was leaving.

Hands tingling, he tensed with the realization that he'd already heard it. Or *hadn't* heard it. For the last thirty seconds,

Shirai had failed to interrupt the crowd to continue his tirade. Savage's nerves felt jolted.

He motioned to Akira and hurriedly went outside. As Akira joined him, they swung to the right toward the barrel-chested guards thirty yards away and saw the gangsters adjust their sunglasses, straighten their suitcoats, and *come to attention*. Most directed their gaze toward the door to the building, two men holding it open, flanking it. Two others opened doors on the limousine. Only a few continued to scan the street.

Unprofessional, Savage thought with relief. The confused situation reminded him of the lack of discipline that had allowed John Hinckley, Jr., to get close enough to shoot and wound President Reagan, his press secretary, a Secret Service agent, and a Washington policeman in 1981. Reagan had been in a downtown D.C. hotel, giving a speech. A cordon of guards had waited to protect him as he left the hotel to get into his car. But as the President stepped into view, his guards had been unable to resist the impulse to turn and look at their movie-star leader. While their attention wavered, Hinckley had made his move, firing repeatedly.

Savage flashed back nervously to the intensive training Graham had given him after Savage had left the SEALs. Graham had ordered Savage to study the films of that attempted assassination and other attacks—tragically successful—on major politicians, to study them again and again. "Keep your eyes away from your principal!" Graham had insisted. "You know what your principal looks like! No matter how famous that principal is, your job is *not* to be a tourist, not to admire someone famous! A protector's job is to watch the crowd!"

Which the men in the white ties and double-breasted blue suits weren't doing.

Maybe we've got a chance, Savage thought, aware of the irony that he as a protector was using the tactics of an assassin.

3

Savage's neck muscles thickened, arteries swelling, blood soaring through them.

A group of guards exited the building, with Shirai at their center. All the protectors on the sidewalk swung to face him, giving Savage and Akira the chance to approach within a few feet.

Savage inhaled, straining to free the imaginary hands that squeezed his aching throat. He thought he'd prepared himself for this desperately needed confrontation. But recognition startled him. Reality fought with illusion.

Dismayed, he relived the slaughter, the wide-awake soul-destroying nightmare at the Medford Gap Mountain Retreat. He had no doubt now. Though cameras could lie and the newspaper photographs and television footage of Shirai might have made the politician only *seem* to be Kamichi, the man Savage now stared at was unquestionably the principal he'd seen sliced in half in the hotel's corridor. Even surrounded by a commotion of guards, the *face* was vividly close. Shirai *was* Kamichi. Kamichi was Shirai!

But Kamichi was dead! How could he . . . ? Reality rippled. Memory, like a camera, could be a liar.

Shirai—gray-haired, droop-jowled, fiftyish, somewhat short and overweight, but for all that, astonishingly charismatic—sweated from the exertion of his energetic, impassioned speech. Striding rapidly but with effort toward his limousine, using a handkerchief to wipe moisture from the back of his neck, he darted his eyes toward the crowd beyond his guards.

And stiffened, his brown complexion turning pale, riveting his startled gaze on Savage and Akira.

He shouted, blurting staccato Japanese phrases of terror. He stumbled back, pointing in horror.

His bodyguards whirled.

"No!" Savage said.

Shirai kept wailing, stumbling back, pointing.

Spotting their quarry, the bodyguards snapped to attention.

"No, we've got to talk to you!" Savage said. *"Do you know us? Do you recognize us?* We know you! We need to talk, to ask you some questions! We have to find out what happened at—?"

Shirai barked a command.

The bodyguards lunged.

"Listen!" Savage yelled. "Please! We—"

A bodyguard struck.

Savage dodged. "We don't want trouble! We just want to talk to—"

The bodyguard chopped with a callused hand.

Leaping backward, Savage escaped the blow. The guards attacked in a wedge, making Savage feel as if the Dallas Cowboys, dressed incongruously in sunglasses and double-breasted suits, were about to crush him. He scurried a dozen steps farther backward, seeing Shirai's terrified face as the man Savage knew as Kamichi scrambled into his limousine.

"No! Just let us talk to you!" Savage said.

Jabbing with his elbow, Savage struck the solar plexus of his nearest assailant. The impact was shocking, as if Savage had hit a sack of cement. But the force of the blow was sufficient to make the assailant grunt, bend forward gasping, and stagger back, colliding with another guard.

Shirai's limousine sped from the curb, rubber smoking, tires squealing.

The guards continued rushing Savage, some of them pulling out blackjacks. Akira spun, kicking.

A guard's leg buckled. Another guard's wrist bent, the blackjack falling from his broken hand.

In a frenzy, Savage bolted, escaping, flanked by Akira, hearing urgent footfalls and angry voices behind him. As they sped through an intersection, Savage's pulse skipped. To his left, he saw demonstrators disbanding from the protest on the parallel street swarm into view.

Jesus! Savage thought, racing harder. A blackjack, flung in desperation, whistled past his head. It walloped onto the sidewalk, the leather-sheathed lead core making a brutal thunk that caused Savage to flinch at the thought of what the blackjack would have done to his skull.

His lungs burned. His legs strained. Heart pounding, he could only hope that the guards would be professional enough to stop soon, having accomplished their task of protecting their principal. For all the guards know, Savage thought, we're a diversion and the real threat's supposed to come from another direction, farther down the street.

But we injured three of them. Maybe the guards are pissed off enough to want to catch us and pound our skulls to get even.

Or maybe they want to find out who we are! A protector ought to know who's after his client!

But how can we make them understand? We don't want to hurt Shirai! We only want to talk to him!

The guards roared closer. As Savage dodged confused pedestrians, a heavy object whacked his shoulder. Another blackjack, hurled in desperation. The impact made Savage stagger forward, wincing. Repressing a groan, he managed to regain his balance, correct his stride, and lunge faster, the footsteps behind him thundering nearer.

Akira charged across the street, through dense stalled traffic toward another side street, away from the site of the demonstration. Savage kept pace, chest heaving, legs stretching, pounding. Sweat drenched his shirt. His shoulder throbbed.

But all he cared about was the sudden realization that he and Akira had a better chance of maneuvering through the congested pedestrians they faced than did the herd of angry guards, whose solid mass would impede their rush.

He was wrong. As he darted around pedestrians, a hand reached to grab his sleeve. He twisted away. But at once another hand grabbed, and his stomach plummeted. Dear God, he'd been thinking like a Westerner, as if this were

New York! In Manhattan, pedestrians would scramble to avoid two men being chased. *But not here*. Savage had forgotten what Akira had told him! The Japanese were among the most compliant, law-abiding people on earth. *Tribal*. The group against the individual. Status quo, harmony, order, meant everything. Two men being chased by a mob, especially when one of the men was American, *had* to be at fault, a threat to society, because the majority by definition was in the right.

A third hand grabbed for Savage. Akira turned and grabbed Savage, yanking him through a doorway. They found themselves in a brightly lit department store. Outside, the guards slammed against pedestrians, the chaos of their impact blocking the entrance. Racing past counters and astonished clerks, Savage saw an exit on his left. It led to another street. So out of breath he could barely speak, Savage blurted to Akira, running, "We've got to separate."

"But . . ."

"*You* can disappear among the crowd! They're after a Japanese and an *American!* If you drop out of sight, they'll keep chasing me because I'm conspicuous."

They reached the side exit, scrambling through, hearing the guards burst into the store through the entrance Savage and Akira had used.

"There's no way I'm leaving you," Akira said.

"Do it! I'll meet you at Taro's!"

"No! I won't abandon you!"

Spotting a uniformed messenger about to get onto a Honda motorcycle, Savage lunged, thrust the messenger aside, grabbed the motorcycle, and leapt onto it.

"Give me room!" Akira leapt on after Savage, clasping his arms around Savage's chest.

Putting the motorcycle into gear, twisting the throttle, Savage sped onto the street, veering past cars. He no longer heard the guards pursuing him. As his chest swelled, all he heard was the suddenly reassuring din of traffic, the roar of the motorcycle, the deafening clamor—so unexpectedly normal—of Tokyo.

"We'll have to get rid of the bike soon," Akira said as Savage rounded a corner and increased speed. "Before it's reported stolen and the police come after us."

"Right now, what I'm worried about are those guards."

"I thank you for offering to be a decoy so I could escape," Akira said behind him.

"It seemed a friendly thing to do."

"Yes," Akira said, his voice strange. "Friendly." He sounded puzzled.

Three blocks later, they left the motorcycle on the sidewalk outside a subway entrance, hoping the authorities would assume that Savage and Akira had hurried below to escape on a train. Strolling tensely through an intersection, they hailed a taxi and didn't need to discuss that this would be the first of *many* taxis they'd use in their zigzagging evasive tactics that would hide their trail back to Taro's.

"That messenger will probably never see his bike again," Savage said.

"Not true," Akira replied. "Someone might move it so it doesn't interfere with pedestrians. But no one would dare to steal it. This is Japan."

4

"I don't understand. What did Shirai say?" Savage asked.

He sat on a chair in a small infirmary on the fourth floor of Taro's building. His shirt was off, the old man examining the back of his shoulder. Akira and Rachel stood to the side, and Rachel's narrowed eyes made clear to Savage that the bruise the thrown blackjack had caused was considerable.

"Raise your arm," Taro said.

Savage did, biting his lip.

"Move it back and forth."

He managed to do so but not to its full extent and not without effort.

"Describe the pain."

"Deep. It aches. At the same time, it throbs."

"Nothing feels sharp?" Taro asked.

"No. I don't think anything's broken."

"All the same, you ought to consider going to a hospital and requesting an X ray."

Savage shook his head. "I've attracted enough attention today already."

"*Hai*," Taro said. "I'll give you something to reduce the swelling. Your shoulder's too stiff to be of use in a crisis."

"If I have to, believe me, I can use it."

Taro's wizened lips formed a smile. He rubbed a cotton ball soaked in alcohol against Savage's shoulder.

Savage felt a sting. Taro removed a needle.

"Novocaine, epinephrine, and a steroid," the old man said. "Sit with your hand on your thigh and give the arm a rest."

The shoulder began to feel numb. Savage exhaled and glanced at Akira. "But what did Shirai *say*? It was all in Japanese. I didn't understand a word, although I did get the message. He was terrified by the sight of us."

Akira scowled. "Yes . . . Terrified. And not because he feared we might be anonymous assailants. And not because after delivering his anti-American speech, he found an American close to him. Clearly he recognized us. 'You. No,' he shouted. 'It can't be. You're . . . It's impossible. Keep them away from me.' "

"And that's *all* he said?"

"A few more outbursts as he scrambled into his car. The gist was the same. 'You. How did—? Stay away. Don't let them near me.' "

Savage brooded, the injection taking effect, the pain in his shoulder replaced by a total lack of sensation. But his mind felt numbed as well, stunned by the morning's events. "So what are we supposed to conclude? That we were right?"

"I don't see any other explanation." Akira sighed. "He remembers us, just as we remember him."

"Even though we never really saw each other before," Savage said. "Like us, he recalls things that never happened."

"But *what* things?" Akira demanded. "Because he recognized us, that doesn't mean he saw us killed just as we imagine *he* was killed! We can't assume that *his* false memory is the same as ours. For all we know, in *his* nightmare we were assassins from whom he barely escaped."

Rachel stepped closer. *"That"* would explain the look of terror you described and his desperation to get away from you."

"Perhaps." Savage squinted. "But he might have acted the same way if he suddenly found himself confronted by two men he'd seen die! Preoccupied, exhausted, leaving the demonstration, eager to reach the safety of his limousine, he sees two ghosts and panics. In *his* place, would you want to stick around and chat, or feel so shocked that your only impulse would be to get away?"

Rachel considered, then gestured. "Probably the latter. But by now, if I thought I'd seen two ghosts, my shock would have changed to bewilderment. I'd want to know why you're still alive, how you survived, what you were doing at my car. And I'd be furious that my guards didn't catch you so I could learn the answers."

"Good," Savage said. "Good point." He raised his eyebrows and turned toward Akira. "So what do you think? Maybe he'll be ready to talk to us."

"Maybe . . . There's one way to find out."

"Right. Let's give him a call."

As Savage stood, his arm dangled uselessly. He rubbed it, preoccupied, and at once reminded himself that they had yet another problem. "Taro-*sensei*, your men still haven't come back? There's still no word about their attempt to infiltrate Akira's home and rescue Eko?"

The old man's face seemed more wrinkled, his body apparently shorter, thinner, dwarfed by his loose karate *gi*. For once, his appearance of frailty was not deceptive. "Almost twelve hours, and they haven't reported."

"That might not mean a disaster," Akira said. "Taro-

sensei trained us not to attempt a mission unless we were confident of accomplishing our purpose. They might be in position, waiting for their chance to move.''

"But wouldn't they have called to report?" Savage asked.

"Not if their plan required all of them to stay in place, prepared to make a coordinated effort," Taro said. "We don't know the obstacles they face."

"I should have gone with them," Akira said. "They're doing this for me, to get Eko. I ought to be sharing their risk.''

"No," Taro said. "You must not feel ashamed. *They* went so that *you* could be free to contact Shirai. You haven't failed in your duty. You cannot do more than one thing at once."

Akira's lips trembled. He straightened, his back rigid, bowing deeply. *"Arigato, Taro-sensei."*

Taro gestured. It seemed as if he knocked a burden off Akira's shoulders. "Go. Make your call."

"But not from here," Savage said. "We mustn't allow Shirai to be able to trace our call to this building."

"But of course," Taro said. "I never doubted that you'd follow the correct procedure." He narrowed his wrinkled eyes. Despite his concern for his absent students, his wizened lips again formed a possible smile. "Your *sensei* deserves respect.''

"He's dead," Savage said. "I don't know his part in this, but yes, like you, he deserves respect." Savage grimaced. "I have a request."

"My home is yours."

"My Beretta. I want it back."

5

Akira chose a pay phone in another ward of Tokyo, making doubly certain that if the call was traced it wouldn't attract

Shirai's bodyguards toward Taro's building. The pay phone was located at the rear of a *pachinko* parlor, a harshly lit huge room crammed with rows of what resembled vertical pinball machines. *Pachinko*, Savage learned, was one of Japan's most popular entertainments, with over ten thousand parlors and millions of machines throughout the country. Players crowded next to each other. The pervasive clatter of steel balls dropping through the machines made it impossible for anyone except Savage, standing close to the phone, to overhear Akira's conversation.

Though Akira spoke in Japanese, Savage knew what he was saying, both men having agreed on the essence of Akira's remarks.

The first call was to Shirai's political headquarters, but the receptionist claimed that Shirai had not returned there after the demonstration. The next call was to Shirai's corporate office, but again the receptionist claimed that Shirai wasn't present. While Savage and Akira had been at the demonstration, Taro had used his many contacts to obtain the unlisted number for Shirai's home, but yet once more when Akira phoned, he was told that Shirai wasn't available.

Akira set down the phone and explained. "Of course, any of them could be lying. But I left our message. 'The two men he saw at his car this morning are extremely anxious to speak with him. Please relay that information.' I said I'd be calling back every fifteen minutes."

"So now we have to wait again." Savage's chest ached with frustration. He wanted to move, to do something, to confront his problem and finally solve his nightmare. "Should we go to another pay phone?"

Akira shrugged. "Each call took no longer than forty seconds. Not enough time for anyone to trace it."

"But all the same," Savage said.

"Hai. Let's go."

6

The next calls were made from a pay phone across from a crowded playground in a small wooded park that contrasted starkly with a traffic-jammed overhead highway. The receptionist at Shirai's political headquarters repeated that Shirai had not returned from the demonstration. Persistent, Akira dialed Shirai's corporate office, and after a few remarks, his features became alert, though he permitted no trace of excitement in his voice. Breathing quickly, Savage stepped closer.

Akira pressed the disconnect lever. "Shirai's at his business office. We have an appointment to see him in an hour."

Savage's pulse quickened. Elated, he started to grin.

Abruptly his mood changed. His grin became a frown.

"What's the matter?" Akira asked.

Traffic blared in the background.

"Just like that?" Savage said. "He didn't explain why he was terrified when he saw us, why he scrambled into his limousine and rushed away in horror? Or why, despite his terror, he's agreeing to see us?"

Akira left the phone and walked with Savage. "He didn't explain because I never had a chance to speak with him. His secretary relayed the message."

Savage frowned harder. "No."

"I don't understand," Akira said. "What's wrong?"

"That's the question, isn't it? That's what *I* want to know. It doesn't make sense. After the demonstration, Shirai's reaction to us was so extreme I have trouble believing he'd adjust this quickly and agree to meet us right away."

"But that's exactly what *makes* it believable," Akira said. "He *was* upset. Frightened to the point that he lost control. Whatever he falsely remembers . . . it may be he thinks he saw us killed, or else he imagines we tried to kill *him* . . . whatever the reason, in *his* place I'd be desperate for answers, the same as *we* are. I'd want to know how dead men were resurrected, or in the latter scenario, why my protectors turned against me.''

''Desperate. Yes.'' Savage kept walking, scanning the crowded street, on guard against possible danger, his protective instincts at a nerve-straining zenith. He'd never felt this vulnerable. ''*That's* why I'm suspicious. If his secretary told him you were going to call back every fifteen minutes, why would he simply instruct her to make an appointment an hour from now? Instead of risking a face-to-face meeting, he should have ordered her to put your call through . . . so he *wouldn't* be in danger, so he could speak to you *safely* from a distance.''

''I take for granted he'll have protectors at the meeting,'' Akira said. ''He'll guarantee his security.''

''And what about *our* security? If his guards are the same men who chased us after the demonstration, they might be waiting for us with big grins and blackjacks.'' Savage rubbed his throbbing shoulder. The painkiller had dissipated. He felt as if he'd been hit with a baseball bat. ''I don't know how much damage I caused to the first man who rushed me, but I know I heard you break another man's hand. They won't be happy.''

''They're professionals. They were doing their job. But an hour from now, they'll have *another* job, and their emotions shouldn't interfere. Their principal's wishes take precedence.''

''And what if *Shirai's* wishes are the same as theirs? To get us out of the way,'' Savage asked.

''I'm convinced''—Akira paused—''that Shirai wants information.''

''You mean that *we* want information and we're prepared to *trust* the man we saw killed.''

''What is it Rachel likes to say? Her favorite quotation?'' Akira asked.

'' 'Abraham believed by virtue of the absurd.' ''

"In other words, faith is a mystery. Sometimes, if we're confused enough, we have to trust," Akira said.

"Graham would have called me a fool. Trust? That goes against everything I was taught. And if Taro heard you talking this way, he'd be appalled."

Akira hesitated. Shaking his head, he chuckled. "My *sensei* would insist on retraining me."

"We don't need retraining. What we *need* to do is step back and be objective, to pretend we're protecting someone else."

"Oh, in *that* case," Akira said.

"Right. Let's pretend we've got someone else, *not ourselves*, for clients."

"All of a sudden security, not answers, has priority," Akira said.

"So let's do what we *know* how to do, what we do best."

Akira's voice reminded Savage of the ominous polished hiss of a sword being drawn from a scabbard. "Inspect the danger zone."

7

Shirai's corporate building, one of few multileveled structures in earthquake-prone Japan, was made of gleaming glass and steel but with resilient defensive innovations of design, Savage assumed, that made it impervious to assault. The equivalent of an executive protector's code. He studied the glinting edifice from an intersection two blocks away, slowly approaching from the south, nervously aware that no matter how many chameleon tactics he used, he'd still be conspicuous. A *gaijin*.

At the same time, he knew that Akira approached and, with equal caution, assessed the potential trap from two blocks in the opposite direction. In case of a threat, they'd agreed to retreat to a fallback position. Indeed they had *several* fallback positions . . . to allow for contingencies. The care with which they'd planned their surveillance made Savage feel proud. For the first time since he'd arrived in Japan, he felt in charge, in control, like Graham's disciple, not like a victim.

A block from Shirai's towering building, Savage stopped. As traffic and pedestrians passed, he noticed that in addition to the large main entrance to the building, there was a slightly less large side-entrance. The streets were so congested that parking wasn't permitted, though vehicles with a legitimate purpose were allowed to stop briefly, for example a delivery van outside the front entrance. Below the ideograms on the van, a drawing of a floral arrangement made clear the purpose of the delivery. At the side entrance, a truck was parked, a bored looking man in a cap and coveralls leaning against a front fender, reading a newspaper, occasionally glancing at his watch, then toward the side entrance, sighing, shaking his head, as if waiting for his partner to come out. All seemingly natural.

Except that Savage's neck prickled when he noticed that instead of thick, heavy workman's boots, the driver wore shiny, stylish loafers.

Shit, he thought and turned to stroll tensely southward, in the direction from which he'd come. A prudent distance away, he crossed the busy street, proceeded east for several blocks, then swung around a corner and headed north toward Shirai's building to assess its rear and eventually the side he hadn't been able to see from his initial position.

This time, at the back, a dark limousine with opaque windows was parked near the entrance. And at the side, Savage saw a truck with a telephone symbol.

He clenched his fists. Determined to do this properly, he made a second circuitous inspection of the building, then retreated toward the rendezvous site.

8

A long line of ticket holders filed into the movie theater. On the clamorous sidewalk, Savage pretended to study a poster for a U.S. action film. It amazed him that a country with one of the lowest violent-crime rates in the world would be fascinated by a muscular, bare-chested American aiming a rocket launcher.

Akira appeared beside him, his voice low. "All the entrances are being watched."

Savage kept studying the poster. "At least Shirai didn't insult our intelligence by keeping the same vehicles in place. The second time I circled the building, there were different trucks, vans, and limousines."

"But we have to assume that several men are hidden inside each vehicle."

"Oh, absolutely," Savage said. He pivoted to face the street, to make sure he hadn't been seen and followed from Shirai's building. "The question is, are they merely a precaution or does Shirai want us picked up and eliminated?"

Akira spread his hands. "Are you prepared to risk stepping into the building to find out?"

"I've lost my faith," Savage said.

"As have I."

" 'Abraham believed by virtue of the absurd?' No way," Savage said.

"Then what should we do?"

"Phone Shirai's office," Savage said. "Tell his secretary we're sorry but we've been detained. Ask to speak to him."

"It won't do any good. Given the trap he seems to have arranged, he'll refuse and keep attempting to entice us into the building."

"That's my assumption," Savage said. "But it's worth

the attempt. Assuming he does refuse, try to reschedule the meeting for later today. My guess is he'll agree.''

"No doubt. But that only postpones the problem. It doesn't solve it," Akira said. "We still need to talk to him, and we don't dare go into that building."

"So we arrange to meet him somewhere else, somewhere he doesn't expect," Savage said. "While I circled the building, I had an idea. But it won't work unless we keep Shirai in his office until we're ready to make our move. So we keep calling him, postponing the meeting, and in the meantime we phone Taro."

"Why?"

"To ask if a few more students can graduate early."

9

Static crackled. In the rented Toyota, Savage straightened, muscles rigid. Frustrated by his unfamiliarity with the Japanese language, he hoped that the garbled male voice that squawked from the two-way radio wasn't so distorted by poor reception that Akira found it as intelligible as he did.

Steering with effort through rush-hour traffic, continuing to drive north, east, south, and west in a square two blocks adjacent to Shirai's building, Akira picked up the walkie-talkie. He spoke briefly in Japanese, nodded to the staticky answer, and said something further.

His face hardened when he heard the reply. *"Hai. Arigato."* Setting down the walkie-talkie, Akira gripped both karate-callused hands on the steering wheel and veered toward a sudden opening in the lane beside him. He veered yet again, this time around a corner, struggling through traffic, approaching Shirai's building.

Though Savage felt swollen with questions, he made a

deliberate professional effort not to interrupt Akira's concentration.

Akira broke Savage's frustration. "They've seen him."

"Ah." Savage leaned back. But his tension wasn't relieved. He imagined Taro's students, expertly trained in camouflage, blending with pedestrians, keeping a wary surveillance on every side of Shirai's building. Akira had described Shirai's car and provided the information on the license plate that he'd memorized as the car sped away from this morning's demonstration. Taro in turn had supplied his students with magazine photographs of their quarry. The students had previously seen Shirai on television reports about his radically conservative politics, his belief in the Force of Amaterasu, and his insistence that Japan return to the cultural quarantine of the Tokugawa Shogunate. They'd known precisely whom to watch for. "So Shirai's limousine finally came out of the underground garage?"

Akira steered urgently, slipping into another break in traffic, too busy to answer.

"The trouble is," Savage said, "Shirai's limousine . . . whether we like to admit it, this is still an act of faith . . . Shirai might not be in the car."

"He is. There's no doubt," Akira said. His eyes assessed traffic. His hands responded, veering the Toyota.

"No doubt?"

"He was seen," Akira said.

"What? How? That's not possible. The rear windows are shielded, and we couldn't get any of Taro's students into the underground garage to see who stepped into the car."

"But Shirai *was* seen stepping into the car. Not in the underground garage."

"Then how . . . ?"

"Two minutes ago," Akira said, "the limousine appeared at the northern exit from the building. Shortly after, guards emerged on the sidewalk and formed a cordon. Shirai came out, passed through the guards, and got into the limousine. They're driving west."

The walkie-talkie crackled again. Akira picked it up, listened to another static-distorted Japanese voice, said, "*Hai*," and returned the walkie-talkie beside him. "They're still headed west. An escort car filled with guards is before and behind the limousine."

"Standard procedure." Savage imagined Taro's students using motorbikes to follow the limousine while taking care to keep an unobtrusive distance. They'd maintain surveillance and continue reporting by radio until Akira had a chance to catch up to the motorcade and cautiously follow. No matter which street Shirai's driver used, Akira would be informed.

"As we expected, Shirai finally became impatient," Akira said. "He realized we had no intention of arriving for our constantly postponed meeting."

"He's either confused or furious. The main thing is, we've got him responding to us, not the other way around," Savage said. Subduing tension, he watched Akira steer around a corner, then attempt to proceed through another stream of dense traffic. "But if Shirai goes into a public place, we won't be able to get him alone to talk with him."

"No matter," Akira said. "We'll continue to follow. Eventually we'll find our opportunity. Where he's least expecting us. Where he doesn't have an army of guards."

"So in other words, relax and enjoy the ride."

"Relax?" Akira glanced at Savage and raised his eyebrows. "I'll never get used to American irony." A voice spoke from the walkie-talkie. After responding, Akira glanced again at Savage. "At the next street, when I turn left, I should be two blocks behind the limousine."

"In this traffic, we won't be able to see the car," Savage said.

"Taro-*sensei*'s students will continue their surveillance. They also have motorbikes keeping pace on each parallel street. If Shirai's driver turns, we'll be alerted."

10

They continued struggling through traffic, heading west, though sometimes changing to a parallel street, guided by walkie-talkie reports from Taro's students. As dusk thickened, traffic dwindled. They reached a highway, increased speed, and suddenly saw the limousine ahead of them, two Nissan sedans providing protection, one in front and one in back. Akira radioed to the surveillance team, thanking them, telling most of them to return to Taro. Only a few would now be needed to help follow Shirai. Keeping several cars between the Toyota and the motorcade, Akira drove warily.

Savage rubbed his aching shoulder. "Wherever Shirai's going, it looks like he'll soon be out of the city."

Akira shrugged. "There are many adjacent ones."

"Even so, this is taking so long Shirai must have an important reason to drive this far." Savage brooded and added, "Those people at the demonstration—I can't help being surprised that Shirai's been able to attract so much support."

Akira kept his eyes on his quarry. "Don't be misled. He still has an upward battle. Most Japanese don't agree with him, although his influence is growing day by day. The economic miracle, the new prosperity, makes my countrymen delighted to do business with outsiders, as long as the bargain's in our favor. Cultural contamination, however much it incenses Shirai, is something that Japanese born after the war find intriguing."

"Then why are the demonstrations so large?" Savage asked.

"Large compared to what? In nineteen sixty, hundreds of thousands protested the renewal of the defense treaty with America. A pro-American politician was killed publicly with a sword. The demonstrators wanted the U.S. military to leave

Japan, principally because they didn't want nuclear weapons on Japanese soil. As Taro explained last night, we can never forget that we're the only nation *ever* to have suffered atomic attacks. In nineteen sixty-five, a U.S. aircraft carrier lost a hydrogen bomb off the coast of Japan. Your government didn't admit to the accident until nineteen eighty-one but claimed that the bomb had fallen five hundred miles offshore. A lie. In nineteen eighty-nine, we finally learned that the bomb was only *eighty* miles offshore. Such incidents and deceptions fuel right-wing anti-American resentment. . . . Have you ever heard of Mishima?''

''Of course,'' Savage said.

Mishima had been one of Japan's most famous novelists. In terms of his personality and subject matter, the closest American equivalent Savage could think of was Hemingway. Mishima's code of discipline had attracted a devoted core of followers, what amounted to a private army. On special occasions, they'd worn an elaborate version of the Japanese military uniform, a costume that Mishima himself had designed. Because of the novelist's fame and influence, the officers at one of Japan's Ground Self-defense Forces bases had permitted Mishima and his men to practice martial exercises there.

In 1970, Mishima and a handful of his closest worshipers had arrived at the base, requested permission to speak with its commander, subdued the man, taken over his headquarters, and demanded that the soldiers on the base be assembled so that Mishima could make a speech to them. The authorities—unable to rescue the hostage—agreed to Mishima's demands. The speech turned out to be a disturbing, ranting, rambling harangue, the basis of which was the decline of Japan, the country's need to regain its purity, to assert its greatness, to pursue its god-ordained destiny: militarism combined with a pre-Shirai version of the Force of Amaterasu. The soldiers, compelled to gather for Mishima's tirade, jeered.

Humiliated, outraged, Mishima returned to the commander's office, unsheathed the sword he wore—a vestige of the samurai tradition—knelt . . .

And committed *seppuku*, impaling his bowels.

But not before he commanded his most loyal follower to stand beside him with *another* sword, to complete the ritual and chop off his head.

"The incident created a controversy," Akira said. "Many Japanese admired Mishima's principles and courage. At the same time, they questioned the futility of his suicidal outrage. What purpose did it serve? Social pressure hadn't forced him to do it. Couldn't he have found an effective, constructive way to express his despair? Or had he truly believed that his suicide would prompt others to take up his cause?"

Savage didn't know what to answer. He thought of his father, not the stranger he'd met in Baltimore, but the man he remembered from his youth, the man he'd so loved, the man who one night had put a bullet through his brain. Oh, yes, indeed, a part of Savage could very much empathize with Mishima's desperation.

But Savage was conditioned by American values. Pragmatism. Survival, even with shame. Endurance, no matter the cost to pride. Don't let the bastards get you down.

Christ.

Akira broke the awkward silence. "Mishima's a perfect example. A symbol. Twenty years after his suicide, he's still remembered. Respected. So maybe he *did* achieve his purpose." Akira lifted a hand from the steering wheel to gesture. "Not right away, as Mishima hoped. But eventually. You have to understand. In Japan, left-wing demonstrations are squashed. They're equated with communism, and communists are hated. Everyone is equal? No. Japan is based on levels. *Shogun* to *daimyo* to samurai to . . . This country's a hierarchy. But *right*-wing demonstrations. They're another matter. The authorities tolerate them—because those demonstrations advocate a system of control, of social order, every element in its place, master to servant, husband to wife, parent to child, employer to subordinate."

"You sound"—Savage frowned—"as if you agree with that."

"What I'm trying to explain is that the right wing is a minority here, but it's nonetheless powerful, and it forms the base of Shirai's followers. What he needs, of course, is to turn huge numbers of moderates into extremists, and so far he hasn't been able to do that. So the majority of Japanese watch the demonstrations with interest and perhaps with sympathy . . . but not with sufficient conviction to act.''

''Not yet.''

Akira shrugged. ''We can try to learn from history, but it's almost impossible to reverse its trend. As much as I hate Commodore Perry's 'black ships' and what they did to my country, I don't believe Shirai can take us back to the cultural purity of the Tokugawa Shogunate. He needs a catalyzing issue, a rallying cry, and he hasn't been able to find it, no more than Mishima could.''

''That's not to say he isn't trying.''

Eyes dark with melancholy, Akira nodded, staring ahead toward Shirai's limousine. The sun had disappeared. In the gloom, passing headlights revealed the motorcade. Only occasionally was traffic so sparse that Akira had to rely on the taillights of the limousine and its Nissan escorts to guide him. He stayed well back.

Savage saw no indication that the motorcade knew it was being followed.

''To reply to your earlier comment,'' Akira said, ''I condemn Shirai's tactics but respect his values. It disturbs me. A man with whom I'd normally identify . . . Circumstances force me to treat him as a potential enemy.''

''Or maybe he's a victim. Like us.''

''We'll soon find out. *His* nightmare will perhaps at last explain ours.''

11

The motorcade left the highway. With increased caution, Akira followed, maintaining a greater distance from the lim-

THE FIFTH PROFESSION / 429

ousine. From time to time, cars passed, breaking the pattern of traffic, preventing Shirai's guards from noticing a constant pair of headlights far behind them.

One road led to another, then another, twisting, turning. Like a maze, Savage thought, his sense of direction confused. The glare of cities had given way to glowing lamps in windows of isolated villages. Uneasy, he peered out his passenger window. In the night, huge shapes loomed beside him.

"Are those *mountains?*" Worms of apprehension squirmed through Savage's bowels.

"We're entering a branch of the Japanese Alps," Akira said.

Savage squinted toward the hulking crests with greater dismay. He tensed as the Toyota crossed a narrow bridge beneath which moonlight glimmered off a rushing river. The gorge veered sharply upward toward dark wooded bluffs.

"*Alps?*" Savage asked.

"The term exaggerates. These aren't like the craggy mountains in Europe, more like the high rolling hills in the eastern United States."

"But don't you . . . ? I suddenly feel . . . My God, it's like we're back in Pennsylvania." Savage shuddered. "Dark. Not April but October. Instead of leaves beginning to appear, they're starting to fall. The trees look as bare as when . . ."

"We drove Kamichi to the Medford Gap Mountain Retreat."

"Which we never did."

"Yes," Akira said.

Savage shivered.

"I've been sensing it, too." Akira's voice sounded thick. "The eerie conviction that I've been here before, *though I haven't.*"

The Toyota crossed another precipitous gorge. Seized by vertigo, Savage's mind swirled.

But this time, it wasn't *jamais vu* but *déjà vu* that assaulted him. Or a combination, the former triggering the latter. His intestines roiling with fear, with a terrifying sense of unreality, Savage studied Akira, the man he'd seen beheaded.

The road kept winding, rising and dipping through the impossibly familiar wooded mountains.

Japan. Pennsylvania.

Shirai. Kamichi.

False memories.

Ghosts.

Savage's terror worsened. Deep in his soul, he desperately wanted to blurt to Akira to stop, to turn around. Every protective instinct warned him to abandon the search, to go back to Rachel, to retreat, to learn to live with his nightmares.

Because his guts slithered with a horrible foreboding that a much greater nightmare awaited him.

Akira apparently read his thoughts, or maybe felt the same stomach-wrenching terror.

"No," Akira said. "We've come this far. We've been through too much. We *can't* stop. I need to know. *For the rest of my life, I refuse to be haunted by phantoms.*"

As Savage flinched, remembering the flash of the blade that had sliced off Akira's head, another intense emotion erupted within him. The surge overpowered his fright and seized his body, every part of it, his torso, his limbs, his veins, his blood.

Anger. A rage beyond anything he'd ever felt. Astonishing.

He'd never known such fury. Graham would have been appalled. Avoid emotion, his mentor had always said. It's unprofessional. It keeps you from being objective. It leads to mistakes.

Not this time! Savage thought. *It'll keep me from making mistakes.* I'll control it! I'll use it! To cancel fear! To give me strength! To persist!

"That's right," Savage said. He dug his fingernails into his palms, drawing power from the lancing pain. "Someone messed with my mind, and by God, I want to know who and why. And someone, damn it, is going to pay."

12

Steering around a curve, Akira abruptly pointed. He stamped a foot on the brake. Disturbingly, the road ahead was totally dark. No taillights glowed in the distance. Savage tingled.

The motorcade had vanished.

Savage drew his Beretta. "A trap. They realized they were being followed."

"No. I was careful."

"But for the last ten minutes, we've been the only headlights behind them. Maybe, on principle, they decided to investigate. They pulled off the road, switched their lights off, and now they're waiting. If we drive past, the escort cars will try to flank us, force us onto the shoulder, and find out who we are."

Akira stared toward the darkness beyond the Toyota's headlights. "Assuming your assessment is correct, they know now for sure that they were followed—because we stopped when we no longer saw their taillights."

Savage rolled down his window. "Switch off the engine."

Akira did, not needing to ask what Savage intended.

In the sudden quiet, Savage listened for sounds on the road ahead, for the rumbling of engines, the crunch of footsteps stalking along the gravel shoulder, the scrape of branches in the shrubs that flanked the road.

But all he heard were the natural nightsounds of the forest—crickets screeching, occasional fluttering wings, boughs swaying in a gentle breeze.

"I may as well turn off the headlights, too," Akira said. "We don't want to be an obvious target."

A cloud drifted over a three-quarter moon. The darkness ahead became absolute.

Apprehension made Savage's mouth dry. His grasp tightened on the Beretta. "Even without the headlights, they know where we are."

"If they're waiting," Akira said.

"We have to assume. And if they've got weapons, they might decide to strafe this section of the road."

"Imprecise, unprofessional."

"But an excellent distraction while someone sneaks at us from the forest and empties a pistol through this open window."

Akira started the engine, put the car in reverse, and backed along the road, around the curve. When he stopped, he couldn't do anything about the glow from his brakelights, but presumably the Toyota was now out of sight from potential hunters, and the brakelights at least served the purpose of allowing Akira to see a space where he could park at the side of the road. He took his foot off the pedal, extinguishing the brakelights, and shut off the engine once more. Darkness again surrounded them.

"We might be overreacting," Akira said. "I kept a prudent, nonthreatening distance from the motorcade. It's possible that they were far enough ahead of us that they rounded a curve down the road before we rounded *this* curve. That would explain why we don't see their lights."

"Yes." Tension squeezed Savage's voice. "It's possible." His voice became thicker. "The thing is, do you want to take the risk of trying to catch up to them when in fact they might have arranged a trap along the road?"

"Not particularly." Akira tapped his fingers on the steering wheel. Pensive, he nodded, suddenly picked up the walkie-talkie, and spoke in Japanese. A moment later, he received a static-distorted response. The mountains were obviously interfering with the radio waves. Akira concentrated, spoke again, listened to the crackly reply, said one more thing, and set down the walkie-talkie.

He turned to Savage. "They'll let us know."

"The sooner, the better," Savage said.

Two hours earlier when Akira had instructed most of Taro's

students to drive back to Tokyo, their surveillance duties having been completed, he'd asked that two of them remain in case there were complications in following Shirai.

The tactic they'd agreed upon was that the two men would leave Savage and Akira and drive their motorcycles farther ahead, increasing speed, passing Shirai's limousine and its escorts, then roaring into the distance, staying well ahead of the motorcade, to all appearance just two young Japanese on a late-night expedition in a hurry to reach their destination. Now Akira had told them to stop and double back in an effort to learn if the motorcade was still on the road, to determine if the limousine and its escorts had indeed outdistanced Savage and Akira.

Of course, the two bikers would attract the motorcade's suspicion if they passed it again, this time in the reverse direction. Worse, they might be caught in the trap that Savage suspected was down the road on the shoulder just around this bend.

But Savage subdued his misgivings by reminding himself that motorcycles had the advantage of being small targets, speedy, easy to maneuver. In case of trouble, the two young man had an excellent—be honest, he told himself; what you mean is decent—chance of veering from assailants and darting away, especially if the cyclists turned off their headlights.

He admired their bravery. He acknowledged his debt to them. He prayed for their safety.

And hated the necessity that forced them to risk their lives.

But what's the alternative? Savage thought.

None.

He swallowed sour bile and opened his passenger door. "While we're waiting . . ."

Akira opened his own door. "The forest is a great deal safer than this car."

Outside, Akira gently *closed* his door, as did Savage.

Thinking as one, the two men crouched, crept toward a ditch, and disappeared into bushes. Silent, straining to listen, Savage's fingers taut on his pistol, they waited.

13

Beyond the curve, an echo became a drone.

Savage raised his head.

The drone increased to a roar. Motorcycles.

In the night, Savage stiffened, dreading that any moment —now!—he'd hear shots and screams, the squeal of tires, the scrape of metal crashing, flesh and steel skidding on concrete.

But the roar continued, louder, nearer.

The cyclists would soon reach the curve! Bent over, Savage rushed from the woods toward the road. Akira, who'd brought the walkie-talkie from the car, blurted instructions in Japanese.

At the same time, Savage reached the Toyota, yanked open the driver's door, and flicked the headlight lever. Once! Twice!

Satisfying himself that the flashing glare—aimed toward, reflecting off, the trees on the far side of the curve—would be visible to anyone approaching, Savage ducked behind the Toyota, ready with his Beretta in case these motorcycles were a subterfuge, themselves a trap.

Two bikers swerved into view. As the glare of their headlights revealed the Toyota, the bikers abruptly reduced speed and stopped behind the car, their engines rumbling. Savage stayed behind the Toyota, cautious. The bikers turned off their engines but left their lights on, aiming them toward bushes. The reflected illumination was sufficient for Savage to see the two young men on the motorcycles, but their helmets and Plexiglas visors concealed their faces. Not that Savage would have been able to recognize them—they'd been wearing face masks the first and only time he'd met them, the night before at Taro's *dojo*.

As they took off their helmets, revealing their shadowed features, Akira spoke in Japanese from the cover of shrubs at the side of the road. One of them answered, and Akira emerged, telling Savage, "It's all right. They're ours."

Savage lowered the Beretta. The bikers shut off their headlights.

Akira approached and spoke again in Japanese. After hearing their replies, he turned to Savage. "They didn't pass Shirai's motorcade when they drove back."

Savage tensed. "Then we were right. The motorcade stopped down the road beyond this curve. Shirai's guards suspected they were being followed and set up a trap. They'll be tired of waiting. They're probably stalking us right now. We have to—"

"No." Akira sounded baffled. "The bikers also looked for cars parked along the road, especially near this curve. But the side of the road is deserted."

"*How?* That's *impossible*. Shirai's men must have found a place to hide the cars. Taro's students missed them."

"The bikers assure me they were meticulous. They're certain. No cars are hidden along the road."

"Well, that motorcade didn't just vanish. It has to be *somewhere*," Savage said. "No disrespect to Taro's men, but we don't have a choice—we need to check for ourselves."

In a crouch, Savage crossed the road, followed by Akira. Staying close to bushes, they proceeded warily around the curve and continued down the road, prepared at any moment to dive toward the cover of the forest.

But the farther they crept along the road, the more convinced Savage became that Taro's students were right. When they reached the next curve, Savage was certain. The motorcade was definitely not hidden along the shoulder.

Then how the hell—?

His attention was so fiercely directed toward the opposite side of the road that he wasn't sure what made him look up. Perhaps his subconscious had detected and warned him about a vague detail in his peripheral vision. For whatever reason, he glanced up toward the mountain beyond the road and felt a chill when he saw the small glow of headlights far up the bluff. Three sets of them, so distant and diminished, they resembled flashlight beams. Turning right, then left, they curved higher, dimmer.

"Jesus."

Akira stared up in the direction of Savage's gaze. His murmur needed no translation—a curse in Japanese.

At once they hurried across the road. There was always the chance that the cars had left guards behind, that the headlights far up the mountain were intended to be an enticement, to tempt Savage and Akira into getting careless, to force them to hurry and lure them into an ambush, so Savage continued to aim his Beretta toward the murky forest, prepared to shoot at the slightest sign of trouble.

But instead of guards attacking from the forest, what they found—midway along this section of road—was a narrow lane flanked by dense bushes, its entrance so carefully disguised, so seemingly natural, that it blended with the landscape. Savage frowned toward the blackness beyond the lane, then jerked his gaze up toward the top of the mountain, though from this perspective the trees prevented him from seeing the faint, ghostly headlights getting smaller as they curved along the lane toward the summit.

"Sure as hell, they're not sight-seeing," Savage said.

"A meeting perhaps. So sensitive it requires a remote location and utmost secrecy."

"In the middle of nowhere? At night in a forest on top of a mountain? Even *I'm* not that paranoid," Savage said. "Shirai's too busy to come this far and waste this much time for a meeting that could easily be arranged in equally safe, closer, and much less primitive conditions. Suppose he has to relieve himself? I can't imagine that arrogant politician pissing in the woods. . . . And then there's the long drive back to Tokyo. No matter if he manages to sleep in the car, he'll still be exhausted."

"This lane," Akira said.

"It must have a purpose. No one would clear it, maintain it, and disguise its entrance just to provide access to a view from the top of a mountain."

"Something's up there."

"A building," Savage said.

"That's the only explanation I can think of." Akira pressed a button on his watch, producing a digital glow. "What time is it? A little after eleven. *Shirai plans to spend the night up there.*"

Savage's veins throbbed.

As if thrust by electrical current, each man began to run, racing along the road, charging toward the curve beyond which the two bikers stood guard against potential assassins stalking the Toyota.

Though Savage sweated from exertion, he also shivered, but not from the damp chill of night in October in the mountains. *Déjà vu* again made his mind swirl. "A little after eleven? But isn't that just about the time we reached—"

"The Medford Gap Mountain Retreat," Akira said, running next to him. "It's all a lie. We never—"

"Went there." Savage breathed.

"But I remember it so—"

"Clearly." Savage rushed. His heart beat so fiercely it made him sick. From fear. From rage. "It's happening—"

"Again." Akira increased speed.

"But it never happened the first time!" A premonition scalded Savage.

"Tonight," Akira said.

"We'll find out why."

They rounded the bend, racing toward the Toyota. The two bikers stepped from bushes, Akira blurting instructions to them as he opened the Toyota's trunk.

The light inside the hatch showed Savage two knapsacks. In Tokyo, where Taro had arranged for them to use this car, Akira had explained that Taro always made sure to equip a surveillance vehicle with emergency kits. Weapons. Microwave, infrared, and voltage detectors that in turn would warn about *intrusion* detectors. Dark clothing. Tubes of camouflage grease.

"Should we use the lane?" Savage quickly put on a black pajamalike garment over his clothing.

"We have to assume that the lane is monitored," Akira said.

"Yes." Savage smeared camouflage grease on his face and hands. "The lane's too tempting. Too easy. We'd be in the open. An obvious perfect trap. . . . So we have to do this the hard way."

"Is there any *other* way? Ever?" Akira examined a pistol he withdrew from a knapsack.

"Not that I know of. Upland? Right? We climb the mountain?"

Akira made sure that the pistol's magazine was loaded. "Yes. Upland. We climb. Can you manage that?"

"Are you saying you want to race? How much do you want to bet?"

Akira pulled back the pistol's slide to chamber a round. "Our lives."

"In that case—I know I'd outrace you—I suggest we do this cautiously."

"*Hai*." Akira thrust the pistol into a holster on the hip of the garment he'd slid over his clothes.

"Ready?" Savage asked.

"Not yet." Akira turned to Taro's students and spoke to them in Japanese.

Savage waited, nerves primed.

The students responded. Akira nodded.

"What?" Savage asked.

"I told them to wait," Akira said. "But first, while we climb, one of them will drive the Toyota to the nearest village. To leave it there. In case Shirai's men check the road along the lane. Taro's other student will follow the Toyota on his motorcycle. They'll return on the bike and hide. If we don't reappear by tomorrow night, they'll report to Taro."

"And Taro will avenge us," Savage said.

"He's my *sensei*. My substitute father. He'll destroy"— Akira swallowed—"whoever killed me."

"Enough. No talk about dying. The hardest part is the climb. The rest is . . ."

"I'm not a Christian. But I'll use your Western word," Akira said. "Salvation."

"Yes," Savage said. "The end to our mutual nightmare. The start of peace."

Savage strapped the knapsack onto his back. For another eerie moment, he felt as if he'd been here before—but not approaching the Medford Gap Mountain Retreat, instead preparing to infiltrate Rachel's husband's estate and rescue her. With a shudder of terror, he sensed that everything was coming full circle. Then his rage again insisted. If a circle was being completed, as well for months he'd felt that he'd been trapped in a maze . . . like the one on Mykonos. Except that *this* maze was in his tortured mind.

And *tonight* he intended to escape.

14

They entered the forest. Clouds drifted, freeing a three-quarter moon, its illumination helpful. But Savage and Akira didn't need it. Because they both wore infrared goggles and aimed infrared flashlights ahead of them. The beams, invisible to unaided eyes, cast a green glow through the trees when viewed through the goggles. The trees were remarkably similar to those in the mountains of Pennsylvania: chestnuts, oaks, and maples, many of their leaves having fallen. As Savage climbed higher, he saw pines, their resin scent reminding him of turpentine. But the predominant odor came from the damp, spongy earth beneath him, a loamy smell that widened his nostrils.

The ground was soft, carpeted with dead leaves and pine needles, but while they eased the pressure on Savage's feet, they also made it difficult to climb without making sounds. Whenever possible, Savage stepped on slabs of rock. The slope was gentle at first but soon became steep, and he felt the weight of his knapsack bite into his shoulders. His *right* shoulder, the one that had been injured by the blackjack, continued to ache. He worried that its stiffness would impair him in case of a fight and stopped briefly to swallow several painkiller pills that he took from a bottle Taro had given him. Working higher, he felt sweat trickle down his back. At the same time, paradoxically, he noticed puffs of misty breath come out of his mouth, the cool night air condensing them.

Akira led the way. They emerged from trees and discovered a grassy plateau. Crossing it quickly, they reached another wooded slope. The next ascent was more difficult, steeper, with boulders and deadfalls obstructing their progress through the forest. Because they didn't have compasses and a terrain map, they had to stop periodically, look for a break in the trees, and stare up toward the top of the mountain, correcting their course. The landscape became more rugged. They waded through icy streams, crossed razorback ridges, climbed walls of rock, and finally rested.

Above, the mountaintop was a hump against the increasingly clouded, starless sky. Savage took off his infrared goggles to rub sweat from his eyes and felt puzzled that the moon seemed inexplicably brighter. The peak of the mountain appeared to have a halo. The illusion made him frown. With a start, he suddenly realized that the halo wasn't caused by the moon but instead by *something on the mountain.* Lights. There were lights on top. We were *right,* Savage thought. There's a building on the summit!

Akira noticed as well. With stronger resolve, he gestured upward, eager to continue. Savage wished that Taro's emergency kits had included sturdy ridge-soled boots for outdoor walking, but there'd been no way to anticipate their ultimate destination. Urban obstacles had seemed more likely. As it was, Savage's street shoes provided no traction. Often their smooth leather soles came close to slipping off a rock and making him topple backward. He placed each step with caution. Briefly a game trail provided an unimpeded way through dense trees up a slope, allowing them to quicken their pace. Abruptly the trail disappeared, and they struggled through brush.

Under Savage's black pajamalike garment, his other clothes now clung to him, sweat-soaked. But after the long drive to reach these mountains, his muscles enjoyed the exercise, the strain on them perversely satisfying. He reminded himself that this climb would have seemed just a hike when he'd endured the final "hell week" of his training in the SEALs. He forced himself higher, resisting exhaustion. Indeed the closer he came to the mountaintop, the more adrenaline fueled his body. His need to reach his destination, his desperate urge to find answers, to end his nightmare, gave him ever-growing strength.

He paused again with Akira, this time not to rest but to take off their knapsacks and prepare their intrusion-detector sensors. Savage noted with approval that the voltmeters and microwave monitors that Taro had given them did not have glowing dials, a target for snipers. Rather they came equipped with earplugs. If sensors that gave off microwaves or an electrical field were ahead of Savage and Akira, a muted wail through the earplugs would warn them but not give away their position to sentries.

Despite his satisfaction with Taro's professionalism, Savage felt troubled, however. Because this equipment was the same type he'd used when he'd infiltrated Rachel's husband's estate. It seemed as if he'd *been* here before, gone *through* this before. The clouds thickened. Rain began to hiss through the forest, oddly reminding him of the storm he'd used for cover when he'd rescued Rachel. Memory, real and false, haunted him. The Mykonos estate. The Medford Gap Mountain Retreat. Shivering, he scowled toward the glow on the peak.

Time. Yes. Definitely time, he thought. To cancel the past. To *hell* with the past. The present mattered. And the future. Rachel.

With fierce resolve, he restrapped his knapsack onto his shoulders and adjusted the microwave detector's earplug. Akira did the same with the plug for the voltmeter. Savage studied him through his infrared goggles, aiming his flashlight. Akira, eerily green, hardened his jaw muscles.

Savage nodded firmly, the message clear. Let's finish this.

15

Their arduous climb had taken two hours. Relentless, determined footsteps had brought them forcefully to a clearing a hundred yards below their objective. But now caution overcame urgency. Savage and Akira took for granted . . . No need to bother discussing it. Both just knew, as one, that they had to creep instead of stride, to examine every obstacle, to heighten their senses, to anticipate threats. Sensors would no doubt surround the glow on the mountaintop. Sentries, perhaps with dogs, would likely patrol.

Muscles compacting rock hard with tension, Savage stretched out his left arm to aim his microwave detector and skirted the clearing, hugging the trees, avoiding the obvious trap. The rain fell harder, colder. Akira snuck next to him, matching Savage's steps, extending his voltmeter, prepared as Savage was to jerk up a hand in warning the instant he heard a wail from his earplug.

The glow on the peak intensified as Savage neared it. Through his infrared goggles, he studied the trees for closed-circuit cameras, scanning his infrared flashlight across the forest. He reached a chain-link fence and reminded of the fence at Mykonos, felt doomed to repeat the past.

The fence, green through Savage's goggles, had no boxes on its posts, no wires, no vibration sensors. Uneasy, Savage climbed it. Akira landed beside him. The rain increased. They crept higher.

Savage suddenly knew what they'd find next, and his premonition worsened. He was right! Ahead, through the trees, the next obstacle was another fence, but this fence *did* have boxes on its posts with wires from one to another!

It's the same setup I found on Mykonos, Savage thought.

The man who designed Rachel's husband's defenses also designed them for Shirai! Do Shirai and Papadropolis *know* each other? Coincidence?

No! *Nothing's* a coincidence! *Everything's* connected! Mykonos! Medford Gap! Kamichi! Shirai! Papadropolis! It's all a pattern!

Déjà vu and false memory! We thought we were free, but our every move was controlled. Predicted.

We're rats in a maze. A labyrinth. And with every dead end, we were forced to run for—guided toward—the most promising path, the line of least resistance.

Here. On this mountaintop.

Like Rachel's husband's estate. And Medford Gap. And . . .

Savage reached for Akira, determined to grab him, spin him, and urge him back down the mountain. *We've got to get away from here. It's a trap! It's what Shirai wants! We were tricked into coming here! It's* . . .

Akira sensed—and spun from—Savage's grasp. Even through his goggles, Akira's glare of confusion was vivid. He spread his arms. *What?* he wanted to know.

Savage couldn't risk revealing their position by speaking. Frantic, he motioned that they had to leave.

Akira spread his arms again. He shook his head in confusion.

Savage almost whispered hoarsely, *We have to get out of here.*

But the sounds past the fence made him freeze.

On the peak.

Amid the glow.

Shots. The rattle of automatic weapons. The crack, crack, crack of pistols. The boom of shotguns. Men screamed. Wails pierced the night.

Drenched with rain, Savage spun toward the fence. The shots—the *shrieks*—persisted. Jesus. Savage lunged toward the fence. Shirai was being attacked! If he dies, Savage thought, if we don't get there in time, if we don't protect him, we'll never know . . .

A pistol barked. A machine gun burped. More screams. No!

Savage resisted the impulse to grab the fence. Control! He had to keep in . . .

A hand's length away, he stared at the fence. At the post before him.

And cringed. The box, the vibration sensor. The wires that led from this box to another. They'd been severed! Someone got here before us! Savage thought. A hit team went after . . . !

We've got to . . . !

Savage leapt, grasped, scrambled, scurried, climbed. Amid the hissing rain and the jangling chain links, he heard Akira clamber after him. They struck the ground and tumbled, rolling to their feet. Pistol ready, heart thundering, Savage charged toward the crackling shots, toward the agonized screams.

And the night became deathly silent.

16

The silence was paralyzing. Time seemed suspended.

Abruptly Savage and Akira dove toward the mud. Careful to keep their weapons from being clogged, they squirmed forward on their stomachs, approaching the glow that radiated from the top of the bluff.

This final slope was bare. It reminded Savage of the slope he'd climbed to reach Rachel's husband's estate. And again he anticipated the next obstacle he'd encounter, a line of posts that would transmit microwave beams from one to another and trigger an alarm if an intruder passed through them. An invisible fence. But even with a microwave detector, an intruder would have to find a way to avoid the beams, as Savage had done on Mykonos. Crawling higher through the mud, scanning his infrared flashlight, Savage tingled when he saw the posts.

Above, the bark of another gunshot broke the silence. Freezing, Savage aimed his Beretta toward the left side of the peak, the direction from which he'd heard the shot. Rain drenched his back. Mud soaked his chest. He scowled through his goggles, straining to listen for anyone creeping toward him.

But what he heard instead, from beyond the rim of the peak, were car doors being slammed, the sudden roar of an engine.

Then *another* engine. The roars intensified, tires crunching over gravel, spinning through mud.

Akira jabbed Savage and pointed. Far to their left, headlights glared, glinting off raindrops, rushing down the lane from the peak. Two cars flashed by, blurs speeding down toward the valley, disappearing among trees.

The roar of the engines diminished, the rain and forest muffling them. Thirty seconds later, Savage couldn't hear even their far-off drone.

He slowly rose to a crouch. Mud slithered off him. He shuddered, his nervousness sharpened by the cold. Wary, he approached the line of posts, straining to listen for a wail from his microwave detector. But his earplug didn't wail.

He hesitated, frowning. Was it safe to assume that the system had been disabled?

What difference did it make? he suddenly thought. Who'd respond to the alarm? Nobody fired at those cars as they sped down the lane. The hit team did its work. That final shot, just before the cars sped away, was a *coup de grâce*. Everyone's dead up there!

He stepped through the open space between the posts and flanked by Akira, ready with his pistol, climbed the open rain-swept hill, sank to the mud near the top, then crawled the last few feet to peer over the rim toward the glow.

17

What he saw astonished him. His heart skipped. Beside him, Akira exhaled.

Shock. Although climbing this mountain and proceeding past the various security barriers had been a disturbing reminder of when Savage had infiltrated Papadropolis's estate on Mykonos, he now felt sickened with a terrible memory of another building. Dismay made him gasp. He took off his goggles. With horrified recognition, he found himself staring at the Medford Gap Mountain Retreat.

No! A bizarre Japanese facsimile of it!

The place was huge, stunningly long, an eighth of a mile. Arc lights glared all around it, every window illuminated, shrouded by rain. Its central portion made Savage think of a Japanese version of a castle, five stories high, each with a parapet beneath a downward-slanting roof that curved upward at the rim. But joined to it on either side were sections with different heights and radically different styles. A traditional thatch-roofed Japanese farmhouse was linked to what looked like a slate-roofed shrine. A ceremonial teahouse abutted a cypress walled pagoda.

Savage shook his head, fighting the dizziness that attacked his sanity. Most of the sections—their function—he didn't have the knowledge . . . he couldn't identify. But of this much he was sure. They all shared a common denominator. The entire surreal structure depicted, was a monument to, a meticulous re-creation of, the various stages of Japanese architecture.

Overwhelmed, he lowered his eyes from the impressive, grotesquely concatenated building. His dismay increasing, he squinted from the glare of the arc lights and frowned so severely that his brow ached, seeing bodies across the lawn.

Men.

Japanese.

Some wearing suits, others martial-arts costumes. Each had bloodstains on his chest . . . or else on his back, depending upon which agonized position the man had assumed when he struck the ground.

Savage counted ten.

All were Japanese. All had pistols or automatic weapons beside them.

None was moving. Fishhooks seemed to tear at Savage's guts.

Despite the cleansing rain, the stench of gunfire continued to hang in the air. And another stench, which became more pronounced as Savage stood and wavered, approaching the aftermath of the massacre. The stench of body gasses vented through bullet holes, of bowels that had voided in death throes.

The coppery smell of blood soured Savage's mouth.

Akira frowned toward the pattern of the scattered corpses. "Some," he said, "the men wearing suits, were sentries. When the shooting started, they ran to confront the attackers. The others, those who wore a karate *gi*, must have rushed from the building to help."

"And they all got taken by surprise." Subduing a tremor, Savage picked up a pistol and sniffed its barrel. "It hasn't been fired."

Akira examined an Uzi. "Nor has this one."

"The hit team was organized. Efficient. Extremely skillful."

"They snuck up through the trees," Akira said.

Savage nodded.

"They did their work and used the cars in the motorcade to make their escape."

"But we didn't see any vehicles on the road," Savage said. "How did they get here?"

"Days earlier perhaps. If they knew their targets would eventually arrive, they could have waited patiently. I once stood guard on a principal for forty-eight hours."

"And I was trained to lie motionless in a jungle for days,"

Savage said. "Yes." His throat burned from bile. "For all we know, they managed to infiltrate this place quite a while ago. They hid and . . . A matter of discipline."

"But who was their *daimyo?*"

Savage shrugged in disgust. "A fanatical left-wing group. The Japanese 'Red Army.' Who knows? We lost our chance. We got here too late. We'll never, damn it, find out." He stared from one corpse to another.

"But I do know this." Savage swallowed. "These men were our obstacles, the barriers between us and Shirai. As much as we needed to get beyond them, to question Shirai, *they* were compelled to protect him. The fifth profession. They obeyed the rules. They knew their duty. They did their best to fulfill their obligation. They died with honor. I . . ."

"Yes." Akira wiped rain from his melancholy eyes, stood bolt-straight, and bowed.

He murmured, as if praying.

"What did you say?" Savage asked.

"I commended them to their ancestors. I promised to respect them until my *own* death. I swore to do my best to sense them, their *kami*, in the wind and the rain."

"Good," Savage said. "In America, the equivalent—at least if you're Catholic, as *I* was raised—is 'God bless. God speed.' "

"Their spirits will understand."

Savage abruptly added, "Shirai . . . Maybe he isn't dead." Hope made his heart pound. "Maybe the hit team only wounded him. Maybe he managed to hide." He walked, then raced toward the building. "We've got to find him."

Akira surged next to him. "Don't hope. As much as I want answers . . . It's futile. The assassins knew their work. They didn't have a reason to run away. They wouldn't have left unless they accomplished their mission."

"But there's always a chance!"

18

They reached the building, the central area, the five-story structure with parapets beneath sloping roofs that made Savage think of a Japanese castle. The door was open. Light spilled out.

Savage darted toward one side, Akira the other, peering crossways through the opening, checking the interior in case not all the members of the hit team had gone, or in case some of Shirai's guards had survived and were braced to shoot at what they thought were more assassins coming through the door.

Detecting no threat, Savage lunged inward on an angle, Akira sprinting sideways, taking the opposite direction. They crouched, aiming tensely, spinning this way and that, muscles rigid, checking everything around them.

No danger.

Because everyone was dead. The room, a great hall made of burnished teak, with chandeliers shaped like Japanese lanterns, was littered with corpses.

Savage cringed and lowered his pistol. Again the coppery smell of blood, the stench of excrement thrust forcibly past traumatized sphincter muscles during violent death, made him want to gag.

To his right, near an open panel, five bodies lay in pools of blood. Three others sprawled near the back. Four others were slumped on a staircase to the left, just about where the Medford Gap stairway had been situated, and like the stairway at the Mountain Retreat, *this* one crisscrossed upward.

"Dear God," Savage said. He forced himself farther into the hall and, subduing vomit, stared at the carnage. "How many more will we find?"

In horror, they searched adjoining rooms, finding more bodies.

"It's almost too much to . . ." Savage slumped against a wall. Beside him, pen-and-ink drawings hung next to swords. The arts of peace and war. He wiped moisture off his brow, sweat mixed with rain. "I've been in combat zones, too many to mention. I've killed so many times I dream of legions of corpses. But this is . . ." Savage shook his head fiercely, as if strong enough denial would erase the carnage around him, would made the corpses disappear. He scrunched his eyes shut, reluctantly opened them, and winced again from the horror. "Too much. When this is over, when we're finally able to give up, to back off, to retreat, I welcome what you yourself called . . ."

"Salvation."

"What I want is . . ."

"Peace?" Akira asked.

"And an end to threats."

"But there'll *always* be threats," Akira said. His melancholy voice dropped. "It's the way of the world."

"The difference is . . ." Savage breathed. "I'll no longer risk my life for strangers. Only for Rachel."

"Your training still conditions you. You look after someone else," Akira said. "From now on, I will be my principal. I'll protect *myself*."

"You'll be very lonely."

"But not with you as my friend."

Savage felt a surge. "Did I actually hear you say that? Friend?"

Akira gestured, closing the topic. "We need to find Shirai. This won't be finished . . ."

"Until we do." Savage pushed himself away from the wall. "But where would—? We've checked these rooms. He isn't—"

They turned toward the stairs. Surrounded by death, oppressed, Savage crossed the hall, stared at the blood trickling down the steps, and climbed, passing one body after another.

They reached a landing and pivoted, following the reverse direction up the next set of stairs.

Savage's voice broke, as if wedged with gravel. "Remind you of anything?"

"The stairs at the Mountain Retreat."

They cautiously reached the next floor.

And *again* found more bodies.

"It won't end," Savage said.

"If he's not in this building, we'll search the others," Akira said. "I don't care how long it takes."

Savage spun, aiming his pistol right, then left, seeing a corridor on each side that seemed to stretch on forever.

"It must connect with the other buildings," Akira said.

The silence of death thickened the air. It pressed against Savage's face. He had trouble breathing. "Notice the rooms along the corridor. . . . Sliding panels, not doors. But . . ."

"The same arrangement as the Medford Gap Mountain Retreat," Akira said.

"I know where we'll find him. Kamichi. Shirai."

"*Where?*"

"Where he's *always* been! In my nightmare! Where we took him! Even though we didn't!" Savage pointed up the stairs. "Third floor. That's where his room was. And that's where we'll find him. Where he *was*. Where he *will* be."

They climbed the stairs.

19

And found more bodies. Savage's heart shrank. Blood. The floor was . . . He couldn't avoid stepping in . . . Everywhere. Slippery. The soles of his shoes made a squishing sound. Ice seemed to squeeze his chest. With greater foreboding, he stooped to feel each man's wrist. No pulse. He picked up the weapons that lay beside them, smelling the barrels.

"None of them was fired."

"What? But . . ."

Savage nodded. "I can understand the sentries on the grounds being taken by surprise. But . . ."

"These guards must have heard the shots from outside."

"And in the rooms below us and on the stairs. The hit team had to kill all those other men before they could reach these guards."

"And yet despite the commotion these men didn't have enough warning to fire even one shot?"

"Something's wrong," Savage said.

Back-to-back, he and Akira aimed tensely along each section of the corridor. They inched toward the right of the staircase, darting nervous glances up the steps as they passed. Savage's shoes made bloody footprints on the floor. They entered the right wing of the corridor, wary of the panels on either side, and stopped at the fifth one on the right, where—

—if it had been a door instead of a panel—

—and if this had been the Medford Gap Mountain Retreat—

—they would have reached Kamichi's room.

"A blast from the past," Savage said.

"I don't understand."

Savage realized he'd begun to babble. Trembling, he fought to get control. "Ready?"

"Always."

"Cover me." Chest heaving, Savage grabbed the edge of the panel, shoved it sideways, and lunged toward the wall, aiming through the open door.

Akira, who'd surged toward the opposite side of the opening, aimed inside as well—and let out a gasp.

Savage's eyes widened.

Kamichi . . . Shirai . . .

The names merged. *The past and present* became identical. With a terrible difference.

Wearing a black karate *gi,* Kamichi-Shirai sat cross-legged at a low table across from them, sipping tea. The fiftyish, gray-haired, slightly overweight, somewhat slack-jowled businessman-politician raised his head and studied them. He didn't flinch at their sudden appearance. He wasn't startled or surprised or confused. He merely nodded, set down his cup, and sighed.

Placing his karate-callused hands on the table, he pushed himself upward and slowly stood.

"At last," he said.

"But how did—?" Savage stepped forward. "Where—? You should have stayed hidden. We might have been other assassins coming back to—" Numb, Savage faltered. He suddenly realized that Kamichi (*Shirai*) had spoken in English, and with greater shock, he realized something else, that his questions were useless, meaningless. Kamichi (*Shirai*) had never been in danger, had never been forced to hide.

"Oh, Jesus," Savage said.

"Please accept my humble compliments." Kamichi bowed. "My utmost respect. You are indeed professionals. You obeyed your code to the limit."

Savage breathed and sighted along his pistol. "Everything led us here."

"Yes."

"*Why?*"

"If you'll lower your weapon, I'll tell you," Kamichi said.

Savage kept aiming. "No, you'll tell me now, or else . . ."

"You'll shoot me?" Kamichi debated the question and shrugged. "I don't believe so. In that case, you'd never—"

"Tell us!" Akira's grip trembled on his pistol. "*Have we ever met before?*"

"In a sense."

"What the hell does *that* mean?" Savage's finger tensed on the trigger.

"Please lower your weapons," Kamichi said. "We have many things to discuss." He shook his head. "But I don't feel . . . conversational? Is that the proper word? . . . under these threatening conditions."

"But maybe I don't care," Savage said. "Maybe if I shot you, my nightmares . . ."

"No." Kamichi approached. "They wouldn't end. They'd

persist. Without answers, you'll always be haunted. Both of you. For the rest of your lives.''

Savage straightened his aim toward Kamichi's approaching chest. ''But you'd be dead.''

''Would that give you satisfaction?'' Kamichi reached toward Savage's pistol.

''Stop.''

''Would killing me relieve your torment? Think clearly. What are your priorities?'' Kamichi grasped Savage's pistol. ''You need answers!''

''Yes. But right now what I need is, get your hand off the gun! Before I—!'' Savage pried Kamichi's fingers away, stared into Kamichi's dark, unblinking eyes, then lowered the weapon, aware that Akira still aimed his. ''So *answer* my question. Have we met before?''

''I prefer to answer another question, one you *haven't* asked.'' Kamichi guided Savage toward the corridor. ''Your name is . . .''

Compelled by phantoms, Savage allowed Kamichi to guide him, reassured that Akira backed out of the room, his pistol aimed toward Kamichi's chest.

''Your name . . . Would you like to know your name?'' Kamichi asked as they entered the corridor.

Savage decided to trust the word of the friend and former fellow SEAL he'd seen killed in the alley in Virginia Beach. ''I'm Robert Doyle.''

Kamichi looked disappointed. ''You learned more than I thought.''

''The alternative was 'Roger Forsyth,' but I knew that couldn't be right, because I used that name in my nightmare, and nothing in my nightmare happened.''

''Ah, but you *have* used 'Roger Forsyth' on occasion. As a pseudonym.''

''I guessed that as well,'' Savage said. ''A man I saw in my nightmare—he called himself Philip Hailey—came after me in Tokyo. As he chased me from the Meiji Shrine, he kept calling me Forsyth. When I didn't respond, he called me Doyle. I finally decided that if one name was false, he might use that first, and only when I didn't respond to it would he take the risk of shouting my real name in public.''

"Astute," Kamichi said.

"So who *is* he?"

" 'Philip Hailey' is not his real name. Like 'Roger Forsyth,' it's a pseudonym."

"I asked, *who is he?*"

"Your CIA contact."

20

"*What?*"

As Savage gaped from Kamichi's answer, shock was added to shock. He heard the smooth slide of wood. Repeated. Overlapping. Along the corridor, panels opened. Men stepped out, Japanese, wearing suits, holding weapons.

"Please set down your pistols," Kamichi said.

Akira spoke harshly in Japanese.

Kamichi responded, his tone patient, then turned to Savage. "Your associate insists he'd sooner shoot me."

"He's not alone," Savage said, aiming. "If those men come any closer, you're dead."

"But I thought you wanted answers," Kamichi said. "Besides, if you kill me, they'll kill you. What purpose will that serve? No, it's better if you cooperate."

The men took a wary step forward.

Savage lunged behind Kamichi. Temples throbbing, he pressed his back to the wall and his pistol against Kamichi's skull. Akira rushed next to him, pointing his handgun toward the men.

"*Hailey's my CIA contact?*" Savage asked.

"You're not aware that you work for the agency?"

"Do I sound as if I am?"

"Good. The deception had its effect," Kamichi said. "And you?" he asked Akira. "Did *you* become aware that you work for Japanese Intelligence?"

Akira looked stunned.

"Yes," Kamichi said. "Excellent. The plan remains intact."

"You son of a bitch, what did you *do* to us?" Savage pressed the pistol harder, wanting to crush Kamichi's skull.

"You answered that question earlier."

"How?"

"I led you here," Kamichi said.

"I'm beginning to understand," Akira said. "Tonight. You were never in danger."

"True. Can you guess why?"

Akira sounded as if on the verge of vomiting. "The corpses. So many. This place . . . it was never attacked. Assassins didn't shoot all those men, try to find you, fail, and then flee. *There were no assassins*. Those men . . ." Disgust choked Akira, cutting off his words.

"Died willingly. Bravely. With honor," Kamichi said. "For their *daimyo* . . . for their country . . . their heritage. Above all, for Amaterasu."

"My God," Savage said. His mind swirled. The corridor seemed to tilt. "Oh, Jesus, you're crazy!"

The men stepped closer, weapons raised. Savage grabbed the back of Kamichi's suit, tugging him toward the staircase.

Akira aimed rigidly. "Tell your men to stop. I'll kill them."

"But don't you understand?" Kamichi was disturbingly calm, unnervingly rational. "They're *prepared* to die, to sacrifice their lives for their *daimyo*, for the spirit of their nation, for the land of the gods. They want to fulfill their duty, to join the *kami* of their fellow samurai."

Savage trembled. Horrified, he realized the scope of Kamichi's madness. He thought of the Jonestown massacre, of followers so devoted to a charismatic zealot that they'd do *anything* for him, even force their children to drink poisoned Kool-Aid and then swallow it themselves.

At once, he shifted perspective, changing his logic, reminding himself that the utterly mad, the hopeless psychotics, convinced themselves that they alone were perfectly sane.

But with equal abruptness, he reminded himself of something more. This wasn't the West but the East. He thought of Mishima disemboweling himself after haranguing Japanese soldiers to return their country to its former imperial greatness, to pursue its god-ordained destiny.

He thought of the legendary forty-seven *ronin*, who waited two years to avenge their insulted dead master and who, after cutting off their enemy's head and setting it on their master's grave, committed *seppuku*. In America, the zealot of Jonestown was considered a monster. In Japan, Mishima was remembered with respect as someone willing to die for his principles. And the forty-seven *ronin* were revered for their absolute loyalty to their *daimyo*.

Somehow, though a *gaijin*, Savage could understand, perhaps because his father had blown his brains out.

But that didn't mitigate the horror that continued flooding through him.

"Now I know why their weapons hadn't been fired. They willingly . . ." Savage shook his head. Appalled yet consumed with respect, he imagined their bravery, their dismaying confidence, their belief in Amaterasu, a conviction more powerful than fear.

He forced himself to keep talking, his throat so tight he felt strangled, his voice hoarse. "They willingly stood at attention. And let themselves be shot. Solemnly gave up their lives . . . honorably committed a unique form of *seppuku*. So their nation would think that its—*your*—enemies had killed them."

"For a *gaijin*, you understand our values more than I expected," Kamichi said.

"Who shot them?" Akira asked. *"You?"*

"Their fellow samurai, who in turn were shot by others, until this final group remains," Kamichi said.

The guards took another step, weapons poised. Savage desperately tugged Kamichi farther along the wall, keeping his pistol against Kamichi's head while Akira aimed at the guards.

"But this conversation *is* beneficial," Kamichi said, more eerily rational. "I realize now I made a mistake."

"Damned right," Savage said. "Those men didn't have to die, not for the sake of your crazy—"

"I mean their weapons," Kamichi said.

Savage jammed his pistol harder against Kamichi's skull, dreading yet another insane attack on his own fragile sanity. *"Weapons?"*

"I thought I'd anticipated every detail," Kamichi said. "But I understand now that they should have fired toward the trees before they were killed—to litter the ground with additional ejected cartridges, to make their deaths much more dramatic. To emphasize the loyalty and determination with which they strained to the limit to defend me."

With his pistol thrust against Kamichi's head, Savage almost pulled the trigger.

So tempting.

No, Graham's ghostly voice whispered. *Avoid emotion. It causes mistakes. A professional must always be objective, rational, in control.*

Rational? Savage thought. Like Kamichi? He's so fucking rational he's a lunatic!

But you're not. Endure. Remember your obligation. To me. To yourself. To the fifth profession.

Yes! Savage thought.

He knew too well that he and Akira remained alive only because Kamichi's guards wouldn't dare to attack while their *daimyo* was threatened.

Nonetheless he was tempted, he imagined the pleasure . . . it would feel so right, so good, so just, so *satisfying* to pull the trigger.

Kamichi's unnervingly rational tone distracted him. "I'll take care of that problem later. I'll make sure that the weapons are fired. The fingers of the corpses of my loyal followers will be placed and tugged on the triggers while the weapons discharge, to leave powder residue in case forensic tests are performed. Every aspect of the plan must be correct."

"What did you hope to accomplish?" Akira asked.

Kamichi turned, resisting the pressure of Savage's pistol against his skull. "I'm disappointed. You've managed to guess so much, and yet you haven't understood the ultimate noble motive?"

"Apparently we're just too stupid," Akira said.

"So tell us," Savage said. "Convince us how smart you are."

Kamichi straightened. "The record will show . . . History will record . . ."

"Just tell us," Savage said.

"Tonight," Kamichi said proudly, "it will seem that assassins, hired by enemies of Amaterasu, felt I was such a threat that they committed a massacre to get at me. . . . But they failed. A devoted core of brave samurai managed to force them away, though not before the leaders of the massacre were destroyed. You." He gestured toward Savage. "A member of the CIA. And *you*"—another gesture, toward Akira—"a member of Japanese Intelligence.

"I needed an incident, so dramatic, so symbolic, so *national*, that it would catalyze my followers, urge them, *compel* them into greater action and like a magnet, attract new members to the Force of Amaterasu. The scene of the massacre, this shrine to Japanese history and architecture, will intensify the significance."

"Of?" Savage asked.

"The American government, the assassins they sent to kill me, with the help of Japan's own corrupt establishment. The incident will arouse such anger, such resentment, such . . ."

"No one will believe you," Savage said.

"No one in America. But in Japan? They'll believe. In the next few days, the course of history, the course of this nation, will change. I'll erase the mistake of the Meiji Restoration and return my country to the cultural purity, the cleansing quarantine of the Tokugawa Shogunate. All foreigners will be expelled, their contamination eradicated."

"And you're the great man who'll lead the shogunate, I suppose," Savage said bitterly.

"In the name of the emperor, who will no longer have to renounce his divinity."

"You're so crazy"—Savage tugged him closer to the stairs—"you'll spend the rest of your life in a padded cell."

"The strangest part," Akira said, aiming toward the guards, "is I agree with him."

"*What?*" Savage said.

"Then *join* me," Kamichi said. "I can change the plan so that only the *gaijin* would die. Other evidence can be manufactured to link this man and his CIA employer with Japanese Intelligence. Your talents would be useful to me."

"Agree with you? Yes," Akira said, aiming. "I wish I lived in another time. I wish history could be reversed—not just the American occupation and the constitution it forced upon us, but the Pacific War and the militarism that caused it, and the Meiji Restoration, and above all Commodore Perry's 'black ships.' The Tokugawa Shogunate. That was our finest flower. When we stayed to ourselves, when we shut out the world, looked inward, and perfected our spirit. I wish we had nothing to do with America. The atomic bombs they dropped on us were modern versions of Perry's 'black ships.' And because of them, we now try to dominate economically instead of militarily. Greed, the hunger for power, a work ethic so severe that it leaves us no time for contemplation— we learned these vices from America. They're destroying the beauty of our spirit. We're no longer the land of the gods. We've *forgotten* the gods."

Savage couldn't tell if Akira meant what he said or was merely trying to distract Kamichi and his men. In turmoil, he tugged Kamichi closer to the stairs while Akira aimed.

"Then *join* me," Kamichi repeated.

"No!" Akira said. "What you've done tonight is . . ." Disgust filled his voice. "Obscene. Nothing good can come of this. All those men didn't have to die. You *perverted* the code of loyalty. You're not a savior. You're a monster."

"Then die with the *gaijin*."

"Like hell." Savage reached the stairs, tugging Kamichi. "We're getting out of here."

Kamichi spoke in Japanese to his men.

They stood rigidly and bowed.

"Akira, what did he say?"

"He told them, 'You know what must be done. Obey your oath. I honor you. I commend you to Amaterasu.' "

"Oh, shit," Savage said.

He heard a sudden creak on the stairs below him and, glancing sharply downward, saw eight men stalking toward him, aiming.

"The guards who pretended to be assassins and drove away," Kamichi said. "They had orders to come back after you arrived. One of my men contacted them by radio."

"Tell them to stay away," Savage said.

"Or you'll shoot me? That argument no longer matters. You see, the final stage is about to begin."

"The final stage?"

A man below fired at Savage.

Cringing from the feel of the bullet zinging past his head, Savage jerked his pistol away from Kamichi and fired in return.

The gunman toppled.

But at once the other men started firing, the corridor filled with ear-ringing thunder, bullets splintering the banister, walloping walls.

Savage kept pulling the trigger . . . again and again! . . . empty cartridges flinging from his pistol, men falling, screaming. Next to him, he heard other shots, from the guards in the corridor, from Akira. But even as Savage shot and shot, he sensed . . .

Something was horribly wrong! Bullets kept hitting the wall behind him. Akira kept shooting. Men kept screaming, falling. Blood kept spraying. And suddenly, when the last men dropped—

—the corridor and the staircase a hideous shambles, the stench of cordite, blood, vomit, and excrement reeking around him—

—Savage realized in horror what it was that he'd sensed was wrong.

I shouldn't be alive! Those men were ten feet away.

Kamichi dove when the shooting started so we couldn't use him as a shield.

And in all that shooting, with all those bullets flying, Akira and I weren't hit even once?

Impossible!

Unless . . .

He shuddered.

Unless they never meant to, never *tried* to hit us!

Dear God, they wanted to force us into killing them!

They committed suicide!

Madness had been added to madness. Too much, too long. Savage doubted that his mind could withstand another assault. He wanted to scream. He felt his sanity tilting, on the verge of a breakdown, about to crack!

Rage made the difference. "Kamichi, you son of a bitch!"

Savage spun to confront him, aiming toward the floor where Kamichi had dove when the shooting started.

But Kamichi was gone.

"Where did—?"

"There!" Akira shouted, "He's running down the corridor!"

Savage raced after him, dodging the bodies on the floor.

Akira chased him as well, blurting what sounded like Japanese curses.

As Savage neared the entrance to Kamichi's room, suddenly everything seemed in slow motion, *jamais vu and déjà vu* colliding in his brain. I've been here before! I know what's going to—!

Before he could stop and react to his premonition, a fierce blow deadened the nerves in his wrist and slammed the Beretta out of his hand. Behind, he heard a bone snap, Akira wail, a pistol thumping on the floor.

He spun, and now his nightmare was complete.

He faced three men. Muscular. Midthirties. Japanese.

Wearing dark suits.

The assassins from the Medford Gap Mountain Retreat. They'd lunged from the room across from Kamichi's and struck with wooden swords at eye-blink speed, disarming Savage and Akira.

Aruptly Savage recalled that there'd been *four* men, not three!

And the fourth had gripped a samurai sword instead of a *bokken*.

His terrified confusion dissolved as Kamichi reached into a room and pulled out a gleaming sword.

"Full circle," Kamichi said. "In your end is your beginning."

A man swung a *bokken*. Savage pivoted to escape the blow, but too late. The wooden sword whacked his arm with such force that he was slammed against the wall.

"I promised a conclusion to your nightmare," Kamichi said.

Another man swung at Akira, who doubled over from the impact of the *bokken*'s blunt end being driven into his stomach. Agonized, Akira sank to his knees, holding himself.

"Answers," Kamichi said. "That's what you wanted. . . . I arranged for you to shoot all those men so the authorities would be convinced of—and the media would spread the word about—a major battle in which my bodyguards fought bravely to defend me. The bullets had to come from your pistols. The powder traces had to be on your hands. And when at last you confronted me, only these three samurai remained, armed with wooden swords."

"And you," Savage groaned, "not with a *bokken* but a *katana*—because you're the *shogun*, the hero of your story."

"As I explained, I need an incident, something so dramatic, so symbolic, so catalyzing, that the nation will follow my lead. You're about to be a part of a legend. The people will talk about this moment for a thousand years—how the wicked *gaijin* and a traitorous Japanese led a team of mercenaries to try to kill me. And indeed you killed all my men. Until at last, after the rest of your team had been forced to retreat by my brave dying samurai, we confronted each other, you and I, firearms against a *katana*."

"Who gets to win?" Savage dove for his pistol, grabbed it, and screamed as wooden swords struck his skull, his back, his arms and legs.

Again!

It was happening again! He felt helpless!

Everything was preordained!

No, *post*ordained! Time was being reversed! He was living backward!

And history couldn't be changed!

He screamed again, but not from the agony of the wooden swords pounding him, instead from the greatest fury he'd ever known.

"You bastard!"

Rolling, Savage kicked. He felt the satisfying crunch of a kneecap breaking. A guard wailed, dropping his *bokken*, grabbing his knee, toppling.

Savage continued to roll. He heard a rush of air as a *bokken* swept past his head.

The wooden sword slammed the floor. Savage kicked again, heard a grunt, and grabbed his Beretta, surging upward.

But another *bokken* struck him with brutal force, behind his right shoulder, where the blackjack had left a massive bruise. Reinjured, his arm lost its power, muscles paralyzed, the Beretta slipping from his useless fingers.

Anguish increased his fury. He jabbed his left elbow backward, struck a guard behind him, and heard a wheeze, ribs cracking, the man doubling over.

Savage pivoted, prepared to kick the third guard, but the man leapt clear, swung his *bokken*, and connected with Savage's side, just above his left kidney, the pain so excruciating that Savage's vision blurred. He kept pivoting, disoriented, banging against a wall. The guard swung toward his skull. Savage raised his left arm, desperate to shield his head, though his arm would likely be shattered.

A blur intercepted the *bokken*. Akira! He'd been slumped, on his knees, clutching his stomach from the devastating impact of a wooden sword's blunt end rammed into his guts. The guards had apparently assumed that Akira was sufficiently disabled for them to concentrate on Savage.

They'd been wrong. Thrusting a karate-callused hand upward beneath the third guard's wrist as the man swung his *bokken* toward Savage's skull, Akira impeded the blow, chopped another hand across the guard's nose, spun him, and kneed his groin. The guard fell, blood pulsing out of his nose.

Savage strained to steady his consciousness. He managed sufficient awareness to realize that Akira was charging toward Kamichi, and as Savage turned to help, he felt his legs give out. The guard with the shattered kneecap had crawled and struck with his *bokken*, whacking Savage's shins. The force of the blow shocked nerves and knocked Savage's legs from under him. He fell. The floor rushed toward him. His jaw struck wood. Stunned, for a moment he couldn't see.

Then he could, and peering up . . . dazed . . . in agony . . . he saw Akira attacking Kamichi.

Kamichi raised his *katana*.

No! Savage inwardly screamed. *Jamais vu* had become reality! What never happened was now occurring! Full circle. Living backwards. *In your end is your beginning*. Except that the beginning had been a lie, and *this* was unbearably actual.

As if watching a movie he'd seen too many times . . . witnessing a nightmare he'd endured too often, Savage cringed as Akira attacked Kamichi.

The fourth assassin.

The man with the gleaming sword.

If the present had become the past—Savage kept inwardly screaming—was it also a forecast of the future?

No! Akira! Don't!

Sprawled in pain on the floor, Savage focused his delirium-distorted vision . . .

And felt his heart stop, swollen with hope, as he realized that Akira had grabbed the third guard's wooden sword after knocking the man to the floor and preventing him from striking Savage's skull.

The past that had never occurred was *not* taking place identically in the present! In Savage's nightmare, Akira had *not* been armed with a *bokken*. This wasn't full circle! Reality did *not* conform to false memory! The future did *not* have to match the lie of the past.

Kamichi swung his gleaming sword.

Akira dodged. He parried with the *bokken*.

Kamichi swung yet again.

Again Akira parried.

They circled, testing each other, lunging, twisting, darting.

Akira feinted to the left, then the right, and saw an opening! As he swung, a guard on the floor threw his *bokken*. It glanced off Akira's shoulder, deflecting his aim.

Kamichi's sword sliced Akira's *bokken* in half.

Now Savage did scream.

Akira jumped back.

Kamichi's sword hissed. The razor-sharp blade seemed to miss Akira's neck.

Savage prayed. I'm wrong. Oh, please, dear God! No, I didn't see . . . !

His frantic plea went unanswered.

Akira dropped the *bokken*. His head toppled off his neck. It struck the floor with the thunk of a pumpkin, rolled, and came to a stop, resting upright in front of Savage.

His eyes blinked.

And Savage lost all control, which in this case meant that he *gained* control, the shock to his mind overcoming the pain that paralyzed his body.

He rose to his knees, staggered to his feet, and stumbled toward Kamichi, shrieking.

But Kamichi shrieked as well.

Because Akira's headless torso impossibly kept moving, lurching toward Kamichi, grabbing the hands that grasped the *katana*. Pulses from Akira's severed brain seemed to persist and compel his decapitated corpse, hate lasting longer than life. At the same time, gruesomely, blood fountained from Akira's neck. His body vomited crimson. Gushing, the blood cascaded over Kamichi, drenching his skull, veiling his eyes, soaking his clothes.

His shriek more intense, a high-pitched shrill of insanity and revulsion, Kamichi released his grip on the blood-drenched sword and pushed Akira's struggling, headless, crimson-gushing torso away from him.

And that's when Savage finished stumbling across the corridor. He grabbed the sword, which came with startling, eerie, tingling ease from Akira's formerly rigid hands—

—as if those hands communicated with Akira's severed head—

—as if those lifeless fingers recognized the touch of the compatriot who gripped them—

—and with all his might, Savage swung the *katana*, wailing in victory as the blade entered, sliced through, and swept from Kamichi's abdomen.

Kamichi whimpered.

Blood trickled.

Spewed.

His torso parted, the top half falling to the right, the bottom half to the . . .

Savage's vision turned black. A blow to his skull made him double over.

The guards! One of them must have managed to stand, struggle toward him, and swing his *bokken*.

Savage fell to his knees but reflexively swirled with the sword. Vision clearing, he saw the guard falter backward.

Savage crept on his knees, aimed the sword, lost strength, and fell.

He landed in front of Akira's head. He couldn't move. Helpless, wincing from pain, he struggled to focus on Akira's face.

I'll miss you.

We tried, my friend.

We learned answers.

But not enough.

There's so much else to know.

A lingering electrical impulse made Akira's eyes blink yet again. Melancholy as ever, though clouded with death. But tears beaded out of them, no doubt a reflex after death, yet almost . . . impossibly . . . in good-bye.

A guard swung a *bokken*. Savage's consciousness exploded.

But not before he heard gunshots.

EPILOGUE

λλλλλ

THE KEY TO
THE MAZE

FORTUNE'S
HOSTAGE

What seemed an eternity ago, when Savage had met Rachel's sister, Joyce Stone, in Athens and gone with her to the Parthenon, he'd quoted from Shelley's "Ozymandias" to describe the lesson of those ruins.

> *"Look on my works, ye Mighty, and despair!"*
> *. . . Round the decay*
> *Of that colossal wreck, boundless and bare,*
> *The lone and level sands stretch far away.*

Joyce Stone had understood: "Nothing—wealth, fame, power—is permanent." Indeed. Take nothing for granted. The future confronts, interprets, and more often than not, mocks the past. History. False memory. Disinformation. These issues, as much as his nightmare, haunted Savage. The paradox of, the relentlessness of, the deceit and treachery of time.

The truths of Shelley's poem soon became evident. After

471

the discovery of the massacre at Kunio Shirai's mountain retreat, the Japanese news media inundated its readers, viewers, and listeners with reports and speculations for seemingly endless weeks. Intrigued as much as baffled, the nation demanded increasingly more details.

One item that attracted obsessive attention was the discovery of a diary that Shirai had kept. As he'd said to Savage and Akira, he intended to create a legend, convinced that the nation would talk about it for a thousand years. Of course, in his diary Shirai did not reveal the lie at the core of the legend. Instead he attempted to bolster the legend by comparing himself to great historical figures, to Japanese heroes who'd so boldly altered the course of their nation's history that they'd achieved the magnificence of myth. Shirai's intention had evidently been to release the diary shortly before or after his death, so his followers could revere his written legacy just as they worshiped his *kami*.

The hero whom Shirai most identified with was Oshio Heihachiro, a political activist in the nineteenth century. Outraged by the poverty of the lower classes, Oshio had organized a revolt, so committed to his cause that he'd sold his belongings to buy swords and firearms for starving farmers. In 1837, his rebels sacked and burned rich estates. The city of Osaka was soon in flames. However, the authorities managed to defeat the revolt. Oshio's followers were executed, but only after being tortured. Oshio himself was caught and avoided dishonor by committing *seppuku*.

Shirai's decision to compare himself with this particular hero seemed puzzling at first, and Shirai admitted as much in his diary. After all, Oshio's rebellion, though brave, had ended in defeat. But Shirai went on to explain that the cause for which Oshio sacrificed his life had consequences of which Shirai greatly approved. After Commodore Perry's "black ships" anchored in Yokohama Bay in 1853, a new generation of rebels protested America's demand that Japan lift its cultural quarantine and allow foreigners to import mechandise, to become a satellite of the West. Inspired by Oshio's principles, these new rebels reaffirmed the cultural purity of the Tokugawa Shogunate. They insisted on the mystical uniqueness of their nation, their god-ordained *nihonjinron*, their divine Japaneseness bequeathed to them by the sun goddess, Amaterasu. Warriors, masterless samurai who called themselves *shishi*, swore to expel all intruding foreigners and in some cases slaughtered Western settlers. Shirai emphasized deceitfully in his diary that he didn't advocate bloodshed but rather an overwhelming political movement in which the Force of Amaterasu would accomplish the dream of Oshio's later followers, "Expel the barbarians," and return Japan to Japan.

When put in this context, Oshio did seem the proper hero for Shirai to emulate. But there were ironic disturbing implications that Shirai either didn't recognize or didn't want to admit, for his diary abruptly changed topic and described its author's patriotic zeal in conceiving, organizing, and unleashing the Force of Amaterasu, which his diary took for granted would be successful. The implications that Shirai's diary ignored were that Oshio's later followers had taken their dead leader's principles—"Feed the poor"—to such an extreme that "Expel the barbarians" and "Keep Japan pure" became synonymous with "Revere the emperor." Since 1600, the Tokugawa Shogunate had insisted on keeping the emperor in the background, in Kyoto, far from the *shogun*'s center of power in what is now called Tokyo. But the zealots, who unwittingly perverted Oshio's intentions, so identified their Japaneseness with the former sanctity of the imperial institution that they insisted on reinstating it, on bringing the emperor from Kyoto to the *shogun*'s capital, and on reaffirming him as a symbol of the greatness of Japan.

Thus in 1867 the Meiji Restoration occurred. After more than two and a half centuries, the Tokugawa Shogunate fell, and calculating bureaucrats realized that they could benefit financially and politically from this amazing shift in power. Secluding, surrounding, and above all controlling the emperor and his attitudes, they embraced what they saw as the lucrative pronationalistic consequences of Commodore Perry's "black ships." In the words of Masayoshi Hotta, who'd seen the future in 1857, four years after the "black ships" arrived:

I am therefore convinced that our policy should be to stake everything on the present opportunity, to conclude friendly alliances, to send ships to foreign countries everywhere and conduct trade, to copy the foreigners where they are at their best, and so repair our shortcomings, to foster our national strength and complete our armaments, and so gradually subject the foreigners to our influence until in the end all the countries of the world know the blessings of perfect tranquillity and our hegemony is acknowledged throughout the globe.

Shirai—attempting to change history—had been blind to it. *Akira*, though, had recognized the truth. As he'd told Savage en route to their destiny at Shirai's mountaintop retreat, "We can try to learn from history, but it's impossible to reverse its trend." In other words, we move forward, Savage thought. Relentlessly. We can try to build on the past, but the present—a wedge between then and soon—makes all the difference, contributes new factors, guarantees that soon will be different from then.

We can never go back, he sadly concluded, recalling the innocent happiness of his youth and the night his father shot himself. But what does that say about ambition, hope, and especially love? Are they pointless, doomed to fail? Because the present emerges, is programmed by, but at a certain point is divorced from the past . . . and the future is by definition a change, controlled by unanticipated circumstances?

Jamais vu. Déjà vu.

False memory. Disinformation.

For months, I relived a past that wasn't true, he thought.

I then confronted a present that seemed to replay the past. But with a difference. Yes . . . Savage swallowed . . . Akira died. (*Dear God, how much I miss him.*) But his death was not an exact replication of my nightmare. He was . . .

Beheaded. Yes.

And his head struck the floor, rolled toward me, and blinked.

(How much I miss him.)

But before his body toppled, his lifeless hands gave me the sword.

It wasn't the same! It *wasn't* the past!

So maybe we *can* reverse, change, alter, *correct* what's behind us.

But in *that* case, the past was a lie. It never happened. It was all a damned trick played on our memory.

Isn't everything? Remember what you read in the book Dr. Santizo gave you. Memory isn't a year ago, a month ago, a day ago. It's a second ago, as the past becomes the present, about to change to the future. I'm trapped in my mind, in my momentary perceptions. The past can't be proved. The future's a mystery. I exist forever now. Until I'm dead.

So what about hope and love? What about Rachel? What about . . . ?

Tomorrow? Will my dreams collapse, my hopes fall apart, my love dissolve?

I don't think so.

Because Rachel knows the truth. She's told me often enough.

Abraham believed.

By virtue of the absurd.

The alternative is unacceptable. As long as I act with good will—

—and I know there'll be pain, disasters—

—as long as I struggle forward—

—with good will—

—despite the disasters—

—despite the pain—

—with the help of God—

—by virtue of the absurd—

—I won't be fortune's hostage.

A COMPLICITY
OF LIES

1

Now Savage's nightmare was twofold, a hideous double exposure, Akira being killed not once but twice, Kamichi dying twice as well. Sprawled paralyzed in a pool of blood, seeing Akira's severed skull, the melancholy, tear-beaded eyes blinking, Savage screamed and struggled upright.

But hands restrained him. A soothing voice reassured him. For a moment Savage wondered if he were back in the hotel in Philadelphia, where Akira had calmed him after Savage wakened screaming from his nightmare. Hope abruptly changed to fear, because Savage groggily realized that if he were still in Philadelphia, then the final disastrous confrontation with Shirai had not occurred. The present was the past, and the horror of the future had yet to be endured.

This terrifying murky thought made Savage want to scream once more. The gentle hands, the soothing voice, continued to reassure him. At once Savage recognized that the voice belonged to Rachel, that he sat weakly on a *futon*, that bandages encased his skull, that a cast weighed down his right arm, that tape bound his chest. He shuddered, recalling the hospital in Harrisburg, where he'd never been, the casts that had imprisoned his body, though his arms and legs had not been broken, the blond-haired doctor who'd never existed.

"You mustn't excite yourself," Rachel said. "Don't move. Don't try to stand." She eased him gently back onto the *futon*. "You have to rest." She leaned down and kissed his beard-stubbled cheek. "You're safe. I promise I'll protect you. Try to stay quiet. Sleep."

As the mist in Savage's mind began to clear, he realized the irony of the change in circumstance, Rachel protecting *him*. Though confused, he almost grinned. But his head felt as if a spike had been driven through it, and he closed his eyes in pain. "Where am I?"

"At Taro's," Rachel said.

Surprised, Savage looked at her. He struggled to speak. "But how did . . . ?"

"The two men who stayed with you when you followed Shirai brought you here."

"I still don't . . . How . . . ?"

"They say that you and Akira told them to wait at the bottom of the mountain while you went up to investigate."

Savage nodded despite the pain in his head.

"Two hours later, they heard shots," Rachel said. "Handguns. Automatic weapons. They claim it sounded like a war. Shortly after, two cars sped down the lane from the mountain and raced away."

Savage inhaled, fighting to concentrate. "And then . . . ?" His voice cracked.

"Save your strength. I'll do the talking. Are you thirsty? Would you like a—?"

"Yes," he managed to say through parched, scabbed lips.

She set a glass of water beside his head and placed a bent

straw between his lips. Weak, he sucked water over his dry swollen tongue. He had trouble swallowing but kept sucking the water.

She took the glass away. "You'll get sick if you drink too quickly." She studied him, then continued. "The two men decided to investigate."

Savage closed his eyes again.

"Are you sleepy? We can talk about this later."

"No." Savage breathed. "I want to . . . have to . . . know."

"They assumed that the men in the cars had done the shooting, so because it would have taken them too long to go up the mountain on foot, Taro's students risked driving their motorcycles up the lane."

With his good hand, Savage gestured weakly for her to keep going.

"Near the top, they hid their bikes and snuck through the forest," Rachel said. "They found a huge building, or rather all kinds of different buildings weirdly joined together. It reminded me of the way you described the Medford Gap Mountain Retreat." She hesitated. "There were bodies all over the lawn."

The memory made Savage grimace.

"Then the cars came back, and the two men hid. The men from the cars went into the building. Taro's students waited, then followed cautiously. They found more bodies."

"Yes," Savage said. "So many." His nostrils flared, retaining the coppery stench of the blood. "Everywhere."

"They heard more shots. On an upper floor. They didn't know what they'd be facing. Only two men, they had to go up warily. By the time they reached the third floor, they found it littered with corpses." Rachel bit her lip. "Akira had been beheaded. Shirai had been cut in half. And three men with wooden swords were about to crack your skull apart. Taro's students grabbed guns from the floor and shot the three men before they could kill you."

Savage's concentration wavered. He fought to keep his mind from swirling, desperate to know the rest. "But you still haven't told me. How did I get here?"

"One of Taro's students drove his motorcycle to a nearby village where they'd hidden your car. He brought the car back, put you and Akira in it, and drove you to Taro's while the other student followed on his motorcycle. Taro ordered them to return to the mountain, to retrieve the remaining motorcycle, and to arrange the bodies so it seemed as if some of Shirai's men tried to kill him while others tried to defend him. According to the newspapers, the authorities believe the deception, though no one can explain what caused the rebellion."

Savage's consciousness began to fade.

"Taro took care of you," Rachel said, "cleaned your wounds, set your arm, did whatever he could. It would have been too risky, have attracted too much attention, to take you to a hospital. But if you hadn't wakened soon, I'd have insisted on taking you to a doctor."

Savage grasped her hand. His mind dimmed, turning gray. "Don't leave me."

"Never."

He drifted, sank.

And reendured his nightmare, or rather both of them, one on top of the other.

2

The next time he wakened, he felt stronger, more alert, though his body still ached and his skull throbbed.

Rachel sat beside him, holding his hand. "Thirsty?"

"Yes . . . And hungry."

She beamed. "I have to leave you for a moment. There's someone who wants to say hello."

As Rachel left, Savage expected that she'd bring in Taro. Instead, to his delight, he saw Eko come in, her aged face strained with grief for Churi, but her eyes aglow with the pleasure of serving, of bringing Savage a tray upon which, he soon discovered, were a cup of tea and a bowl of broth.

Rachel stood next to her. The women exchanged glances more meaningful than words. With a gesture, Rachel invited Eko to sit on the futon and spoon broth into Savage's mouth. Occasionally Rachel helped by giving Savage a sip of tea.

"So Taro's men finally rescued you," Savage told Eko, the warmth of the broth and tea making him sigh. At once he remembered that Eko didn't speak English.

Rachel explained. "I don't understand what the problems were in accomplishing the rescue, but the night you followed Shirai to the mountain, Taro's students arrived with Eko."

"Akira"—emotion prevented Savage from speaking for a moment—"would have been overjoyed, immensely grateful. At least one good thing came out of this. . . . God, I miss him. I still can't believe he's . . . Does she know Akira's dead?"

"She helped prepare his body for the funeral rites."

"I wish I knew how to tell her I'm sorry," Savage said.

"She understands. And *she* feels sorry for *you*. For your grief."

"*Arigato.*" Close to tears, Savage touched Eko's arm.

She bowed her head.

"Taro's students came back with someone else," Rachel said.

"What? Who?"

"It's complicated. When you're strong enough, you can see for yourself."

"I'm strong enough now." With effort, he managed to sit.

"You're sure?" Rachel asked. "I'm worried about . . ."

"Now," Savage said. "Help me to stand. Too many questions haven't been answered. If this is who I think it is . . . Please, Rachel, help me."

It took both Rachel and Eko to raise him to his feet and steady him. Each woman supporting him, he shuffled toward the sliding panel.

Light hurt his eyes. He faced a room in which cushions surrounded a low cypress table. Taro sat, legs crossed, on one side. And on the other . . .

Savage glared at the well-dressed, fiftyish, sandy-haired man he knew as Philip Hailey.

But Hailey looked haggard, unshaven, his suit wrinkled, his tie tugged open, his shirt's top button undone.

Hailey's hands trembled worse than Savage's did, and his eyes no longer were coldly calculating.

"Ah," Savage said and sank to a pillow. "Another closing of a circle. Who *are* you?"

"You know me as . . ."

"Philip Hailey. Yes. And you were in my nightmare at the nonexistent Medford Gap Mountain Retreat. And you chased me at the Meiji Shrine. And Kamichi—Shirai—told me you're my contact, that you and I work for the CIA. Answer my question! *Who the hell are you?*"

Savage's anger exhausted him. He wavered. Rachel steadied him.

"If you don't remember, for security reasons it's best that we don't use real names, Doyle."

"Don't call me that, you bastard. Doyle might be my name, but I don't identify with it."

"Okay, I'll call you Roger Forsyth, since that's your agency pseudonym."

"No, damn it. You'll call me by my other pseudonym. The one I used when I worked with Graham. Say it."

"Savage."

"Right. Because, believe me, that's how I feel. What *happened* to me? For Christ's sake, who did what to my mind?"

Hailey tugged at his collar. Hands trembling, he opened the second button on his shirt. "I don't have clearance to tell you."

"Wrong. You've got the best clearance there is. My permission. Or else I'll break your fucking arms and legs and—" Savage reached for a knife on the table. "Or maybe I'll cut off your fingers and then—"

Hailey's face turned pale. He raised his arms pathetically. "Okay. All right. Jesus, Savage. Be cool. I know you've been through a lot. I know you're upset, but—"

"Upset? You son of a bitch, I want to kill you! Talk! Tell me *everything!* Don't stop!"

"It was all"—Hailey's chest heaved—"a miscalculation. See, it started with . . . Maybe you're not aware of . . . The military's been working on what they call bravery pills."

"*What?*"

"The problem is, no matter how well you program a soldier, he can't help being afraid during combat. I mean, it's natural. If someone shoots at you, the brain sends a crisis signal to your adrenal gland, and you get terrified. You tremble. You want to run. It's a biological instinct. Sure, maybe a SEAL like you, conditioned to the max, can control the reflex. But your basic soldier, he suffers a fight-or-flight response. And if he runs, well, the ball game's over. So the military figured, maybe there's a chemical. If a soldier takes a pill before an anticipated battle, the chemical cancels the crisis signal that triggers adrenaline. The soldier feels no emotion, just his conditioning, and he fights. By God, he fights.

"The thing is," Hailey said, "when they tested the drug, it worked fine. *During a crisis.* But afterward? The soldier's memory, the stress of what he'd been through, caught up to him. He fell apart. He suffered posttrauma stress disorder. Eventually he was useless. Haunted."

"Yes," Savage said. "Haunted. I'm an expert in that, in being haunted." He aimed the knife toward Hailey's arm.

"I told you, Savage. Be cool. *I'm telling you what you want to know.*"

"Then do it!"

"So the military decided that the bravery pill worked fine. *Memory* was the problem. Then they got to thinking about posttrauma stress disorder, and they figured they could solve two problems at once. Relieve the agony of vets from Vietnam who couldn't stand remembering what they'd been through. And at the same time, guarantee that the bravery pill would work if something else removed the memory of the horrors that the bravery pill had forced them to think was normal."

"Psychosurgery." Savage's voice dropped.

"Yes," Hailey said. "Exactly. So the military experimented on removing traumatic memories. It turned out to be easier than they expected. The techniques existed. Neuro-surgeons, treating epileptics, sometimes insert electrodes into the brain, stimulate this and that section, and manage to find the neurons that cause the epilepsy. The surgeons then cauterize the neurons, and the epileptics are cured. But they have memory loss. A trade-off for the patient's benefit. What the military decided was to experiment with the same technique to remove the memories of combat that gave soldiers post-trauma stress disorder. A brilliant concept.''

"Sure," Savage said, tempted to plunge the knife into Hailey's heart.

"But somebody realized that the soldiers had a gap in their minds, a vacuum in their memories. They'd always be confused by the sense that something important had happened to them that they couldn't remember. That confusion would impair their ability to fight again. So why not . . . as long as the surgeons are in there . . . find a way to *insert* a memory, a false one, something peaceful, calming. Drugs combined with films and electrode stimulation did the trick.''

"Yeah," Savage said. "What a trick."

"Then somebody else thought, what if the memory we insert isn't just peaceful but motivates the patient to do what we want, to program him into doing . . . ?''

"I get the idea," Savage said, stroking the knife against Hailey's arm. "Now talk about *me*. Where do *I* come in?''

"Japan." Hailey fidgeted, staring at the knife. "They screwed us at Pearl Harbor. But we beat them. We stomped them. We nuked them. Twice. And then we spent seven years teaching them not to screw with us again. But they are! Not militarily. Financially! They're *buying* our country. They dump their merchandise onto our markets. They own our Treasury bills. They control our trade deficit. They're responsible for our national debt.''

Taro's wizened face turned red with fury. He glared, unforgivably insulted.

"Just get to the point," Savage said.

"A group of us in the agency, not the agency itself," Hailey said. "It's too damned cautious. But a *group* of us decided to correct the situation. We knew about Shirai. For quite a while, he's been trying to undermine the status quo in Japan. Last year's influence-buying scandal, the Recruit corporation giving top politicians bribes in the form of undervalued stocks that would soon be worth a fortune . . . Shirai was behind that. Through intermediaries, he controlled Recruit. And through the newspapers he owned, he leaked the information. Politicians fell. Party leaders. *Former* party leaders. One prime minister and then another. The system verged on collapse. And Shirai intended to step in, to use his wealth and power to take control. But he needed an incident, a symbolic, catalyzing sensation, so outrageous that it would attract sufficient followers to unite the nation and achieve his goals. Inward, though, not outward. A rejection of the world. Japan for itself. And my group within the agency loved it.''

"So you decided"—Savage clutched the knife—"that you'd help him."

"Why not? Shirai's goals coincided with ours. If Japan turned inward, if the country established a cultural quarantine and refused to deal with outsiders, America wouldn't be smothered with Japanese merchandise. We'd have a chance to correct our trade deficit. We'd reduce, hell, maybe eliminate, our national debt. We'd balance our budget. Jesus, man, the possibilities!''

"You were prepared to help a . . . ? Surely you realized that Shirai was crazy."

Hailey shrugged. "Everything's relative. We preferred to think of him as idealistic."

Savage cursed.

"The agency's been watching Shirai for quite a while," Hailey said. "One of his lieutenants was on our payroll. He kept us up-to-date on what Shirai was doing, and we sent information through the lieutenant—scandals involving bureaucrats and politicians—that helped Shirai continue disrupting the Japanese establishment. Shirai knew nothing about our help, of course. And then we waited to see if our investment would pay off."

"That still has nothing to do with me."

"Well, yes," Hailey said and wiped sweat off his cheek, "I'm afraid it does. I didn't find out till recently, but some of the men in our group formed their *own* group. We're conservatives, proud of it. But these other guys . . ." He swallowed nervously. "They're the kind that thinks Oliver North's the best thing since microwave popcorn, and they had what North would have called a 'neat' idea. They figured, why not go all the way? Why not give Shirai a chance to stage an incident that would be so sensational he'd gain all the support he needed? What if it seemed that America felt so threatened by Shirai's anti-American attitude that we sent an assassin to shut him up? A CIA operative. The attempt would fail. The operative would be killed. Shirai would reveal the assassin's link with the agency, and Japan would be incensed. If tens of thousands of Japanese demonstrated because we lost a nuclear weapon eighty miles off their coast, how many *hundreds* of thousands, perhaps even millions, would demonstrate against an assassination attempt engineered by America?"

"But that's . . . Those guys are as nuts as Shirai was. What in hell made them think it would help America if Japan turned against us?"

"Don't you see? If Japan rejected us, if relations between our countries were severed, Japanese imports would stop. We'd have won the economic war," Hailey said.

"Yeah, and suppose Japan then sided with the Chinese or the Soviets."

"No. It wouldn't happen that way. Because Japan doesn't get along with the Chinese and the Soviets. The Japanese-Chinese feud goes back hundreds of years. And the Japanese are angry that the Soviets won't give up a string of northern islands that used to belong to Japan until after the Second World War. Shirai would turn anti-American sentiment into universal anti-foreign sentiment, and we'd be back in business."

Savage shook his head. "Absolute madness."

"The splinter group in the agency arranged for Shirai's lieutenant to promote the idea, and Shirai loved it. Mind you, Shirai still didn't know that Americans were suggesting it or that the nutso group in the agency believed that America would gain a lot more than Shirai would. Now,'' Hailey said, ''this is where you come in. Illegal or not, it's one thing to tell an operative to assassinate someone. It's quite another to order him to go on a suicide mission. No one would do it. What the splinter group needed was an operative who wouldn't know what he faced and, better yet, wouldn't even know he worked for the agency so he wouldn't have second thoughts, contact his control, and back out.''

''And you were—are—my control.''

Hailey sweated more profusely. ''We recruited you when you were in the SEALs. In nineteen eighty-three, you pretended to be outraged by America's invasion of Grenada. Politically motivated, pointless and needless, you said. Fellow SEALs died so a movie-star president could bolster his image, you said. You got drunk. You made speeches in bars. You fought with your best friend.''

''Mac.''

''Yes,'' Hailey said. ''He was part of the plan. Sworn to secrecy. The two of you trashed a bar. Mac swore in public if he ever saw you again he'd kill you. You left the SEALs and became an executive protector.''

''Trained by Graham.''

''He was also part of the plan. With your cover established, an American who hated his government's policies, no one would suspect that you actually worked for the agency and that every powerful client you protected was actually a target, a means of obtaining information. A protector, pledged to be loyal, has access to a lot of dirty secrets. The information you gave us helped us put pressure on a lot of important people.''

Sickened, Savage turned to Rachel. ''You suggested that as a possibility. Remember? After Mac was killed? But I didn't want to believe it.'' He glanced back at Hailey. ''So for all these years I've been''—bile stung his throat—''a blackmailer.''

''Hey, it's not that bad, Savage. Don't be hard on yourself. You saved a lot of lives. You're a talented protector.''

"That doesn't change the fact that I pledged allegiance to my clients and then betrayed them," Savage growled.

"Not all of them. Most were legitimate assignments, to maintain your cover. . . . But *some* clients . . . Yes, you betrayed them. You've got to believe me, Savage. They *deserved* to be betrayed."

Savage stared at the glinting knife in his hand. He almost slammed its point through the table. "And you were my contact. That's how the splinter group learned about me."

"Your background was perfect. A man with superior military skills and with protection abilities that enabled you to understand and bypass security systems. An operative in deep cover who wouldn't be missed by the agency if you dropped out of sight for a while. And one other item, a crucial detail about your past."

"*What* detail?"

"Now here's where we pause for a moment, Savage."

"Tell me! *What detail?*"

"No, first it's deal time," Hailey said. "I'm not telling you all this for fun. The guys who brought me here would just as soon kill me as let me go. I'm walking a narrow line. My price for telling you that crucial detail about your past is my freedom. You're so concerned about honor. Okay, I want your *word*, I want you to *swear* that if I tell you, I walk out of here. And this is your incentive—the information's about your father."

Savage clutched the knife so hard his knuckles whitened.

"What *about* my father?"

"You won't like it, Savage."

"He shot himself! If that's your filthy secret, I already know it!"

"Yes, he shot himself," Hailey said. "The question is why."

"My father helped organize the Bay of Pigs invasion. When it failed, the government needed a fall-guy. My father, God bless him . . . Incredibly loyal, he agreed. So he took the heat and resigned. But humiliation ate his soul. The agency meant *everything* to him. Away from it, he had no purpose. He started drinking. The booze intensified his emptiness. He blew his brains out.''

''Yes and no.''

''*What are you talking about?*''

''A deal,'' Hailey said. ''I want to walk out of here. And what I'm selling is the truth about your father's suicide.''

''The truth? My father's dead! What other truth can there be?''

''Plenty. Let me walk out of here, and you'll find out.''

''Maybe I don't want to know. Maybe if I killed you right now . . .''

Hailey shook his head. ''You'd regret it forever. You'd always want to know the secret. And I'll be honest with you. The truth will tear you apart. But that's why you'll want to know.''

Savage glared. ''You . . .'' In horror, he remembered the night he'd found his father's body, a towel placed beneath his father's head to minimize the spatter of blood and brains. ''You have my word.''

''Not just yours. I want *this* man's word.'' Hailey pointed toward Taro. ''*He* has no obligation to me. And after all, I'm a *gaijin*. I doubt he'd feel remorse or bound by your word if he killed me.''

Savage slowly turned, directing his gaze toward the bald, wrinkled, stern-eyed Japanese. ''Taro-*sensei* . . .'' Struggling to choose the proper words, Savage bowed. ''Taro-*sensei*, I ask a formal favor of you. Akira explained the significance of such a request. I'm willing to put myself in eternal debt to you. I accept the obligation of *giri*. I ask you . . . with respect, I beg you . . . to spare this man's life if he tells me what I need to know.''

Taro squinted, assessing.

''I ask you this,'' Savage said, ''in devotion to Akira's memory.''

Taro squinted harder, staring from Savage to Hailey, then back again.

''For Akira?'' the old man asked. ''*Hai.*'' He bowed in grief.

"All right, Hailey, it's a deal. You have our word," Savage said.

Hailey debated. "I've worked for the agency too long. I'm not used to acts of faith."

"Tell me!"

"Okay, I'll trust you. Your father committed suicide. Yes. But not for the reasons you think. It had nothing to do with the Bay of Pigs."

"What?"

"Your father, Savage, was in charge of the agency's attempts to assassinate Castro. He kept trying and trying. And every plan failed. But Castro found out what the agency was doing. He warned the United States to leave him alone. But your father, under orders, kept trying. So Castro decided enough was enough and arranged for President Kennedy to be shot in Dallas. Your father killed himself because of grief, because he was responsible for Kennedy's death."

"Oh, Jesus." Savage's strength failed. He slumped, falling backward. Rachel supported him.

"I told you you wouldn't like it," Hailey said. "But that's the truth, and I expect you to fulfill your bargain."

"I promised." Savage could barely speak. "You'll walk out of here."

"And that's the piece of your background that made you an ideal candidate for the assassin who'd fail to kill Shirai. Like father, like son. Shirai could not only implicate the United States in an attempt against him, but he could link that attempt all the way back to the Kennedy assassination and the U.S. attempts against Castro. Shirai would dredge up garbage from the past and convince his nation to call us a pack of killers. Oh, you were perfect, Savage, and all that needed to be done was erase crucial portions of your memory, so you didn't know you were CIA, and then implant a hideous nightmare that compelled you to track down Shirai."

"What about Akira?" Savage exhaled with grief. "How did he fit in?"

"Shirai needed to compromise the Japanese establishment as much as he did America. So why not use a Japanese

Intelligence operative who also had executive protection as a cover? If the two of you thought each other had died, and if you both discovered you were still alive, you'd each want to know what caused your nightmare. Certain choices were predictable—that you'd go to the Medford Gap Retreat and discover it didn't exist, that you'd go to the Harrisburg hospital and discover you'd never been there. Et cetera. Et cetera. But as soon as Shirai made his move and it was publicized, on television, in the newspapers, you'd recognize the principal you saw cut in half, and you'd run to him to find out what he knew about your nightmare.''

''But some things *weren't* predictable,'' Savage said. ''My decision to go to Virginia, to talk to Mac.''

''Exactly. After you were conditioned . . . it happened in Japan, by the way, at Shirai's estate . . . before the casts were put on your arms and legs, a location transmitter was inserted in a cap that was put on one of your teeth. That site was chosen because you and Akira, like many people, already had a dental cap. On an X ray, the replaced caps wouldn't attract attention. And because of those location transmitters, Shirai's men knew about—could follow you—everywhere. In case they had to nudge you in the right direction.

''But seeing Mac in Virginia was *not* the right direction.''

''Yes,'' Hailey said. ''Shirai's men feared Mac would tell you too much and erase your conditioning. They had to kill him.''

''And try to grab Rachel because she was the reason Akira and I came together but after that she didn't belong in the plan.''

''Unfortunately that's true.''

''What about the man and woman I thought were my parents?''

''The ones in Baltimore?'' Hailey asked. ''Window dressing. Further confusion. Shirai's intention, with prodding from the splinter group in the agency who used Shirai's lieutenant, was to so confuse you that when you saw Shirai on television or in the newspaper, you'd race to get in touch with him. Of course, the alternate plan would have been to abduct Akira and you, drug you, take you to Shirai's estate, and kill you while Shirai's men sacrificed their lives for their leader's ambitions. Mind you, that plan has the merit of simplicity.'' Hailey shrugged. "But it wouldn't have been convincing— because you and Akira had to leave a trail. In Greece. In southern France. In America. Most of all, in Japan. You *had* to leave evidence—the stamps on fake passports you carried, not to mention the conversations you had with taxi drivers, hotel clerks, and immigration officials—that showed your determination to get to Shirai.''

"And Graham's death?" Savage trembled.

"The agency had nothing to do with that. After Graham arranged for both you and Akira to be on Papadropolis's estate, Shirai's men decided he was a liability. They killed him, attempting to make it appear a suicide.''

"But Graham *knew* what he was doing when he sent Akira and me to Mykonos. His ultimate loyalty was to the agency. Not to us.''

"Savage, you ask too many questions. Don't dig too deep. He was your friend. Yes. But he was also a professional. He obeyed his masters. Why else would he have traveled back and forth from Maryland to Massachusetts to nurse you and Akira back to health? He loved you, Savage. And he loved Akira. But he loved his profession—not protection, but espionage—more.''

Nauseous, Savage leaned back against Rachel, welcoming her warmth. "You're right. I ask too many questions.'' Despite his multiple painful injuries, he managed to straighten. "But I do have one more question.''

"Ask it. You're entitled. We made a bargain. But after that, I'm out of here.''

"Okay,'' Savage said. He struggled to stand. Rachel— ever dependable Rachel—helped him. Wavering upright, with Rachel's arms around him, Savage glowered down at Hailey. "Okay, here's my question. At the Meiji Shrine, did you try to stop me or urge me forward?''

"Hell, man, I wanted to stop you. The plan was out of control.''

"And the van, was it yours?''

"You said just one question.''

"Damn it, answer me!''

"Yes, it was ours."

"Who shot the driver?"

"Shirai's men. The transmitter in the cap on your tooth. They were able to follow you. And they didn't want us stopping you!"

"And what about . . . ?"

"That's *two* more questions," Hailey said. *"Don't tell me you're breaking your bargain."*

"I'm almost finished." Savage's knees sank. Rachel held him up. "What about . . . ? Who invaded Akira's home and tried to kill us? Who *ordered* . . . ?"

"Man, your guess is as good as mine."

"No," Savage said. "My guess is better. *You* did. You ordered the assassins to take us out! Because the plan was *out of control!* Because you'd discovered what the assholes in that splinter group were up to! And you felt it had to be stopped! So you made the choice to have us terminated! And when that didn't work, you followed us to the Meiji Shrine to try to kill us there! *You're* my enemy, the same as those jerks! The difference is, apparently I once trusted you! Apparently you were my friend!"

"Hey, Savage, business and friendship . . . as much as I'd like it . . . sometimes . . ."

Fury canceled weakness. Anger canceled pain. With every force he could muster, Savage used his good arm—and it felt so wonderful!—to punch Hailey squarely in the face.

Teeth snapped. Hailey's nose crunched. Blood flew.

Hailey lurched backward, groaning, sprawling.

"I ought to . . ." Savage grabbed him, jerking him upward. "Kill you."

"Giri," Hailey muttered through swollen lips and broken teeth. "You gave your . . ."

"Word," Taro said and stood. "So did I. A formal favor. An eternal obligation." Taro restrained the knife in Savage's hand. "Obey it. Or you're worthless. You have no honor."

Trembling, seething, sobbing, Savage gradually lowered the knife. "Something has to mean *something*. Get out of here! Now!" he told Hailey. "Before I change my mind. Because of you my friend is dead, you . . . !"

Hailey ran, clutching his broken face, yanking a panel open, disappearing, his footsteps dwindling.

"You did the proper thing," Taro said.

"Then why do I feel like hell?"

"Because he might come after you."

"Let him," Savage said. "I'm better."

"For a *gaijin,* you're a noble man."

"But are *you?*" Savage spun. "Our business isn't finished. I refuse to believe that you weren't aware . . ."

"That Akira belonged to Japanese Intelligence?" The old man nodded. "That's correct."

"And you *knew* what Shirai was trying to do! You *knew* that Akira and I were supposed to die!"

"For Japan."

"*Giri,*" Savage said. "Thank God for *giri.* For the solemn promise I made you. If you allowed that bastard to leave, I swore I'd be eternally in your debt. Otherwise . . ."

"You'd try to kill me?" Taro chuckled.

"Yes." Fueled by ultimate rage, Savage overcame his weakness, pressed a paralyzing nerve in Taro's neck, and tickled the point of his knife against Taro's jugular vein. "Your problem is you're arrogant. Even a *gaijin* can be . . ."

"A worthy opponent. Savage-san, you have my respect."

"And your word that there'll be no recriminations? *Giri?*"

"Yes." Taro's face became more wizened. "*Giri.* Friendship. Loyalty. Obligation. What else is there to believe in?"

"Love." Savage lowered the knife. "What did you do with Akira's body?"

"It was cremated. The urn with his ashes is in my room. But Japanese Intelligence can't know about his death. The investigation would be disastrous. To us all."

"May I have them?" Savage asked.

"Akira's ashes?"

"Yes. If his interment must be a secret, Eko and I know what to do with them."

Taro studied him.

And bowed.

FESTIVAL FOR
THE DEAD

Before Akira had brought Savage and Rachel to Japan, as he'd explained the complexities of his divinely born nation, he'd referred to a summer ritual known as the Feast of Lanterns and otherwise called the Festival for the Dead. During three days, involving incense, prayers, and funereal meals, traditional Japanese obeyed the Shinto custom of revering— one might almost say worshiping—the dead.

Savage complied, though this was autumn, not summer. But he didn't think Akira would mind. After three days of scrupulous devotion, he and Rachel embraced each other in the garden at the rear of Akira's home.

Night surrounded them.

But a glow reflected off their faces.

For Savage had placed a lantern on the garden's pool. Throughout the afternoon, he'd drained water from the pool, removing the assassin's blood that tainted it. He'd refilled the pool and drained it.

And refilled it again.

And *drained* it again.

And cleaned it *again,* determined to purify it, to exorcise its desecration.

At last he'd been satisfied that the ritual would not be corrupted. He lit a match and set fire to the lantern's paper.

"God, I miss him," Savage said. The flames reflected off his face.

"Yes," Rachel said. "So do I."

"His eyes were so sad."

"Because he belonged in another time."

"Commodore Perry's 'black ships,' " Savage said. "Akira was a samurai. He belonged in a time before samurais were outlawed. Before America corrupted Akira's nation. You know"—he turned to Rachel and kissed her—"before he died, he called me . . ."

Savage choked on emotion. He gagged on his tears.

"He called me . . . oh, Jesus . . ."

Rachel held him. "Tell me."

"His friend."

"And he *was* your friend," Rachel said.

"But do you understand the effort, the sacrifice, it took him to say that? All his life, he'd hated Americans. Because of Hiroshima, Nagasaki. Yokohama Bay. Perry's 'black ships.' Akira belonged in another century. When Japan was pure."

"It's always been pure," Rachel said. "And it always will be. Because if Akira . . . if he's typical . . . this nation is great. Because it understands honor."

"But he's dead."

"Because of honor."

Savage kissed her, the flames of the lantern blazing higher. "What I wonder . . ."

"Is?"

"America. Our Civil War. We made a myth of the South before the war. The magnificent mansions. The dignity of the lifestyle."

"Except for the slaves," Rachel said.

"That's what I mean," Savage said. "Myth. Sometimes, for *some* people, myth hides ugliness and becomes its own reality."

"Like disinformation?"

"Like memory. But memory's a lie. Above all, Jesus, that's what I've learned. *Now* is what matters."

The lantern flamed brighter.

"Not love? Not the future?" Rachel asked.

"Don't I hope."

"But not the past?"

"Akira would have *hated* the past," Savage said. "The Tokugawa Shogunate. From everything I've learned, it was fascist. An oppressive system of control, *shogun* to *daimyo* to samurai to . . . Akira would have desperately craved the present."

"And what do *you* crave?" Rachel asked.

"You."

The lantern flared to its brightest. Sadly its flames diminished.

"In Greece, after we rescued you," Savage said, "I asked Akira if we could be friends. . . . But he refused."

"Because of his background. He was conditioned. And you were . . ."

"A *gaijin*."

"But you love him," Rachel said.

"Yes."

"Should I be jealous?"

"No," Savage said. "Our love was different."

"Can I be a substitute?"

"No." Savage straightened. "You're unique. I'll always worship you."

"Always?"

"I know what you want to say."

"Don't presume." Rachel frowned.

" 'Abraham believed by virtue of the absurd.' "

Now Rachel smiled. "You did know."

"So what are we going to do?" Savage asked. "Hailey didn't admit it, but your *husband* was a part of this."

"What?" Rachel paled.

"Yes," Savage said. "Akira and I. Both sent to Mykonos. Both sent to meet each other during your rescue. Japan for Japan. That's fine. But Japan needs oil. And that means ships. And I think your husband made a deal to guarantee those ships. That's why Akira and I were sent to Mykonos. Because your husband's estate was convenient, since he was involved in the conspiracy."

"So he beat me and raped me for political reasons?"

"From everything I learned, I think he did it . . ."

"Oh," Rachel said. She clutched him.

"Because he liked it. A bonus in the midst of business."

"So . . ."

"I think . . . ," Savage said.

"What?"

"I might have to kill him. Otherwise," Savage said, "he'll keep chasing us."

Rachel shook her head in fury.

"What?" Savage asked.

"No more killing. Too much! Too damned much!"

"He's a very proud man."

"So are *we* proud," Rachel said.

"Then what's the answer?"

"You mentioned a beach near Cancun."

"Where I'd like . . ."

"To make love to me?"

"In fact I'd like to do that right now."

"In spite of your grief?" she asked.

"*Because* of it. In memory of . . . in celebration of . . . life. That's all we have. Not the past, not the future. My past, I discovered, was a lie. But I prefer the lie to the truth. And the future . . . ?"

"Faith."

"And that's absurd."

"And don't I love it."

"And don't I love you," Savage said.

The lantern's flare sank, extinguished by water.

"I'll remember you, Akira, your *kami* in the wind and the rain," Savage said.

They turned and saw Eko, who bowed.

Savage and Rachel bowed as well.

And turned toward the carefully raked and groomed sand of the Zen Buddhist garden, which Akira's father had spent years arranging, and which Akira had persisting in attempting to perfect after his father's death.

Neither man had achieved his obsession.

But as Savage scanned the meticulous design that he'd labored to recreate after the assassins had despoiled it, he grinned with melancholy, sensing that his eyes were as sad as Akira's.

For Akira's ashes had been scattered.

And raked among the sand.

One with nature.

"I know . . . I'm sure," Savage said, "he's at peace."

"And what about us?" Rachel asked.

"Will you . . . ?"

"What?"

"Will you marry me?"

"Jesus, Savage, I'm *already* married, and the bastard's chasing me."

"Trust me. We don't need a *legal* ceremony. Just a private one. You and me."

"Right now?"

"Damned right." He kissed her. "I promise to love, to honor and cherish you."

"Sounds wonderful."

"And a final promise." He kissed her again.

"What's that?"

"To protect."